# WHEN THERE WAS US

## CALIFORNIA DREAMING

### BOOK ONE

## K.C. LAKE

OPEN BOOK PUBLISHING CO.

For anyone who's ever found family among friends—
and clung to them like a life raft. Found family is a
potent, beautiful type of friendship, one which
graces us with the love, acceptance, and safety we
desperately need... even if it's just for a heartbeat
in time.

# PREFACE

In California, circa 1982, modern technology was in its infancy, illegal drugs (especially cocaine, marijuana and LSD) were easily accessible and popular, young adults rarely used condoms, tattoos were worn mostly by criminals or hippies, theaters had one screen and played the same movie for weeks or longer, and muscle cars abounded as part of a vast car culture that has long endured in the Golden State. I have vivid, fond, reckless memories of this time in my life—and it provided the perfect backdrop for this story.

"The sea, once it casts its spell, holds one in its net of wonder forever."

— Jacques Cousteau

# PROLOGUE

## 1989

It's been five years since I've seen Mick or Remy. My best friends. My lovers. The men who left a gaping hole—one that's been hard to repair—in my heart.

I'm not naïve enough to believe what we shared could last forever, especially with the complications of our...*unusual* relationship.

But god, I miss them.

Shifting in my airline seat to gaze out the tiny oval window, patches of landscape blink through the clouds as this titanium contraption hurtles across the earth, California drawing me to my native shores.

Even though I've moved on, the nagging feeling something tangible is missing lingers, like the soldier who experiences a phantom limb after an amputation.

Maybe a part of my heart will always be missing because it will always be theirs. Or perhaps seeing them will heal this fissure and make it whole again.

Inhaling a fortifying breath, I resettle against the headrest.

Endeavoring to open the box we shut all those years ago may very well be a fool's errand, but with my wedding on the horizon...I need to close that box once and for all.

# ONE

## 1982

As I monitor the balding man with a pronounced beer gut fuel his equally unglamorous Pontiac, I'm reminded—again—my life is not where I'd planned.

Four days ago, I finished my freshman year at the local community college. I was supposed to attend UC Santa Barbara, situated a glorious five hours south of here and right on the beach. But instead, stupid me redirected my application in the eleventh hour, trying to keep a relationship—already on life support—afloat. A relationship that ended two weeks before senior prom...and took all of my so-called friends with it.

Forced to attend CCC means I'm stuck living at home for another year with a father who has his thumb pressed to my windpipe and a mother who doesn't care whether I live or die. Okay, that may be a tad melodramatic, but she is, at best, ambivalent.

Now I'm on day three of working this tedious, brainless summer job at a self-serve gas station. My duties include sitting in a dingy office for eight hours, making change or grappling with the carbon-smearing, knuckle-busting credit card machine. After every transaction, I trudge out to the pumps, which must be manually reset with a key. As the new hire, I'm mostly saddled with the late shift, not getting off until nine.

Service stations are notorious targets for robbery, making me a hapless sitting duck behind this not-bulletproof plate glass window. It may be the nicer Lakeshore area, but it's *still* Oakland, known for top tenning the annual "Most dangerous cities in America" list. How much is this little panic button seriously going to help if some asshole points a gun at my head?

The customer approaches, eyes dropping to my chest, and I complete his transaction with the bare minimum of enthusiasm since all I really want to do is kick him in the balls.

I'm resetting the pump when a candy-apple red Camaro roars past and screeches into the Chevron next door, which is a combination gas station/auto repair shop. My boss, Leo, owns both.

Inching toward the low hedge separating us, I peer across the lot. A tall, copper-haired guy exits the Camaro, which is parked among other muscle cars. My glands salivate at the sight of his Z/28 and those fat black rally stripes gracing the hood and rear...I would give anything for a hot car. Instead, I'm the less-proud owner of a faded yellow 1972 Volkswagen Beetle, which is cool but so damn slow ("Economical," my father said when he gave it to me. It *does* save on gas, but good luck beating anyone off the line).

A second mechanic dressed in work coveralls walks from the garage and says something that makes the redhead laugh.

He's got wavy chestnut hair almost kissing his shoulders. He runs a rag over the wrench he's palming and his forearms flex, the navy sleeves he's pushed to his elbows showing off tanned skin. I drag my gaze up to his face just as he turns my way. My heartbeat pulses faster. He's *gorgeous*.

When he jerks his chin—a microscopic acknowledgment

—I freeze then startle as a shrill ring resounds from behind, announcing a customer. Hustling back to my post, I'm both grateful and irritated for the distraction, but a smile plays at my lips. Maybe this summer won't suck as much as I thought.

THE CLOCK'S PERSISTENT TICKING IS THE ONLY sound in this grease-stained office with permanent dirt in the corners. I stare at it for the umpteenth time. Three hours to go. My fingers tap on the grimy metal desk overlooking the station, once again devoid of customers. Tomorrow, I'm bringing a book to pass the time. Tipping my Coke can to my mouth, the last tepid gulp slides down my throat.

Those unmistakable muscle cars fire up, slicing through the tedium, and I jump to my feet, straining for a glimpse. They roar in different directions, their thundering engines sending heat straight to my center. When the Camaro rumbles into my station, I bolt back to my chair, attempting to play it cool.

The redhead's frame soon fills the doorway. He stares at me with vivid blue eyes, a striking contrast with his hair, cropped short on the sides but long on top—and dark in color, closer to brown. Freckles paint his skin, also tan, although not as dark as his coworker's.

"Hey, new girl," he says, leaning against the jamb with a beguiling smile.

"*New girl?*"

"I'm assuming, at the risk of making an ass of you and me." He fishes a pack of smokes out of his back pocket and silently offers me one.

"Sure. Thanks," I murmur, getting a pleasant whiff of pine and motor oil when he leans over to light it with a green disposable. "I started Saturday."

He blows out a stream of smoke and the way he does it is sexy as hell. "If you need anything, holler." He flips his thumb to the left. "I work next door. Just look out for those other baboons."

My lips quirk. "They're wild animals?"

His eyes shine with amusement, softening his sharp features as he crosses one ankle over the other and leans against the doorway. "Sounds about right." He lifts his jaw my direction. "What's your name, sweetheart?"

"Jacqueline." Why did I say that? I'm not formal by any stretch. "Jacqui for short."

"Hmm...pretty."

"You gonna leave me hanging?"

He smirks. "Remy."

"Never heard that one before."

"It's Randolph Richard Remington the third," he says with dramatic haughtiness, "which is a bit too stick-up-your-ass-rich-prick for my liking." One of his eyebrows hikes as he flicks hot ash on the floor.

"I love your car," I blurt.

"Me too, new girl." His pointed gaze goes straight through me, and goosebumps ripple across my skin as he lets loose another affable grin. "Want to go for a ride when you get off?"

"Hell yes." I don't give it a second thought. My father would be pissed at my impulsive decision to joyride with a relative stranger. Ask me if I give two shits about that. (I don't.) But how bad can Remy be? He works next door. And he appears friendly. "If I don't die of boredom by then," I add.

He chuckles, dropping the butt and extinguishing it with his work boot. "Be back to get you at nine." He turns to leave and stops, knocking on the doorjamb twice. "Don't die."

Seconds later, he leaves in a cloud of smoke from an epic burnout, a flash of red skidding onto the avenue—while a giddy smile I can't erase plasters itself to my face.

# Two

Remy screeches to a stop in front of the office the minute I finish reconciling my drawer. With one hand slung over the wheel, his lips split into an inviting grin when our eyes meet through his open window. Rock music pumps from his stereo, competing with the rumbling engine. I shove the money and credit card receipts into the bank pouch, drop it through the slot safe, and lock up.

He leans over and pushes the passenger door ajar. My pulse races as my ass slides into the black bucket seat. Dropping my purse, I grope for the seatbelt ends and cinch them over my lap. The vibration from the loud, sputtering idle holds nothing but promise.

"Ready?" Remy revs the engine three times, the amplified growl bouncing into the car.

There's no chance of stopping the mile-wide smile on my face. "Born ready."

"You've got spunk, new girl. I like it." After an appreciative glance, he fishtails into the street then burns rubber down Lakeshore Avenue. We whiz by a few residential blocks followed by more jammed with stores and restaurants before whipping onto the freeway.

When he opens it up, we fly.

An exhilarated shriek leaves my lips. Holy fucking shit, I've never gone so fast in my life! The roar of the Camaro as we jet down the highway is a total rush, the intermittent lights strobing overhead.

My honey-blond tresses float around me like Medusa, and I laugh into the balmy night. Every cell in my body crackles with energy—a crazed combination of absolute glee coupled with a side of completely freaking out.

Remy gets off at Redwood Road, giving me the opportunity to wrangle my flyaways. He glances over at me, all smiles, and I return it tenfold.

"Oh my god, this car..." Slapping my hands on my bare thighs, bereft of words, my head tips back in unbridled elation.

"Looks good with you in it," he finishes, my gaze snapping to his in time to catch a rakish wink. Stroking his jaw, his gaze turns predatory, reminding me of a wolf. *A handsome wolf ready to eat Little Red Riding Hood.*

That does something else entirely to my insides and vocabulary escapes me again.

Smirking, he pushes in the chrome dash lighter and flicks a cigarette out of his pack, silently offering me another.

"No thanks." I'm way too amped to smoke.

The lighter pops, the glowing element illuminating Remy's face when he inhales. He huffs out a stream of smoke, clamps the cigarette between his lips, and guns the gas.

Accelerating expertly through all four gears, Remy rockets into the hills. My heart beats wildly against my ribs as a loud whoop escapes my lips, reveling in every shift, every mile, every minute. He turns onto Skyline Boulevard, and we race past Skyline High, bringing with it a flurry of memories I long to leave in the rear view, like this ruby machine does in mere seconds. Navigating through the curves at top speed, my hands clutch the seat, trying not to flap around like a caught fish while AC/DC's live version of "Shoot to Thrill" thunders from the speakers.

"You up for a stop?" Remy yells over the music.

I give him a thumbs up.

He cops a left a few miles later, and we meander slowly through a quiet, upper-class neighborhood, the kind where dependable vehicles are tucked safely behind tidy, two-car garages. Moments later, he parks among a handful of enviable muscle cars. I pull a brush from my purse and rake it quickly through my tangled hair.

Flutters ricochet through my belly as we approach the two-story shingled house. Am I walking into trouble? I'm not getting *Friday the 13th* vibes. We're in the Oakland hills, and the manicured yard has flowerbeds, for chrissakes.

"Who lives here?" I ask.

"Terry Walton. One of my buds." Remy doesn't bother knocking, pushing through the door like he owns the place. Zeppelin blares, two people make out on the sofa without breaking spit, and shit-talking taunts and insults from what sounds decidedly male erupt from another room.

Remy pauses by the couple, planted on an oversized, upholstered chair in a chic living room decorated in ivory, taupe, and onyx hues. "What's up, brother?"

The couple untangles their mocha limbs, revealing a striking pair. The guy shifts his date across his lap, his navy Cal Baseball shirt stretched around arms of solid muscle. "Livin' the dream, Red Man." The friends give each other some skin in a practiced greeting ritual.

"Hey, Remy," the pretty girl says, all doe eyes and coifed hair. "Who's your friend?"

"This is Jacqui. New girl, meet Terry and Kendra."

"Make yourself at home," Terry says with an expansive array of white teeth before his dark eyes fixate back on

Kendra. "Now if you'll excuse me, I've got business to attend to."

Laughing, I follow Remy into the dining room, where three guys play Quarters.

The mechanic with the long chestnut waves stands front and center. His huge gray eyes lock on mine, trapping me. I swallow the sudden knot in my throat as he breaks the connection and tells Remy something I don't catch for the all-consuming buzz in my ears. My neck heats, and I tear my eyes away from Mr. Incredible to glance at the others, who are all staring at me with open curiosity.

Remy catches a can of Bud thrown his way with one hand. "Everyone," he says, grinning at me, "this is Jacqui."

"The new girl?" asks a blue-eyed fox nearly as tall as Remy. Thick sideburns inch down his jawline, framed by perfectly feathered hair a gleaming towhead white.

"Yep," I answer, wondering how long I'm stuck with that stupid moniker.

He flips his chin. "I'm Jeremy."

A shorter, buff male with sable hair and hound dog eyes lurches toward me with his hand out. "Vinny. Nice to meet you."

"Likewise," I murmur before letting my hand drop.

My breath hitches as *he* steps forward in all his six-foot glory, our gaze colliding again. "Hey," he utters softly, hand outstretched. "I'm Mick."

His palm is warm, fingers wrapping around mine with a sure grip as I squeak out a "hi."

My gaze fixates on his unusual eyes, a stormy gray. They pop against his brown hair with sun-brushed strands framing his face, the rest cascading in loose waves. It's only a heartbeat until I'm hypnotized by the shape of his mouth. Full lips punctuated by an alluring cupid's bow. Mick is masculine with a touch of boyish that all adds up to irresistible.

*Look away from the lips...*

Our hands part, jarring me back to reality as Mick steps back. What *is it* with this guy? And really, all of them. They're ridiculously hot—and built, like we're in some alternate universe of only beautiful people.

"You all work at the Chevron?" *If so, I'm a lucky girl.*

"Everyone but Terry and Jeremy," Remy explains. "Terry plays baseball for Cal, and—not to swell his bloated ego—he's probably headed for the bigs, so when he's not in school, he's training and practicing."

"I can't wait to hear what you have to say about me," Jeremy says.

Remy points at his friend. "Another inflated ego."

Jeremy scoffs with exaggerated volume.

"But," Remy continues, "our resident pretty boy is busy brown-nosing, I mean interning, for a state representative, so he's not the kind to get his hands dirty...right, Jer?"

Jeremy reaches down, grabs his privates, and waggles the whole wad at Remy. "This is what I'm interning at this summer, dickhead. I know you're jealous." Zeroing in on me, he asks, "You playing?"

It's a pivotal moment: dive in or become the wallpaper.

I dive. "If you're ready to lose."

The boys erupt in a chorus of guffaws and hoots.

Jeremy hands me a quarter, a sly smile inching up his lips. "Time to put your money where your mouth is."

Making my way to the game set-up, the distinctive, musky aroma of pot hits my nostrils, and my eyes dart toward the source. Vinny takes a drag off the joint and passes it to Remy as I arrive at the end of the table directly in front of Mick. I'm hyper aware of his presence and hope these cutoffs do my ass justice.

Time to put up or shut up. Settling my nerves, I position the quarter between my thumb and forefinger and bounce that sucker right into the cup. *Thank fucking god.*

Jeremy chugs the beer and retrieves the coin, wiping it off

on his shirt, never breaking eye contact. With a wink, he flashes me a roguish grin. "I think you're going to fit in nicely around here."

I wink back. But underneath my cocky assurance runs a current of something foreign but welcome—the hope and possibility I've made some friends.

Remy offers me a Budweiser, nodding with approval. "That's the way you do it, new girl."

As he takes his turn, I inhale a few fortifying gulps.

Someone bursts through the front door, shouting, "Where is that motherfucker?"

My body flinches so intensely, I sway backward, heart lurching in my chest.

Remy lunges away from me a second before a petite strawberry-blond enters. She fastens her glare on him, then scans the crowd, pausing on me.

"Who the fuck is this?" she demands. "Is she the reason you stood me up tonight with your bullshit excuse?"

What? *Oh, shit.*

"No, babe," he croons. "You've got it all wrong."

Hands planted on her hips, she purses her lips like she doesn't believe him at all. She's ferocious for someone half his size. "If you're stepping out on me, we're going the rounds right here, asshole."

He moves toward her, palms up. "Come here, sweetheart. Don't be like that."

She bats his hands. "Don't *sweetheart* me. Who the fuck is she?" The girl scowls my way, her round face and upturned nose giving off pig vibes. A little, *angry* piggy.

"She works next door to us, Karin," Vinny interjects, sliding an arm around my shoulders in a casual yet protective way. "Just started. Put your claws away and say hello to Jacqui."

I meet her stare, breathless from the adrenaline spiking in

every direction, attempting to cipher the mess playing out. "Hi."

Karin's glare narrows. "Huh," she mutters, and swivels back to Remy. "Why the fuck are you here then, if you told me we weren't going out?"

He closes the gap between them. "The guys asked me to swing by for a beer. That's it, K. It wasn't planned, I swear. And I was about to leave...come with me."

Wait a minute. *Seriously?*

Now I'm screwed. How will I get back to my car? Fucking lying asshole men. I'm not *with* Remy, but he didn't tell his girlfriend the truth, either. The way Vinny acted makes me realize there's more to this whole story.

Remy steers Karin into the kitchen—I'm sure murmuring more lies and platitudes in her ear—while inside my body, the roar intensifies. I turn away from the others and drag a hand through my hair, silently weighing my options.

The unexpected smell of the ocean fills my senses—a mix of salt and fresh air. I jerk my head toward the scent and find Mick standing next to me.

"I'll drive you wherever you need to go whenever you want." His voice is deep, quiet, sincere.

"Thank you," I manage, still reeling.

He dips his chin once, gaze still fastened on mine. His eyes are more striking up close, the iris ringed with a dark gunmetal gray, offset by lashes I'd kill for. A scar slices through his right eyebrow, which only adds to his appeal.

Before my gawking embarrasses me further, his buddies harangue him to take his turn. He returns to the game, landing his quarter into the target with ease. Biting down on a smile, my anger dispels as a different type of vibration zings through my body.

Remy pokes his head back into the room. "See you, guys." His eyes flicker over to me briefly before landing on Mick. They appear to share a nonverbal exchange before the

redheaded douchebag bolts without so much as an explanation, I'm sorry, or fuck-you-very-much.

Then again, maybe he did me a favor. My eyes gravitate to
Mick again, roving over his build, appreciating how he fills
out those faded Levi's, the effortless way he carries himself,
and the face God gifted him. This stunning man is driving me
home.

# THREE

Mick opens the passenger door to his sky-blue Mustang fastback, and I slip into the flat bucket seat. No guy has ever opened my car door, and it strikes me as...romantic. Or maybe that's wishful thinking. A streetlight casts enough illumination for me to admire the pretty dash, oversized steering wheel, and matching blue interior. A miniature chrome horse frozen in a gallop greets me from the glove box. And something akin to badass airplane controllers sit midway on the dash, I'm guessing for adjusting temperature and the defroster.

My eyes fixate on the shifter. "Three speed?" I ask when he's seated next to me. I've never even heard of three on the floor.

He grins, the first real smile he's displayed, and my heart splutters. As if he could get any better looking, the dimple popping in his left cheek is boyishly adorable...and probably ruinous to hearts everywhere.

"It's a 1965 2+2. She's a keeper."

"What's the 2+2 mean?"

He motions to the seats. "Two up front and two in the back."

I'd bet all the money in my savings account these front seats recline all the way, and my brain fills with images of the two of us embroiled in a make-out session.

He fires up the ignition, turning down the radio when a song by The Police blasts through the speakers, and a grin pulls my lips wide. While not as loud as Remy's Camaro, it's got a decent growly purr that goes straight to my girlie parts—also awake and idling thanks to Mr. Incredible.

We roll down the windows, letting out the stale air. Mick pulls out a pack of cigarettes and offers me one. My occasional smoking is about to escalate to a habit, I can tell. When I say yes, he surprises me by lifting two to his mouth and igniting them with his Zippo, puffing to get them started before handing me one.

*Holy shit.* My lips are now where his lips were seconds ago. It's clear he's oblivious the move is beyond seductive. And...chivalrous. Insides crackling, my lungs exhale smoke into the night air along with a held breath.

Mick revs the engine a couple of times, whips a U-turn, and guns it down the street. A new high surges through my veins. Another fast car, and I couldn't be happier about the change of driver, especially after the earlier shitshow between Remy and his girlfriend. The cherry glows in the darkness with my next drag, creating enough ash to flick out the window. My hair rustles as we gain speed on the boulevard, and I'm doing my damnedest to disguise the bundle of nerves churning inside.

"I love how smooth she rides," I finally say.

He glances at me. "You a gearhead?"

My shoulders lift for a beat. "I dig the cool wheels. Hard to top the muscle cars, though. I'd kill to have one, instead of my Bug."

"Don't knock the VWs. They're good vehicles, and a hell of a lot more economical than these gas hogs."

Oh my god. I *cannot* believe he just said *economical*, parroting my stupid father. "Who cares about fuel efficiency over design and speed?"

He smirks.

I will my nerves to settle—and stop popping like corn kernels hitting hot oil. "Is Mick a nickname or is that your real name?"

He nods, then tilts his head my direction. "My mom's a diehard Stones fan."

*Ah.* "I applaud her good taste." I glimpse my driver, who's holding one hand on the wheel with the other resting out the window when he's not pulling on his cigarette.

As we drive, it's clear Mick's a man of few words. I get the feeling if I don't say anything, he won't either.

"So...what's the deal with Remy and all the bullshit that went down earlier?"

"Not sure I can comment."

*That's how we're playing this?* "Does he cheat on her?"

"That'd be a question for Remy."

"Oh, I fully intend to ask him."

Silence.

Getting a boy's club answer irks the fuck out of me. Then again, maybe they're best buds—and I'm just the *new girl*.

"Did he hit on you?" Mick asks this so softly I almost don't hear it.

My head swivels his way, already reading too much into it. "Not really. He offered to give me a ride in his Camaro. I had no idea we'd end up at a party. Thought we'd be gone twenty minutes and he'd drop me back at work."

He appears thoughtful.

"But he also never mentioned a girlfriend." I tuck my bare foot under my leg.

"Surprise, surprise," he mutters.

"I'm not saying he should have. We just met. But lying?

Leaving me stranded? Not cool." We enter the freeway, and I roll my window up three quarters of the way. "Karin seems like a real prize."

Although shadows obscure Mick's face, I catch a smirk when he's briefly illuminated by a streetlight.

"Do you have a girlfriend?" Better to know now, so as not to pine in vain.

"Nope."

He doesn't offer more, and my gaze shifts toward the bay I can't see but know is there.

Mick turns up the radio. Van Halen and my resulting squeal fill the silence. I'm rewarded when a sidelong glance at my cute driver shows a small smile playing on his lips, which pleases me more than it should.

All too soon, we arrive at the gas station, and he pulls the Mustang alongside my VW. I slide on my flip-flops and collect my purse from the floor. "Thanks for the ride, Mick. I know you went out of your way, and I appreciate it. A lot."

"No problem," he says, lifting two fingers from where they rest on the wheel. Our eyes collide and his hold mine, a persistent quickening pulsing through my veins. He breaks away first.

A part of me resists getting out of the car, away from this mysterious man, but it's time. "See you around."

"I'd say that's likely since I work next door."

"Ha...right." *Get out of the car.*

Mick waits for me to get in my Bug and crank it up, following me when I drive out of the parking lot. More chivalry. But broody, cryptic, and smacking of unavailable. Fits my fucked-up template perfectly.

I'm not exactly hitting it out of the park with boyfriends. Or friends. And especially not family. But—with vivid recollection, Mick's intense eyes blaze in my memory—I've *never* experienced such heady infatuation before. Maybe love at first sight is real, instead of my preconceived notion it was fabricated ridiculousness.

Gripping the wheel with both hands, I exhale a long, slow breath. *Whatever the hell this is, it's intoxicating.*

# Four

Fifteen minutes into my shift the following day, Remy strolls into the office wearing greasy coveralls and a guarded expression.

My gaze snaps up and returns to the book splayed in front of me at the desk where I'm seated.

"I can tell you're pissed," he says. "I deserve that."

Sitting up, I cross my arms and pin him with a death stare.

He flashes a big grin. Why is his stupid smile so disarming? Ugh.

"I'm sorry about how everything went down," he adds.

"Yep...pretty much a dick move on your part. Or rather, *dickless*."

"Ouch." He places a hand over his heart. "My dick and I are offended. And we suggest you withhold judgment until you see for yourself." He has the audacity to wink.

My eyes roll, but damn if it doesn't make me curious what he's got under the hood. "What's the deal with you and your girlfriend?"

He shoves a hand in his pocket and hangs his head as if debating how much to reveal. A new customer drives in, dinging the service bell as another finishes pumping gas and walks toward the office.

Remy backs out, another stupid grin on his face. "You're busy. I'll talk to you later."

"Saved by the bell. Literally!" I call after him.

The bastard saunters away, still grinning.

The hours creep by agonizingly slow. I wonder what the guys are up to next door. *Working, obviously*. It makes the tedium and isolation only seem bigger.

Turning on the transistor radio, I locate KMEL, midway through "You Can't Always Get What You Want" by The Rolling Stones and chortle. Got that right.

My boss calls, informing me he's moving the tow service communications from the Chevron over to the self-serve, and to expect Vinny shortly to set it up. I welcome the additional responsibility. A girl can only read so many Danielle Steel and Sidney Sheldon novels.

A couple of hours later, Vinny shows up holding a cardboard box stuffed with machinery. His coveralls are unzipped and hanging over his waist, giving me a view of his barrel chest, covered by a T-shirt barely restraining his bulging muscles.

"Ciao, bella. Did Leo give you a heads up on this?"

Another sweet talker. I can't help smiling. "He did and said you'd walk me through it."

"Piece of cake. Smart girl like yourself won't have any trouble."

He scouts the office and begins installing the two-way radio while I shamelessly check out his biceps and forearms.

"You Italian?"

"Vincente Murano, at your service."

"Great name. Can you speak any?"

"Mostly cuss words." He chuckles. "My grandparents are

fluent, but my parents are first generation American. Some things were lost in translation, like language. But not the food. Never the chow." He plugs in the black box, microphone, and power.

"My heritage is as white bread as it comes. Scotch-Irish, a splash of Norwegian. Boring, compared to you."

He glances at me with those huge brown eyes then faces me, propping an elbow against the shelf. "Bellissima, you are anything but boring. Long golden hair with eyes that somehow match. If last night was any indication, you're fun, sweet, and know how to dish it back. And don't get me started on your body. A straight up ten. Bo Derek's got nothing on you."

My neck heats from his candid praise.

He jerks his chin my way. "Don't ever think you're less."

"Thanks, Vinny," I mumble, wondering if he's saying that last part because of what Remy did.

He returns his attention to the task, fiddling with the knobs as I absorb his flattery.

A few minutes later, he motions me over. "Let me show you how this works."

I lift off the desk and stand beside him, getting a whiff of mint from his gum. He shows me how to receive and initiate communication, explaining only one person can speak at a time. His thick fingers adjust the volume and other settings, his nails ridged a pronounced black. Basically, when a tow's needed, I'll get the call, log the details, and communicate the data to the truck driver, who has a receiver on his end.

"Who's the tow driver?" I ask.

Vinny rubs his jaw between a thumb and forefinger. "A mean SOB named Gooch."

"That's his first name?"

"Last. It's his company, but he has an arrangement with the boss. Transmit the correct information as fast as you get it, and you'll be fine." He pats me reassuringly on the shoulder.

Worry blooms, but this should only be a challenge if tow customers call while I'm juggling gas customers.

"Let's do a quick test before I split." He leans into the mic, presses the lever, and says, "Base to Gooch."

The response is a series of crackling static, then, "Gooch here."

"Testing. We're set-up at the self-serve."

"Roger. I'll swing by in ten."

"Roger and out."

I glance at Vinny. "He's coming here?"

He nods. "He'll probably show you everything again. His way of ensuring you don't fuck it up. Listen and learn."

"Let the mean SOB do his thing. Got it."

"I'm sure you'll dazzle him like you have everyone else." He nudges my shoulder and walks out the door.

Gooch arrives in a big white truck with "Cradle Snatcher" emblazoned on the top of the tow mechanism. He's a weathered old man who rasps like he's chain-smoked since age ten. His hair's slicked back with some kind of old-school pomade.

I survive his personal train-up and veiled threats about not getting him calls in a timely manner. An hour later, relief reigns after a call comes in and I successfully transmit the first communication, although it takes near screaming into the microphone to be heard.

WHEN THE CHEVRON CLOSES AND THE COLLECTIVE roar of muscle madness fires up next door, I lament still having three hours to go. I'm stuck here by myself and desperately want the company of my newfound work neighbors.

My spirits lift when Mick's Mustang pulls in alongside the gas pump I'm resetting, Remy grinning at me out the passenger side window.

"You hungry, new girl? he asks. "We're getting burgers and I'm happy to bring you one back." He dips his head. "On me. I owe you one." Instead of appearing chagrined, his eyes spark with mirth.

I shove a hand in my front jeans pocket and tilt my head, attempting a bitchy nonchalance. My stupid lips twitch. Damn if I can't stay mad at the lying snake. Plus, I'm starving —with two hot guys offering up dinner. That's called a no-brainer.

"That'd be awesome." I rattle off my order, adding fries and a Coke. Leaning in closer garners me a better view of Mr. Devastating—which is distracting—and I force myself to focus on Remy. "And if you forget the ketchup and extra salt, you're never getting back in my good graces."

He chuckles. "Duly noted."

The boys return a half-hour later, Remy clutching a greasy paper bag exuding a smoky, chargrilled aroma and Mick holding a cardboard tray wedged with fountain drinks. We dig in, and it's tasty...but nothing compares to sitting across from the ridiculously attractive Mick, who's blind to his effect on me. Polite but not solicitous, he's the opposite of Remy's aggressive charm.

It's on the tip of my tongue to press about the girlfriend situation, but I think twice about doing that in front of Mick, not wanting to spoil the mood.

We finish, and Remy sparks up a joint, taking a long hit before passing it. Mick inhales a drag and hands it to me. I'm no stranger to pot and wouldn't normally get high on the job, but as my position requires zero brainpower and my shift ends soon, what the hell. I take a pull, holding for a few beats before exhaling.

A mellow high kicks in and conversation turns to what we want to be or do when we grow up.

"You first, new girl," Remy prompts.

"I want to be a writer. I love books—always have. Writing them would be a dream come true."

Mick's gaze shifts from fixating on the floor to me. "Do you write anything now?"

Nodding shyly, a swath of my golden hair falls into my eyes, and I shake it back. "Short stories. Mostly stupid love stories."

"Stupid?" he challenges.

Shrugging self-consciously, I pull my knees up into the chair and wrap my arms around them. My true love story has yet to happen. "What about you?"

"I want to be on the water," he says, gray eyes thoughtful. "Captain a boat, work with boats, something to get me out on the ocean."

"Working outside would be cool," I agree.

"I'd prefer it. Being stuck inside all day working on cars sucks."

"Especially with smelly coworkers," Remy adds.

Mick flips him off.

Remy belches loudly, seeming pleased with himself. "I'm gonna party 'til I'm dead."

"*That's* your life plan?" I ask.

"Essentially."

"Your parents must be so proud."

Remy leans so far back in his chair I think he'll tip. "They're the ones who turned me onto drugs and booze in the first place."

"No shit?" I hug my legs tighter.

He hums. "My mom comes from money and my dad doesn't do squat except mooch off her and flirt with every skirt he can. My mom has her overbearing moments but neither one acts much like a parent. Our house has been one long party since I was born. I've been watching adults get lit for years."

My mouth gapes.

"Eventually, I joined in, like my older brother. Inevitable." Remy stares at the ceiling, unperturbed.

"That's terrible," I sputter.

He brings his chair back to the floor and cocks his head. "Is it?"

*It is, right?* My brain can't process something so outlandish. "I don't know."

Remy's eyebrows raise.

"Hold up. Your rich parents want you to be...what, a playboy?"

Mick snorts, glancing at his best friend.

"Not exactly. But for now, they're not hassling me."

"Why work at all? Why as a mechanic?" I ask.

He shrugs. "I dig cars, and I'm required to be gainfully employed. Any job will do."

I'm still trying to wrap my head around his reality. "So, you're happy?"

He smirks. "Hell yeah. Are you?"

Mick groans, pressing his fingers to his temples like we're giving him a headache. "That's a loaded, existential question. Happiness is fleeting. No one is happy all the time."

I stare at Mr. Handsome, wondering why he's so jaded.

He flips out a pack of smokes and offers me one, lunging over to light mine with his Zippo. My hair falls dangerously close to his flame, and he catches it and lifts it over my shoulder.

My lips pull on the cigarette, hoping to tame the jolt to my system from his hand on my hair. I swear, every simple, unassuming thing he does comes with a side order of sex appeal, and I might drown in its allure.

"I love the idea of happily ever after," I admit. "We all deserve that."

Mick shakes his head, lips quirking. "You're a romantic, Jacqui. We deserve nothing we don't earn."

His comment stings initially but swiftly recedes as I wonder if he's been hurt. The thought makes my heart ache.

Maybe the pain in me connects with the pain in him. Or I'm just high.

"Careful, new girl. You're about to uncork Philosophical Mick, and he's almost impossible to turn off," Remy taunts, getting another bird flipped his way.

"But if we aren't bloodsucking assholes spreading discord throughout the land," Mick continues as if never interrupted, "we have the opportunity to be happy, at least some of the time."

*Bloodsucking assholes?* What the hell's happened in his life?

Raising my fists, I throw some air punches. "Hallelujah. Thought we were going to have to take it outside."

He unleashes one of those incinerating, gray-eyed stares that turn my insides molten. "Think I can take you."

*You can have me. Period. No fight whatsoever.*

Paranoid Mick can hear my thoughts, I excuse myself to use the bathroom and get my bearings.

When I return, the guys are about to head out, and my spirits drop. This pair is growing on me. *Fast.* Whatever they are, or will be, they're filling a desperately wide and empty void. And there's not a cell in my body even questioning it.

# FIVE

I wake up Friday morning at eleven, elation washing over me. I'm off work for a couple of days *and* I'm joining my new group of friends tonight to see *Poltergeist*. Would you looky there, Mick...*happiness!*

I'd like a shot at making Mr. Broody happy, but he seems uninterested in anything more than our budding friendship. While that blows, I'll still take it—because I crave interaction with these literal "guys next door." Correction: *hot guys* next door.

The unwelcome flashbacks of my best friend flirting constantly with my boyfriend, finding out other gal pals were talking shit behind my back, and the general catty, jealous, competitive nature of chicks—as witnessed in Remy's girlfriend—makes it natural to distance myself from women altogether. In the short time I've been hanging around Mick and Remy, it's already just...easier. I don't even have to try.

Shuffling into the kitchen, I rummage in the fridge and pour a glass of orange juice. The house is quiet, my parents at their respective jobs. My father works in finance for a big corporation in San Francisco, and my mom is a secretary for a nonprofit organization in Walnut Creek.

A muffled sound steers me to my mother's bedroom, where she's prone in her king-size bed, hand flung over her forehead, flaxen hair fanned out across her pillow.

So, not at work after all, which happens with such regularity I'm not surprised or alarmed.

"You alright, Mom?"

"Migraine."

Right. *More like made-up reason of the day to huff down another Valium.* Mother's Little Helper has been her go-to for years now. Since the accident...or basically my entire life.

Call me judgmental, but if tragedy strikes, at some point you've got to get out of bed, get dressed, and get on with it. Maybe think about someone other than yourself, *like your kid*.

"Will you shut the door? And keep it down?"

"Sure. I'm leaving soon to go shopping anyway—and I'll be out tonight. A bunch of us are going to the movies."

"That's fine," she whispers, retreating into her tranquilizer haze.

Shutting her door, I quietly enter the bathroom, turn on the shower, and strip down, irritation chafing.

The rumination begins as warm water cascades through my hair, running in rivulets down my body. When's the last time my mother acted like one? She'd at least *tried* early on, despite her paralyzing grief. She baked cookies for class parties, took me shopping for new school clothes, dutifully attended my choir concerts. She still cooked. Decorated at Christmas. Sang happy birthday. Now that I'm older, she's basically a zombie. Her eyes—devoid of light. Her smiles— rare and forced. And her affection, once desperate and almost suffocating, became nonexistent, retreating over the years until she inhabited a vacant shell, incapable of showing any emotion.

The fact is, she's never really been present. Never been a mother except in name only. Never figured out how to pull herself out of the bog of despair in which she's so thickly mired.

She hardly pretends anymore. And my father—who tried to pick up her slack initially—has only grown more bitter, rigid, and unloving as my mother succumbed further into her swamp.

Dwelling on these negative thoughts only makes me resentful. Stuffing them back into the dark corners of my mind, I shift gears, considering where to shop. My first paycheck is burning a hole in my wallet and finding something cute to wear tops my agenda. Something Mr. Wonderful can't ignore.

Jeremy picks me up in his Starlight Black GTO Judge. As I round the front, admiring the scoops, there's no missing a totally rad hood tach.

"Like what you see?" he asks, his mouth settling into a smirk.

"It's alright, I guess." I'm unable to keep a straight face, and he smacks me playfully on the butt.

"Get in." He flips up his seat and I climb into the back with Vinny.

Jeremy introduces me to his date, Cora, whose brunette mane is teased to the ceiling. We take off to meet the others at the theatre and when I say *take off,* I mean like a jet. This GTO has serious giddy-up.

Relief sags through me with every mile put between me and my comatose mother and asshole father. I'm at ease with these new friends for some inexplicable reason and wonder if the universe is finally on my side.

The line for *Poltergeist* wraps around the block. After parking, we find Remy and Karin, Terry and Kendra, and Mick at the midway point. Angry piggy barely acknowledges me, but at least she's not spewing venom. She shrieks when she sees Cora, the pair launching into private conversation. After experiencing a momentary pang of odd woman out, Kendra steps up with an enthusiastic "Hi!" and we shift comfortably into our own dialogue.

Through it all, I'm acutely aware of Mick's every move. Where he stands. Whether he can see me. When he speaks. If he's noticed my new rainbow halter top.

Finally, our eyes meet, his again sweeping through me like a hurricane until I'm dazed.

The theatre opens and the line steadily inches forward. Inside our group splits. The couples get in line to buy concessions while Mick, Vinny, and I are tasked with saving seats. We enter the auditorium, nab a row halfway up, and spread out. I bust Mick checking out my ass, hugged nicely by my favorite pair of Levi's 501s. After breaking in these suckers for months, the button fly rips open with ease and they're hella comfortable—and flattering.

He meets my gaze for only a second, letting out a low laugh as he stares at the curtained screen. *But he looked.*

I'm anxious about seating arrangements as the remainder of our group filters in. Ten bucks says Remy won't be sitting next to me, but there's only one guy I desperately want on my left. There's a smidge of confusion but when the dust settles, Mick remains on the aisle seat with me by his side, then Vinny, followed by the couples.

The lights dim, the curtains open, and my heart thrums in my chest. A light sheen of sweat coats my skin as energy crackles in the dark from the proximity of my crush. I fan myself with the box of Milk Duds Jeremy tossed me and take a few sips of grape soda.

The previews highlight a funny little extraterrestrial stuck on earth called *ET* which looks promising, and *Blade Runner* with Harrison Ford, who stole the show in *Star Wars*.

The movie begins, and when Mick and I bump into one another on the armrest, we both flinch like we've been singed.

*Burn me again, please.* Now hyper aware, my hand rests on my leg. Glancing down, I realize he's done the same, and my lips curve into a smile.

I return my attention to the screen, where it's all happy family and neighborhood scenes...knowing it's the calm before the storm.

Carol Ann puts her hands on the TV and says, "They're heeeeeeere," and my heart rate ticks up like I'm at the top of the drop on a roller coaster.

Goosebumps ripple across my skin—frigid air and fear, and I rub my arms vigorously.

"You cold?" Mick's deep voice whispers in my ear, his warm breath setting off another wave of raised flesh while something else entirely clenches in my belly.

"Mm-hmm."

Without a word, he wraps his arm around my shoulders and tucks me in close, assaulting me with his ocean scent. He's only in a T-shirt but burns like a furnace. My heart threatens to beat out of my chest. I force out an exhale and let myself settle into the glory of being in Mick's orbit.

"Thank you," I whisper, sneaking a glance his direction.

He nods once and returns to watching the flick.

I do the same, even though my palpitations have every-thing to do with Mick Callahan and not the terrifying scenes playing out onscreen.

His arm stays put until the end, and I'm screaming on the inside more enthusiastically than a rabid Elvis fan. The magic ends when the house lights turn on and we all stand. The loss of his warmth is palpable, and Mr. Aloof acts as if nothing happened. *But it did.*

It just might not mean anything.


WE CONGREGATE IN THE LOBBY AND MICK INVITES everyone over. He's staying at his mother's home most of the summer while she traverses Europe, writing travel articles for the magazine where she works—a job I'd kill for.

Our bitchin' collection of vehicles race into the winding Montclair hills, throwing me into Vinny around the hairpin turns. Jeremy parks in a cul-de-sac on a dead-end street and we hike the stairs up the embankment to Mick's house.

I wander the modern, very California structure built of redwood, cement, and slate. Huge windows and sliding doors overlook a breathtaking view of the bay and San Francisco beyond. A long deck spans the house and out back, there's an intimate stone patio with a few chairs and a fire pit sheltered by the hill.

It's easy to love the minimalist, chic décor with enough plants to make it feel homey. Based on how his mom's put the home together (and naming her kid after a rock legend, the epitome of cool), I like her already.

My self-guided tour ends in the living room, where the whole crew is hanging out. Music blares from an impressive stereo system surrounded by a vast record collection I'm dying to flip through. Terry fires up a joint and does a super hit with Kendra. Remy pulls out a vial of cocaine and a razor blade and cuts a dozen lines on the glass coffee table.

Mick hands me a beer after twisting off the top, and I nearly drop it. Being near him makes me absurdly nervous, especially after the theater situation. Tipping the bottle, I chug a third to help me calm the fuck down before reaching into my purse for my cigarettes.

I avoid Karin's brittle, suspicious stares as Remy offers me a line. I've snorted blow a few times and liked it—not enough to buy it myself, but enough to jump on the party hardy express that's underway.

The coke burns up my nostrils, flaring and subsiding, the residue dripping slowly down my throat and leaving a trail of numbness. It's not long before the rush emerges, surging through my system like a firehose on full throttle.

Remy regales us with funny stories, his vivid blue eyes expressive, and I can see why women—and dudes—flock to him. Naturally charming, engaging, fun...and easy on the eyes. He sets people at ease, welcomes you into his world.

But what about his moral compass? He lied to his girl-friend, and I don't get the impression it was the first time. Does he cheat on her? Oddly, I don't care. Of course, I'm not dating him either.

After snorting several more lines, my heart beats like rapid gunfire, the edginess gnawing at my skin. I grab another beer and ease onto the deck, shutting the sliding door and dulling the sounds within. The trees shoot skyward, offering a framed scene that could be a painting. The Milky Way blazes a path overhead, leading to those dark, murky bay waters and lit city skyline.

The door opens behind me, and my head whips around. Mick shuts the door and moves next to me, resting his fore-arms on the rail.

"You've got a hell of a view," I say. It's a far cry from our modest, ranch-style home with a panorama of mostly other houses.

"Agreed." He tilts the beer to his mouth.

"Just your mom lives here?"

"I stay here a lot."

Gazing straight ahead, I briefly wonder where else he calls home but tuck it away for later. "Where is she now?"

"She's hiking in Italy, headed to Portugal soon. She loves doing outdoor stuff, and always combines it with her travel-writing gigs."

*A travel writer.* "Sounds glamorous. Adventurous."

Mick shrugs. "She digs it. I'm sure I get my love of nature from her."

Wow. Mr. Man of Few Words is conversing. "Are you an only child?"

"Nah. I'm the youngest of three. All boys."

"Are your siblings good looking too?"

*Crap. Did I say that out loud?*

He shifts toward me. "You think I'm good looking?" There's an amused half-smile on those inviting lips.

I lick my own, and his gray eyes track them intently. "Um...yes?" *Oh my god.* I jerk my gaze back to the skyline, wanting to leap into it.

He chuckles.

"Where's your dad?" I ask, my eyes finding their way back to his face, like they have a mind of their own.

He sighs and scratches his chin, tips the bottle, and drains it. His Adam's apple undulates in the dim light, and I'm riveted.

"Yeah...that's probably too much for this conversation."

"I'm sorry. I don't mean to pry."

"You're not. I just don't like talking about him." He absently picks at his beer label.

"I don't like talking about my parents either."

He swivels, as if wanting to say something, and my gaze snags on his eyebrow scar. Finally, he nods toward the house. "Come on. Let's get another drink."

I learn more about my friends as the party rolls into the wee hours, including that I'm the youngest of the bunch. Most graduated in 1979, one in 1978. It surprises me the majority went to Skyline, placing us there at the same time for one year. Although seniors and sophomores don't often mix, I can't imagine not noticing them before.

Terry tells me a sweet story about how most of them met through Young America baseball in their youth. Somehow, that's the glue that's held them together. The *Bad News Bears* springs instantly to mind.

Vinny throws out an invite to watch a handful of them play rec league softball, and I get an instant visual that brings a smile to my lips.

Some of the couples start making out, getting far too

handsy for my comfort level. I scoot over to the record collection and sift through it, busying myself admiring the album art. It's brimming with rock and Blues, and Mick's mom's cool quotient rises still higher.

My dreaded curfew looms along with blooming disappointment. No one else here has curfews (or wardens), reminding me—humiliatingly so—I'm the baby of the group. I also need a ride and don't want to wreck someone else's night by asking for one. Worst of all, I'm not ready for the evening to end. Especially when I'm in this kind of proximity to Mr. Gorgeous. An internal debate about blowing off my curfew ensues, but that will only result in penalties probably worse than the crime.

Relief hits when Terry and Kendra say they're splitting and I quickly bum a lift, explaining I'm only ten minutes down the hill.

Mick's cryptic expression, which I catch seconds later, remains unreadable as always. But his gaze on me is palpable as my fingers grip my denim purse and sling it over one shoulder.

Dejection seeps further into my bones as Mick ushers us to the door.

My eyes meet his. "Thanks for..."

He cocks his head and waits.

"You know. For the arm..." *For the arm? Seriously?*

Mick's lips break into a one-sided smile, but he utters nothing. No lifeline. No help.

I huff out a breath. "I *mean*, I had a nice time tonight. So just...thanks, okay?" *Kill me now.*

He bites his lip like he's trying not to laugh and nods. "Goodnight, Jacqui."

Fleeing, mortification stings every step until I catch up with the couple. Kendra flips up the passenger seat, allowing me to squish into the back of Terry's Trans Am.

It's a quick trip home. After thanking them, Terry grins as

brightly as his white car and Kendra waves from the open T-Top before they speed into the night.

Tiptoeing to my room, I collapse on the bed, wide-fucking-awake from amphetamines and all things coming with soulful gray eyes framed by long, dark lashes.

# Six

After a near-sleepless night, I haul my useless and bleary-eyed self out of the rack, already obsessing about what the guys are up to. Fetching the phone book from the kitchen drawer, I sift through the lightweight pages, find Remy's number easily enough, and write it down. Flipping back to the C's, my lips form a silent prayer Mick's mom still goes by Callahan, or I'm screwed. When her name leaps out, corresponding to the right street, my toes tap dance against the linoleum floor.

Should I call? Not call? Will it come off as desperate? The debate persists, even when my zombiefied mother nags me to clean the house. It's not like *she's* going to—or my father, who's planted himself in front of the TV drinking beer and watching sports. Hell will have a blizzard before he lifts a finger.

Two hours of chores later, in full "make the voices stop" surrender mode, my fingers dial Remy's number. He's far less daunting than Mr. Incredible, and I don't get tongue-tied around him. My face burns thinking about the inane babble that came out of my mouth saying goodbye to Mick last night.

Ten rings. No answer. Disconnecting the call, my eyes flick between the receiver clutched in my hand and the other seven digits staring back at me.

*Oh, fuck it.*

Once again, I depress the tiny, block-shaped keypads, each one resounding with a musical tone, and wait for the call to connect. My insides swirl with tornado-esque energy as each unanswered ring tolls. Once. Twice. Three ti—

At Mick's quiet hello, I unleash a rambling mishmash of words begging him to save me from suffering any further parental oppressiveness.

Not again. *What is wrong with me?*

To my dismay and delight, he green lights me coming over to hang out. I'm behind the wheel of my Bug in minutes, whooping loudly.

"C'mon, baby," I croon, downshifting on the steepest hill as we crawl up it like the train in *The Little Engine That Could*. My excitement overrides my usual exasperation at how little torque she has.

Coasting to a stop in front of Mick's, my internal buzz rivals a frenzied swarm of bees. The car sputters when I kill the ignition, and I waste no time bounding up the steps by twos. My flip-flop snags on one of the jutting stones, nearly taking me to the ground, but my hands save me. This is why someone invented the term chill pill. I need twenty.

The front door is wide open upon reaching it, the only sound aside from my heavy breathing coming from the television.

I tentatively pop my head through. "Hello?"

"Come on in," Mick beckons.

The guys lounge in the living room, each hogging a couch, the table before them littered with beer bottles and food debris. Mick's reclined, one arm crooked under his head. His eyes shift away from the baseball game on TV to lock on mine. Even tired, this man looks like a gazillion bucks. His bare feet poke out of faded jeans, a black T-shirt bringing out the gray in those bloodshot eyes.

His lips quirk up on one side. "Hey, Jacqui."

Remy sits with his long legs splayed, one elbow slung over the sofa ridge. He's wearing hunter green Adidas sweats with white pinstripes and a white undershirt, auburn locks askew. He flashes me a big grin. "There's our girl."

"Can I get you a drink?" Mick says, rising, revealing art from Pink Floyd's "Dark Side of the Moon" album on his shirt.

"Whatcha got?"

I follow him to the kitchen, trying—and failing—not to stare at his ass. Because just like every-fucking-thing else, his is superb.

"Beer, white wine, ginger ale…water."

"Wine, please." Might as well hair-of-the-dog it.

My gaze flicks around this stylish, open concept house where the main rooms connect unobstructed. A house I could get used to hanging out in. With a certain someone.

Mick extends classy stemware filled with pale gold liquid and our hands graze, jolting my insides and burning a hole straight through me. If his flinch is any indication, he felt it too. I take a long swallow of the chilled Chablis as Mick grabs two beers, and we return to the living room.

I slide into a burnt orange lounge chair, its quilted tufts deceptively firm. "How you guys doing?"

"Ready to roll, sports fans," Remy says, that perpetual grin plastered on his face.

Mick gives his friend a sideward glance and shrugs.

My finger circles the rim of my glass. "I hardly slept, thanks to you. You're both a bad influence."

Remy smirks. "You're a big girl—even if you *are* the baby. Mick, I'm not sure we should be corrupting her. She's not of legal drinking age yet."

Reaching behind me, I snatch the pillow and throw it at him. Remy bats it away easily.

"We've been drinking since we were fourteen," Mick deadpans, clearly for my benefit.

So have I, give or take, including sneaking it out of my parents' liquor cabinet—which, *shocker*, they've never noticed.

We laze for hours, hanging out, casually talking about nothing of importance, and I settle into actual comfort. My heart palpitations remain at bay in exchange for companionship without expectations, and it's...natural, unforced. Like a puzzle piece clicking into its counterpart.

Buzz going strong by late afternoon, I suggest we play I Never. I'm shocked when Mr. Broody doesn't shoot it down.

I start. "I've never had a threesome."

"Damn, girl. Throwing down the gauntlet first thing," Remy says. He's the only one to drink, which means he has. My mouth splits into a grin. Scoundrel.

He goes next. "I've never had sex outside."

All three of us drink.

Mick's turn. "I've never gone on a blind date."

We all stare as no one drinks. "Cheers to that," I say, and we lean in and touch glasses.

I fish out my pack of smokes and a matchbook. The match screeches across the strike pad, filling my nostrils with the sharp stench of sulfur. "I've never given someone a fake phone number."

We all sip again and burst out laughing.

Remy's expression turns wicked. "I've never whacked off more than once in a day."

The guys share a smirk and drink. My eyebrows hike with my deliberate swallow of wine.

Their mouths drop, staring as if uncomprehending, and I revel in every second.

Remy shakes his head. "I call bullshit."

Tucking my bare foot under my other leg, I drag on my cigarette and blow out a stream of smoke. "Sorry, loser, but you're wrong." My shoulders lift in a shrug. "I have needs." And since I'm the only person who's been able to give me an orgasm, I'm all I have—a tidbit I'll keep to myself.

They chuckle...but their eyes visibly darken as I see them mentally contemplating it.

"I read once ninety-eight percent of men whack off daily and sixty-five percent of women. So, you know, it's a thing," I quip, like I'm talking about the weather.

They stare at me like I'm from outer space. Eventually, Remy breaks the silence. "Girl, you're a trip. But I dig you."

My lips stretch into an unstoppable smile. "Your turn, Mick."

"I've never been arrested." Both guys drink.

Hiding my shock, I lean forward in my chair toward Mick. "What for?"

"DUI. Spent the night with a bunch of smelly assholes. Don't recommend it."

My eyebrows lift toward Remy.

"Busted with marijuana...after urinating in public," he answers sheepishly.

My brows furrow.

"I was wasted, and the cop had a Napoleon complex, so it escalated. Whatever," he says, blowing it off, "I was underage, got out of it. My record's sealed for life."

These bad boys. I'm not sure what to make of them.

It's my turn again. While taking another puff, it comes to me. "I've never cheated on someone."

Remy groans, dropping his head back against the sofa. "Just won't leave it alone, will you?" After a sideways glance, he tips back his beer. He's the only one, which makes me think Mick is a stand-up guy, even with the drunk tank visit, an infraction that could easily happen to any of us.

Tiny embers spark and fizzle stubbing out my cigarette. "Why *do* you cheat?"

He takes another gulp but has the good sense to look embarrassed. "I like variety...and there's a lot of fine tail out there."

"Why not break up with your girlfriend and sample the smorgasbord to your heart's content?"

He rakes a hand through his disheveled hair. "Because I love Karin, okay? I don't expect you to understand, but it's true."

He's right. I don't. "How often do you—"

"Nope. Not answering that."

An unladylike snort leaves my lips. "You're a fucking dog...but I still like you."

Remy grins, but Mick is strangely silent, making me think he doesn't condone his buddy's behavior. I don't either, but I'm not his lover—nor imagine that scenario *ever* happening.

My heart beats harder for the guy sitting next to him.


Driving to Laney College the following day has me gyrating in my seat. After parking beside the baseball diamond and grabbing my Coke, I settle on the bleachers and study the warm-up in progress. Remy, Mick, Vinny, and Jeremy wear blue shirts with "Commanders" scripted on the front, bold numbers on the back. They've got matching ball caps, but everything from the waist down is their choice, a combination of athletic shorts and fitted baseball pants.

Remy's at pitcher, lobbing softballs at Vinny, who's crouched behind the plate with pads strapped to his chest and legs. Mick plays shortstop, fielding grounders and hurling them to designated bases straight and fast. Jeremy stands in left field, long tossing with the other outfielders.

Seeing my boys in action gives me a natural buzz, and I'm ready for my role of cheerleader, even though it was never my jam in high school. When their opponents take their turn to warm up, my guys head for the dugout, waving or lifting their chins my way in greeting.

I'm fully absorbed when I hear, "You again." A glance behind me shows Karin barreling toward the bleachers. And yup, she's talking to me.

"Hi," I muster with a politeness she doesn't deserve.

She sits in the row directly in front of me and leans back, forcing me to retract my toes or let her squish them. Such a bitch move.

"You're like a pathetic stray who keeps turning up," she snarks. "Except there's no food for you here."

Ignoring her barbs, I slide down a few feet and stretch out my legs, crossing them at the ankles while resting my elbows on the bleacher behind me, taking up more space than before.

"Did the cat lose her tongue?" she goads.

"What's your problem, Karin? You don't even know me, nor have you tried, but you give me serious attitude. I totally don't get it."

"I don't trust you."

*Me...or your boyfriend?* "I've given you no reason not to."

"I don't like how chummy *my* boyfriend has become with you. You somehow have all these dudes brainwashed into thinking you're something special."

My snort resounds in the tepid air. As if. "Remy and the others are my friends, nothing more. We only know each other because we work right next door. It's no biggie."

"Don't kid yourself—or bullshit me. It's not natural for a girl to be *just friends* with guys."

Sounds like she's projecting her own insecurities. "It's a hell of a lot easier than dealing with chicks and their crazy shit," I mutter.

"What did you say?"

"You're wrong." *Maybe your pea brain can process that.*

"I bet you're hoping for a gang bang." She chuckles.

It's tempting to say something about how I hope Remy's involved, but I won't stoop to her level. "You're way out of line, and I'm done talking to you."

"Aww...did I hurt the widdle baby's feewings?" She scrunches her hands into fists on either side of her face, bobbing her head with each word and punctuating it with an exaggerated pout.

My silence suffices as my response even while my insides roil. Let the death fantasies begin. *No wonder* Remy cheats on this cunt. She's spiteful. Mean. Insecure. And a bully. What could he possibly see in her...aside from her body, I guess. But who cares when the inside is so ugly?

Swiftly ditching Karin and the bleachers, I walk to one of the fenced sides to cheer my guys on. I'm going to get loud.

And I do. Screaming, clapping, or whistling every time they enter the batter's box, make a play in the field, or strike another player out. I drown out Remy's pathetic excuse of a girlfriend—not that I'm trying. Much.

The team impresses me, especially my players. The catches they make. The saves. The steals. The hits. The home runs...plural, with Mick and Vinny each hitting bombs. Remy's amazing on the mound. Two innings straight, he sits down three batters in a row, with plenty more strikeouts. The game lasts seven innings, the Commanders dominating 12-2.

I hug every sweaty, dirt-stained one of them afterwards, their warm muscles bulging, their scents musky. Not even Mick flinches when I hurl myself at him. That ocean I'm growing addicted to fills my senses, and I drink it in, loving the way-too-brief moment I'm in his arms.

"Here we go again," he grumbles when we part.

I follow his gaze. Karin and Remy argue, their voices escalating by the minute. Angry piggy's upturned face shouts at Remy's, her finger pointing my direction. His hands fling out and hold steady as he dishes it right back. She shoves at his chest, and he looks like he wants to return the gesture. My heart drops. I don't mind pressing her buttons one bit—but not at Remy's expense.

You know what? Not my problem.

My problem is standing next to me with absorbing gray eyes and a one-sided dimple.

# SEVEN

My brain stalls mid-conversation with the tow customer, struggling to remember what to ask. The assholes lounging across from me got me mega stoned—an increasingly regular occurrence on weekday afternoons. They snicker while the distressed woman repeats her location, and now I'm laughing at them laughing. Collecting myself, I apologize to the caller, finish, and hang up.

"If you cretins don't shut up, you're going to get me in trouble—or fired."

Mick and Remy laugh harder, and my fingers close around a roll of paper towels and hurl it at their heads.

Slugging down a few gulps of Tab to slice through my cottonmouth, I glare a warning to the guys and depress the communications button on the unit. "Base to Gooch."

The radio crackles. "Gooch here. Got a tow?"

A grape whizzes past my head, and I turn, dodge another, and flash the boys a withering stare. They howl.

"What BS is going on over there, Jacqui?" Gooch barks. "Finish giving me the information. Right now."

More grapes are hurled my direction. I'm going to kill these motherfuckers.

"Uh...sorry." I relay the pertinent facts.

"What's the cross street?"

My stomach drops as my wasted eyes scrutinize the paper...where I failed to write it down. *Shit.* "I forgot."

"Goddamn it. Stop all that grab-assing and do your job!"

The guys stumble outside, bent over from laughing so hard.

"Yes, sir. My apologies."

"Your apology doesn't help me find this stranded woman."

*Shit. Shit. Shit.*

"I'll try and locate her. Contact me if she calls back," he grumbles. "Out." The communication goes dead, and I swivel, glowering at my friends lounging by the door.

"Seriously?" I say, folding my arms.

Remy walks over. "That was fucking funny." When he circles his arm around my shoulders, I violently shrug it off, and he feigns hurt.

My eyes stare at Mick expectantly. Maybe he can act like a grown-ass man.

"Grape?" he says, holding one up in his fingers.

"Oh my god! You two are going to be the death of me." But my lips quiver, fighting to curve up like the traitors they are.

"You love us," Remy teases.

He's not wrong. These idiots have endeared themselves to me in a matter of weeks. I don't remember having this kind of connection with most girls, and never guys. And certainly not my fucking family. We're one month into summer, and I'm already dreading going back to school and how it will change...everything. I wonder if they feel the same.

Mick shakes his keys. "Let's go, Rem." His gaze swings to me. "You coming up later?"

My heart surges. He may not be asking me *out*, but he's still asking me *over*. I yearn for more, but he doesn't seem to despite the energy sizzling between us—unless that's all in my head. There's no denying I love hanging out with them. Maybe too much.

A smile spreads. "Yup. After I close."

"Be careful," he says in that disarmingly caring way of his, and they split in their way-cooler-than-mine cars.

BY THE TIME I GET TO MICK'S, THE PARTY'S rocking, music's loud, and drugs and alcohol flow like a river.

Passing the kitchen, I spy Vinny sucking on a beer bong with Jeremy holding the funnel.

A game of Quarters is underway on the dining room table between Remy, Karin, Terry, Kendra, and a girl I don't recognize. Mick's in the living room speaking earnestly to some chick in a tight pair of Dittos jeans—the kind with the horseshoe stitching that leave nothing to the imagination. And she's *pretty*.

I'm struggling not to stare while also tempering the hot, roiling angst in my gut. Unsure what else to do, my feet backpedal into the kitchen.

Jeremy shakes the hair from his eyes, which falls back into perfect, feathered layers, and references the contraption he's holding. "You look like you could use one of these."

"You have no idea," I mutter. "Hit me."

He grins diabolically. "I've got you, new girl. Open wide."

The salacious way he says it obliterates the jealousy coursing through my veins. I place my lips around the tube. Jeremy pours a beer in the funnel and lifts it overhead, the liquid crashing into my mouth and down my throat at record speed. Swallowing the waterfall, let alone with grace, requires concentration. Some dribbles out, but I manage most of it.

"Impressive, Jacqui."

Licking the foam from my upper lip, I wink. "I've got a big mouth."

He tracks my tongue, then leans in close. "I'd like nothing more than to find out everything about your mouth. Just say the word."

A knowing smile etches across my lips. Jeremy's super fine, but he's a total player, and I only want the affection of one person in this house. And he's talking to another chick. I will fucking die if he makes a move on her, not that I have any claim. *Someone show me how to override my damn heart.*

A FEW HOURS LATER, I'M HAMMERED. AND UTTERLY miserable. Mick has spent most of the night with Mystery Girl, who is cute, built, and hangs on his every word. Her only obvious flaw is being friends with Karin.

Mick's gaze lingers on mine, and I worry what my face broadcasts. Hopefully not *desperately in love with you*, but who knows? I'm drunk. He's drunk. Everyone's drunk.

"Fuck you!" Karin's shrills, and I jerk toward the sound in time to witness her shove Remy with both hands. She's such an asshole.

They're outside on the deck, words muffled, but her body language transmits her fury loud and clear. I'd feign concern except this seems like a weekly phenom for them. Still...it's not looking good for Randolph Remington III, and I empathize. *It's not looking good for me either.*

They verbally duke it out for another twenty minutes before Karin storms inside, declares to her friends they're leaving, and yanks open the front door. "Assholes!" she screams, to—I guess—all of us, then slams it shut behind her.

I join Remy outside as he finishes chugging his beer. "You okay?"

He scrubs the back of his head in vigorous strokes. "I don't fucking know."

Giving him time to elaborate, I light a cigarette and slowly release the smoke, tracking the wisps as they evaporate. The world spins, and my fingers grip the railing. I'm trashed to the point sitting is probably a smarter bet.

"Gimme one of those," he says.

I hand over mine and fumble sparking up another. "Wanna talk about it, good buddy?" Now "Convoy" lyrics are bouncing through my head.

He glances over at me, expelling smoke with a forced breath. "She's jealous. She's uptight. She's never happy. I can't do anything right." His words come out garbled, but somehow, I decipher it. Maybe drunk is a whole language, only understood by other drunks.

My forearms prop against the railing. "Are you tired of trying?"

Remy mimics my position. "Fuckin' A. It's like being on a demented merry-go-round. Sometimes the ride's so good, and other times we spin, trapped, unable to get off the motherfucker."

"But you don't want to end it," I say.

He takes a lengthy drag. "I don't know. We've been together a long time..."

"And?" Teetering, my fingers clutch the railing again.

"And it feels like a lot of fucking work these days."

"Bummer."

"You know the weird thing? I can talk to you ten times easier than her. I don't know if I've ever truly been friends with a girl before. You're different somehow." His lips quirk up on one side, and he nudges me with his shoulder. My body sways dramatically, and he lurches to catch me.

"I love being around you guys," I admit.

"Yeah?"

"Way better than chicks." Totally true.

Remy shifts, knocking into me so our shoulders are touching, but he doesn't correct. "Good."

Mick appears out of nowhere, grabbing my arm and hauling me behind him. "Not her," he slurs.

"What the fuck, man?" Remy scowls.

*What's happening?*

"Keep your goddamned hands off her."

Remy's eyes narrow. "What's it to you? Not like you're gonna make a move."

*What?*

Mick's gray eyes turn even stormier...and dangerous. "Just fucking leave her alone."

"You're being a dick."

"And you're only thinking with yours," he spits out as he lunges for Remy, spins him toward the house, and drives him against the exterior wall. He shoves his forearm to Remy's throat, but Remy breaks away and throws a right hook into Mick's side.

The breath leaves my body, replaced by a flood of adrenaline as they scuffle.

"Stop it, you guys!" I scream.

They weave precariously across the redwood decking, fists flying at each other, trading blows.

They topple to the ground just as Terry and Jeremy charge outside. Terry pulls Mick off Remy, and Jeremy presses a knee into Remy's torso. Chests heaving, Mick and Remy shoot murderous glares back and forth, bucking against their restrainers, not ready to quit brawling.

"Drunken idiots," Terry mutters.

He glances at me as if looking for an explanation. I shrug, open-mouthed, the sudden turn of events sobering me faster than a cold shower.

"Let me fucking go," Mick thunders, his death stare squared on Remy.

Remy shakes his head, looking more puzzled than angry.

"Time to kiss and make up, girls," Jeremy says, hauling Remy to his feet.

Remy flings his hands out. "What the fuck was that all about?"

"Nothing," Mick mutters, and the two friends exchange hard stares for a long minute.

Remy breaks the stalemate. "Whatever, dickhead. We good?"

"Yeah, man."

He strides past Mick into the house and Terry and Jeremy follow, leaving the two of us alone.

We're silent, although a thousand thoughts race through my head. Blood smears his cheek, and when he lifts his hand to push the hair off his face, he winces, his right hand shredded across the knuckles.

"You're hurt, Mick. Let me help you."

"I'm fine," he mumbles.

"Let me help you anyway."

He shrugs.

"Where's the first aid?"

"Hall closet." He trudges inside, losing his balance and crashing into a row of plants, then landing hard against the wall.

I guide him to the living room sofa, and he falls against the cushions, closing his eyes. I locate the medical supplies, grab what's needed, and walk back to find Mick passed out and Remy locking the front door. It's two in the morning and the fight served as a party-ending buzzkill.

Kneeling by Mick, I gently clean the blood from his face using a warm, wet paper towel, and do the same with his injured hand, squeezing antibiotic ointment on it before adding a dressing. When I check his other hand, my brow furrows. Strange scars mar his knuckles, but these look ancient.

Not finding any other obvious wounds, my gaze turns to Remy, inspecting him for injuries. A bruise blooms on his left eye, the swelling apparent. He's already holding a bag of frozen peas. Caressing his arm, I ask, "You alright?"

"Never been better. Great fucking night." He plops down on the adjacent sofa, tilts his head back, and presses the cold pack to it.

Carefully, I slide my body underneath Mick, resting his head in my lap. My curfew is now officially broken but I doubt I'm legally sober enough to drive despite clarity reigning.

Except in one area.

"Remy?" My fingers comb lightly through Mr. Incredible's chestnut waves, which are every bit as glorious as I'd imagined.

"Hmm?" he grunts.

"What the hell was that all about?" My fingers trace along Mick's face, more angelic in sleep, my gaze snagging on his eyebrow scar and the tiny mole on his forehead above it. Sensing Remy's unswollen eye aimed at me, I look up.

"What do you think? He was jealous."

My mouth drops. "Of what? *Us?* But...he doesn't even act interested."

Remy resumes his former position and exhales forcefully. "He's interested," he mutters, almost like it's painful. "He's gun-shy. And a dick."

My brain sticks on *he's interested,* replaying it. "What do you mean? Why is he apprehensive?"

He removes the peas to look at me. "You know...walking wounded. He's still got shrapnel from the last relationship."

*Ohhhhhhhh.*

"You've got it bad, don't you?" He scours my face with his good eye.

My neck heats. Am I so obvious? A shaky breath releases, my head bobbing in admission. "Is it a lost cause?"

He shrugs and offers a weak smile.

"I don't want to mess this up either." My hand waves between the two of us.

"This what?" he croaks, leaning forward on his knees, his stare boring into mine.

"The three of us. Our friendship. Our whole Musketeers thing." Gazing at Mick's gorgeous face, my fingers stroking his hair, I float on a cloud. My throat knots replaying the earlier deck scene. Was he protecting me? Defending me? Being territorial? Whatever it was, it was *something*.

"Jacqui, there's no crystal ball for any of this shit. Carpe diem. You only live once."

"That's deep," I tease.

"Stop worrying about the what-ifs and go after what you want. And if it's Mick, you might have to make the first move." He lets his head loll back, grimacing when the frozen vegetables touch his injured eye. "That motherfucker is such a moron."

Am I brave enough to act...*if* what Remy says is true and Mick's attracted to me?

Mick stirs, mumbling incoherently. I caress his arm, and he unconsciously reaches for my hand, the warmth of his pressing into mine. And here we are, holding hands. Even if only one of us knows it.

# EIGHT

Intrusive sunlight beams through the sliding doors, burning my eyes when they open with a jolt. It doesn't take long to realize I'm prone on the sofa with a blanket draped across me. Mick's nowhere in sight. Remy's crashed on the other couch, a shiner in shades of green and purple blemishing his handsome face. My head throbs as I sit up, then I'm hit with a disgusting gummy texture coating the inside of my mouth.

Staggering into the kitchen, I fill a glass with water, sag against the counter and chug it, emotions swirling. What did last night mean? And what kind of trouble am I in for staying out all night without making a phone call? *Colossal.*

Torn between hightailing it home and tracking down Mick, I opt for the latter. I stealth down the hall in my bare feet, find his bedroom door ajar and peek inside. He's sprawled face down on his bed, fully clothed, softly snoring. Indecision plagues me. Wake him...don't wake him. Questions loom, but clueless about what I'm ready to do or say or expect, I do nothing but stare.

I'm officially a head case.

Absorbing one last lingering look of Mr. Sleeping Beauty, I back away. After pulling myself together and quietly cleaning up some of the train wreck we made of the house, I drive home to face the firing squad.

My dad arrives home at the same time as I do. By his disheveled appearance in yesterday's wrinkled navy suit—part of a paisley necktie hanging out of one pocket—it's clear he also stayed out all night. I'm struck speechless. He's *never* done this before...although I've harbored suspicions he's cheated on my mother.

"What?" he challenges as we start up the walk.

"You're...just getting in?" *Does mom know? How could you?*

"Yup. Pulled a Jacqui," he says with zero remorse.

*Jackass.* My purse slips from my shoulder, and I fantasize about swinging it hard at his head. "I fell asleep by accident at a friend's house. I would've called, not that it would have mattered..."

"Don't give me any lip. You still have a curfew and if you don't adhere to it, you'll lose all privileges."

*Power tripping prick.* God, I'd love to say those words out loud. I fucking hate him. And this house. And my life. I'm filled with disgust. He blows through the front door with me trailing behind, and I clamp my mouth shut and go straight to my room.

When my parents start screaming at each other, I wrap my headphones around my ears and crank up Fleetwood Mac on my turntable, wishing I lived anywhere but here.

An hour later with my head still aching and shrouded in fog, I shower and leave for the late shift at the self-serve. My long, listless hours are consumed with what the hell Mick was thinking last night...and reliving my fingers in his soft hair and the peaceful way he slept in my lap, like he belonged there.

Frustrated, exhausted, and with nowhere else to go once work ends, I'm forced to return home. Minutes after crawling into bed, I crash hard.

# Nine

On Sunday, Kendra invites me to swim at Terry's, and I jump at the chance. She's sweet and genuine, making me want to know her better, especially after detecting no hidden agenda or cattiness. My parents don't argue with me with World War XVII still underway—they've segued from shouting to silence.

It doesn't take long to put on my suit, slip into a pair of hot pink Dolphin shorts, a white tank top, and matching flip-flops. I unearth my beach bag and shove in a towel and suntan oil.

My Bug winds back into the hills to Terry's affluent neighborhood, and I park out front.

Kendra opens the door, gorgeous in a mesh cream bikini, hair pulled up into a high ponytail, doe eyes rimmed with kohl eyeliner, and mascara taking her lashes to extremes. She greets me with a big hug as if we didn't see each other two nights ago.

I follow her out back, where Terry's already lounging on a deck chair in trunks and a pair of Ray-Bans. The sun glints off the water in a sizeable rectangular pool, diving board jutting over the deep end.

"What's good?" he asks.

"Same ol', same ol'." Even though it's not. "Thanks for having me over." I drop my bag and drape my towel on a lounge next to Kendra's—trying not to gape at the muscles rippling across every part of the athlete sitting beside her like a god. *Jesus.*

Terry points toward a cooler. "Beer's in there. Sodas are in the fridge. Help yourself to anything. Mi casa es su casa."

"Somebody paid attention in Spanish."

"You think only my baseball cred got me into Cal?" He flashes a panty-dropping smile.

Smirking, I strip down to my vivid yellow string bikini. I'm toned, not muscular, and the opposite of petite at five-foot-eight, sporting generous curves (my hips reached maturity in eighth grade, but the rest of my body finally caught up). A killer tan and Heather Locklear lookalike hairstyle fuels my confidence wearing this skimpy suit.

"Don't you be looking at this fine-ass white girl," Kendra warns.

Her boyfriend chuckles and holds up his hands.

Giving her a pointed stare, I say, "Um...there's no competition—look at you."

Terry leans over and outlines Kendra's lips with his finger. "She's right. You're all the sugar I need."

As they make out, I sink back against the chair and close my eyes, groaning contentedly as the sun coats my body. Muscles relax, tension dissipates—and I try really fucking hard not to think about how long it's been since my last kiss. *Not that I've been fantasizing about it with a certain someone at all.*

Other friends trickle in as we talk, swim, and bask. First comes Jeremy, who wolf-whistles at Kendra and me—despite the Flavor of the Week by his side. Vinny shows up next with a girl named Camilla, who sports lips painted red and wavy black hair reaching almost to her waist. Finally, Remy and Karin saunter in like they're the life of the party. They obviously worked out their issues. *For now.* Mega downer for me, though...I'd rather guzzle pool water than deal with that bitch again. And why can't Remy see her for what she is? It's disappointing. Anxiety floats freely within me with each new arrival, waiting—hoping—for Mick while also unsure about...everything.

Someone lays on their horn in the street with obnoxious, relentless enthusiasm and curiosity has us all moving toward the front. An extended Cadillac in a deep merlot sits on display, so long it's practically a limo. A dude sporting a seven-inch afro and maybe the same width grin cackles out the window from the driver's seat.

Guffaws and exclamations erupt as the guys dap with the grinning driver.

"Leland," Terry says, scoping out his buddy's ride and shaking his head with an incredulous laugh. "Where'd you score this pimpmobile?"

They banter while the rest of us gawk, speculating how many people it seats.

I complete a full revolution around the vehicle. "That's some car."

"That's some bikini," Leland answers, groping me with his eyes.

Giving him an eye roll, I meander back inside, taking an impromptu tour and fighting my disappointment Mick's still not here. Maybe he's not coming. Maybe he's avoiding me, or Remy, or both?

Night descends and Terry fires up the grill. There's food, booze, cannonballs...and Leland, who hits on me like it's his job.

In escape mode, my feet sink into the plush hallway carpet taking me to the refuge of the bathroom. My hair's a wild mess after dips in the pool, and a slight sunburn kisses my skin. Deciding it's a lost cause, I head for the kitchen, hoping there's something tasty whirring in that blender.

Mick rounds the hall corner as I'm nearing the midway point, and my heart stutters. His gray eyes rake over my body before burning into mine. My breath catches and stays lodged in my windpipe. He's staring. *Hard.*

"Fuck," he mutters.

"What's wrong?"

He closes his eyes and scrapes a hand through his hair. "Nothing."

*It's not nothing.*

"You okay?" Because I'm not.

"Yeah." He appears to compose himself.

"I wondered if you were coming," I venture a step forward and he immediately retreats, like I'm aiming a blow torch his way. What the hell?

"I had shit to do."

My eyes drift from his face to his hand: he stripped off the bandages, and his cuts are still a deep red.

"Hope your house wasn't too trashed. I tried to clean up before splitting yesterday but didn't want to wake you."

His eyes slide down my body and snap back up. "Right...thanks. Most of these slobs don't care. Assholes."

My shoulder lifts and drops. "Men."

He laughs softly, not meeting my eyes. "So, I need to use the head..."

"Gotcha." I shift out of the way, and he strides past.

Dazed, my feet move of their own volition, winding up in the kitchen where Camilla and Kendra pour margaritas. They offer me one and I take it gratefully, inhaling a few sips of the tart mixture.

Kendra raises her eyebrows at me in silent question. She knows I'm crushing on Mick from my earlier confession and must have seen our interaction.

Tears glass my eyes, and my throat tightens staving them back.

She offers me an encouraging smile, grips my waist, and pulls me close for a side hug.

Shuffling outside and inhaling some deep breaths, I'm more confused than ever over my moody not-boyfriend. People are in the pool, others in the hot tub or near the grill. I sit on my lounge and tuck my feet underneath me, getting lost in the moonlight dancing on the water and trying not to over-think my life.

Leland slides into the seat next to mine. "You are *fine*, girl."

"And you're...not shy."

He snorts. "Did you *see* the Lelandmobile? What about that screams 'timid' to you, Special J?"

An insincere chuckle pushes from my lips. "It's a cool ride."

"I'd like to take you for a ride." He leans in, teeth gleaming in the dark.

"Behave, Leland."

"Why? You taken?"

*"Jacqui."*

That voice. I'd know it in my sleep...hell, *my grave*. My head swivels and finds Mick looming, his eyes glued to mine.

"Can I talk to you for a minute?"

"Homey...why you gotta do me like that?" Leland gripes. "I was just getting somewhere."

The way Mick grins is almost feral.

I leap to my feet and Leland grumbles in my wake. "I'm snagging your digits before you leave."

*Hate to break it to you, but you're not.*

I follow Mick inside, my pulse ticking up with every step. His broad shoulders lead the way, his Levi's hugging all the right parts. He coaxes me into a room lined with crowded bookshelves.

My kind of place, under normal circumstances...but I can only focus on one marvel at a time. And when mine shuts the door, my rapidly thudding heart threatens to pop out of my chest.

It's dark, the only light filtering in from a streetlamp. He's standing close enough that his ocean scent floats around me. Faint laughter echoes from the backyard, eclipsed by the echo of my heartbeat.

"Jax," he murmurs.

My insides soar. *He called me by a pet name.* I'm stunned into silence, all cohesive thoughts and responses scrambling in my head.

His deep voice stays low, quiet. "I'm sorry."

"For what?" I breathe.

"I've tried to stay away from you, but..." He scoffs, leaning his head back. When he snaps it forward, his eyes blaze, searing me like a brand. With one step, he bridges the gap between us and his hand captures my face. "Why do you have to be so fucking gorgeous?"

My heart launches into a full gallop.

"I'm done fighting."

"Why are you fighting it?" I whisper.

"Not sure I can give you what you deserve," he murmurs. His focus shifts to my lips, as if asking. "I'm not looking for a commitment. Or complicated. But damn I want you."

I tear my gaze away from his tantalizing mouth before forgetting to respond. I don't know what he means or whether to heed his warnings.

Not that it matters—my answer's the same. "I want you too."

Both of his hands frame my face, drawing my lips to his as electricity sizzles and crackles between us. His lips grace mine softly, a zing of molten heat shooting through me with meteoric force. My whimper collides with his groan, and his strong arms pull me flush against him. He kisses me breathless, our heads tilting as we discover how we fit together. His full, supple lips are *everything* I imagined and more. Overcome with his heady scent, the putty I am in his grasp, I'm completely, instantly under his spell.

His kisses turn decisive and demanding, and my knees wobble so forcefully, I clutch his sturdy frame tighter. I'm overwhelmed in the most delirious, welcome way. With Mick's hand cupping the back of my head and the way his mouth possesses mine, he tells me I'm his without uttering one syllable.

*I'm yours. I'm yours. I'm yours.*

His tongue roves along the seam of my lips, and my body quakes with new explosions as our tongues tangle and explore. My mewls escape unbidden, and his resounding guttural rumblings only fuel the inferno melting my core.

His large, rough hands roam *everywhere* as his lips glide down my neck. I gasp when his teeth focus on one spot, marking me.

*I'm yours. I'm yours. I'm yours.*

My fingers stroke his biceps and up his broad shoulders, threading through his glorious hair. I'm consumed by the tidal wave of his ocean, and happily drowning in it.

His mouth returns to mine while his hands grip my hips, fusing us together. His erection presses into me, and we both moan with pleasure, grinding against each other, our bodies saying everything.

I'm in a haze of lust-filled bliss, unsure I could stop this cyclone if I tried. It's highly possible I just made a deal with the devil, because my soul is lost to this man.

Our frenzied lips part and our foreheads touch, keeping us connected. Heavy breathing punctuates the air and slows —but not the need simmering between my thighs. I'm on fire.

He pulls back to look me in the eyes. "Fucking hell, Jax.

You're driving me insane. And that bikini? That's not even playing fair."

Swimming in potent, undiluted joy, my smile beams. "You're one to talk." *You hijacked my heart months ago.* I was Micknotized on day one.

He cocks his head as if oblivious to his effect on womenkind.

I caress his smooth face, wondering if he shaved before showing up here, and grapple with how to express my feelings. "I've been waiting fifty lifetimes for you to kiss me like that."

His gaze deepens, then darkens. "I want to keep you in here all night doing everything I've imagined to your perfect body."

His words send more heat to my already soaked bikini bottom. I audibly swallow. "Sounds good to me."

He slips his hand in mine, his thumb's caresses sending tingles down my spine. "But this isn't the time or place."

I'm sure he's being logical, but it still smarts. "Rain check?"

He grins, tracing my jaw with his knuckles. "Baby, we're just getting started."

My insides surge with hope and longing, stomping on my unanswered questions. He palms the back of my neck and draws me closer, kissing me tenderly. It's short-lived as the spark quickly reignites and we hurtle into feverish yearning.

When he finally forces us apart with a frustrated groan, he adjusts the obvious bulge in his jeans. If I'm uncomfortable, I can only imagine what it's like on his end.

"Hot tub?" I suggest.

"Only if you're sitting next to me." The husk in his voice sends more tremors through me.

Ten minutes later, we climb into the circular redwood tub, fresh drinks in hand. We sink into the steaming water, bubbles covering our legs as they wedge together, his hand discreetly stroking my thigh. From the surface, no one's the wiser, but inside, sheer elation threatens to break out like a caged tiger.

# TEN

Mick saunters over halfway through my shift and leans on the door frame, arriving moments after I've peeled a banana. My mouth hovers over the tip and stalls, my insides jolting to attention. The mere sight of him snatches the breath from my lungs, even more so with the memory of his lips on mine burned into every one of my cells.

My internal engine revving, a wicked idea emerges. Returning my phallic fruit to my mouth, I insert several inches—achingly slow—and finally bite it off, groaning from its sweetness. His gray eyes turn stormy as he watches the show.

He approaches like a beast stalking his prey and my insides shift. *First gear.*

"Two can play at that game," he purrs.

He whips me around in my chair and in one fluid movement, claims my mouth with his, unleashing his talented tongue. *Second gear.*

I whimper in supplication, and he consumes it, a low, throaty growl leaving his throat. *Third.*

Every sweep of his tongue, every suck on my lip, every

demand his body makes ignites my nerve endings and floods my center. We're at max horsepower now, flying in fourth gear, as he burns me to the ground.

Abruptly, he stands, wearing a satisfied expression.

My body crackles with need, desperate for more, more, more. I'm panting like a dog, responding like a bitch in heat.

"Mick..." I whine.

"Hmm?" He shoves a hand in his coveralls and cocks his head.

Realization dawns. "You motherfucker. You did that on purpose!"

He smirks. "Who, me?"

I fling my banana skin at him as a customer pulls in the station.

He dodges it, laughing. "Come over for dinner tonight."

*Mick Callahan is asking me on a date.*

Melting further into a warm, gooey mess, I smile. "I'd love to."


I'M A BASKET CASE DRIVING TO MICK'S. I SPENT most of the afternoon planning my outfit to make it quick and painless after work but I'm still waffling about my choices. Glancing quickly into the rearview mirror doesn't help. And my appearance isn't really the issue...this man turns me into a nervous wreck.

Our first, second...twentieth kisses are out of the way, and I'm greedy for more. God, *his lips*. I trace mine with a finger, savoring the memory. This is still so new—his revelation he's been fighting me, us, the idea. He *was* jealous of Remy. He thinks I'm *beautiful*.

It's a dream come true.

But there's a lot about Mr. Mysterious I don't know...and, of course, I'm choosing to ignore those flashing caution lights. *He's not looking for a commitment. He doesn't want complicated. He's not sure he can give me what I deserve.* Whatever all that means.

I still don't care, hopeful it will just work out.

My brain conjures up his mental image. Those lips. Eyes. Build. Bulge. I've never wanted carnal knowledge of someone so much in my entire life. Thank God I stayed on birth control, even though I've engaged in zero sex since my break-up with Robbie. I've gone on a few dates, but none that even warranted a second round. There were also one-night stand opportunities, but those aren't really my style. I'm monogamous by nature, wanting more than just physical release or one night of fun (and is it fun if the sex isn't great? How do you know what you're getting?).

Going all the way with Mick tonight would be fast. So far, we've only kissed...except there's nothing *only* about it. His kisses obliterate me, turn me upside-down, consume me. Anything beyond that will probably kill me. A death I welcome.

But we've grown closer these past several weeks spending so much time together. We may not have been *together* together, but I've craved him from minute one and now I'm pretty sure it's been the same on his side.

Which brings me back to *will he think I'm easy if I jump his bones?*

I'm way too chicken for that. I'll let him take the lead, go with my gut, show restraint if necessary. One body part laughs out loud, and I silently whisper for her to shut up.

After parking and climbing the stairs, the stupid organ in my chest jackhammers at a ridiculously frenetic pace. *Calm the fuck down.* My knuckles rap on the open door and an answering shout beckons me in.

Mick's barefoot, in Levi's, with a white T-shirt emblazoned with the Dr. Zogs Sex Wax logo stretched over what I've envisioned to be delectable pecs. I could ask for no more perfect attire for this specimen. Now I'm salivating. For real.

"Hey," he greets, circling me with one arm and planting a soft kiss on my lips. Just like that, I'm rocketing into space.

"Hey yourself," I breathe, miraculously forming words. I need to stop the hero worship. And I will. Any day now. But not today.

His fingers graze my cheek, his stare intense, making tingles zing to all my parts. "You have the most extraordinary eyes. They're the color of honey," he says, kissing me again.

I'm floating when we pull apart. "I love yours too. The gray changes with your mood." Like the sea. Calm. Stormy. Every iteration sexy.

His lips lift in a half-smile.

There's a smoky sweetness in the air. "I don't know what you're cooking, but it smells damn good in here."

"It's nothing fancy, but I think you'll like it. Make yourself comfortable." He hooks a thumb toward the kitchen. "I need to check on things."

Dropping my purse on the nearest sofa, my gaze fixates on the sky framed by the sliding glass doors, painted in dazzling golden hues as the sun inches closer to the horizon. An album spins on the turntable, B.B. King crooning out his signature Blues while manipulating his legendary guitar.

Mick offers me wine. I'd drink the entire bottle if it would unknot my stomach. Drifting to the counter, I sip from the stylish stemware. It's another refreshing, crisp white. "You're a chef too?"

"A competent cook—yes. A chef—no. What about you?"

"It's been my responsibility for many years although my parents never taught me much in that department. My mom's not often...up to cooking, and my dad works long hours. I've mostly taught myself but doubt it's anything to brag about."

"Good skill to have if you appreciate eating well. My mom schooled me right up." Mick's eyebrows wing up. "She was concerned I'd starve as a bachelor."

I bark out a laugh. "Smart lady."

He guides me to a fully set table and pulls out my chair, chivalry in full force. He disappears, returning with a spread of barbecued chicken, rice pilaf, and salad.

"Looks delicious. You're a man of many talents." Thoughts about his mouth on mine flash in my memory and the heat ignites. *Get your head out of the gutter, girl.*

"Dig in," he says.

We're quiet, the formality awkward as we eat. A couple of hours ago he had his tongue in my mouth, and now we're making polite conversation. Probably not for long. *Hopefully not for long.* We're sitting near enough that I'm devastated by a close-up of those gray eyes with the dark ring, his lashes creating a shadow against his cheek when he focuses on his plate. Those nearly symmetrical lips, a kissable shade of rose. The cupid's bow my tongue begs to trace. That wavy hair my hands crave to touch again. His looks should be illegal.

He stares at me like I'm the meal, which keeps the pool of heat swirling at record temps. He smirks like he knows *exactly* what I'm imagining.

"Not hungry?" he asks, noticing I've pushed more food around than eaten.

"I'm nervous," I admit, setting down my fork.

He leans in. "Why?"

Goosebumps ripple across my skin from his penetrating stare. My mouth goes dry. It's like he's aware of everything I'm thinking and feeling and wanting.

His eyes flick to my heaving chest, up to my lips, and those exquisite eyes hood. In seconds, he's lifted me flush with his body. He kisses me hard, and an unintentional whimper releases from my throat again as the persistent ache between my thighs intensifies.

He grips me still tighter, closer, his hands drifting south, squeezing and exploring as my arms encircle his neck. When his own tell presses against my abdomen, inferno status hits.

Pulling back, he asks, "Better?"

I thread my fingers through his hair and pull his face to mine, kissing him hungrily. Mick chuckles into my mouth as our hands rove. My hands slip under his shirt, coasting appreciatively across the planes of his back while his surf under my shirt and run along my midriff.

His hands squeeze my ass through my jeans, then he lifts me off my feet. My legs wrap around his hips, my hands clutching his flexed biceps. Our mouths stay connected as he walks us down the hall and into the bedroom. He places me on the bed and climbs up my body until our faces nearly touch.

"You are so fucking gorgeous, Jax."

Every molecule in my body swoons from his praise—and that nickname I want to hear the rest of my life. "Not sure I hold a candle to you..."

He scoffs.

"Seriously, Mick, I can barely speak in your presence, I'm so under your goddamn spell. You should come with some kind of disclaimer warning."

He gives me a big smile, flashing his single dimple that turns me to mush, then bends down and melds our mouths together once again.

"I want to do everything with you tonight," he whispers while licking my earlobe and down my neck, fanning the flames incinerating my entire being. "Only whatever you're comfortable with. Okay?"

"Yes," I breathe.

His fingers roam across my breasts, skirting the outer layer of my halter top, and my breath hitches. Nipples stiffening from his touch, my body trembles as he pushes up the clinging material and his hands caress my bare skin. He dips his head, taking my right breast into his mouth, his tongue circling, sucking, and teasing. I arch off the bed, wanting more, and Mick groans around my flesh.

I've never responded to anyone like this, never been more turned on, never *quivered*. It's intoxicating—and electric.

My fingers weave into his hair as he continues exploring my breasts. Writhing beneath him, heat shoots straight to my center, flowing like a waterfall. Mick's free hand snakes down my torso, fondling me through my jeans with enough pressure that I gasp. *Oh my god.*

"Goddamn," he utters. "So sexy. I want to see all of you."

I nod through nearly shut lids, want screaming from my cells.

He slides off my pants and peels off my underwear, and I wriggle out of my top. Looming at the foot of the bed, he takes his time drinking me in, his eyes absorbing every detail. "You are everything I imagined and more."

He whips off his shirt and I'm lost in his beautiful, striking masculinity, my gaze mapping the expanse of his muscled body.

Reaching underneath my hips, he pulls me to the edge and gently spreads my legs. His tangible desire shoots me into another stratosphere, one I never want to leave.

But as he kneels, a twinge of doubt slithers through me. My body stiffens, head dumping all the detritus from my last relationship into my lust-filled brain.

"What's wrong?"

*Fuck.* I sigh with frustration. At myself. The situation. And Robbie, my asshole ex.

In an instant, Mick's back, bracing his distractingly strong arms on either side of me, coaxing me to meet his questioning gray eyes.

"I'm sorry. My former...boyfriend...didn't like doing that. He said I..."

His gaze turns soft. "What?"

"It's embarrassing."

"Tell me. Please." It's a request, not a demand.

I stall. He waits.

"He said he didn't like the way I...smelled. That he couldn't stand the taste." My neck heats with shame—quickly replaced with alarm. I'm ruining everything by stopping this insane chemistry we're experiencing. Tears threaten, and I squeeze my eyes shut, choking them back, emotions swarming that I'm single-handedly messing up the only thing that matters to me in this world.

"Jax. Look at me."

Slowly, my gaze lifts.

"I don't know what kind of jackass you dated before, but he was an idiot. I can't wait to taste you." He kisses me softly, flashes me a brash grin, and returns to the apex of my thighs.

My breath shallows, hope swirling with want.

Mick gently pushes my thighs open. "This is the prettiest pussy I've ever seen." When he slides in a finger, then two, I mewl—and he hums in unison. "And the wettest. *Fuck*." He removes his fingers and licks me slowly, intentionally, exploring my depths and contours.

*Wow. WOW. Holy fucking wowwwwww.*

Between my quivering thighs, he zeroes in on all that is holy, and I convulse beneath him, the pleasure wild and unconstrained. He's absorbed, attentive...voracious. I can't believe I've been deprived of something so potent, and I'm euphoric it's Mick Callahan devirginizing this orally starved apparatus right now.

His tongue-assault continues as the pressure mounts. Fisting my hands in his hair, I use the leverage to thrust toward his beautiful mouth. He's like a maestro conducting his orchestra, and he knows how to maximize every instrument.

The tension builds, his masterful strokes commanding a thrilling crescendo, and my breathing ceases for several seconds, the pressure building in my chest. A thunderous orgasm rips through my body and my lungs gasp for oxygen.

Vision blurred, eyes squeezed shut, colorful orbs dance beneath my lids like its own exquisite golden hour.

In the aftermath, my center twitching and spasming as Mick draws out the delicious pleasure even longer, I can only whisper a hushed mantra of "Ohmygod, ohmygod, ohmygod." Because OH. MY. GOD.

Mick reclines alongside me, his low voice serious, coating me like a blanket. "I'd consider myself a lucky man if I could taste you every day for the rest of my life."

*Yes, please. You can. Where do I sign?*

Although I won't begin to give those words the weight he probably didn't intend, my unrestrained smile radiates. My palm finds his face—something I could easily stare into for the rest of *my* life—and he leans into my touch.

"That was...*indescribable*," I say.

I'm shocked when he bends to kiss me, unsure about tasting myself. His tongue won't take no for an answer as it seeks mine, my essence commingling between us. It's tangy but not unpleasant, and damn if it isn't revving me up another notch.

"Take your pants off," I murmur, hungry to get him out of those jeans and have my turn.

My heart skips at his answering grin, his sexy dimple making an appearance. He shucks off his remaining clothes, and I get a look at what he's packing. It's as mouthwatering as every other physical component of this insanely gorgeous man—robust and *ready*, a perfect size.

I push him back against the pillows and kneel between his legs, admiring him up close before stroking his firm, silky length for the first time. He lets out a harsh breath when I lick the leaking tip, and another when my tongue explores. When I slide him all the way into my eager mouth, he loses it.

"Goddamn you're perfect," he groans, lacing his hands into my hair.

I continue exploring, savoring, playing...and finally pick

up speed. Opening my throat, I take him deep, my gaze fixated on his enraptured face. His blown pupils and unguarded expression display a rare vulnerability—and it's a *massive* turn-on.

Gripping his base, I revere his rock-hard cock, reaching my other hand lower to gently stroke the boys downstairs with a feather-light touch. It elicits another groan, another plea, and I whimper around his length. My nether regions salivate sucking this beautiful man and I'm lost again in his beauty and strength.

"Jax, I'm…" Mick warns seconds before he tightens and tenses. He detonates a moment later, and I savor every salty drop, relishing his blissed-out expression.

I crawl back up to his side and he grips me to him, kissing me deeply.

"You're going to be the death of me," he murmurs. "That is one talented mouth."

Likewise, handsome.

His breathing steadies as we lay entwined. His fingers coast along my spine and I bask in his touch, astounded we're finally naked together. Something tells me I'll never get enough of this man.

Mick's hand strokes my hair. "Jax?"

"Mm-hmm?"

"You on birth control or—"

"Covered." All systems reignite, my rapid pulse gearing up for the main event so fast I'm lightheaded.

"Good," he says, rolling me onto my back. "Because I need you right fucking now."

His gaze is intent, pupils dilated, and my heart wants to burst in this moment.

*He wants me.*

"Yes," I whisper, my need desperate.

He shifts between my legs, his erection so rigid, my body trembles with anticipation, my pussy throbbing, slick, wanting. He lifts my right leg over his shoulder and presses a kiss to my calf. It's caring, tender...and caresses my volatile heart. Rubbing his tip against my drenched entrance, his eyes smolder. Our gaze locked on one another, he sinks into me. His expression—surely mimicking mine—is worth the price of admission. He eases in, reverence and bliss crossing his face as I stretch to accommodate him. Our bodies fully merge, and he stills. All thoughts obliterate.

There is only us, and now.

"Yesssssss," leaves my lips in a long, breathy exhale as my eyes squeeze shut from the sheer fullness I'm experiencing...everywhere. My mind, my heart, where we're joined.

"You feel so fucking good, Jax," he murmurs.

He lets out an audible breath and begins to move, finding a rhythm as we join for the first time in the most intimate of ways. My other leg lifts to straddle his neck so he can go deeper. He gives me every inch, and I take it as he fills me sublimely. Entirely.

When he thrusts, my hips meet his, our bodies working in tandem. I soar with each stroke, reveling first in the slow pace then losing my mind when he takes me harder and faster. Our uncensored moans and breaths fill the room.

The crescendo builds, our tempo wild and fierce. My incoherent whispers mingle with his grunts as we topple over the edge. He explodes, his warm essence commingling with mine.

Mick hovers over me, his head buried into the pillow inches from my face, chestnut waves obscuring most of his. My heart slows, possibly ruined for life. The rightness of us together reigns with clarity. Until my gut twinges, reminding me I have no idea if he feels the same. Or ever will.

"Heroin," he murmurs, so softly I almost don't catch it. He lifts his head, kisses my cheek, and shifts to lay beside me. "You're like goddamn heroin."

# Eleven

I'm logging another workday in paradise at the self-serve, the kind where business creeps by at an excruciatingly slow pace.

I've already fended off Dirk (codename Dork), who shows up weekly in his sparkly blue Mercury Cougar, flirting with me and acting like God's gift to women. Every time he's finished filling his tank, he opens the driver's side door, pushes the vehicle to get it rolling, running alongside until he can slide in, pop the clutch, and jumpstart the engine. First, fix your car, loser. Second, not interested. Take the fucking hint.

It doesn't help that Mick's not working today. I miss him. Pathetically so. We have another date tonight. It's been one glorious week since our first kiss—and everything between us from that moment has me floating on puffy clouds I hope never evaporate. Nothing could be better than this. *Nothing.* He is still Mr. Broody and Mr. Enigma, but he's also Mr. Kiss Me Breathless and Mr. Sweetheart.

While I learn more about him every day, the questions mount.

Why isn't he good for me?

Why doesn't he want a commitment?

Why doesn't he like talking about his dad?

How did he get the scars on his beautiful body?

Does he like me as much as I like him?

I'm scared to burst this bubble by asking any of them.

I reset the pumps after a burst of customers, grab a soda from the vending machine, and sit back in my office chair, contemplating.

Remy wanders over, leaning against the door and lighting a cigarette. "What's up, new girl?"

My eyes roll. "Been here half the summer, douchebag."

"Touchy."

I flip him the bird and his eyebrows raise.

Remy's not acting like his larger-than-life self, his mood registering about a quarter-speed. "Something wrong?"

"No," he says a little too quickly.

Fishing a smoke out of my own pack, my head cocks. "I call bullshit. What's going on?"

He turns sideways and kicks a boot against the doorjamb, looking down at the floor as he flicks his ash. "Fucking Karin. What else?"

"I wouldn't want to fuck her either," I snark, biting my lip to keep my laugh from bubbling out.

Remy tosses me a playful glare, but it's forced.

"Sorry." Attempting sincerity, I school my features. "Trouble in paradise?"

"I dumped her last night."

My eyes search his striking blues. "What happened?"

He shakes his head, sucking in another deep drag. "I'm just...done. Tired of the fighting, the accusations, the work it takes trying to keep her happy."

It takes restraint not to leap in the air. Remy may have faults, but Karin in two words: supreme asshole. "You okay?"

He shrugs. "I think so. Or I will be."

"I know you love her." *Not sure how, but to each his own.* "Breaking up is hard...and sucks."

"Love stinks," he deadpans, referencing the epic J. Geils Band song.

*"Yeah, yeah,"* I say, finishing off the chorus.

"So...you and Callahan, huh?"

A big grin stretches across my face and Remy laughs.

"Good for you. Hopefully he won't be a jackass."

"Thanks, Rem," My face beams like a lovesick sap, obliterating the last half of his remarks and stilted expression.

He turns and props a hand above him on the side of the door and it illustrates how tall he is, those coveralls camouflaging solid muscle. "Hope you don't mind, but I'm crashing your date tonight."

"Of course not. You know I love hanging with you both. He hasn't told me where we're going."

"That makes one of us," he says with a wink, then retreats and walks back toward the shop.

By the time Mick and Remy arrive to pick me up, my dad is four-deep on highballs and my mom is passed out after chasing her "Vitamin V" with half a bottle of Zinfandel. Despite my protests, my father insists on meeting my date, and I shove my irritation about it away, hoping he doesn't embarrass me.

Mick shakes my dad's hand, turning on full Mr. Manners (one of his finest qualities and a personal favorite). My father asks the standard questions (which Mick nails), but he's totally judging my date's chestnut waves (also one of my personal favorites) because my dad thinks only degenerates wear their hair long.

We finally escape.

Mick tucks me into the Mustang, and we race toward downtown Oakland. After dipping under the MacArthur

Freeway, he parks. We're in an unrecognizable section of the city that kicks my nerves into high alert—but my chaperones are big, strong dudes, making me feel safe.

We walk one block and arrive at Eli's Mile High Club. I'm relieved when my fake ID passes and we're granted entry. The instant we're through the doors, it's an assault to the senses. Seductive Blues penetrate the club, the low-lit dance floor gyrating with tangled bodies moving to wailing guitars, horns, and throaty male vocals.

Mick takes my hand and guides us through the throng. We pass a counter selling soul food, and I'm hit with delicious aromas before we navigate through the haze of cigarette smoke.

We find a small table and sit while Remy heads to the bar to snag our drinks. Mick's hair falls forward as he lights two cigarettes simultaneously and hands me one. It's still one of the sexiest things in his repertoire, making me fall a little harder each time he does it.

Remy returns ten minutes later with a pitcher of beer for them and a tequila sunrise for me. The cool drink refreshes from my first sip in the already steamy club.

Six musicians cram on stage, belting out kickass music. As they begin another number, Mick tugs me onto the dance floor. Mr. Broody surprises me again as he moves to the sultry tunes with laid-back appeal, even grabbing my waist and spinning me around. The touch of his skin against mine is like a drug—I doubt I'll ever get enough. We stay out for a couple of songs and the second I'm back, Remy takes his turn.

The three of us dance for hours—sometimes I'm with Mick, other times Remy, and occasionally, both at once. Mick's attentive, kissing me when the mood strikes, throwing an arm across my shoulders as we enjoy the band, and lighting me cigarettes without asking. I've got a mellow buzz rolling from the alcohol, the carnal music, and Mick's presence. Sweat clings to my skin, plastering strands of hair to my face, and I roll my icy glass across my hot cheeks. I've never felt so alive, and so cherished.

Momentarily startled at how strong the bond between the three of us has become, a lucid thought rings through the clutter.

*I love them.*

I'M ON SUCH A HIGH WHEN WE LEAVE THE CLUB, I don't want to go home. Mick and Remy make plans to score some blow, and I stare out the window, my mood dampening by the second. Once again, my choices are: 1) missing all the fun or 2) breaking curfew.

Mick's free hand squeezes mine, jolting me from my reverie. "Want to come over? I know it's late."

"You know I do. Let me think."

All too soon, he rolls to a stop next door to my house, where the neighbor's hedges afford us extra privacy. He opens my car door, and I take his outstretched hand.

"I have an idea," I say. "If it works, I'll be there soon."

His knuckles brush my cheek. "Don't do anything stupid." He kisses me, stoking the embers always burning for him. My arms snake around his neck and he pulls me flush against him for a long kiss.

When he releases me, I'm still sulky, wanting the night to continue and hoping my plan doesn't backfire. "Wish me luck," I mutter over my shoulder.

Resting a hand on his car roof, he watches me retreat. "Be careful, Jax."

Stealthily, I enter the house, pack some clothes and jot a note about spending the night at Kendra's. Neither parent wakes—lost in their own drug comas.

I scoot up to Mick's in my Beetle, and the guys pull in ten minutes later with cocaine and beer.

"Atta baby," Mick says, planting a kiss on my lips.

"Our little girl has a pair," Remy adds.

We hike upstairs, and Remy promptly dumps an entire gram on the glass table, chops it up, and portions out several lines. We snort one up each nostril, which jumpstarts my high like a direct hit of lightning. My brain clears, the world zooming into focus, and after a few more lines, I'm flying.

Mick loads a Pretenders album on the turntable, and when "Precious" queues up first, I sing along, bouncing across the living room to the beat, not even embarrassed after realizing Mick and Remy are tracking my every move. Bathing in their attention, I put on more of a show.

Although it's past one in the morning, Remy makes a call and twenty minutes later, Cora walks in like she was sitting around in full makeup and Aqua Net-sprayed hair, waiting for the invite. I'm surprised but mask it—this is Karin's friend, after all, and wasn't she dating Jeremy? When my eyes question Mick, he gives away nothing.

We snort more lines, and in short order, Remy and Cora start making out on the couch like it's an everyday thing.

Not that I really care. He's single, despite his breakup with Karin not even dead body cold. It's not my place to judge—and maybe my guys trust me enough to be themselves now.

As much as I try to look away, I'm riveted...the way Remy kisses Cora stirs something between my own legs.

Mick takes my hand and leads me down the hall into the primary bedroom suite, fast becoming our favorite place. He pulls off his shirt, and although I'm already skyrocketing from the drugs, the sight of his tanned chest, corded muscles, and smattering of hair trailing to a Levi's bulge—all for me—is heart attack category.

He undresses me, his hands roving my curves, before kissing me intensely, the heat from his touch setting me aflame.

"Heroin," he mumbles.

Ditto, Mick. *I'm completely, irrevocably addicted to you.*

# TWELVE

I wake at two in the afternoon with a fuzzy head to an empty bed. The four of us stayed up past dawn, inhaling cocaine and copious amounts of alcohol. Cora and I even found common ground, and it turns out she's not nasty like Karin.

After pulling on my clothes, I head to the living room. Mick and Remy look like the living dead, sprawled on separate couches watching football. Maybe it's the hangover, but they're both quiet, giving me a third-wheel vibe. Dragging ass into the kitchen, I down a glass of orange juice. My stomach instantly roils.

I'm probably in all kinds of trouble and dread going home. Forcing myself to get this over and done with, I make my way over to Mick and stand behind him.

My fingers glide into his hair. He tilts his head back and our tired eyes meet. "I'm splitting. I'm probably dead meat."

He nods. "Call so I have proof of life."

I plant an answering kiss to his forehead.

"YOU'RE GROUNDED," MY FATHER SAYS CALMLY once I'm past the foyer. He's planted on the mustard and cream patterned couch watching a muted game on TV, his dreadful classical music blaring from the hi-fi.

"Why?" I know damn well why.

He sets down his beer, and his brown eyes bore into mine. "Whether you like it or not, you are still our daughter, living in our house, under our rules. You leave here with a date last night, and later slink in and out, thinking *a note* will suffice? We don't know Kendra—"

"She's a friend I made this summer. You'd like her."

"Don't interrupt. We don't know these new friends of yours, and you do not get to *inform* us of your plans. You still need to *ask* for permission. If you're even telling the truth about your whereabouts, which I highly doubt."

I cross my arms, fuming inside.

He returns his attention to the game, waving a hand as he speaks. "This is not some way station for you to stow your clothes. You live here. We're supporting you. In exchange, you must contribute, be responsible, and treat us with respect."

*You don't even respect yourself. And speaking of clothing, you're wearing the dorkiest Bermudas ever. Who wears plaid shorts?*

His eyes swing back to me. "Is that understood?"

My head nods in the slightest increment possible. "How long am I grounded?"

"To be determined. No TV or phone—nothing but work and home."

I'm almost twenty and on restriction. What bullshit. Mick's going to punt, thinking I'm too young and not worth the trouble.

Time to backpedal. "Look, I'm sorry, okay? During my date, we met up with a bunch of people, and I figured you wouldn't mind me staying over at Kendra's. It was late and I didn't want to wake you"—*and you were passed out*—"so I took a chance despite debating whether it would upset or worry you. I *am* a mature adult capable of making good decisions, you know."

Not that sex, drugs, and all-nighters are my dad's idea of good decisions. *But naked, sexy Mick may be the best decision I've ever made.*

My father's eyes flare, mouth pinching into a taut line, and my gut tightens in warning. "You're barely of age, Jacqueline, and you've been pushing the envelope lately—and my patience. You're only a few years from finishing school. Don't blow it when you're so close. Because in case it's not clear, if you don't shape up, I'll throw you out on your ass so quick it'll make your head spin. And you will no longer be the recipient of my generosity to bankroll your college education, put gas in your car, feed you, and buy the clothes on your back."

My mouth drops. He's such a fucking asshole.

"Your choice," he snaps.

I turn to go to my room, defeat and depression permeating every step, and he stops me.

"One more thing: clean up this place before your mother gets home."

I would rather pull my toenails out one by one. I'm so hungover, the thought of bleach makes me gag. More than anything, I'm worried about what happens now with Mick.

# Thirteen

I t turns out, hell is a real place—and I'm in it, grounded,
hungover, and inhaling cleaning products on four hours
of sleep. Worry blooms as I wield a long-bristled brush
to scrub the pink toilet in my parents' bathroom. Shoving
away the negativity, the more pleasant memory of how Mick
worshipped my body last night replays.

I've fallen so hard so fast—hurtling over the cliff and
enjoying the ride—but wonder if I'm about to hit the earth
sideways. Hard. I'm also in the dark about whether Mr. Stunning's falling too. If so, will it override all the reasons he stated
for not pursuing me initially?

Obsessing about him—us—through my chores, I spiral in
this miserable fucking purgatory with no expiration date,
unable to even make a call to tell Mick I'm fine.

*What a joke. Everything's far from fine.*

After finishing my servant duties, I recede to the solace
and privacy of my bedroom. Falling onto the bed, my eyes
flutter closed.

THE PHONE TRILLS, AND I JOLT UPRIGHT OUT OF A deep sleep, automatically reaching for it before remembering it's off-limits.

My father's heavy footfalls pound toward the kitchen. I make a snap decision and pick up my receiver as he answers, clamping my hand over the lower half to smother any noise.

"Hello, Mr. Hall. It's Mick Callahan. Is Jacqui there?"

My heart surges. *He's checking on me.*

"She's unavailable."

*Not exactly, Dad.*

"Will you tell her I called?"

"No, I won't."

*Dick.*

"I don't know what happened yesterday evening," my father continues, "but you were the last one I saw with my daughter, and I have a strong hunch she was with you—and not this *imaginary friend*—all night."

"Well, sir—"

"Frankly, you don't impress me. You're a garage mechanic, and a few years older than Jacqueline. This leads me to believe you're taking advantage of my daughter."

*What the fuck, Dad?*

"No, sir, I'm not."

"Here's the thing, sport. What's your life plan? Do you have one? Jacqueline does, and I intend to help her stick to it. She's got a bright future if she keeps her head on straight, which would include avoiding guys exactly like you."

Adrenaline surges through my veins, and it's a struggle to remain silent. Mick is probably thinking he should jump ship. Paralysis sets in, and my fingers grip the phone tighter.

"Maybe you're right, Mr. Hall."

*Noooooooooo! He's wrong, Mick, so totally and completely wrong!*

"No 'maybe' about it, pal."

*Condescending motherfucker.*

"Guess there's not much else to say other than good night," Mick says quietly, respectfully—although I don't know how. He hangs up without waiting for a response.

My dad mutters something indiscernible and slams the phone against the cradle.

Tears roll down my cheeks, all my hopes dying with the finality of that dial tone. The unknown stretches like a barren desert, nothing visible for endless miles.

Fuck. Fuck. Fuck!

As soon as my parents are asleep, I'll call Mick and straighten this out. My father doesn't get to decide who I date or screw or love. I've half a mind to march out there and tell him these very things, but self-preservation prevails.

At ten-thirty, assured my parents are sleeping soundly, I stealth into my closet with my phone cord stretched as far as it will go without unplugging from the wall. Fumbling my flashlight in the dark, I finally switch it on and dial Mick's number. It rings twelve times before I give up. Reluctantly. I'm tempted to phone back...maybe he's in the shower or something? More likely he's avoiding me. Cutting bait. Getting out while the getting is good. Afraid of coming across as a psycho, I don't call again.

Instead, I crawl back to bed and cry myself to sleep.


SUNDAY IS SPENT WORKING AT THE SELF-SERVE. IT'S slow, torturous, with the minutes ticking by slower than grass grows. I call Mick's house every three hours (in fully aware psycho mode). It rings and rings, one of the loneliest, hollowest sounds on earth.

Each time a car pulls in, I'm hopeful it's my gray-eyed ocean, but he neither stops by nor calls. By closing time, devastation sets in. Best case: he's busy. Worst case: my father scared him away.

Time will tell. And tomorrow, we'll both be working. Surely, he won't ignore me then.

Monday, I'm relieved to see Mick's Mustang at the Chevron after parking for my shift at the gas station. There's also an undercurrent of dread, the unknown, all the unanswered fears and questions strangling me and whispering *it's over.* Textbook basket case.

Once again, the hours tick by without any sign of Mr. Callahan, and I fight off tears, sinking into heartache. Being this close in proximity, but disregarded, is hard to fucking accept.

When the Chevron closes, Remy roars past in his Camaro, laying on the horn and waving an arm out the window. At least he's acknowledging me. My heart's trapped in a cage, my throat tight, waiting to see if Mick takes off too. I get my answer ten minutes later as his frame fills the doorway.

My pulse ticks up as the hornet's nest in my gut swarms. I'm a major mess and trying desperately not to show it. My fingers grip the chair edge to prevent launching myself at him.

"Hi," I croak. *Smooth, Jacqui. Real smooth.*

"Hey." His eyes are soft but distant, not meeting mine.

He stays planted in the same spot, leaning against the jamb, taking a few pulls off his cigarette. Gorgeous, gorgeous, gorgeous.

"I tried to call." *Eight hundred times.*

His expression remains unreadable. "We had a game yesterday and a bunch of us went to Jeremy's after."

"I've missed you." *The eight hundred calls, replaying every kiss, look, grin you've ever given me...* My lip quivers, and I bite it hard.

He nods, thoughtful.

"Look, my dad is an asshole. I heard what he said to you. None of it is tru—"

"All of it's fucking true," he cuts in, acid lacing his tone.

My eyes water, damn them. I stand on shaky legs and brace my hands on the desk. "No, Mick. It's not. I see you. What little part you let me see, *I see.*"

He shakes his head. "Jax, I'm no good for you. Or anyone."

I clear the desk, moving toward him. "Don't do this. Please."

"Don't." He glares at me, and I halt in my tracks, watching as he stomps on his cigarette butt and grinds out the embers.

It's painfully symbolic...but I'm not giving up.

"I care about you. I *want* you. And I think you feel the same."

His gray eyes pierce mine. "I do fucking want you. More than I should. That's not enough—and I'm..." He stalls. "You deserve better."

My hand reaches for him, then falls back to my side. "You're perfect for me," I whisper.

He shakes his head and when his eyes meet mine, those gray pools penetrate. "You don't know me. I'm only going to disappoint you."

My knees buckle at those declarations. Straightening, I gulp down the new knot in my throat. "You deserve happiness, you know."

He cups the back of his neck and smiles ruefully. "We're back to that shit now, are we?" His gaze turns steely. "Some people find happiness and others don't. It's probably not in the cards for me. Just move the fuck on, Jax."

His words spear my heart. "Is this why you warned me? No *commitment.* No *complications.* Is that what this fucking is?"

He keeps his mask in place, his silence an arctic blast, and my emotions bleed out.

In a final mad dash to penetrate his new coat of armor, I advance toward him with every intention of kissing him and reminding him what we have is undeniable, *real*.

He thwarts it, pinning my arms against my sides. "I've got to go." Abruptly, he turns and walks away.

I crumple, my sobs filling the room.

# FOURTEEN

My breaths come in huffs and gasps amidst a downpour of tears. With shaky hands, I call Kendra and blubber into the phone. She arrives at the station twenty minutes later to help pick up the pieces Mick scattered on the floor.

Kendra commiserates and listens, providing the right amount of outrage and sympathy. She has few insights on Mick because he's a fucking mystery who rarely reveals anything about himself.

She remembers his last girlfriend, recalling they dated about a year before things went south, but doesn't know the reasons why. Remy once told me Mick had "shrapnel" from a past relationship, not that his history matters or helps me now. Besides, I'm guessing his ominous assessment of himself goes deeper than some ex-girlfriend pain.

Kendra wraps her arms around me. "It'll be alright, Jacqui," she says. "You know what? You hold your head high and come with Terry and me to Remy's party on Saturday."

If possible, I sink further into hopelessness. First, I'm on stupid restriction. Second, there's no way I'm ready to face Mick after this—and everyone else. Third...

"I have a confession. My parents think I spent the night at your house last Friday. I lied so I could stay overnight with Mick." It seems like weeks ago instead of three days. "Admittedly, I wasn't smart in how I went about it and that's why I'm grounded. I'm sorry I dragged you into this."

"*Pshh.* No biggie, girl."

My heart lifts a little. "My dad also thinks you're imaginary, that I just conjured you out of thin air."

"I ought to stop by and say hello. Make him eat those words." Her mouth quirks into a pursed '*How do you like that?*' expression.

A chortle huffs from my mouth. "Oh my god, would you? I'd pay good money to see my dad's face when he realizes you're a real person."

"It's on. Maybe he'll let you come out with me...I'm nice."

My half-smile and shrug conceal my pessimism. "You're super nice, Kendra, the most genuine girl I've ever known." My eyes well all over again. "I'm lucky to have you as a friend."

She wraps me in a big hug. "Aww, pumpkin...same."


My week is agonizing.
1. Mick-less.
2. Excruciating at work.
3. House arrest with menial labor.
4. Pity parties galore.
5. Buckets of tears.
6. Did I say 'Mick-less' already?


Remy comes by Thursday afternoon, relief flooding me when he appears in the doorway of the self-serve. Thought I'd lost him too. *Shrapnel.*

We share a doobie, and he somehow makes me belly-laugh. His crazy personality, funny stories, and impersonations lighten the heavy load I'm lugging around.

He turns serious, his blue eyes zeroing in on me. "Sorry about Mick."

I shrug, not trusting my words.

"He's an idiot," he asserts.

It's way more complicated than that, and Mick's not remotely stupid. "He doesn't believe in himself." Voiced, it rings even more true.

Remy bobs his head once.

"But why?"

Remy stares through me, quietly lost in thought. "His dad did a real number on him. It was rough, Jacqui." His eyes reconnect with mine. "Imagine watching your father beat the shit out of your mother...and feeling powerless, afraid, royally *fucked*. But then the old man doubles down and beats the crap out of his kids too. It's hard for Mick to trust anyone, including himself. And it sure didn't help when his first girlfriend screwed him over. Put it all together and that'd fuck up even the best of us."

A knot forms in my windpipe, telltale pricks knocking behind my irises. "Damn," I murmur. My brain immediately calls forth the scars marking Mick's body, and I see them through a new lens—wondering how he really got them.

Remy clears his throat, wincing. "It wasn't my place to tell you all that."

My forehead sinks against my hands, my eyes squeezing shut as I attempt to block out the emotion flooding every cell. "God, this hurts." A sob escapes. "I care about him, Rem. And you. It's been hard this week."

"Hey...you and me?" He leans over the desk to gently grip my chin, forcing me to meet his gaze. "We're good, okay?"

I nod with watery eyes, chest pinched like it's trapped in a vise.

Remy's fingers smooth my hair. The affection dissipates some of my angst.

"I thought you were avoiding me." *Which killed me.*

He *tsks* me, cocking his head and giving me one of those one-sided smiles. "Never, sweetheart."

I reach for my smokes and flick two from the pack. Remy ignites them with a red plastic lighter before flopping back in the chair across from me.

He takes a drag and exhales, his gaze never leaving mine. "What's taken up all my time this week is Karin. She came crawling back, begging to get back together."

*Fucking figures.* My brows raise and stay there. "What'd you say?"

He's sheepish now, all bravado gone. "I caved."

*Bummer.* "Should I be happy for you? Is that the high-road answer?" A laugh bubbles out, which causes Remy to join in.

"Damn, Jacqui...*harsh.*" He rakes a hand through his copper hair, his biceps bulging against his shirt.

"Just looking out for you, Rem. You guys constantly go the rounds. Someone's getting KO'd at some point."

"For real," he says.

"Plus, it's not like you don't have options," I dig, alluding to his *extracurricular* activities. Pulling the ring top from my soda, it cracks and sighs.

He raises a brow. "Are you offering?"

My drink sputters from my mouth and sprays the desk. "Ha ha."

He winks and spreads his arms wide. "I know you've thought about it. Handsome guy like me. Open book. Excellent in bed. A good time, all the time."

I cackle. "Ooh, and a philanderer."

His blue eyes flare, and I squirm under his intense gaze. "Might straighten up if I was with you, beautiful girl."

Breaking eye contact, a nervous laugh escapes my mouth.

I'm reading too much into what he said. He's probably trying to yank my chain as usual. "In your wet dreams, buddy."

"Busted," he says under his breath, quietly chuckling. Thankfully, he drops it.

I slug down more soda, eager to switch topics, and remember his party. "Kendra invited me to your party Saturday."

He waves a hand my direction. "You know you have a standing invite."

"Even if Mick doesn't want me there?"

"You're projecting shit." He leans back and props a boot on the desk, crossing his long legs. "Mick doesn't *not* like you. Quite the opposite," he mutters.

I shrug, my go-to avoidance move. In this case, to avoid crying. Taking a deliberate drag, I force my lips into an O and exhale a line of smoke rings, watching them float toward the open door and into the night air.

"I'm in jail anyway. Kendra's trying to bust me out, but my dad's a douchefuckhole." *And so much more.*

Remy barks out a laugh. "A what?"

"You heard me."

We visit a while longer before he stands to go, professing he's off to meet Karin. "Come here," he says, gesturing me over.

He pulls me in for a hug, my cheek hitting his broad chest and giving me a whiff of his piney, musky scent. He kisses the top of my head, filling me with a comforting warmth and emotion like...love. Because I do love him, and our friendship. His absence added to my angst this week, just in a different way than Mick's.

"Thanks, Rem," I murmur.

"For you, new girl...anything."

And I'm pretty sure he means it.

# FIFTEEN

Saturday finally arrives, my sentence looming large as I force down breakfast with my parents and try not to think about Remy's party today. I've avoided looking at my father out of spite, resentment, and the debilitating powerlessness he creates in our lopsided dynamic. Instead, my fantasies abound. Like me walking out the door and never coming back...or sometimes a bus running his ass over. I will *never* forgive him for ruining things with Mick.

Grating classical music plays in the background as we eat in silence, aside from my father flipping the newspaper and clacking his coffee cup on his saucer. Brown liquid dribbles down the sides, not that he cares. *I* do all the dishes because *I'm* a captive slave. My mother appears less comatose than usual...but hey, the day's still young.

"No work today?" she asks, taking a bite of toast smeared with apricot marmalade.

I curb my irritation, especially since it's not directed at her, and muster polite conversation. "I'm off until tomorrow."

"I remember when businesses were closed on Sundays," she muses.

"Pretty sure those days are over, Mom." I fork through my scrambled eggs, pushing them around my plate, my stomach roiling with free-flowing distress.

My father peers over his paper. "You still seeing that boy?"

My fork slips from my hand, clattering to the plate. How can I summon an earthquake which swallows only him? C'mon, Mother Nature. Do your thang. Shake it for me.

"I'm not *seeing* anyone...I'm grounded. As for Mick, he broke up with me on Monday for some inexplicable reason." *You, fucker. You're the reason.*

"Huh," my father muses.

My mother stays mute, aside from crunching her stupid toast. Typical.

"You can consider your punishment fulfilled, Jacqueline, but I won't hesitate to ground you again if you lie or push the boundaries of respect. Clear?"

"Crystal."

"You're welcome," he says.

"Thank you," I grit out as nicely as possible.

TRUE TO HER WORD, KENDRA KNOCKS ON OUR DOOR midday while Terry idles out front in his Trans Am.

When I introduce her to my parents, my dad's jaw visibly twitches as he realizes she's real, not a figment of my imagination. Kendra is the first Black friend I've had over, and I register my parents' surprise. They've never voiced prejudice to me before but worry creeps in. Maybe this was a bad idea— my dad is obviously a shallow, judgmental asshole.

Kendra displays her natural charm—genuine and friendly. When she talks about going into her second year at Cal and considering pre-law, my father's posture relaxes. She may as well have walked on the moon with a *life plan* like that. I'm probably a disappointment in comparison.

"I know it's late notice, but I'm hoping Jacqui can come

swimming with us. Would that be alright?" she says, addressing my father.

He hesitates, his stare sharpening as it flicks to me. "If she wishes."

"I'd love to! Let me grab a few things." I've only walked a few steps before I pause and address my parents. "Thank you." This time, it's sincere.

Hurrying to my room, my mind whirls. I'm getting sprung! God bless Kendra and the universe for saving me today. Avoiding thoughts of who might be at this party (as if I could), I pull on a bikini, throw on a short, casual sundress and sandals, and snag a beach towel. My excitement runs rampant...getting out of here, checking out the loaded Remington household, and the possibility of reuniting with a certain gray-eyed someone and hoping he's had a change of heart.

I climb into the back of Terry's Pontiac, heart stupidly fluttering at the thought of seeing Mick.

# Sixteen

Remy's parents own a sprawling estate in Piedmont, where some of the wealthiest reside. Terry parks along an expansive circular driveway in front of the white mansion. which towers in gleaming glory. As we approach, laughter and music echo from behind the house, and we pivot to follow the brick herringbone walkway around back.

Two dozen people mingle in the lushly landscaped backyard. Some are in the massive pool, others gather on couches shaded under a chic cabana, and a few bikini-clad girls lounge on chairs soaking up rays.

My scan for Mick comes up empty, and I'm relieved...and disappointed. At least I don't have to worry about how to act this second because I'm clueless.

Remy greets us, beer in hand, and tells us to make ourselves at home. My brain buzzes with anticipation—I can only imagine what living here would be like. Our house is a Cracker Jack shack by comparison. My parents are firmly middle class, and while we live in a nice neighborhood in the Montclair hills, it's a far cry from this opulent spread.

Craning my neck to survey more of the yard, I experience a momentary twist of envy.

Remy's voice finds my ear, his hands squeezing my shoulders from behind. "Glad you came."

I toss a smile back at him. "Me too. Are your folks here?"

He shakes his head, his expression suggesting I'm crazy to ask. "Greek Islands."

"Must be nice." Mansion life, trips to Europe. I'm working for scraps to have spending money, totally reliant on my increasingly oppressive wardens for support. "Mind if I check out the inside later? I love seeing how the other half lives."

He lifts his beer in toast. "Knock yourself out, Jacqui."

Kendra touches my forearm. "Let's grab a few chairs."

"Cool with me."

We set up across the pool from the other girls, spreading our towels on strap chaise loungers and peeling off our outer layers. I'm sporting my red string bikini today.

"I'm going in search of drinks. What do you want?" Kendra asks.

I tilt my shades down and meet her expectant stare. "Anything but beer. I can't take another beer."

She laughs. "Ugh. I know...these boys. That's all they drink." She saunters off in the mesh cream number that looks stunning on her, and I sink into my happy place. Or rather, the best I can do under these circumstances. Happy remains far out of reach, but this is a hell of a lot better than just a couple of hours ago. Off restriction. Warmed by the sun's golden rays. Grateful for a genuine female friend.

Kendra returns with strawberry daiquiris in sturdy plastic tumblers resembling real glass.

"I totally want to kiss you right now. Do you swing both ways?"

She giggles, visibly flustered, and purses her lips playfully.

Remy and Karin exit the house, appearing at ease.

"Incoming," Kendra singsongs under her breath.

Karin's sigh reaches audible levels when she spots me. I ignore her. That shrew is the least of my problems.

Remy sets down his beer and leaps onto the diving board, bellowing a rally cry. I brace for a splash, and he delivers, landing a cannonball that shoots water into the sky and nails us with precision. Kendra squeals on impact, but I don't mind—the water's refreshing.

A whole line of guys queues up to the diving board, including Vinny, Terry, Jeremy, and a few others I don't know. Their buff bodies perform flips, can openers, nutcrackers, and cannonballs, putting on a hell of a show.

Ready for another daiquiri, I grab my glass and head inside, using it as an opportunity to take a self-guided tour. Wandering through the expansive main level, my feet sink into plush carpeting or glide across pristine hardwood floors, depending on the room. Big spaces, high ceilings, contemporary paint colors, abstract art—and not a speck of dust to be found. Safe to assume they have cleaning staff and gardeners and maybe a damn butler. Everything is manicured, curated, and smacks of money, yet there's something sterile and soulless about it all, like no one enjoys living here.

I stumble across a library, immediately calling forth every detail that went down between Mick and me at Terry's house. There's also an office, and a music room with various instruments, including a grand piano. Spotting the stairs heading to a lower level, I hesitate just a moment, then follow them.

They lead to a fully finished space brimming with games —air hockey, ping-pong, foosball, and a smattering of upright video games and pinball machines. *So cool.* Venturing down the adjacent hallway, I discover an entire cinema set-up with comfy recliners stacked in rows, and my mouth drops. I've never seen anything like it. Do they rent real movies? Maybe they use the new Betamax technology people talk about?

I shut the door and proceed to the next, finding myself in

a sizeable personal gymnasium. The music's on and my gaze skirts around, wondering if I'm alone.

I'm not.

As if propelled by a magnetic force, my feet inch toward the bench press, which is partially obscured. The grunts of the individual become louder as recognizable legs come into view. My calm heartbeat ratchets up to a jackhammer pace, and I stall.

Fight...or flight?

The decision made, I close the gap, standing before Mick just as he re-racks the barbell, his bare chest coated in perspiration, muscles glistening in all their ripped glory.

He startles when he realizes I'm there, sliding from under the bar to sit, strong thighs straddling the padded bench. The edges of his wavy hair cling to his face, those gray eyes darkening as they rake over me in my cherry-red bikini.

His sweat only adds a saltier tang to his ocean scent, and I inhale it, *him*, unable to look away from the most handsome man I've ever known in my life, the one who can strum my body into pleasure oblivion, the one my heart is leaning toward with a yearning so loud it echoes.

"Fuck," he mutters, squeezing his eyes shut.

"Hi to you too," I retort, an edge to my voice. I pivot to leave but he grabs my hand, sending electric volts shooting through me.

"I don't mean anything by it, Jax. Stay."

I slowly turn, and our eyes meet with the force of a head-on collision.

"How've you been?" His hand drops, and I want so badly to feel it in mine again.

"You want the truth or a lie?"

"Truth."

"Terrible. But things are looking up," I say with a small smile.

His lips curve into a grin too, flashing me that goddamned dimple. "Guess you're out of jail?"

I nod, eyes skirting to nearby apparatus. "What are you doing down here?"

He cocks his head. "Working out?"

My eyes roll. "*I mean*, why aren't you at the party?"

He shrugs. "Not feeling very sociable. I haven't had the best week either."

My heart tugs, and I tamp down those lurching hopes. Worse, with him sitting there, I'm suddenly picturing getting on my knees and—

*Down, girl.*

I physically shake myself back to the present.

It's like he knows, his expression turning animalistic.

"You still like me?" I ask.

He growls low and slow, dragging a hand through his hair. "I more than fucking *like* you."

My insides soar. Before I can think it through, I'm climbing on top of him, pushing his chest to the bench, and straddling him. He's already hard, and I'm already soaked. We both groan as our bodies come in contact, knowing exactly how well we fit together.

"Goddamn," he utters. "You're making this impossible."

"Stop fighting," I whisper. "Whatever your reasons."

His eyes close and reopen, focused. "Jax, wait."

Reluctantly forcing myself upright, I brace for the potentially agonizing words he's going to speak.

He shifts to sit, but his arms loop around me, keeping me on his lap. Just that small act has my insides swooning, glowing...hoping.

My eyes search his face, waiting.

"I want to be fair to you. Honest with you." His throat works and my eyes sidetrack right to where it bobs.

"Okay."

"You're probably going to think I'm an asshole, but the

reason I don't want a commitment, or anything complicated," he says with a grimace, "is because I'm leaving at the end of summer."

The roaring in my head obliterates all thought as my elation and hope...sink. One of his hands strokes my back, while his other arm holds me firmly on his lap. It's intimate, although he's, what, letting me down easy? *There's nothing easy happening here.*

I finally manage a word. "Where?"

"Florida. I got a job that'll get me on the water. They'll teach me to operate their fleet, enable me to get my captain's license, and lead excursions—scuba, fishing, recreational stuff."

"That's...great, Mick," I force myself to say, despite the words ringing hollow. "How long have you known?"

He glances away before swinging those gray eyes back to mine. "I've been trying to put it together since the beginning of summer. After the call with your father, it motivated me to increase my efforts."

Rage burns through me. *Meddling motherfucking father.*

"Hey," he says, bringing me back to the present. "It has nothing to do with your dad. I want, *need*, to get out of here, Jax. I've dicked around for months, years really. I want to be on the water, captaining boats. Florida is logical—it's warm year-round, surrounded by ocean and the Gulf, and there are lots of jobs."

I nod, swallowing the heavy disappointment lodged in my throat.

"Thank you for telling me," I murmur, trying to unscramble my thoughts. Is he giving me a choice? But what about the rest of it...the crap about not deserving me? And why didn't he tell me about Florida up front? *Because he doesn't owe you anything. It was supposed to be casual.*

"I'll spend every last minute of my summer with you, but

only if you want to, and only knowing the truth about where this is going." A glimmer of sadness crosses his face.

"And my father's…impression of you? That you believed enough to break up with me?"

He pauses, as if debating. "I'm not saying he's one hundred percent wrong—but your dad can go fuck himself. He doesn't know me or dictate what I do or believe."

Studying his face, all I find is sincerity, warmth, respect. *Fuck me.* "Now what?"

"The ball's in your court, baby. I'm in, even if it's going to hurt like a sonofabitch when I split."

His words ricochet around my brain as I mull them over —as if it's even necessary. I've been screwed from the first glimpse of his face. The intimacy we've shared. The moments he's let me in. I love him, possibly from the very first moment, falling hard and reckless. It was unstoppable, like preventing a tornado from ripping across the plain. And never a choice, still not one now. But if it is, I choose us. For as long as us can exist.

My fingers lift to his forehead, shifting the hair obscuring one stunning gray eye. "I'm in."

His eyes trace my face. Then he reaches up with both hands and guides my mouth to his. He kisses me tenderly, the emotions churning between us. I let go of sorrow, regret, and expectation, and allow myself to drown in everything Mick Callahan.

His lips turn demanding, claiming what belongs to him. My whimpers escape, and he swallows them hungrily. Pleasure and heat surge through me at his every touch—the swipe of his tongue through my mouth, the grind of his pelvis into mine, his fingers roving my skin, leaving it pebbled in his wake. I tremble, under his spell, lost to any semblance of control.

He lifts us both to standing and lays me flat against the bench. With a hooded gaze, he deftly tugs the strings on my bottoms undone and the material falls away. Mick kneels and licks me right through my soaked center. I grab onto the weighted steel barbell for leverage as he spreads my thighs, licking and sucking until I arch off the padded seat. I pant his name like a mantra. When his fingers join the party below, my orgasm combusts without any warning, blowing with rocket force. *Holyohmygod-dddddddddd.*

Whisking me out of boneless bliss, Mick frees his erection, lifts my legs and splays them around his pelvis, suspending me in the air, his hands firmly gripping my hips and ass. He thrusts into me with a crazed vengeance, stealing all my words as I'm lost in sensations too powerful to describe. Our gazes collide as he drives himself through my clenching center with delicious pressure, the passion palpable, binding us as one.

My orgasm continues unabated, shockwaves pulsing through me with each stroke as a steady stream of moans leaves my lips. He stakes his claim over and over, the pleasure almost too much to bear.

"I'm not going to last," he says in a strained voice. His smoldering expression shifts as he nears release, his pace quickening. I cry out his name, and he rams his cock inside me to the hilt, grinding and stilling, grinding and stilling, his warmth coating my throbbing canal.

Mick lowers us to the bench, staying lodged within me, and presses a lingering kiss to my lips. I'm utterly dazed—and dazzled. He leans over and picks up his workout towel, pressing it between my thighs once he eases out of me.

Wordlessly, he pulls on his shorts, then hangs his forearms across the adjacent barbell rig, watching me tie my bikini back into place. I've never seen a more glorious sight than his taut, shimmering muscles on display, his equally glorious, satisfied eyes locked on mine.

Standing until our bodies touch, I gaze up at him.

His arms wrap around me, pulling me in tight. "You are irresistible."

"Not compared to you."

He huffs, his breath shifting my hair. "What am I going to do with you?"

"I've got a few ideas."

He pulls back, cups my cheek, and kisses me gently. More questions knock at the door but there's no way I'm ruining the moment by asking. Yet.

"Heroin," he murmurs, shaking his head.

Not waiting for a response, he takes my hand, and we walk upstairs and out into the sunshine. Mick's hand in mine purposefully broadcasts I'm his, causing some internal backflips. Not only can everyone see, but *they're looking*.

"I see you finally got your head out of your ass," Remy mutters when we find him fishing a beer out of the cooler.

Mick scoffs. "Not sure why you're staring at my ass, but while you're down there, give me one of those."

Remy hands him a bottle with a smirk. "So...where you kids been?"

"Working out," he says without missing a beat. I bark out a laugh and Mick's mouth forms a telling, sinful grin.

Remy smiles wide. I want to hide behind a bush.

Mick's hand slides around my waist. "You set-up somewhere already?"

I motion further down poolside, where Kendra flashes us her megawatt smile.

After Mick and I settle in our recliners, she reaches over and gives my hand a firm *I'm so happy for you and you better tell me everything later* squeeze.

I grip hers back. *I will.*

As Mick and Terry banter, I float on the fumes of Mick's desire, him wanting *me*—and the palpable, burning reminder of him buried inside me minutes ago. It's preferable to thinking about the rest.

Mick lights two cigarettes, his dark lashes fluttering against his cheek, and hands me one. He asks Terry about his summer training routine as his free hand lightly strokes my thigh.

My glow is hijacked after sensing open hostility. I glance across the pool to find Karin glaring at me from behind gaudy, gold-framed sunglasses. Okay, I can't see her eyes, but her entire posture spews her special brand of rancor.

Maybe it's petty, but I hope her days with Remy are numbered. *For good.*

Remy howls from the diving board, showering us seconds later with chlorinated water.

Mick leans over and kisses me. "Watch me put that to shame."

I ogle Mr. Kissed Me in Public as he saunters to the board and executes a textbook can opener, raining more droplets our way in the biggest splash of the day. He breaks the surface, flipping his long hair out of his face, and I melt. He's insanely good looking in every iteration.

Remy grabs a football and like a well-oiled machine, the pair toss each other the ball while they execute backflips, gainers, and other moves. A half-dozen guys get in on the action, and Kendra and I aren't the only females clapping when they succeed and laughing when they miss.

Afternoon gives way to sunset, flames of color licking the sky. Remy fires up the grill, and the smoky scent of char burgers and dogs fills the air. My skin's a bit charred too after several hours in the sun, but I couldn't care less. I'm the epitome of elated sitting on Mick's lap eating a cheeseburger.

Once we're finished, he leads me to the hot tub, where we're alone for a whopping one minute before others pile in. His arm rests on the outer edge, providing a cushion for my head, while conversation turns to A's baseball.

My leg hooks over Mick's, his closeness reassuring. Seconds later he snakes his hand underwater, his fingers traveling across my thigh and toward the promised land. My breath hitches when he finds the seam of my bikini. I lean my head back and close my eyes, practicing an Academy Award performance of *Nothing Happening Here*.

Mick says something about Vida Blue, a former beloved Oakland pitcher now playing for the Royals, as his index finger wiggles under my suit and begins teasing my entrance...while no one else in the hot tub has a clue. It's all I can do to keep my composure as I thrust carefully against his hand, keeping my feet planted.

*Oh my god.*

I can't do this.

*Those fingers.*

I can't do this.

Someone alert Command Central—she's opening wide and ready to take no prisoners.

I open my eyes and tilt my head. He senses my gaze and meets it, his twitching lips giving away how much he's enjoying every second. Pushing Mick's hand away, I straddle his lap, a satisfied grin crossing my face as it becomes apparent how happy *he* is I'm here. Wrapping my arms around his shoulders, I press my mouth to his, my tongue demanding entry and granted it. Our tongues swirl as he grips me tightly to him.

Someone mutters, "Get a room!" Another narrates, "We now bring you back to the game where a heated tonsil-hockey match is in progress. I believe he's going for the goal, ladies and gentlemen..."

We laugh into each other's mouths, breaking apart. Mick leans in close to my ear. "Let's go back to my place. I want you alone and undressed."

Heady elation erupts, igniting every nerve. *He wants me.* He *more than likes* me. It's enough to obliterate the niggling background whisper that our days are numbered...for now.

# SEVENTEEN

Rain pelts the roof, gloomy clouds casting a soft light into the bedroom on this lazy Sunday. After Mick cooked us breakfast, we made unhurried, toe-curling love. I wish we'd never leave this bed.

My head rests on his naked chest, reassured by the rhythmic beating of his heart as my fingers glide along the planes and valleys of his torso.

My mind drifts to all the time we've shared this past week. Our sex only gets better the more time we spend together and figure out what turns each other on, like fine-tuning a radio until all the static's gone. I dig playing house and the decadent alone-time it affords—sharing meals, sunsets on the deck, tangled up on the couch watching TV, our conversations.

Every ounce he gives, I take. My lovesick self can't bear to think about his mom coming home, bringing all this to a screeching halt...before it officially ends when he moves to Florida. And I don't tell my parents we're together, since clearly my father has it out for Mick. Adhering to my curfew and completing expected chores prevent his questions and ire.

As if privy to my thoughts, Mick's voice rumbles through his chest. "Did you ask?"

Mick invited me for a weekend away of camping and canoeing on the Russian River, and I'm still figuring out how to swing it. It irritates me I can't go on my own say-so. I'm still required to get permission for such things from my parental wardens, as if I'm a toddler instead of nineteen.

Of course, this poses problems for more than one reason. I have no idea how to tell him.

"Not yet. I'm worried they'll say no. I'm strategizing my best angle for success."

"Is it me?"

Ugh. "They're not going to let me go somewhere with a guy overnight. It doesn't matter which guy," I hedge. "I'd love to tell them I can have plenty of sex without spending the night with someone, but that's probably not a smart tactic."

His chest shakes with soft laughter. "Definitely not."

"Also, because...my sister—"

"You have a sister?" He shifts, searching my face.

I lift my head to meet his. "Had. I *had* an older sister. She drowned when we were little. I was only four. Honestly, I don't remember her." Is that terrible to admit?

He moves a swath of my honey-blond hair behind my shoulder. "I'm sorry, Jax. That's awful."

Sighing, I sit up, cross-legged style, wrapping the sheet around my waist. Mick leans over and lights us cigarettes, moving the ashtray from the nightstand to the bed.

"It was...*is*. We were at my grandparents' house in Ventura. My sister and I were supposed to be napping. No one realized she'd wandered down to the pool, and by the time they did, it was too late. My parents were devastated. Never recovered. My dad turned into even more of a jerk and my mom...checked out. Pops pills and sleeps most of the time."

Mick tilts his head, blowing out a stream of smoke, his gaze intent on mine. "It must be hard for them. I can't imagine what it's like for a parent to lose a kid, especially an accident, where they probably blame themselves."

"I get it, but at some point, you've got to pull your shit together. I'm still alive. I've needed my parents the whole time. Not ghosts. I've basically raised myself. How is that right?"

He shrugs. "It's not. But no one said life was fair, and you get dealt the hand you're dealt. It's up to you to play your hand, figure it out, try to come out on top. You're an adult now. It's on you."

His words sting, accurate or not.

"You're tough," he says, gentler. "You'll transcend it, probably be a great mother when the time comes."

I'm not so sure. It's not like there's a roadmap from my mother. A picture emerges of Mick as a father, and I shake the thought away. "You were dealt a bad hand too, weren't you?" The secrets Remy shared about Mick's past echo in my head and heart. I silently beg my ocean to trust me with it.

He swallows would-be words, his Adam's apple bobbing, staying silent so long I'm positive he won't answer.

"My dad was—is—a sadistic motherfucker." Spite laces his tone as he stubs out his cigarette. "I fucking hate him."

My eyes drift from the slash in his eyebrow to the odd-shaped scars marring his knuckles. I've seen another—straight and thin, stretching about five inches—on his back below his shoulder blade.

"What did he do?" I ask softly.

He stares at me hard, and my emotions simmer beneath the surface. "He was...terrible to my mom. He hit her, berated her, screamed at her. He beat the crap out of me and my brothers. Frequently." He roughly rakes a hand through his hair. "He's nothing but a fucking bully and coward. To pick on someone a fraction of your size, to harm *your family*, is deplorable. And unforgivable."

No amount of swallowing can stop the tear that escapes.

"I'm so sorry," I murmur, wrapping my hand across his and stroking the scarred skin. "These are from him, aren't they?"

He nods once, a terse dip of his rigid chin. "I've got plenty of his fucking battle scars." He tilts the hand I'm holding. "These came from his belt buckle, a special treat repeated numerous times for various infractions." Mick traces his eyebrow with a finger. "This is from him slamming my face into a kitchen cabinet. Splintered the wood and gave me a concussion." He jerks his forehead toward his shoulder. "That one is from him throwing a shovel at me in the backyard. Hit me with the blade side, cutting me deep enough for eight stitches. I've got another one on my leg where he flung a jack stand at me."

"Mick..." I breathe, devoid of words. Hurting your child —*any* child—is unfathomable, heart breaking, *fucking evil.*

He shrugs, like it no longer matters. But it does matter. *To me.*

"How long did you live with him?"

"Too long. It took my mom years to find the guts to leave him. She worried about how she'd support us and hated the idea of sharing custody knowing there'd be weekends we'd be alone with him. Not that she protected us. She couldn't even protect herself. None of us could. She finally summoned the courage—to fight for herself and us—but after an ugly battle, the courts awarded them joint custody. It was a hard road of back and forth," he says, scrubbing his jaw.

So much about Mick's cryptic, brooding nature makes sense now. Especially his take on happiness. His trust issues.

"My god. How have you dealt with it? I mean, have you...transcended it?" I'm not trying to be an asshole throwing his phraseology back at him, but if he has a roadmap, I want it.

"I don't fucking know. Some of it, yeah. It hasn't been easy. I'm not implying it's not difficult, Jax. I'm saying we've got to try or else they win. And I don't know about you, but

I'm not knuckling under one more second for overbearing, abusive assholes."

My eyes well as I fight the lump in my throat. "I needed that." The rain picks up, pounding against the roof and sounding as angry as I feel. "So, you don't see your dad ever?"

"Not if I can help it."

Mick swings his legs over the side of the bed, effectively letting me know he's done talking. I'm grateful he shared anything. It's major.

I shift to press my bare body against his back, viscerally aware of his pronounced scar, and wrap my arms around his chest, whooshing out a held breath. "I'll figure out a way to come with you to the Russian River. I want to."

He turns, his beautiful masculine profile on display, and dips his head. "I want you with me. I love it there and want to show you why."

His sculpted muscles flex as he heads toward the bathroom. While I can't help admiring the view, it pales in comparison to knowing Mr. Closed Book just cracked the door open. A little.

I fall a little harder.

# Eighteen

After I lie to my parents again (Kendra coming to the rescue like the hella cool friend she is), I pack for the trip and load my car. After working first shift at the self-serve on Friday, I drive to Mick's, and we get on the road around six p.m.

It's less than two hours to the Russian River, northeast of the Bay Area, and once we pass San Rafael, the congestion clears. The last Led Zeppelin song fades and I haul Mick's case full of cassette tapes on my lap and figure out which to pop in next.

I pluck out ZZ Top's "El Loco" and push it in the player. Their signature ragged vocals and southern blues rock guitar fill the Mustang. I prop my bare feet on the dash and move my upper body to "Tube Snake Boogie," earning me a genuine smile from my stone-cold fox, whose hair blows in the breeze like mine.

Windows down. Music cranked. My favorite person whisking me away. Carefree as we can get. Life is totally fucking righteous.

We stop in Petaluma for fast food, inhaling tacos and burritos before hitting the road again. As Mick fires up the

'Stang, the player eats the tape. I pull a Bic pen out of my purse, wedge the tip into one of the two hub reels, and carefully wind the translucent brown plastic film back into the cassette.

"When's your mom due back again?" I ask, watching the last bit of film disappear into the reel.

"Next week."

Conflicting emotions war internally. "I'm psyched to meet her but..."

"You're going to miss having the place to ourselves? Yeah, me too." He shoots me a sideways glance.

I smile.

He pulls my hand to his lips and kisses it, sending tingles shooting down my center.

"What's she like?"

"My mother? A badass. Loves her work, and her playtime. Does a good job balancing life since...being on her own." He quirks his head as he lights a cigarette. "She's my role model."

I have exactly zero of those in my household.

"She infused me with a love of the outdoors. One of the brighter spots of my childhood. She took us camping, sailing, backpacking, and rock climbing—mostly once she left the old man, but even when she was still saddled with all that shit, she showed us how to camp in the backyard, teaching us to pitch a tent and build a fire."

"That's incredible." And I mean it. Here's a woman who not only faced adversity and abuse but righted her ship, overcame it, and pursued her own passions. Despite my inner fist pumps, envy rears its ugly face, pressing on bruises no one can see. My mother hasn't overcome squat; she's succumbed to it. She provides nothing to model myself after—quite the opposite. I'm weighed down by the sadness of it, the missed opportunity. What I wouldn't give to have parents I admire and want to emulate.

"She transcended," he says with a wink, pulling me out of

my spiral. "Reclaimed her life, seized it by the horns, and went for it."

"It's inspiring," I admit. *Maybe there's hope for me yet.* "Tell me about your brothers. Wait," I say, grabbing his forearm, "are they named after musicians too?"

"Sure are. Townshend and Graham."

"Those names are *rad*. She officially wins The Coolest Mom title. Let me guess. Townshend..." I roll it around my tongue then snap my fingers. "That's easy. Pete Townshend from The Who."

"Good job, baby. Now Graham."

I draw a blank no matter how hard I cycle through bands. "I'm not a good test-taker. It's why I suck at Trivial Pursuit."

Mick smirks. "I'll throw you a bone. David Crosby."

I clap my hands once and dance in my seat. "Graham Nash of Crosby, Stills and Nash!"

He laughs and shakes his head, as if I amuse him and he adores it—and it fills me with such warmth, I could melt.

WE MAKE IT TO THE CAMPGROUND AFTER DARK AND locate his cousins. I meet Kirk and his girlfriend Dana, Eric, and Wayne, who resume sitting around the fire drinking beer and roasting marshmallows for s'mores.

I hold a lantern while Mick sets up our tent to a chorus of crickets and the banter of his cousins. Watching him, it's no surprise he's a straight up Boy Scout—getting it pitched in no time. He unrolls the insulation pads and sleeping bags he brought then zips together one enormous bed. I grab our backpacks and cooler, stowing them to the side.

He pulls me down to kneeling and kisses me, my insides liquifying as he presses our bodies together. The flame Mick created stays permanently lit, like a pilot light on a gas stove merely waiting for him to ignite the sucker. He knows exactly what buttons to push.

His arms tug me closer, his steely erection a promise for later, and a moan escapes as more heat shoots through my center.

"Fucking heroin," he mutters, low.

We join the others around the crackling campfire. Sparks fly into a deep blue night sky littered with stars. Mick's easy-going cousins tease him unmercifully, which cracks me up and endears me to them. Dana's kind and solicitous and appears head over heels for Kirk. We stay up past midnight talking, drinking, and laughing.

When we crawl into our tent, a smoky aroma clinging to us, Mick takes me hungrily and possessively from behind and I stuff my face into the pillow to keep from crying out.

The next morning, Mick's gone over an hour, following Wayne downstream to park the van and buy hoagies for our lunch before we regroup. They've rented canoes from an outfitter who partners with the campground. They'll collect the boats at the end, but we're responsible for getting back to our campsite.

The guys haul the canoes to the water, and we don life-jackets. Mick briefs me on canoe etiquette: how to get in so we don't tip, how to sit in it properly, and how to paddle since he'll be in the rear of the boat doing the steering.

The canoe wobbles as I get situated, then Mick climbs in, grinning at me like it's the best day of our lives. Happy Mick is a potent close second to Sexy Mick, and utterly intoxicating.

We paddle downstream at a leisurely pace. The scenery's gorgeous, the river flanked by lush evergreens on both sides, the water a deep blueish green, nary a cloud against azure skies. Our three boats stay in proximity—enough to easily exchange banter, toss beers, and pass joints.

Mick points out a Great Blue Heron standing on a

boulder seconds before it emits a loud squawk and flies over-head, somehow getting its impossibly vertical body off the ground in a hurry, vast wings casting a shadow across our canoe. What a majestic sight.

Just as I spy a turtle sunbathing on a downed tree poking out of the river, Mick splashes me with his paddle, sending cool droplets across my spine. I yelp, flashing him a look that promises to get him back.

We arrive at a metal bridge, and all four guys let out gleeful expressions as they steer the canoes to shore.

"What are we doing?" I ask.

"Jumping," Mick says, eyes gleaming with pre-adrenaline rush.

I scan the structure, which clearly wasn't built yesterday, shooting at least sixty or seventy feet high.

"Are you nuts? That could kill you!"

I'm met with amused eyes as one side of his mouth turns up. "I'll be fine."

He exits the canoe and joins his equally foolhardy cousins in climbing the hillside anchoring the bridge. Dana and I exchange apprehensive glances from our respective boats.

How do they know how deep it is under the bridge? One shallow spot and they're instantly paralyzed. I can't watch.

I can't not watch.

My breath stalls as Kirk leaps—and makes it. Followed by Mick, then Wayne, then Eric. They each protect their precious cargo, cupping their hands over their junk and entering the water hard, fast, and vertical. But no one gets hurt, despite jumping a second time.

The guys are elated, testosterone pumping through their veins as we resume paddling downriver soaking in the sun and scenery.

We stop at one of the beaches for lunch. I relax against Mick's legs, tilting my head back and smiling at him upside-down. He leans forward and kisses me.

"Having fun?" he asks.

"This is totally killer."

"Gorgeous out here, isn't it?"

"Amazing. I don't want it to end."

We spend the better part of the day on the river, arriving back at the campsite crispy from sunshine, burned out from the pot and beer, and hungry. We roast hot dogs over the fire as the cousins swap stories from their youth. I crash before Mick, dragged into a dreamless sleep.

MICK WAKES ME WITH REVERENT KISSES...STARTING with the hollow of my throat, trailing down my breasts, and then tongues my nipple while coaxing me into a shuddering climax with his experienced hand. We make love, his gray eyes fixed to my amber as he thrusts into me hard and slow.

*I love you.*

I yearn to speak these three tender words, but don't, nervous about how he'll react, especially knowing he's leaving, trying to keep us—this—*uncomplicated*. But I swear I see the same sentiment reflected in his.

Mick drives us home via Highway 1, meandering alongside the breathtakingly rugged Pacific coastline. Windows down, I inhale it all. The tang of salt, damn near eclipsed by Mick's natural, intoxicating scent. The crashing waves rolling on shore in sets. The blazing sunlight, breaking through puffy clouds, only to be veiled again. It is everything Mick. And he *is* my ocean: vast, mysterious, powerful.

We wind down to Muir Beach, where he treats me to a lunch of tangy sourdough bread and messy Dungeness crabs we crack open, dredging the sweet meat through melted butter.

Crossing the iconic Golden Gate Bridge, jutting above the water in vivid orange, we finally split from the coastline upon reaching San Francisco and head home to the east bay.

Upon arriving back at the house, Mick and I share languid kisses in his Mustang. Parting is bittersweet after an incredible weekend. I've only fallen harder and deeper for this man as more of his facets have been revealed.

"I will never get enough of you," he murmurs.

"Same," I breathe.

As our lips dance, intrusive thoughts needle their way in, shoving me out of our protective bubble. Summer's swan song has begun, the hourglass sand running out. Next week, Mick's mom returns, and I register for my fall semester. And when classes resume...my favorite man, my lover, my ocean, leaves for shores thousands of miles away.

*Maybe we'll work it all out?*

I sweep the thoughts away, burying them deep. I'm seizing the day, like Remy said. Today. The next day. And whatever comes after. Plus, Mick and I will see each other tomorrow at work, for chrissakes.

Except...we don't.

# Nineteen

Mick's not at work, which I discover after arriving midday for my shift at the self-serve. I'm about to call him when Remy sticks his head through the door wearing a grim expression.

"Hey," he says, tone somber.

My eyes widen. "Is Mick okay?"

"His father had a heart attack, followed by a stroke. It's serious." Remy lights up, smoke partially obscuring his blue eyes.

A barrage of thoughts assaults my brain. How much Mick hates his dad—an abusive asshole who doesn't deserve the title. What he must be feeling right now. And selfishly, that I'm losing precious time with him. "When did it happen?"

"Sometime yesterday."

The day we drove home from the river. Were we scarfing down crabs or kissing goodnight when his father went into cardiac arrest?

"Is his father...going to live?" I drop into the chair, light a cigarette and puff furiously.

Remy shrugs. "Don't know. The sonofabitch would do everyone a big favor if he croaked."

My head bobs in agreement. But it's not really that simple. Mr. Callahan's death doesn't wash away his sins, the residue, or the grief Mick might feel over never having the father he wanted or needed.

I hate myself for it yet can't help asking. "Did he call you?" *And not me.*

Remy nods and lets his head fall back against the plate glass window, taking long, steady drags off his own cigarette.

Ire rears its ugly head despite knowing I shouldn't be upset by this—Remy's his best friend. My self-loathing amplifies when the next question tumbles from my lips.

"Did he have any...message for me?"

He lolls his head my way and gives it a small shake.

*Stop being selfish and petty.* Mick's dealing with a family emergency—involving a man he despises. He's basically in hell. "If you speak to him again, tell him I'm here if he needs to talk."

Remy nods, his lack of words conveying volumes. He's never short on conversation. But he's known Mick his whole life, which means he knows his dad, mom, brothers, and history. He's worried for him.

"I'll keep you posted." Remy drops the cigarette, grinds out the cherry with his boot, and lumbers out the door.

THE WEEK PASSES WITH NO WORD FROM MICK. Then two. Then three.

I rely on Remy for tidbits, devouring them like a food-deprived lab rat. I'm impatient, anxious, heartsick—the unknowing excruciating. My boyfriend's in the trenches, waiting to see if the father he hates, the father who physically abused him, the father who failed him, lives or dies. It's a mindfuck no matter how you slice it.

What about his big move to Florida? Is he still going?

And. What. About. *Me?*

His absence—and if I'm honest, radio silence—stings like a motherfucker. I wish he'd lean on me, let me help, if only as a listening ear. My daily fantasies include driving across the bay to track him down, hugging him fervently, and showing him he doesn't have to go through this alone.

Instead, I trudge through my responsibilities. I go to work, register for classes, and do the minimum required crap at home, all through a coma of heartache.

I refuse social invitations. I'm no fun to be around and can't bear pretending I'm fine.

Remy helps and hurts. Seeing him reminds me of Mick. They're a pair, a team, a dynamic duo. But Remy is also *my* friend. My best friend, lucky for me. His smiles, hugs, and fast Camaro rides are a salve to my wounds. First aid in human form. It doesn't mend the crack in my heart but I'm grateful for any distraction.

Tonight, I'm pressing him about Mick. I need answers.

I'm squaring the receipts when my copper-haired buddy roars up in his Z/28 for our pre-planned joyride, revving the engine to a deafening level. He grins in his signature way—the kind that always elicits one from me. He's like a giant, happy Irish Setter in human form.

Sliding into the passenger seat, I dump my purse on the floor and issue a demand. "Take me somewhere we can talk."

He cocks an eyebrow. "Sounds serious."

I cock mine back. *It is.*

His lips quirk up. "Hold on, sweetheart!"

I brace myself when he peels out in a cloud of smoke, tires squealing as he guns it down the avenue. The wind flies through my hair, whipping it around. Remy enters the highway, still beaming that stupid smile. This car and how it speaks, shifts, and handles never gets old. It's as much of a rush as the first day I got in it.

Twenty minutes later, he pulls into Lake Temescal Regional Park and cuts the engine. "What's on your mind, hot stuff?"

I shift in my seat to face him, tucking one leg under the other. "Tell it to me straight."

"You're going to have to be more specific," he says, copper hair unruly on top, blue eyes bright.

"With Mick. Why the hell hasn't he called me?"

His hands lift as he shrugs, but he stays silent.

"You willing to fork over his dad's number yet?" I'm tired of waiting and Remy's been uncooperative, but I'm determined.

"Jacqui..."

"He asked you not to, didn't he?"

He looks pained. "Yes."

My breath is sharp, like I've been punched in the gut, only that jab landed squarely in my chest. "So it's over? He wants to break up?"

"I'm sorry, sweetheart. Mick's a weird dude, and he's dealing with some fucked-up shit and obviously not handling it well. Right or wrong, he's cutting you loose to save you from it."

"What bullshit! *Fuck!*" My chest tightens, and I choke back sobs. "I love him, Rem. And I don't understand how he can be so callous. This isn't what I want." Adrenaline burns through me, at war with the anguish trying to pull me underwater. "He can't even give me the courtesy of a fucking call?"

Remy shakes his head as if dismayed himself. "He absolutely should. He's just...fucked up right now."

My body shakes as tears flow, and Remy pulls me into his arms. Wrapped in his scent of pine and sweet nicotine, his hands stroke my hair until I'm calmer.

"God, you must think I'm such a loser," I croak, words muffled by his shirt.

"You're the coolest chick I've ever known." His deep voice rings with sincerity.

Extracting myself, I swipe at my damp cheeks. "Why didn't you tell me?"

His eyes implore mine. "I hoped his stubborn ass would come to his senses, change his mind."

*That's obviously not happening.* But I don't get it. Why is he doing this? Is he back to thinking he's not worthy...or am I simply not worth the trouble? "That's it then? He's not coming back?"

He tilts his head to the side and lights a smoke, viscerally reminding me of Mick. "I have no idea. What I do know is you shouldn't wait for him. He certainly doesn't want that for you."

"He lost the privilege to have a say."

Remy nods, reaches over, and moves my hair across my shoulder. "You deserve to be treated like a queen. Don't settle."

My lips tilt into a small smile. I may be in love with Mick, but I love Remy something fierce, more after all he's done for me these past few weeks. My oasis in the storm.

A long, shuddering breath escapes. "You're not going to get in trouble for hanging with me again, are you?" Karin's made a stink several times about how I'm trying to get into Remy's pants and vice versa, which is ridiculous.

He snorts. "Probably."

"You don't have to babysit me." I push in the dash lighter and search my purse for cigarettes, finding the soft pack mangled. *Fantastic.*

"That's *not* what I'm doing."

"You're saving my fucking sanity." The element pops, and I press it against the end of my one salvaged, bent cigarette and puff to ignite it.

My gaze finds Remy, waiting until he returns it. "Thank you. I mean it. Even if you are an asshole."

His lips quirk on one side and he nods.

~

As September begins, Remy and I sneak off to the movies for my birthday, (avoiding the "Karin police") to see *Fast Times at Ridgemont High*. We howl whenever Jeff Spicoli opens his mouth to say anything. When he and his friends roll out of a smoke-filled van. When Mr. Hand thwarts his efforts at every turn. Whoever wrote this flick nailed high school.

When we leave the theater, I realize I didn't think about Mick once in ninety minutes, and *I laughed*. A lot.

A flicker maybe there's life after heartbreak.

Remy treats me to Fenton's Creamery afterward. I order a decadent banana split oozing with caramel and hot fudge, topped with billowy whipped cream and a lit candle for me to blow out.

"Happy birthday, Jacqui," he says, leaning over to press a warm kiss to my cheek.

His gentle treatment and genuine friendship make my emotions threaten to blow in geyser-like fashion.

Remy is truly a bright spot.

But he can't obliterate the loss of Mick. Despite the hurt, the anger, the pulsating absence—I still miss him. I still want him. I still love him.

# TWENTY

My first week of classes blurs by as I navigate where to go, what teachers expect, and what hours are manageable part-time at the gas station, which will mostly be weekends.

I kick myself (again) for not going to UCSB straight out of high school, and everything I missed in the process. Once my sophomore year at community college is put to bed, I'll be able to transfer to a university and get back on track. The *where* remains to be determined—a topic my father frequently harps about.

My heart still smarts from being tossed aside by Mick, doubly so for him not telling me directly, but I've stopped asking Remy about him and moved onto the He Can Go Fuck Himself category. Anger feels more productive than self-pity.

I do my damnedest to forget the way our bodies fit together, his stupid one-sided dimple, his ocean scent, his dreamy eyes, his opening heart, his insightful mind. And how the sex was so *otherworldly*, relegating all prior sexperiences to be firmly filed under "I" for inferior—or worse. All this time I thought *I* was defective, owner of a smelly, unsnackable pussy, with every orgasm destined to be achieved by my own hand.

*Fuckers.* And by that, I mean all former romantic interests.

God help me, but Mick's mouth, hands, and other...*assets* are hard to forget.

One lone ray of sunshine peeks from my schedule: my creative writing class. Most of my other classes are required under general education, but this speaks directly to my passion, to helping me become a real writer.

Except...our first assignment is a short story about *love*.

The universe has a strange sense of humor.

It can be any kind of love: romantic, familial, pets, whatever. Professor Fairchild wants us to bring the emotion, a point of view, and a theme. After she lays out writing structure, understanding clicks into place. I've never considered the framework, but from reading books and watching movies, I already intuitively know there's a basic, three-act structure, necessary conflict, and a climax. Her outline is game-changing, putting it into new context and giving me a roadmap.

Maybe I'll find it cathartic to write about Mick, or perhaps I should make something up, like a real writer would.

Sitting in the student union with two hours to spare before my next class, I whip out a notebook and pen to see what naturally comes out.

Caught in the Undertow
By Jacqueline Hall

He reminded me of the ocean in every way. From his
stormy gray eyes to his salty aired scent, to the force of
his touch crashing over me, I wanted only to drown
in his waves. Caught up in the undertow, he rendered
me helpless and at his mercy. But even on land, my

time with him felt borrowed, like grains of sand slipping away under my feet as the tide rushed out.

Quicksand.

Here one moment, gone the next.

My eyes well, and a tear spills over. Man, this is hard. I'm unprepared to tackle something of this magnitude. I'm a not-ready-for-prime-time player, just like the *Saturday Night Live* comedians, except there's nothing funny about this. The only joke's on me, the punchline where anyone who gets close enough easily discards and abandons me.

The smothering pillow of loneliness descending, I shut the notebook and shove it into my backpack, exchanging it for *Firestarter*, the new Stephen King book I'm reading. A few pages in, I fall blessedly into another world.

# Twenty-One

On the verge of an orgasm, I'm shoved into the present like I've been shot out of a Colt .45. My body vibrates with sexual tension as I slowly realize it was a dream.

About Remy.

Specifically, about sex with Remy.

*Holy hell.*

My insides tingle with unmet satiety. My underwear's damp, my skin slightly sweaty. Need cries from my center.

It's been two months since Mick and I made love at the Russian River. Two months since I've laid eyes on him. Two months since we last communicated. Two months since he murmured, *I will never get enough of you.*

A bitter scoff leaves my lips.

I sink back against my pillow and replay the dream...*whoa.* Intense. Hot. Sexy. My body thrums, my pulsing vagina beckoning me to act. Closing my eyes, my fingers wander, finding the spot and rubbing slow circles.

I need someone to think about, and know exactly who it *won't* be...

*What the hell.*

I allow Remy and the filthy images from the dream to fuel my imagination. My rhythm grows frenzied, the other hand slipping under my well-worn T-shirt, rendering my nipples hard instantly. It doesn't take long before I'm detonating like a bomb, stifling my sounds as heavy breaths leave my lips.

*Damn, that felt good.*

And you know what? Enough of this shit. Starting today, I'm turning the corner. No more moping—or hoping. I'm moving on and leaving Mr. Gray Eyed Tsunami in the fucking ocean where he belongs.

# Twenty-Two

I'm so engrossed in my novel, I flinch when the phone trills next to me and pounce for it, fumbling the receiver.

"Can you come over?" Remy pleads, his voice breaking.

I flip the book upside-down on my comforter and swing my legs off the bed. "Are you okay?" The numbers on my digital clock tip over to 5:23 pm.

"Just...can you?"

Warning bells ring in my head—he's most definitely not fine. I lunge to my closet, the cord stretching taut, and wiggle into a pair of sandals. "Of course. Leaving here in five."

"Thanks," he croaks.

*Something's wrong.*

Snagging my brush, I hurry it through my long hair and corral it into a ponytail when it won't cooperate. I grab a box of Triscuits and my purse and quickly jot a note to my parents.

It takes massive restraint not to floor it to Remy's apartment, not that my Beetle can hit high speeds. While my mind sprints through scenarios—a futile exercise—I scarf down three handfuls of salty, scratchy crackers.

The first identifiable notes of Journey's "Don't Stop Believin'" filter through my speakers, and I crank it, welcoming the distraction.

Seventeen minutes later, I'm at Remy's door. He pulls me into his arms wordlessly, gripping me tight.

Emotion rolls from him in waves. I wrap myself around his torso, trying to reassure him with my presence.

He tries to speak, but incoherent words tumble from his lips. And then Remy—my strong, tall, joke-telling buddy—breaks.

Rubbing soothing strokes along his back, my mind races. Did someone die? Is Mick alright?

"I'm sorry," he sputters, pulling away. He swipes at his cheeks and eyes and shuffles into the living area. He collapses onto the brown leather couch, slumping his head into his hands as he pulls himself together.

"What happened?" I say softly, sitting close enough to rest my hand on his thigh.

"Karin," he croaks. "We broke up."

I exhale a held breath. Internally, I'm relieved. Not to be unkind, but they break up about once a month. Not that he's ever reacted like *this*.

Remy lights a cigarette and leans against the cushion, his head tilting back ninety degrees. "You're thinking this is our everyday breakup drama bullshit, right?" he says, turning to look at me with bloodshot eyes.

I don't confirm or deny, merely sidestep by lighting my own cigarette. "Tell me what went down." Kicking off my sandals, I shift to face him cross-legged.

"She found out everything. *Everything*." He rubs his forehead, pinching the skin together like he has a headache.

"You mean about all the non-Karin notches in your belt?" I'm clueless *how unfaithful* Remy's been—but assume it's significant and includes any number of her so-called friends.

"Yeah," he says with a resigned sigh. "Cora apparently told her—or maybe just confirmed or some shit."

My eyebrow wings up. I'll bet Cora didn't offer up she'd also been a willing receptacle for Remy's penis. Sounds a tad two-faced.

"You should've seen her. She was so angry. Hurt. Devastated." His voice catches. "I did that to her. I'm such a fucking asshole."

What can I say? He's right. He's acted like a scumbag. No matter how much I hate Karin, she didn't deserve that. Still, I won't condemn Remy. He's my best friend, and he's more than been there to pick up my pieces. It's my turn to reciprocate.

"She didn't deserve it," he says, echoing my thoughts.

"No, but she's not wholly innocent in this."

Remy's head jerks my way. "What do you mean?"

The hand holding my cigarette waves in the air. "She's a total bitch to you on a regular basis. She treats you like shit."

His eyes wander behind me, unfocused.

"Honestly, neither of you were happy. You may have had your moments, but normal couples don't break up all the time, or fight so much, or deal with constant drama. It wasn't a healthy relationship, Rem."

His eyes water and his Adam's apple bobs like he's swallowing tears.

"Yeah," he huffs. "I know you're right. I deserve anything I get."

"Look at me."

His blues find my amber.

"You're going to be fine. It'll blow big-time for a while, but in my heart, I think this is better for you, and frees you to be yourself. I might be biased, but that guy in there?" I point at his chest. "He's my favorite person."

He gifts me a small smile.

"Now, you want me to suck your dick or something?"

His mouth drops.

My face breaks into a grin and I snap my fingers at him. "Gotcha!"

He shakes his head. "Goddamn, Jacqui…"

A giggle escapes and I give his arm a friendly push.

"One more thing."

"Yes?" I draw out the word, exaggerated.

"Offer that up again, and I'll hold you to it."

It's my turn to go slack-jawed.

Remy leans over and shuts my jaw, and with his fingers resting lightly under my chin, his thumb traces the outline of my lips, effectively shutting me up.

"Gotcha," he whispers.

My insides zing as if struck by lightning. A hot, sharp, what-the-hell-just-happened kind of strike.

An hour later, stuffed with fast food we brought back to his place, we lounge on the couch watching TV, already through *Happy Days* and halfway through *Laverne & Shirley*. During a commercial break, he grabs us a couple more beers from the fridge.

When he returns, he holds out a bottle, gripping it until I meet his gaze. "Thanks for coming over."

"You don't have to thank me."

He releases the beer. "I don't really have anyone else to talk to. Dudes don't…we don't do feelings and shit, you know?"

"Wait, I thought guys didn't feel?" My lips curve into a smirk.

He fights back a smile. "Exactly. This fucking hurts," he says, his eyes anguished. "I just…I appreciate you being here for me."

"Remy, you've picked my ass up off the floor more times in the past couple of months than I could ever possibly thank you for in one lifetime. You've been a true friend. It's my turn to carry you for a while, so let me. I'm honored you trust me."

"Likewise."

I reach over and squeeze his free hand. "You call me anytime, day or night."

He nods, eyes back on the screen as Carmine belts out, *"You know I go from rags to riches..."*

We sit through the next several shows in the ABC lineup. Halfway through *Hart to Hart*, I glance over and find Remy sound asleep. With effort, I heft his legs onto the couch, then fetch the comforter from his bed and lay it across him. After pressing a kiss to his forehead, I turn off the television and lights and tiptoe to the door, locking it behind me.

Driving home, the heat cranked to take the chill off the night air, fog already rolling in like a blanket, I replay that awkward moment when what felt a hell of a lot like mutual attraction sparked between us. Another shiver rolls through me, and I'm not sure this one's from the temperature.

# TWENTY-THREE

Remy and Vinny lounge in the office of the self-serve, stoned on Columbian Gold while I perform my job duties.

With college classes back in session, I'm only working the Tuesday and Thursday late shifts plus two weekends a month. Remy's a frequent visitor since his split with Karin, but Vinny drops by sporadically too.

We laugh at one of Remy's stories, and when my eyes connect with his, a warmth spreads through me, happy it's one of his good days. I'd be lying to say I'm not worried about him. The break-up sucked the life from him in a way I didn't expect. Karin refuses to speak to him. After years of their volatile relationship, it's definitely over this time. While this girl privately rejoices, Remy stays mired in guilt and genuine remorse.

I offer a listening ear and *platonic* hugs. Because there's no way I'm getting mixed up romantically with Randolph Remington III...*not that he's asking*. Despite the obvious—reckless playboy who cheats on girlfriends—my heart remains locked, still stuck on Mick Callahan like a broken record on repeat. I'm trying, but my brief but potent relationship with Mick left a chasm which refuses to close.

Vinny interrupts my thoughts. "Have you seen the preview for *48 Hours*?"

"With Eddie Murphy? Dude's hilarious," Remy says.

"Camilla and I are going Saturday night if you want to double date."

"Remy and I aren't dating, silly," I clarify.

He waves his hand, blowing me off. "Calling it like I see it. You two are practically joined at the hip."

"We're best buddies!" Glancing at my redhead for backup, he raises his soft drink.

Vinny rolls his eyes.

ON SATURDAY, I MEET REMY AT HIS APARTMENT, and he drives us to the theater, where we catch up with everyone else. It's a welcome surprise when Terry and Kendra join us.

"I'm sorry," I murmur to her as we share a long hug.

"Pumpkin, you fell off the face of the earth. You are not forgiven—you never returned one phone call. I've been worried!"

I let out a whoosh of air and allow her to see the hint of pain in my eyes.

She tilts her head, pursing her lips in her signature way. "I heard."

Tears threaten, constantly lurking in wait, and I blink them back. "One minute, we were so happy. The next instant, he evaporated."

"He never called?"

Shaking my head slowly, a mountain of words assembles to defend his actions, make excuses for him, confess he was leaving anyway. But why bother? I have absolutely no idea what's currently happening in the life of Mick Callahan and intend to keep it that way. The more I talk about him, the worse it is.

Kendra wraps me in another hug. "Oh, sugar, I'm so sorry. He is not worthy of you." She pulls back, still holding my shoulders. "And if his fine white ass shows back up, I've got a few choice words for him."

Her display of loyalty lifts my lips, making me love my beautiful friend even more. "Get in line."

"'Sup, troublemaker." Terry offers me a broad smile as he holds out his palm.

We slap five, which keeps my smile in place. He's treated me like one of the gang since day one. Such a small act of kindness and acceptance, and yet, I doubt he knows the massive effect it's had on me. "It's good to see you two. How's Cal?"

"Brutal," they say in unison.

We chat and catch up as we wait, file in, and find our seats. Remy and I share a buttered popcorn, pack of Reese's Pieces, and large soda...like a couple.

*Whatever.* We're two lost souls weathering a hurricane out at sea. He's my ship and I'm his life preserver. Nothing more.

The flick rocks—a funny back-and-forth with Eddie Murphy and Nick Nolte in a precarious convicted-criminal-helping-a-beleaguered-cop plot. In my humanities class, we study films to dissect their deeper meaning. Between that and learning better storytelling in creative writing, I try to view the film from those lenses but lose myself in it instead.

Afterward, Remy suggests getting some blow and taking the party back to his place. He gets no argument, and we divide and conquer, rendezvousing at his pad with drugs and alcohol.

I SKIP OUT AT 1:45 A.M. TO MAKE IT HOME BY curfew. Totally amped from the coke, my heart pounds in my chest so hard it echoes in my ears. Sleep eludes me, leaving me vulnerable to thoughts of Mick: where he is, what he's doing, what girl he's kissing instead of me.

*Shoot me now.*

How could he so easily discard me? Am I not good enough for him?

Did he lie about how he felt about me?

Was I gullible, hearing only what I wanted?

Why do I care about him so much, still, after all these months?

Why doesn't he want me? Love me?

Why doesn't *anyone* love me?

Despair and self-pity cloak me in darkness, dragging me below the surface, and I descend into their suffocating depths.

# Twenty-Four

A customer cruises in one minute before I'm about to shut off the pumps and close for the night.

"Damn it!" I grumble.

I fucking hate it when that happens. My backpack is already stuffed with my homework and books, the ashtray cleaned, the office straightened.

Tapping my fingers on the cash drawer, interminable seconds eke by as a bearded man with dark hair fills up his battered, blue wagon. I exhale a lengthy sigh...patience is *not* one of my virtues.

He squeezes the gas nozzle in quick intervals, the audible clicks echoing through the deserted station, obviously trying to reach a round number. He must have started well before necessary because he's a dozen clicks in, and I'm ready to beat him over the head with said nozzle. I hope he goes over by one cent.

He finally taps the last drop into his tank and replaces the fuel dispenser in its holster.

*Halle-fucking-lujah.*

He reaches into his vehicle, then strolls with zero urgency to the office.

My jaw grinds as the guy fumbles for his wallet and shoots me a hapless shrug. I glance at the wall to hide my eye roll.

When I refocus, he's pointing a gun straight at me.

The hair lifts on the nape of my neck and arms, flesh rippling into tiny bumps. My throat constricts. Thoughts jumble as my eyes bounce between his face and the gun, my body otherwise rigid and frozen, gripped in the unknown.

He flicks the gun toward the register and back to me. "Give me everything in the drawer. And don't even think of pressing that button."

Right. The police alarm. *Wake up, Jacqui!* My limbs won't move, like they're in dried cement.

"*Now*, pretty girl."

My body shakes so violently, the key slips from my fingers. I retrieve it from the floor and my trembling fingers finally insert it into the opening and unlock the drawer. Sweat trickles down my back and from my armpits. I discard brave and stupid thoughts as quickly as they appear. The street is deserted—not that anyone driving by could see what's transpiring.

He eyes the cash appreciatively, while mine flit wildly, somehow managing to log a few details. Brown eyes. Acne scars. Under six feet. Dodging his gaze, mine lands on his stained, gray hooded sweatshirt and scrolls down his ratty jeans.

"What the fuck are you waiting for? Give me the cash," he orders, keeping the gun trained on me.

My shaking hands pull the ones, fives, and tens from their slots and he grabs them, shoving the wad in the kangaroo pocket on the front of his sweatshirt.

"Lift the drawer out," he commands in his creepy, raspy voice.

I practically throw it across the room, my movements jerky and tense as adrenaline rages through my veins.

"Don't fucking move."

My knuckles whiten clinging to the drawer while he retrieves the bigger bills with his free hand and adds them to the rest.

My heart thuds hard and fast, my breathing shallow as I silently plead to a god I'm unsure exists. *Please don't let him hurt me.* Tears prick my eyes, and I gulp them down.

He waves his weapon at the supply closet. "Get in. Don't make a sound."

My heart beats wilder against my ribs. I don't want to go in there. "Please don't hurt me. I won't do anything."

"Now."

Walking backwards, I stumble over my feet until I'm trapped in the small space.

His gun stays aimed at my chest. "Sit on the floor. Don't move. And not one fucking noise. I'll be right back."

I sink to the dirty linoleum, my limbs vibrating so hard they could snap off. Fear pumps through my veins, consuming every cell. Satisfied, he slinks off, leaving the door ajar but not enough for me to see what he's doing.

*Please, God, please help me.*

He returns holding a brown paper bag. It crinkles as he roots through it before pulling out white nylon rope. My eyes bug. Fresh sweat coats my skin, my uncontrolled quavering revitalized. His resounding scratchy chuckle fills me with dread.

*Please. Please. Please. Please. Please.*

I swallow the urge to beg. Just follow directions. Stay alive.

"Hands behind your back," he barks.

Flinching, I do as I'm told.

He binds my trembling wrists together, his putrid body odor and nicotine stench assaulting my nose.

I whimper when he cinches the rope tight. It burns, digging painfully into my skin.

Returning to my front, he grabs my chin and jerks it

upward, inspecting my face. His teeth are black with rot, and I fight back a gag.

"Sure are a pretty little thing," he leers. "If I had more time, I'd shove my dick down your throat and show you a real good time."

A cry escapes as my eyes widen further, gripped by a whole new paralysis.

Without warning, he clamps his hands around either side of my head and forces his mouth against mine. He shoves his tongue inside, muffling my scream and keeping my face immobilized in his vice grip.

He retreats, saliva sagging between our lips like a web. Bile rises in my throat as he grins, flashing me his disgusting teeth.

"That'll have to do. For now."

My rapid breathing escalates to hyperventilating, and he laughs.

Retrieving a red bandana out of his back pocket, he plunges it into my mouth and duct tapes over it. The tape is tight and heavy against my skin, stealing precious air from my compromised lungs. He stands back to inspect his handiwork, then leans in close. He pets my hair, and I jerk, revulsion rippling through my body.

"I'm leaving now. Don't scream. Don't move. Don't say a fucking word to the police—or I'll be back. And next time, I won't be so nice."

Fresh terror washes through me. Frantic breaths through my nostrils combine with the tears leaking down my cheeks as he shuts the supply closet. I'm eclipsed in darkness, aside from a scant sliver of light beneath the door. The metal office door clangs, echoing against the walls.

Is he really gone?

It's faint, but there's no mistaking his rattling wagon as it starts and slowly fades into the distance.

A fragment of relief breaks through my hysteria.

*He's gone.*

Thank you, God. Thank you, God. Thank you, God.

I'm alive.

And he didn't hurt me really...didn't *kill* me. A fresh sob bursts forth, bouncing against my muzzle and stealing more precious air. I'm instantly sobered.

If I don't calm down, I'm screwed.

Breathe in, breathe out.

Breathe in, breathe out.

Breathe in, breathe out.

Calming as air filters through my nostrils, I'm better able to assess my situation. Can I stand? If I can get to the phone, maybe...

From my seated position, I tip over, my cheek touching the filthy floor, and roll onto my stomach. My concentration shifts, all effort focused on trying to kneel, but I wind up on my side. Using my shoulder for leverage, I try again. Being bound is a liability, yanking my arm out of my socket with every inch gained. And my breathing labors because it's hard to get any fucking air.

I try again.

And again.

Again.

I'm so close, so fucking close. Pain pierces my shoulder, and I let out a tape-muffled cry. My eyes slide closed as the ache recedes.

I try again.

And again.

Again.

My body's in agony. Rope cuts into my bound wrists. My shoulder screams. My airflow trickles. I'm tired. Scared.

Giving up, I sink into the darkness.

# Twenty-Five

A noise jerks me into awareness. I'm horizontal in the supply closet, my hands and wrists numb, my shoulder aching. Everything rushes back, and my body jolts, fresh adrenaline jumpstarting with a vengeance. *Oh my God, is he back? Please, please, please no!*

Remy flings the door open, flooding the space with light. I blink up at him, relief coursing through me as my brain catches up to the realization my savior has arrived in the form of copper hair and sapphire eyes.

"What the fuck? *Jacqui!* No..."

His face contorts with emotion. He drops to his knees and gently peels the tape off my face and removes the offensive bandana.

I gasp, the involuntary shaking reinvigorated as I blubber through tears. "Thank...god...you're...here."

He makes quick work of unbinding me and pulls me into his warm embrace, clutching me to him when I lack the strength to stand on my own. Sobs rack my body as he picks me up and carries me into the office, sitting in the chair and holding me on his lap, pressing my face to his chest.

He tugs me closer and my shoulder zings in agony. A garbled yelp breaks through my weeping.

"Are you hurt?"

"My shoulder," I manage through broken breaths.

Remy loosens his grip but keeps me close. "Fuck!" he seethes. His voice softening, he whispers close to my ear. "I'm so sorry, sweetheart."

Being in his arms is like a hot bath. I want to sink into him and forget everything about the last hour of my life.

A reenactment of that asshole forcing his disgusting tongue in my mouth blazes into my consciousness, and a full body shudder rolls through me.

"I've got you," he murmurs, gently rocking. "I'm not going anywhere."

My face nods into his chest.

"Jacqui? Can you tell me what happened?"

"Some fucking dude robbed me at gunpoint," I bawl.

"Did he...do anything...to you?" His voice wavers, strained.

I sniff into his shirt. "He shoved his tongue down my throat." I blink back fresh tears. "He...threatened to do worse."

"Motherfucker," Remy says through clenched teeth. "We need to call the police."

"No!" I lurch away from him, wincing from the sharp stab in my shoulder. "No cops. He told me if I said anything, he'd come back and finish the job."

He tenderly cups my face in his hands. "He's not coming back. If he does, that fucker's not touching one hair on your pretty head. I promise you." His blue eyes bore into mine. "Trust me."

I nod, eyes welling with fresh tears, hiccuping breaths leaving my heaving chest as he leans over and presses the police alert button.

He clutches me back to him, muttering a string of expletives, and holds me until two squad cars arrive. Reluctantly we part, and Remy's relegated to pacing outside when the officers won't allow him to sit in on my interview.

They insist on calling an ambulance. Before it arrives, I answer their questions and prompts, recounting the details I'd committed to memory: how the man looked, what he drove, what happened, what he threatened.

My voice cracks, those involuntary tremors still undulating through my body.

"Take your time, Ms. Hall," the squat male officer says.

Remy hovers nearby, worry etched in his eyes when they connect with mine.

"I can't remember anything else."

"Under the circumstances, you've done exceptionally well and given us information that will aid our investigation." The officer lowers his pad. "Would you like me to call your parents?"

I shake my head. "They're out of town for the week."

"Do you have a friend or relative you can stay with?"

My gaze shoots to Remy. He is my safe harbor, the only one I want to be with right now. "Yes. Can I go?"

Sirens wail in the distance before an ambulance speeds into the station, bringing the emergency vehicle count to four. Every rotation of red and blue lights serves as a jarring reminder I'm a victim.

"Let's get you checked out first," he says, herding me toward the uniformed paramedics.

"You okay?" Remy mouths.

I bite my lip and nod.

The medics help me into the ambulance and check my vitals, perform a cursory exam, and provide a temporary sling for my shoulder. They're friendly, gentle, calming.

Through the open rear doors, I glimpse Remy engaged in a heated conversation with our boss Leo, who must have been alerted to the robbery by law enforcement.

The male medic offers to take me to the hospital for a proper evaluation but there's no way I'm going anywhere but Remy's.

When I decline, he strongly suggests I follow up with a physician on my own.

I thank him and exit the ambulance, where my boss is waiting for me with a tense expression.

"Jacqui," Leo says, voice laced with remorse, "Are you alright?"

My shoulders shrug noncommittally, and the resulting throb triggers a wince. "I don't know. I'll probably be fine. Right now, I just want to get out of here."

"I understand. You've been through a terrible, stressful ordeal."

I start toward Remy then pause. "Um...I'm sorry about the money."

Leo shakes his head, cuffing the back with his hand. "No, honey. *I'm* sorry. I'll take care of everything."

The overwhelm threatens to suck me under—and then I'm back in Remy's arms, my body sinking into his with relief.

"Where do you want to go—home or my place?" he murmurs.

"Your place."

Remy drives us to his apartment, holding my hand when he's not shifting. He cranks the heat, and slowly my body stops shaking. He suggests I skip school tomorrow. He already told Leo he was taking off work to look after me...and he doesn't want me to be alone. I glance over at him behind the wheel, concern etched on his face, and get a hit of gratitude—and something much more potent.

I'm exhausted and emotionally drained by the time we arrive. Remy leads me inside to his bedroom, outfitted with a king-size waterbed. He gingerly takes off my shoes, sling, and sweatshirt and gives me one of his T-shirts and a new toothbrush.

The images refuse to abate, playing over and over—even while I scrub every inch of my body in a scalding shower trying to rid myself of that vile man's taste, smell, memory. Once I'm dry and my teeth are brushed raw, I don the soft, oversized shirt, comforted it smells like Remy. When I crawl under the covers, he pulls me against his bare chest and holds me until I've drifted into sleep.

I WAKE UP BURROWED INTO REMY, WHOSE SKIN expels heat like the desert sun. A yawn filters through me, extending to my limbs as they shudder into a stretch. Ow... fuck. My shoulder zings, and everything from last night whooshes back like an avalanche. Fear crackles through my cells.

*I'm okay. I'm okay. I'm okay.*

Remy stirs, a slow smile stretching across his lips when he spots me. His gaze immediately turns concerned. "What is it?"

My eyes tear. "I woke up and freaked out."

Wordlessly, he pulls me back into his arms, stroking my hair. "How did you sleep?" he murmurs.

The knot in my throat releases. "Surprisingly...good."

"It's me. I'm the reason." There's teasing in his voice, but he's right.

I pull back enough to meet his gaze. "It is. You make me feel safe, Remy."

He lifts his hand and traces my face. "You want to talk about any of it?"

*Do I?* "Not with morning breath."

He chuckles, and I ease to standing, the waterbed sloshing with my movement. I'm careful of my shoulder. It's still tender, but...better. I attend to private human necessities and five minutes later, Remy's eyes track my naked legs scurrying back to the warmth of the bed.

"Take a picture, it lasts longer," I quip.

"I'd take a thousand pictures of you...or more." His gaze is a combination of molten and playful, and my insides twinge. He flips off the covers and saunters to the bathroom, leaving me undulating in his wake.

He returns looking every bit the sexy stud, unkempt copper hair and all, muscles flexing across his exposed chest and through those athletic thighs with each step. It's impossible not to stare at the bulge bracing against his snug briefs. "Take a picture, it lasts longer," he says with a smirk.

Smirking right back, I flip him the bird, rotating one hundred eighty degrees for dramatic effect.

Remy grimaces. He's next to me in seconds, gingerly inspecting my wrists. "They're bruised."

"They sting," I admit.

He presses gentle kisses to my wrists, and reclines on his side, propping on an elbow.

Images from the robbery flood my memory and panic ricochets through my body. My eyes widen. "I don't think I can work there anymore."

"Understandable. You're like a sitting duck in that office. It's not safe, and that's on Leo."

Those damn tears prick the backs of my eyes again as the events replay on a loop.

"Can you just go to college or do your parents make you have a job, or what?"

*Focus on this minute, the present.* I notice the size of Remy's neck—huge, strong, seated underneath a sharp jaw. He's close enough to make out the freckle patterns on his face.

"Both, and I like having the spending money. Oh god, my parents. They're going to go ballistic when they find out what happened. They'll probably make me quit."

"Probably?"

I worry a loose comforter thread between my thumb and forefinger. "They aren't exactly...caring. I can't always predict what they'll do or how they'll react. Most of the time they don't seem to give a shit."

Remy squeezes my hand. "I'm convinced all parents are fucked up."

The events from last night butt back into my head, intent on replaying, and a tear escapes.

"Hey...hey," he says softly. "You're okay now. I've got you." He rearranges us so we're facing each other, his arms holding me reassuringly against him.

"Will you kiss me?" I murmur.

"Jacqui..." he groans. "What are you doing?"

I find his handsome, tortured face. "Please. I can't stop the thoughts from coming, and I just want to feel something else. Something *good*. I trust you, Rem. So, please...kiss me."

His eyes are searching for a few seconds then he presses his soft lips to mine.

# Twenty-Six

Remy's lips are tentative, testing the waters gently, slowly. Our first kiss is pure exploration, an unexpected melding of our two halves to see how it makes a whole with no idea where the journey may lead. His typically smirking lips are lean, matching his features, but pleasant and...persistent.

There's a rightness to it, even though he's my best friend. And Mick's.

Mick was the jump off the bridge; Remy *is* the bridge.

Tall, sturdy, safe.

I lick the seam across his mouth, and he hums. His entire energy shifts as our tongues explore each other, and desire ignites as I give myself over fully to his dizzying kiss, obliterating all thoughts but here and now.

*Holy hell.*

He closes any gap between our bodies with one strong hand while the other roams my curves. My leg hitches up over his hip, closing it further, and a soft moan leaves my lips.

"Damn, Jacqui," he breathes.

"So good," I murmur, kissing along his neck. I long to

caress those rippling muscles traversing his back and shoulders but my injury holds me hostage. "Don't stop."

*"Jacqui."* It's a plea.

"What?" Pausing, I meet his still-tortured gaze.

"What do you mean by 'don't stop'?"

A playful smile emerges, my head tilting knowingly.

His intense stare scorches. "Are you sure? Not that I don't want to fucking devour every inch of you, but...not if you're under duress."

I press a hand to his cheek, my words earnest. "I want you —and this."

"Thank fucking god." His lips reclaim mine, throwing kindling on the fire. A second later: "Shit, do we need rubbers?"

"Uh uh," I pant. "I'm on The Pill."

His expression turns giddy, like a kid in the candy store. "You're so in trouble. Fuck, you *are* trouble."

Remy flips the covers off. I'm fixated on his briefs, tented and straining from his erection, midpoint of that magnificent build. Shifting back to his face, I gingerly strip off my shirt, baring myself to him.

He towers above me, admiring me with a heated gaze for a long minute before swooping down to sample for himself. He groans, his tongue dancing around my nipples, and pleasure rocks deep into my core. Bucking my hips, his hard length is a jolt to my system, and I thrust again, begging for contact. He refuses me, kisses searing my taut torso and trailing south until he's hovering directly over the thin fabric separating us. His searing breath breaches the material and it's *sublime.*

"Remy..." I cry.

"You need more, sweetheart?"

"More," I gasp.

He pulls my bikini underwear down slowly. "You are stunning. So beautiful," he murmurs.

He kisses his way back up my legs until he lands squarely

between my thighs and explores. Spreading me further, his tongue probes deeper into my most intimate space.

I suck in a breath, arching off the bed when he lands on the magic button.

"Don't stop. That feels so good." *Oh my god.*

He hums, manipulating me into a heady euphoria. The waterbed rocks gently below us, sloshing with our movements and adding to the soundtrack of pants and groans.

His fingers join the party, and all breath leaves my body. In less than a minute, my orgasm grows and unfurls, snapping me in half when it blows, and Remy rides it to the end.

"Damn," he utters, worship in his tone.

He climbs back up my curves and we share a moment somewhere between wonder and triumph as he lingers above me.

"Let me taste you," I whisper.

He's clearly torn. He's hungry for the main event, like I am, but I need this first. He lifts onto his knees, giving me my first look at his untethered cock, rigid and ready to combust. It's a sight to behold.

"Stand up," I say.

Despite his warring expression, he does, helping me to sitting, careful of my injured shoulder.

He positions himself in front of me, a hand reaching over to caress my jawline carefully, tenderly.

Reaching up, I grip his length, strong and sinewy like everything about him. Enraptured by his weeping tip, I draw it into my mouth first, then swallow him inch by inch.

"Holymotherfuckingshit," he curses in one exhale. His eyes blaze into mine as he pants heavily.

I savor the size of him, his silky texture. As my mouth gradually eases back to the head, tonguing him the entire way, the sound he makes is animalistic.

His hands fist in my hair and he takes the reins, pumping into me slowly. My eyes stay fixed to his, reassuring him—and green-lighting it. His thrusts take on a primal intensity. His expression is everything: awe, respect, disbelief.

When tears leak out of my eyes, he stops abruptly and pulls out, shaking his head with unidentifiable emotions. He's probably worried about hurting me. But I'm massively turned on, especially witnessing him like this.

"I'm...*fuck*. I need to be inside of you," he whispers.

"Yes," I rasp, reclining and inching to the middle of the bed.

My legs part and he repositions above me, aligning with my soaked entrance. I hold my breath, the anticipation all-consuming.

He eases all the way in, burying his length to the hilt. He pauses, giving us a minute to gasp and breathe through this new connection, the fullness, and the rightness. Our eyes hazed with lust, we share a languid smile, aware it's not just good—it's fucking bliss.

Slowly, he works us into a rhythm, our eyes and hearts connected, all life outside our two fused bodies ceasing to exist. My moans fill the room, punctuated by his deep carnal grunts. A sheen coats our skin as Remy moves harder, faster. The intensity claims our breath as we ride the crescendo to the finish line.

His head bows into the pillow as he comes down from...all *that*. It takes a few minutes because...*damn*. I don't think either of us can grasp the magnitude of it.

He pushes up on those strong arms, kisses me tenderly, and shifts his body alongside mine.

Our amplified breathing spears the quiet, the only other sounds coming from the muted traffic outside, the world operating as usual while in here, we just went *way* off script.

His hand finds mine and squeezes. "Say something."

A smile erupts. "You're a good fucking lay."

He barks out a laugh. "Uh...not what I was expecting. I mean—"

"That's why you love me."

His gaze finds me and it's calm, steady. "I do love you, even if you're trouble with a capital T."

My hushed tone turns serious. "I love you too, Rem." I'm not *in* love with him, but there's no question about the depth of my feelings. I don't clarify, but neither does he.

"So, you're *not* merely using me for my body?" he jokes.

"Oh, I totally am."

A low laugh rumbles through him.

I rest my leg across his, place a hand on his chest, and meet his blue gaze. "Stop worrying. That's exactly what I needed. Wanted. And I hope we do it again."

He raises an eyebrow, yearning written across his face like a billboard. "Like, a lot?"

"A fuck-ton."

His relief is palpable. I lower my eyes and let my fingers coast along the muscles defining his abdomen. "Not going to lie, I'm worried about ruining our friendship. You're my best friend, and I treasure what we have. No matter what happens from here on out, I want to keep it intact."

He caresses my shoulder. "I can't imagine not being friends, Jacqui, but...we may have just obliterated that line."

"We crossed the hell out of it." My snorted breath sends goosebumps erupting across his skin.

"I've still got you. You're safe with me."

"The philanderer?"

He huffs out a laugh. "Ouch."

"You deserved that."

"I guess I did."

"Not that you owe me, or to lay anything heavy on you, but you should know, I'm monogamous by nature."

He hums and squeezes me tighter.

REMY IS SURPRISINGLY COMPETENT IN THE kitchen, flipping eggs in a skillet sans utensil without breaking the yolks. He whips up sausage and sourdough toast with real strawberry jam, not jelly. He's got fresh orange juice on hand and an assortment of teas in a cabinet.

*Probably for all the women cycling through his bed.*

Ugh, not ready to think about that.

I swallow a bite of the smoky meat smeared with runny yolk. "This is delicious. I'm hungrier than I thought."

"You're learning all the ways I'm awesome this morning." He winks.

I roll my eyes. "I've created a monster."

He assesses me cautiously, like I'm a bird with a broken wing, his tone softer when he asks, "What do you want to do today, sweetheart?"

Good question. I start to consider going...anywhere...and tears immediately spring to my eyes.

Remy's out of his chair and kneeling beside me in a flash. "Hey," he whispers, stroking his knuckles against my cheek. "We can stay here all day, do nothing but eat, watch TV, whatever you want. Whatever you need."

Our eyes meet. "That's what I want," I choke out.

He kisses away the few escapees trickling down my cheeks and holds my face in his hands. "I've got you," he reiterates. "You're safe with me."

Remy makes good on his promise—at turns attentive, giving, and solicitous—and we spend the rest of the day doing all I want and need, which in a word, is him.

# TWENTY-SEVEN

Early the next morning, Remy drives me to the station to pick up my car. Even before he's pulled into the lot, I'm trembling and my heart rate skyrockets so rapidly, it's impairing my breathing. It's clear I can never work here again.

My redheaded knight gets me squared away, wrapping me in his reassuring arms before helping me into the Bug.

I drive home, needing to shower and change clothes before heading to CCC. My shoulder still cries at specific movements, but it's better, enough to ditch the sling—which would have made shifting gears impossible.

Being in the real world again, and alone, sucks. A pulsing anxiety accompanies me at every turn, along with a nagging pull to glance over my shoulder, double-check locks, move swiftly from one space to another. Maybe that supreme asshole from the gas station will track me down and hurt me, rape me, *murder me.*

Remy's apartment insulated me, but this is my new reality. I can't help wondering how long this fear will cloak me, suffocating my every move.

After wasting precious minutes scouring the college

parking lots for something close, I find a spot and jog to my first class.

My creative writing assignment is due, and incomplete. *Crapola.* We're tasked with crafting a poem for Tuesday to read aloud. Topic: fear. *Unbelievable.* Astronomy nearly puts me to sleep when the professor shuts off the lights for a lengthy slide show despite how magical I actually find the sky, stars, and galaxy. In my next class, a B+ on my statistics test brings a self-satisfied smile to my face. I thought this class would kill me, but maybe I'll surprise myself.

My stomach grumbles, pushing me toward the cafeteria. With hours to kill until I meet Remy, may as well hang around longer. My alternatives are limited: go home to an empty house or find something to do. The campus offers safety in numbers, and I don't ponder whether that assumption is legitimate.

I buy a salad and drink and head back outside into the autumn sunshine. A few skateboarders surf the enormous cement octagon at the center of campus. Steps and railings intersect at each of the eight points, giving them more real estate for tricks. Referred to as The Square (ironic, I know), it's a pretty spot to chill, especially right now with the landscaped beds bursting with colorful fall flowers.

Sliding onto a bench, I track the boarders nailing or failing their stunts while picking at my salad. Students and faculty come and go, their chatter and the drone of lawnmowing equipment augmenting the steady grinding and squeaking of skateboards against the pavement.

Tilting my head to the sun, I close my eyes as Remy...and Mick...crash my thoughts. How would Mick feel about Remy and me? Does Remy worry about Mick finding out or getting angry? Is Remy going to treat me like some casual fuckbuddy or does he want more? Do *I* want more?

My parents are due home Sunday, a thought which thoroughly bums me out. I'll have to tell them about the robbery, revert to forced curfews, and endure the oppressive, depressive atmosphere in our cheery dys*fuck*tional house.

It's only for a while longer. I need to figure out whatever in-state college I'm transferring to and apply. If I want to live as far away as possible, I'd choose San Diego. But I can't fathom leaving the new friends I've made, especially Remy—even though we've already fucked it all up by sleeping together. And even though I told myself I would *never again* base my collegiate decisions *on a guy*.

Collecting my belongings, I walk to the guidance counselor's office and readily find a list of all the universities in California and pamphlets for several. I take one of each and stuff them in my backpack.

The library's a building over, and I head there next, finding a table by the windows. I complete my statistics homework and think about working on my "fear" poem but can't muster the courage. It's too fresh, and I'm too fragile.

An hour later, my feet beat a quick path to my car, and I gun it toward my copper-haired safe haven.

My knee bounces as I wait for Remy, head swiveling at every passing car. When the familiar roar of his Camaro hits my ears, followed by those rally stripes coming into view, I exhale in relief.

There's zero grace as I exit the VW, tripping over my feet in my haste. Remy catches me with a huge grin on his face, and I bury myself into his chest.

He wraps me in a hug. "Jacqui, you're shaking. Did something happen?"

"Just...everything. I'm nervous, afraid. It's stupid, I—"

"It's not. C'mon." He leads me by the hand into the apartment and locks the door behind us.

I force out a few big breaths and stifle my inner critic calling me paranoid.

He holds me again, smoothing a hand down the back of my hair. "I've got you, sweetheart."

Wedged against his shirt, my arms around his waist, his piney, masculine scent calms me. Once my breathing steadies, my gaze shifts upwards and meets his sapphire eyes, warm and reassuring.

"Hi, beautiful."

"Hi, handsome."

"Better now?"

I nod, more composed. He does make everything better. *Maybe I am falling a little in love with you, Randolph Remington III.*

Remy leans down and presses his mouth gently to mine. He doesn't push for more.

We make dinner together, rock tunes flowing from Remy's stereo, and my mood lightens. After, I stretch long on the sofa with my head in his lap while a sitcom's canned laughter sounds from the television. His hand grazes along my hair in languid strokes, and my eyes close, my body relaxing into his touch. His fingers lightly trace my arm. Chill bumps ripple across the surface—but underneath, my blood ignites. My eyes open to find him staring intently. Emotions tidal wave as our eyes connect. Love. Protection. Desire. Belonging.

I've only experienced this with one other person. *Ever.*

It ripples irreversibly in my soul, leaving an indelible mark.

My hand touches his cheek, coaxing him toward me, my lips lifting to meet his.

It goes from careful to unchecked in sixty seconds. He hauls me onto his lap and his tongue probes, takes, claims—and obliterates all thoughts in my head as our hands join the party, roaming everywhere.

He breaks the kiss, breathing hard. "You okay? Your shoulder?"

"Fine," I pant, pulling his mouth back to mine.

I straddle him, tugging his T-shirt over his head. Planting kisses along his corded neck and down his chest, my lips pause to wrap around one taut nipple. He groans his pleasure as I test out rolling and flicking my tongue, fascinated by the way it feels. When I pull back, the tint of his areola has darkened a shade.

He takes off my shirt and unclasps my bra, his blue eyes blackening as he drinks me in. "You are the sexiest broad I've ever seen. Smart. Sassy. Beautiful inside and out."

Every one of my cells glows and basks in his praise, anticipation pinging through my body.

Remy's hand grips the back of my head and guides my lips toward his. He kisses me breathless, pulling our bodies flush. My insides go molten, and I moan into his mouth. He bends to suck on my breasts, vacillating between the pair and sucking my nipples forcefully. My back arches, wanting even more. He's hard where our centers press together, and my pussy grinds against him like she has a mind of her own.

"Jacqui, Jacqui, Jacqui," he utters low. "You drive me fucking *wild*."

He shifts me off his lap and stands, kicks off his boots, and ditches the rest of his clothes while I shimmy off my jeans and underwear. I admire his chiseled, naked muscles in the scant seconds before he sits back on the couch.

He tugs me back, adjusting me so I'm straddling him, our bare skin electric.

"I've never done it like this," I admit.

A delicious smile crosses his face. "Get ready for a ride."

He holds my hips as I sink onto him, my eyes shuttering closed as he stretches me inch by ever-loving inch. I gasp at the fullness, thoroughly impaled by his thick cock.

"Breathe, sweetheart," he murmurs.

I can't remember how.

Forcing my eyes open, I wrap my arms around his neck

and kiss him deeply, our tongues tangling, bodies fused intimately together.

Placing my hands on his shoulders, I begin to move, reveling in the pleasurable friction created by this position. Remy's blown pupils stay fixated on my face, taking in my surely glazed expression.

Securing my hips, he takes over, pistoning into me with deep thrusts. My breaths turn to pants as I hang on, my breasts bouncing with each drive. Because this *is* a ride, and the friction is *divine.*

A new sensation mounts. *Wait...whoa...I think I might come.*

"Play with yourself," Remy orders in a strained voice, as if he can read me.

Leaning back enough to snake my right hand between us, I rub myself with the pads of two well-placed fingers as he continues his delicious assault. Moans erupt from my throat. My touch combined with how deep he's buried inside me is otherworldly.

Fixating on the space where we join, he rasps, "That's hotter than fuck."

The intensity flares, pushing into high gear.

"Let go, sweetheart."

My body obeys, a wail escaping as an orgasm rips through me like a thunderbolt.

"Fuck yeah. That's my girl," he pants, holding me as I clench and release around his rigid length, another long wailing moan leaving my lips. I'm euphoric, brain-addled, lost in a haze of mind-blowing sex.

Just when I think I can't take any more pleasure, Remy renews his thrusts, jolting me back to reality. He fucks me like a man possessed. Fresh waves of ecstasy fire through me, my gasps turning to screams as he quickens and explodes, his hips grinding into mine with gratifying, punctuated jolts I feel to my core.

Our sweaty bodies collapse against each other as the shockwaves subside.

"That was…" I mumble into his shoulder.

"Fucking incredible," he finishes.

WE SHOWER AND CRAWL INTO BED, TALKING BY THE lamplight. My head rests on his chest, the covers gathered to our waist.

"Is this weird?" I ask, wondering if his thoughts match my own.

"You're going to have to be a little more specific."

I stroke the place where his abdominal muscles ripple and he quivers. "How comfortable this is."

"A little. You in your head about it?"

"Nope."

His fingers find my hair, lightly stroking. "I like a woman who knows what she wants."

Am I that kind of woman? A weighty pause passes as I coax my lips to speak my burning question. "Can I ask you something sort of difficult?"

"Fire away."

"Do you feel guilty about any of this because of Mick?"

His hand stills. "You mean because he's my friend?"

"Mm-hmm."

He resumes fondling my hair. "Mick bailed. As far as I'm concerned, all bets are off."

"So, there isn't some 'friend code'?"

"I've always been a tad murky about codes," he admits, chuckling softly.

I snort out a laugh and sit up. Remy snags the pack of cigarettes off the side table and we each light up.

He takes a long drag, eyes fixating on me as he exhales. "Having second thoughts?"

I shake my head. Mick did bail, and without a fucking

word. He's in the rear view, painful as it's been. "Have you heard from him?" I ask casually, despite my entire being belying it's far from indifferent.

"Very little. His father's still in bad shape. He's dealing as best he can, basically holding on until the fucker dies."

Words stick in my throat, so I acknowledge with a nod. Why that hurts so much stymies me, but it does. My next inhale is deep, the tobacco burning a path down my throat. Remy contemplates me carefully and stubs out his cigarette. Once mine's extinguished, he moves the ashtray to the night-stand. An instant later, he's pinned me to the bed.

"You're mine now, Trouble—all mine," he murmurs before flashing me a wolfish grin.

# TWENTY-EIGHT

emy drives us to Vinny's apartment Friday night for a small get-together with friends.

The second Vinny sees me, he wraps me in a bearhug. "I'm so sorry about what happened to you, bella. I'm *so fucking glad* you're alright."

Terror flashes from the recall, receding as I succumb to his comforting embrace. "Thanks, Vin," I murmur. "Remy's been a godsend."

We break apart. "Guess the dumbass is good for something," he snarks.

Remy flips him off, but his eyes graze me softly—and I melt into their caress.

We gather in the living room, and when my redhead dumps out the eight-ball of cocaine we scored on the way over, my eyes widen at the glistening crystal mound. I had no idea how much blow this equated to until now, and my heart rate accelerates as if cued. The intelligent part of my brain registers the excess. *Are we seriously going to snort all that?*

Remy sections out a portion, chops it with a razor blade, and forms it into lines. Vinny rolls a crisp dollar bill into a makeshift straw, the vehicle we pass around to eagerly inhale all those lines.

Terry and Kendra arrive, and my girl and I move to the small dining table to catch up, away from the guys. She hasn't heard about the robbery, and her face falls as I provide the Cliffs Notes version. My vision blurs as I tell her about Remy, my affection growing with each detail shared about how he's treated me, cared for me, and dug into my heart.

When I finish, there's zero judgment staring back at me. Kendra genuinely cares about my happiness, and her dazzling smile and warm hand squeezing mine is every bit as comforting as Vinny's hug.

She tells me her news, including a love-obsessed confession about how crazy she is about Terry, hinting she hopes they're a forever couple.

An hour later when someone raps on the door, all heads swivel when Vinny leaps to answer. I mask my surprise when Cora saunters in, hair ratted and sprayed even higher than normal, wearing zebra-striped jeans so tight she must have greased her thighs to shimmy into them. Vinny throws an arm around her, his eyes flitting to Remy's. Cora stares at anything but us.

Awkward.

"Hi," she finally mumbles.

There are polite replies, but I can't be the only one wondering what she's doing here when she's so clearly Team Karin, also known as Team Turncoat. Not to mention, I've seen her with Jeremy, Remy, and now Vinny, so what's her deal? Is this chick offering a good time for anyone interested —or is she desperate?

I'm one to judge. I dated Mick in the not-so-distant past, and now I'm screwing his best friend. Of course, I'd still be Mick's if he hadn't disappeared into thin air like the fucking fog. I loved him. Still love him. The thing is, I love Remy too.

Not with the same obsessive intensity, but...I'm not sure obsessive is healthy.

Remy finishes lining everyone up again and the chatter resumes. Vinny slides on a Mötley Crüe album.

I lean near Remy's ear. "Everything cool?"

"Yeah. Why wouldn't it be?" He presses a kiss to my forehead.

I tilt my head in the direction of Cora and raise an eyebrow.

"Fuck her."

I raise my eyebrow again.

He shakes his head. "It's not what you think. I don't give a rat's ass about her."

"Or anything she's said or done to fuck you over?"

"Yep. Couldn't care less. Now you? That I care about." He chucks me under the chin.

A smile stretches across my face as a familiar warmth spreads through me. My mouth finds his and I attempt to convey what I feel toward him with my lips and tongue, dancing with his.

Kendra mutters to Terry, "Why don't *you* kiss me like that anymore?"

"Baby..." he croons. "I worship the ground you walk on."

Remy and I split apart in time to see Terry caress his girl-friend's face. When my eyes swing back to Vinny and Cora, there's a flash of something sad in her expression.

"Want another beer, Rem?" I ask.

He nods.

In the kitchen, I make myself a vodka tonic, my head bobbing to "Looks That Kill," one of my favorite songs.

"Hi, Jacqui," Cora says from behind.

I spare her a glance, turning back to roll my eyes. *I've got a look that kills for you.* "Hey." I'm not typically a bitch, but I'm furious with her.

"Looks like you're with Remy now?"

"We're..." What the hell are we? "Haven't defined it or feel a need to."

"Gotcha. Well, good for you, if you're happy and all. I mean, you *look* happy." She sighs, loud enough to discern over the pounding rock music, which she's ruining with her presence.

"Yep."

"What happened to Mick?"

I shrug. It's none of her business, and she's the last person I'd confide in.

"Look, can we clear the air? I'm sensing some hostility—and I get it. You think I'm a two-faced bitch, right?"

I whirl and pin her with my stare. "Did you or did you not rat out Remy to Karin, leaving out—of course—how many times you personally fucked him behind her back?"

Cora's head tilts, her hands finding purchase on her hips when she tries to explain. "She had me over a barrel, okay? One of her coworkers outed Remy and then she came crying to me, demanding to know anything I'd heard. I'm supposed to be her good friend, and yeah...what I did with him was wrong. Maybe telling her what I knew was shitty, but she was *devastated* when she found out how deep and wide his deception went. I was picking up the fucking pieces and trying not to break her any further."

"Convenient." I light a cigarette and wave the smoke away.

"This is on Remy more than me."

"Not debating that."

"Then what?"

"If you're on her side, and believe Remy is some asshole—"

"I never said or thought that. What he did to her was wrong, but I've always liked him anyway. Obviously." She reaches in the fridge and grabs a can of beer, popping the top.

"You're still her best buddy, right? Makes me wonder why you're here."

She purses her lips and shakes her head. "I barely like her. I may be her friend, but she's a bossy, demeaning asshole. I'm tired of her crap and sure as hell *not* under her thumb."

Remy pushes through the swinging door, interrupting us. He stands behind me, hooking a protective arm around my chest. "Everything okay in here?"

Cora flinches. "Remy," she says, her voice tentative.

"Cora," he answers, calmly and unaffected. *He really doesn't care.*

She shifts from one leg to the other. "I'm...sorry for all the shit that's gone down."

His fingers splay in the air and tap back against my shirt. "It's for the best. Don't sweat it."

"We're cool then?" She swigs from her beer and attempts to shove her free hand in her front pocket—not an easy feat, but she commits, finally wedging a few fingers partially in.

"We're cool." Remy's mouth grazes my ear, and he whispers, "You are the sexiest fucking woman on legs. I can't wait to get you alone again. How long are we staying?"

I chuckle, and Cora dismisses herself, leaving us. Leaning into him, I gaze up to meet his eyes. "You're incorrigible."

He answers with a kiss.


We stay up all night and into the next day, finishing the last lines near two p.m. We're totally strung out with matted hair, wrinkled clothes, and bleary eyes.

In a desperate effort to come down from the amps pumping through my veins like a disco strobe, I take several hits off the joints making the rounds. I deplore this combination of exhausted but wide awake, shaky but inept, crazed but unproductive.

Vinny and Cora disappear into his bedroom. Remy and I split, leaving a passed-out Kendra on the couch next to Terry.

Back at Remy's, he delivers a manic, punishing type of sex, pounding into me from various positions with his unrelentingly stiff cock. It lasts so long, I know I'll be sore later, maybe limping. But I want it, every inch, every strike, even when it borders on painful. He finally climaxes, pulling out to shoot his wad all over my chest, an almost disturbed expression on his face mixing with relief.

We don't speak, only climb into a hot shower and crawl into bed, drifting off to sleep as the drug-and-alcohol cocktail drains from our bodies.

I WAKE AT A QUARTER TO MIDNIGHT TO AN EMPTY waterbed. My vagina shrieks when I roll over, morphing into a dull ache. Remy was crazed when we got home, and I wanted everything he doled out—every dirty and depraved minute.

My mind sifts back over the last twenty-four hours: the copious drugs, booze, sex, each deranged on its own, more so together. I don't want to wind up an addict or alcoholic. I'm a girl with potential...with wants and dreams. I'm not sure what Remy wants—or if he dreams.

Shifting the covers, I grimace getting upright. Yanking open one of Remy's drawers, I pull on one of his soft shirts, flipping my hair out of the collar on the way to the living room. My boyfriend's prone on the couch watching MTV on low volume, munching on some crackers.

Wordlessly, I lay next to him, my back to his front. His arm encircles me, tucking me in closer.

"Did you sleep?" he says, his voice low and deep.

"Mm-hmm."

His fingers caress me softly, sparking my body to life everywhere he touches despite the soreness. "You hungry?"

"Mm-hmm."

"Me too. I'll rustle us up something." He climbs up and over me, leaping off the sofa with a signature energy he rarely seems without. Minutes later, he's clanging pans, the fridge opening and shutting. My eyes close, my body settling into the warmth he left behind. Videos play in the background, an eclectic mix of Def Leppard, INXS, Grace Jones, Tears for Fears, Falco.

A plate of steaming pancakes in front of my nose pulls me from my semi-coma, and I hurry to sit up. Slathering on butter and drowning it all in maple syrup, I get the first forkful in my mouth and groan. "Oh my god." My eyes flutter closed, savoring how incredible it tastes.

Remy's deep chuckle resounds beside me, his long legs stretched out, ankles propped on the coffee table. "I'm not sure you sound that turned on when you come."

I flash him some side-eye. "Better up your game." *As if.*

He huffs out a laugh. "Challenge accepted."

We finish—me practically licking my plate—and he takes the dishes and leaves them soaking in the sink. He tugs me back into the bedroom where we get naked and crawl under the covers.

Remy strokes my skin softly, lightly, his fingers sending rippling bumps across every surface, causing me to arch and pant as he rapidly coaxes me to orgasm.

"I love to hear you moan," he whispers, "and know I'm responsible."

Knowing I'm too sore for intercourse, I press my hand into his chest and push him back against the mattress. My long hair trails down his torso to his waiting erection, and I let my mouth and hands go to work. He explodes down my throat in short order, bringing me a similar satisfaction.

We fall back asleep for a few hours, then lay awake, limbs tangled, talking and smoking until the morning sun breaks through the curtains.

We make love again—soreness be damned—and I soak in our last moments like this.

When there's no putting it off any longer, I gather my things, kiss Remy goodbye, and drive home, making it in time to straighten up before my parents return. My heart begins its slow descent into depression, anxiety slithering in over the shit about to hit the fan.

# Twenty-Nine

My parents look rested and...normal, a shocking picture of health after a week's vacation in Mendocino. Not to mention *cheerful*. It's like looking at clones. I'm reluctant to divulge what occurred, knowing it's going to spoil their mood.

"Did you have a nice time?" I ask.

The suntan on my mother's skin, her eyes clear and bright, give her a vitality absent for years. "It was wonderful. Just what the doctor ordered," she says, stealing an affectionate glance at my father. It's jarringly out of place. They don't do endearing.

He shrugs the last bag off his shoulder and it thunks against the hardwood floor. "Great weather, incredible scenery. The food and wine were top notch. We already talked about a repeat trip next year. How was everything here? Any problems?"

I sigh internally. *Here we go.* "Uh...one. It's kind of big."

My father's eyes grow steely, narrowing as they fixate on me.

"But it's all handl—"

"What?" he snaps.

"The station was, um, robbed one night during my shift."

My parents reel on their feet, openly gaping at me. My mother's hand flies to her mouth, eyes opening wide.

"Details. Be specific and don't leave anything out," my father commands.

I run through the events as succinctly as possible, watching my parent's mood tank with every word. My mom's probably ten minutes from downing a Valium. My father's lips clamp into a thin line, his jaw ticking along with his pulse.

His expression fills with rage. "I'm calling our attorney first thing in the morning and we're suing. You could have been killed!"

"Dad...I agree, but it's not like I didn't understand the risks. Gas stations get robbed. I don't think we have legal—"

"Horseshit!" he thunders.

My mother steps forward and hugs me with shaky arms, clinging like a drowning victim. "Thank God you weren't harmed, that you're alive."

Now I've dredged up the worst moment in our family archives...yet it's true I could be dead. An involuntary shudder ripples through me.

"How scared you must have been," she murmurs.

I sag into her and this rare display of affection, nodding in agreement against her shoulder. I was fucking terrified. Correction, *am*.

Too soon, she slips away.

"We've already lost one daughter, and almost another," my father says, spittle flying into the air with his words. "With all the yahoos out there, your employer should have thought about protecting his employees. How hard is it to install bulletproof glass? Create a locked office with some sort of slot to exchange money?"

I stammer to reply and realize he's asking rhetorical questions.

"I'll make sure he pays *and* fixes these unsatisfactory work conditions, so it doesn't happen to anyone else! You are absolutely, positively not working there, young lady. Ever again."

"I already quit," I admit.

He glares at me again and scrubs a hand through his hair, muttering, "I need a drink," before stalking off.

My mother smiles meekly, squeezes my hand, and disappears...probably into her medicine cabinet.

Once again, my parents leave me upset...and alone. In a fog, I trudge to my room and shut the door. Flopping back on my bed, fantasies about fleeing to Remy's abound—where his arms, kisses, and tenderness make the world alright.

I hide in my room until it's time to make dinner, then go through the motions to put something on the table. My father is calmer after however many boozy drinks he's downed, and my mother's dilated pupils confirm she's doped up.

"I started looking into colleges," I direct to my father.

He shovels a wad of fettuccine in his mouth, chewing furiously, and I fight back my reaction. His eating habits disgust me—it's always a fast, angry race, and it puts me on edge. "What's the deadline?"

"Late December."

He tears off a hunk of baguette and smears it with butter. "Don't screw it up. You'll have to write an essay and understand all their requirements, pay fees, get your transcripts there. Stay on top of it." He shoves the bread into his jowls.

"I will." I stare at my bowl. "Um, also, if it's okay, I'd prefer not to get another job yet. I'm not saying long, only a while."

My father grunts. I'm guessing that's a yes. The remainder of the meal is silent aside from the wearisome sound of classical music that is no match for Fred Hall's egregious food inhalation.

SPRAWLED ON MY BED IN WELL-WORN SWEATS AND A soft T-shirt, I'm finishing my homework when Remy calls.

"How's everything going?" he purrs, his masculine timbre every bit as toe-curling as his Camaro's idle.

"My dad wants to sue Leo." My tone is hushed, not wanting to wake my parents, whose room isn't far down the hall.

"For chrissakes. Not that I don't get where he's coming from."

"I'll be mortified if he does. It could bankrupt him."

"Might."

"I miss you. I know it's only been a matter of hours, but we spent a lot of time together this week." *I'd be lost without you.*

He chuckles low, the sound going straight to my heart and wiggling in a little deeper. "I liked having you here too. Especially in my bed. You spoiled me."

"Mr. Remington, are you getting domestic on me?"

"Negative. Although you make it tempting."

That elicits another smile. "Then you're just using me for your sexual pleasure?"

"Of course...not," he teases.

"Shame."

He chuckles again. "Like I said: *trouble.*"

"It's time for me to choose a college to transfer into next year," I blurt before holding my breath, wondering if he'll care.

"Yeah? Where you thinking?" I overhear the flick of his lighter and subsequent inhale. Now I'm jonesing for a cigarette.

"Not sure. Maybe San Jose or San Francisco? Far enough away to live near campus, not at home. I can't stand living in this house, Rem." I pick at a loose thread on my black and white checkered comforter. The sudden prick behind my eyes makes me squeeze them shut.

"You'd only be about an hour away? That's not bad."

I gulp down my emotion.

"Jacqui? We'll make it work."

My heart lifts. He wants to stay close? "I'd love that," I croak.

"What...did you think you were getting rid of me so easily?" He sounds mock hurt.

My mood lightens. "Not when I'm still using you for sex."

"You're giving me a boner."

"Mmm...what I could do with that."

He lets out a long groan. "Remember this little conversation the next time I see you—because I'm going to tear you up."

My insides clench. "Promises, promises."

"It's a fucking promise alright."

"I'm going to whack off now..."

"*Fuck. Me.*"

I grin. "Tomorrow?"

"My place," he practically growls. "Six o'clock."

# Thirty

True to his word, Remy delivers—wielding every tool in his talented sexual arsenal to rock my world.

We share a cigarette while basking in post-coital bliss, the sweat evaporating as our breathing returns to normal. Rolling toward him and burrowing into his side, our body musk fills my senses.

I'm once again bowled over by incredible sex—the intensity, orgasms, shockwaves. Mentally sifting through my past experiences, it's all become so clear. My ex-boyfriend Robbie was selfish. Not only wouldn't he get over his issues with giving me head, but he also never gave me an orgasm, saying I was *complicated*, and alluding his dick should provide all the pleasure I needed. What a crock of shit.

Prior to him was Jimmy, with a rather unfortunate, tiny penis that failed to make me feel anything. And I mean literally. Probably owing to the size issue, he lacked confidence in all areas, resulting in an all-around lackluster experience.

Which leaves my first, Matt, a boy I'd pined for through junior high who finally noticed me in tenth grade. He wanted to go all the way even though I wasn't ready. Desperate for his love, I traded my virginity. The asshole dumped me soon after, leaving me devastated.

Honestly, the first sex I've truly enjoyed—or that smacked of earth-shattering like my pot-boiler novels convinced me existed—happened with Mick. And now Remy.

Why did I compromise my principles? Why did I believe Robbie, or allow him to convince me of such bullshit? Why do I regularly settle for less?

"I can hear you thinking," Remy says with a pronounced yawn. "What's going on in that pretty head of yours?"

"Well, actually...I can't believe sex is this fucking great."

His chest rumbles with laughter. "What?"

"You heard me. I've had a lot of lackluster experiences."

He shifts to look at me, his blue eyes sparkling under disheveled copper hair. "Are you saying I'm a sex god?"

Shaking my head, I push him playfully. "You know you are, asshole."

"Happy to be of service. You deserve to be properly laid and fucking worshipped."

I do? *I do.*

"You're dynamite in the sack," he murmurs.

"I am?"

He tucks a lock behind my ear, his finger grazing my jawline. "I love hearing you scream and moan and the way you thrust your hips. It lets me know you're enjoying yourself, and that turns me on more than anything. That, and you give the *best* head."

A shy smile crosses my face, but inside, I'm lapping up his words. And silently thanking *Cosmopolitan* for the blow job tips.

"From the minute I laid eyes on you, I wanted you...and knew I'd turn my world upside-down for you. You're perfect, Jacqui."

His words softly penetrate, like raindrops against withered plants, trickling down the stalks to find the roots underneath.

"So are you." My lips press against his and I settle my head back on his chest, but I'm still not understanding why I accepted how Robbie treated me.

Why don't I let go of people when they're not good for me? It's as if I'm the doormat for everyone to stand and wipe their feet on. *Don't mind me...trample away. I'll still be here, hoping you ring my bell.* There's something broken inside for me to put up with shit like that. Right?

"New subject," I announce, stopping the spiral. "What do you want out of life?"

Remy's chest rumbles again. "I'm loving these light topics. Does sex make you introspective? Because it makes me want to crash."

A quiet giggle erupts. "Answer the question, Remington."

"You're getting bossy, Hall...and I kind of like it."

I circle my thumb and middle finger together and flick his torso.

"Hey! Fine. What I want out of life..." he muses, "is to be happy."

My head lifts for a minute to address him. "You already seem happy. Like, the happiest person on the planet." Irish Setter to the max.

"I am," he says, lighting another cigarette. "And I want to stay that way. I've watched a fuck-ton of people get older and subsequently become miserable. There's something about working every day for the rest of your life, or tying yourself down to the wrong person, or getting so wrapped up in the 'shoulds' you forget why you're living."

I hum in agreement. "Do you know what you're going to do with the career thing?" The last time we talked about it, he was biding his time as a mechanic before beginning life as a rich playboy. As if that's a job.

"Nope."

"Wait a fucking minute..." Pushing up on my elbow, I seek his gaze. "Do you have a *trust fund*?"

He sighs, like he doesn't want to talk about it. "Guilty—but hear me out."

My mouth falls agape.

"First, it's not guaranteed. My parents are jerks about it. They want me to work for it, try and succeed on my own, before they fork over anything. They love dangling that shit over my head and changing the hoops I'm supposed to jump through."

"Remind me why you work at a garage then?"

He lifts his brows. "One, I dig cars, and I'm not afraid to get my hands dirty. And two, to piss them off?" A smile tugs at his lips, and my head shakes.

They probably want him working a *respectable* white-collar job instead of staying a *lowly* grease monkey. "How are you going to 'make it' though? What if it pushes them too far? What if you lose your trust fund?"

"So many questions, beautiful girl." He moves another lock away from my face, his blue gaze spearing mine. "I don't know, and right now, I don't give a fuck. I'm simply having a good time."

"Hmm. You're such a riddle, Randolph Remington III. Maybe that's a good thing."

"A good thing would be fucking this sweet pussy again," he says, reaching down and cupping me there. He stubs out his cigarette and we go again, making me forget about inadequate ex-boyfriends, money, and the future.

# THIRTY-ONE

"Will you zip me up?" I ask Remy, turning around in my body-hugging black dress. We're at his apartment preparing for a Halloween party, going as Bonnie and Clyde—or our modern-day rendition of the infamous thieves. Sexy garter belts hold up my sheer black stockings with a back seam, about which my boyfriend...*is he my boyfriend?*...makes numerous lewd comments.

Remy looks dashing in a coal suit and white button-down, a fedora tilted rakishly on his head. He hands me mine, which I don while he grabs our fake machine guns to sling over our shoulders. We're quite the pair, dangerous in our own right, and we grin when our eyes meet in the mirror.

I let out a sexy groan. "The way you look is criminal." A giggle escapes at my unintended joke.

He smirks, but his eyes sweep me top to bottom. "I pale next to you, sweetheart. Incredible," he says, planting a kiss on my ruby lips. "And those heels? I'm fucking you with those on later."

Deal. "Ready to rob some banks, Clyde?"

"Born ready, Bonnie darlin'."

Remy winds through the hills in his Camaro, a welcome upgrade to whatever jalopy our 1930s bank robbers drove. We pass by Mick's mom's street, and I experience a slight twinge. Within a mile, we hang a right. Both sides of the road are lined with cars leading up to the party, hosted by some Skyline High alumni known for throwing ragers.

Remy cops a U-turn and parks. The Gap Band's energetic funk pumps through the cool night air as we hike up the hill toward the house. A group of already drunk boys dressed as zombie football players weaves past.

The party pulsates with energy, jammed with costumed bodies, the air scented with pot, nicotine, and malted barley. Remy's intent on scoring cocaine and begins scouting the crowd for dealers as we head in the direction of the kegs. I recognize several faces from my high school years, and murmur greetings as Remy guides me by the hand through the throng. My date knows far more people than I do.

We scan the crowd while we wait in line then fill a couple of oversized plastic cups with cheap beer, half suds. Beer is bad enough, but keg beer? Insufferable.

After Remy buys a gram from some guy, we lock ourselves in a bathroom and quickly inhale some lines. Then we hit the dance floor. My mind rewinds to the night we shared at Eli's Mile High Club. I ward off the pang the memory brings and the subsequent wave of guilt washing through me.

Shaking it off, I look around at the costumed dancers crowding our space. A caveman with Snow White. A jailer with a convict. A mobster with a fairy. When I land back on Remy, he returns my big grin.

Terry and Kendra bump into us intentionally and we turn into a foursome, mixing up partners. The synthesized intro to Parliament's "Flashlight" cues up and Kendra and I scream, joining the collective cheers erupting from the dancers around us.

A few songs later, the four of us snag another round of beers and escape into a bedroom to snort blow. My head's damp from dancing and wearing this annoying fedora, which continuously slips into my eyes. I remove it and fan myself with the brim.

Twenty minutes later, we're back in the fracas, traversing the party to see if we can find more friends.

We nearly collide with Karin and Cora, dressed like Playboy Bunnies. Karin glares at Remy, mutters "whore" and turns on her heel, exiting quickly. Her friend gives us an awkward glance before chasing after her. Remy looks like he's been punched, shocking me into silence when he tells me to wait...then bolts after Karin.

My cheeks burn as I'm left standing adrift like a jilted loser, totally bereft of words. Terry and Kendra remain silent while my gut churns, the embarrassment shifting to something more potent. What is he fucking doing? And was Karin calling him a whore—or *me*? A little ironic coming from someone dressed as a Playboy Bunny. My pulse speeds, heartbeat pounding in my ears, fighting the internal debate of what to do.

Oh my god. It's classic Remy, right? When he and Karin face off, it ends in make-ups or break-ups, and there's only one direction they have to go.

I don't want to believe he would discard me so easily.

I'd rather believe that what we've experienced shows we're good together, better than good, fucking incredible really.

But I can't. Because he left *me* here and chased after *her*.

*Fuck it*. I turn, getting one step before Kendra grabs my arm.

"Where are you going, Jacqui?"

"Outside. I need air." I can't just stand here, waiting.

"I'll come with you," she says, her concern obvious.

I shrug her off, shaking my head, and storm away—as best as one can storm in five-inch heels.

My gaze scans the crowd, thick with bodies, as I navigate my way through. Acquaintances try to chat me up, a strange guy in a hockey mask hits on me, and I'm suffocating in a sea of creepy Jason and Michael Myers lookalikes. I want—need—to get the fuck out of here.

Shucking off the infernal contraptions strapped to my feet, I leave the party altogether and stalk out to the main road, the rough asphalt shredding my fine stockings in a matter of minutes. I turn down the hill, my righteous indignation propelling me forward, the irksome festive noises growing dimmer with every manic step.

Facing traffic on a steep decline, I curse these damn hills with their narrow roads and no sidewalks. I must look like a lunatic with my sweeping hand gestures, talking to myself.

Making it to the intersection where Mick's mother lives, I scream "Fuck!" into the night. Ripping the stupid fedora off my head, I hurl it with all my might and watch as it sails into a nearby ravine.

My nose burns as reality slams me in the face. My feet hurt, I'm cold, and this is a dumb fucking idea. I live at least ten miles from here. My impulses—once again—brilliant.

Worse, I'm out here solo, vulnerable to another asshole like the guy who held me at gunpoint, tied me up, and threatened sexual assault—and it's the middle of the night. Anger turns to anxiety like I've flipped a light switch.

That man is still at large. *What if he drives by?*

My eyes well as the enormity of my situation crashes down on me. I'm alone. *Again.*

Forcing myself to stop, I debate turning back and dealing with whatever is happening at the party or attempting to hoof it home in what clearly could be filed under Rash Decisions.

I burst into tears.

Headlights round the corner, paralyzing me. Do I hide? Run?

Before I can act, the car is upon me.
A blue Mustang.
*Mick.*

# THIRTY-TWO

Mick slows, stops, and rolls down the passenger side window. "Jacqui, what are you doing out here? What happened?"

The tears flow as I stare at the mirage in front of me, spluttering incoherently when I attempt to form words.

"Get in." With effort, he pushes the door open on the inclined road.

I allow gravity to swing it soundly shut as new emotions assault me.

*Hurtful, asshole motherfucker.*

*Also, stealing-the-air-from-my-lungs, gorgeous motherfucker.*

"Damn it, Jax. Get in. *Please.*" He again flings the door wide while keeping the car from rolling downhill.

This time, I catch the door, bracing one hand against it to slide inside.

His tires screech as he flies up the hill and turns onto his street, throwing questions my way. "What happened? What are you doing out here by yourself? Did someone hurt you?"

My sobs only intensify. At this point, I'm beyond caring.

His hand tentatively reaches over and squeezes my knee,

exposing my black and white lace garters where they snap to my now useless stockings. I hear his sharp inhale. "And what are you...is this a costume?"

Emotions swirl inside me. "I'm fine," I choke out.

Mick pulls up in front of his mom's house, and I feel the weight of those gray eyes. "You're clearly not...but you certainly don't owe me any explanations."

An ungraceful snort-hiccup leaves my lips. "Damn right I don't."

"Listen," he says, scrubbing a hand through his chestnut hair, "I don't know what you need or where you want to go. I brought you here because it seemed logical, but I'll take you wherever you want."

I rifle around in my purse for something to mop up the veritable river on my face and come up empty. "Is your mom home?" I croak. It may be stupid, but the first time I meet his mother, if that ever happens, I'd rather not be a blubbering mess.

"No. She's coming back Sunday."

A million questions raid my headspace. *Are you back? Living here again? How long? Were you seriously going to ignore me the rest of your life? DID I MEAN NOTHING TO YOU?*

Instead, I say, "If you don't mind, I'd like to come in for a few minutes."

Out of my periphery, he nods, exiting the car. My body turns leaden, the events of the past hour already too much to process.

Mick opens my door. Always a gentleman. *Except when he fucking disappears into thin air without a backward glance.*

My tears dry as we ascend the stairs, and the familiarity of this house—and him—washes over me like a tidal wave. Once inside, he flicks on lights, and I beeline to the bathroom.

A mirror above the vanity helps me assess the damage: mascara smeared around bloodshot eyes and more skidding down my face, faded red lipstick, splotchy cheeks. Turning on the faucet to let the water warm, I collect a handful of tissues and shut down my brain. It's not like I'm clueless about what comes next.

Once I've mitigated the damage, I walk down the hall and into the living room. My footsteps are soundless, not that anything registers above the thundering in my entire body.

Mick stands in front of the sliding glass doors looking out to the bay. Even after all this time, just the sight of him overwhelms me. Will there ever be a day my heart doesn't beat out of my chest searching to find his?

Pushing myself forward, I step alongside him, and he startles. We're both quiet. Gazing at the vastness of the sky, stars, water, and skyline reminds me how insignificant we are.

Unavoidably, his ocean scent fills my senses, reminding me of all there once was between us.

"Are you okay? Do you need me to—"

"Why, Mick? *Why*?" I stay fixated on the twinkling lights from homes dotting the landscape.

His discernible exhale is the only sound.

"Why didn't you call me? How could you leave us the way we were?" My throat closes, forcing a swallow. I'm *not* crying again, damn it.

"Fuck," he says quietly. Out of the corner of my eye, I sense him grappling. "Jax...I'm...I thought I was doing the best thing for you."

"*For me*? Who are *you* to make decisions for *me*?"

"After everything went down and I didn't know when—or if—I'd ever see you again, I didn't want to tether you to my bullshit. You didn't, and still don't, deserve that."

Facing him, my voice rises. "You didn't even give me a chance! You brushed me aside like a...like a speck of lint."

"It may seem so, but you're wrong." He stares at the floor. "I hated every second."

"I loved you!" I wail, my hands rising and dropping. A

tear escapes and when I don't bat it away, Mick reaches up and gently swipes it, his touch jolting me to the core.

"I'm so sorry I hurt you," he whispers, his gray eyes pleading.

His words sink in, but I'm far from okay. "So, now what? Are you back? Are you living here again?"

"No. I'm only here for a few days. Things are...complicated."

My breath catches at the storm raging in his eyes.

"Because of your dad?"

He waves a hand, a frown tugging at his lips.

"Will you tell me what happened?"

He nods. "I need a beer first. You want one, or something else?"

"Beer's fine." Anything to take the edge off. I'm still tense and his proximity is always dizzying, although my heart beats more normally. Choosing the biggest sofa, I settle on one side, curl my feet under me, and wait.

Mick hands me an uncapped bottle and sits next to me. He hard packs a fresh box of Marlboros against his palm, unwraps the cellophane, peels back the foil, and dislodges a few. He gazes my way, eyebrow raised, and I nod. He flicks his Zippo, igniting two, and passes me one.

Our fingers graze in the transaction, a telltale warmth spreading through me like a needed sigh.

He cracks his neck, and I register how tight my own muscles are wound, shoulders hunching toward my ears, bracing for whatever he's about to divulge. *Relax. Listen to what he has to say.*

"I'm sure Remy told you my dad had a heart attack."

*Remy.* He hasn't crossed my mind once since I glimpsed Mick. But that's a problem for a different hour.

"Then he stroked out. A big one first followed by smaller strokes. He became fully incapacitated."

"That's...a lot."

He nods. "Soon after, my stepmother left him, and my brothers wouldn't do shit to help, which meant I was stuck dealing with it." He takes a few more drags, blowing the smoke with force.

"Caring for a father you hate."

"With a fucking passion."

"So now you're responsible for him? How is that fair?"

His eyes swing toward mine, flashing a stormy gray. "No one said life was fair, Jax." He stubs out his cigarette in an ashtray we've shared countless times. It's orange and kidney-shaped, straight out of the 1970s.

"Is he going to make it?"

"No idea. But I fucking hope not."

I cover his hand with my own, understanding more than he realizes. "Is he still in the hospital?" It's been months.

"He's at home, in a patient bed, with some nursing support. Otherwise, you're looking at the help."

I'm visualizing his world, his perspective, seeing the choices he made and why. It doesn't excuse how he handled *us*, but it takes the edge off my hurt. "I'm sorry," I say, squeezing his hand. "You're in a super tough spot. I don't envy you."

He answers with a rueful smile.

"This leaves you in limbo, doesn't it? How can you go forward with your own life if you have no idea how long this will be your situation?"

"Bingo."

"And Florida? "Can you—"

"Jax, just drop it," he says gruffly, yanking his hand away. "I know you want to be helpful, but talking about it only makes it worse. Everything fucking sucks and will until it doesn't."

His words singe, but I can't blame how he feels. Silently, I take in all the features making up Mick Callahan, my broken heart recalibrating, opening, creating space for him again.

Pushing up to my knees, I shift onto his lap and hold him. He goes rigid, fighting my attempt at kindness, reassurance, empathy...but I don't let go. After a minute, he sighs and allows himself to embrace me—and we stay that way a very long time.

"You smell so good," he mumbles.

*Back atcha, my ocean.* I'm lost in it, in him. Nothing is righter than being in his arms.

"I've never stopped thinking about you," he murmurs.

I pull back, meeting his eyes. "Same."

His gaze shifts to my lips. In seconds, his mouth finds mine, desperate and searching, and we reunite like two misplaced souls. Heat rolls through me like a wildfire, obliterating everything in its path. His hand grips the back of my head, drawing me closer, and I whimper, wanting *more, more, more.* As my tongue dances with his and our ragged breaths fill the space between us, my heart leans fully into his.

"I want you," I murmur.

"I've never wanted anything fucking more." The husk in his voice sends another tremor rippling through me. "Not that I deserve you."

"Shut up," I whisper. "I'm no saint." Like a motor stalling, I still in his arms, remembering whose arms were wrapped around me mere hours ago.

He pulls back, cocking his head. "What do you mean?"

I blow out a breath. "You should know something before we go any further."

"Sounds ominous."

*Because it is.* "I slept with someone else. It just sort of...happened and—"

"That's not really my business, is it, after the way I left things between us?"

"It's Remy," I blurt.

Mick shakes his head, huffing sarcastically. "Fucking Remy."

My insides churn, awash with guilt, shame, more. "Are you mad? Does this change how you feel about me?"

Those gray eyes clash with my amber straight on. "Nope."

In one fluid movement, he stands us both upright, kissing me deeply and thoroughly, leaving no doubt.

His hands roam down my torso, under my dress, and across my behind. I arch against him, my entire body throbbing, fingers slipping beneath his shirt and skimming his masculine contours. Every cell is awake and alert, melting into his touch and engulfed by everything Mick. He lifts me, my legs wrapping around his waist. Cocooning me in his strong embrace, he walks us down the hall, stopping halfway to press me flush to the wall and claim my mouth.

It's his. It's always been his.

Our tongues desperately seek and explore, and it's like breathing oxygen after being deprived.

Once we make it to the bedroom, he deposits me on the bed. I lean on my elbows as he stares at me with hooded eyes —a blackish gray now, one of my favorite shades. He peels off his shirt and I'm struck speechless at the gorgeous, blinding display: his broad chest with defined pecs, corded arms, a ripple of abs, and a hint of chestnut hair trailing into his straining Levi's.

God, I missed him. I'm drunk in his presence, wanting to lose myself in his scent, touch...storm.

His eyes travel down my body, absorbing every inch. He lifts my dress enough to expose my garter belts. "I like these," he hums, caressing each thigh before easily unsnapping both to release my shredded stockings. "I think we'll leave them on."

If my thong wasn't already soaked, it is now.

"Let's take off your dress," he says in a low throaty voice that could make me orgasm all by itself. He pulls me to standing and unzips me. Once I step out, he tosses the garment over a nearby chair. He shucks off his remaining clothes, hard cock springing against his abdomen, his dazzling nakedness on full display.

I inch back up the center of the bed, clad only in lace garters and my microscopic thong. He pauses to admire the view, his gaze brimming with heat, want, and something more that knocks against my heart.

He kisses and licks up my calves to my thighs—ignoring the pulsating triangle between them—continuing along my sunken abdomen to my breasts. His breath teases an already erect nipple. My back bows, beckoning him closer. He delivers, his hands and mouth working in concert as he alternates sucking on them both. I writhe beneath him, burning with hunger, overwhelmed we're together, consumed by everything Mick. His name leaves my lips in uttered pants.

His mouth trails upward, stopping at the hollow of my neck, kissing my jaw before using his tongue to do filthy things to my ear. Fresh heat shoots to my core, and I claw at his back with frantic yearning. Grabbing his face, I press my mouth to his, and he inhales my whimpers.

I'm so fucking lost in him again.

My hand winds between us, and we simultaneously groan as I fist his silky length while his hands roam. Too soon, he slides down, taking his beautiful manhood with him. I don't pout long when his mouth hovers over my vibrating center, his hot breath scorching the tiny scrap of material. He slowly drags my thong down my legs, exposing me fully.

He returns, and with his hands framing my hips, he dips to taste me.

I cry out with zero restraint.

He keeps my hips pinned under his mouth. "Fuck, I've missed this," he murmurs, flicking, teasing, and making love to me with his tongue.

*That makes two of us.*

He inserts a finger, then two, and I'm shot into another

stratosphere. Manipulating those thick fingers in tandem with sucking in the perfect spot, I teeter on the brink.

When I combust, a light show explodes behind my shuttered lids. I ride his face, bucking with spasm after spasm of bliss, as he consumes all of me. My body. My mind. My heart.

Before I've caught my breath, he repositions himself and our eyes collide, shining with unsaid words. Never breaking eye contact, he drives himself all the way in.

"*Fuuuuuuuuuuck,*" he murmurs.

We both still, savoring the sensation of him buried deep inside me.

My legs shift, beckoning him deeper, and Mick begins moving in measured, deliberate strokes. His eyes stay fused with mine, and I'm lost in his universe, my heart wide open in offering. Our bodies move in natural, beautiful tandem, remembering each other. Our lovemaking is languid, like molten lava flowing from a volcano, hot and all-encompassing, devastating anything in its wake.

His eyes never leave mine as he claims all of me with every thrust.

*I love you.*

All that I am is his.

*I love you.*

He is everything I want.

*I love you.*

Overcome, my eyes well.

*I love you. I love you. I love you.*

He sinks into me faster, his magnificent face full of rapture. When his release hits, he spills into me with a vengeance, a guttural roar leaving his lips.

# Thirty-Three

Waking up to Mick's warm body spooning mine brings last night flooding back. His scent invades my space as our lovemaking replays, rousing all my cells.

Too soon, those pleasant thoughts dissipate like sand through my fingers, replaced with questions—and the sobering reality of a new day.

Rolling over and facing him, I inhale everything Mick Callahan. His dark lashes rest gently against his face, chestnut hair tousled from sleep, full lips slightly ajar. A thick neck leads to broad shoulders and a glorious chest. I follow the graceful curve down his muscular arm, thrown over the covers. Merely looking at him makes my chest hurt.

He stirs, his eyes fluttering open. A sleepy smile appears, tugging him further into another damning layer of my heart. "Good morning."

"Good morning," I rasp, my first spoken words of the day sounding unintentional sexy.

We stare silently at each other, small smiles playing upon our faces.

"I've missed those eyes," he says.

His have haunted me. "Mm-hmm. I know exactly how you feel."

Our gazes stay locked another minute, soaking one another in, until he breaks the silence. "Hungry?"

*For you.* "Ravenous."

"I've got just the thing." He pulls me toward him, his firm erection greeting me.

We fall back into carnal bliss—and I'm floating, flipping, flying.

We shower after, stealing kisses as we take turns washing one another. He shampoos my hair, revering it as he massages my scalp and runs his fingers through my long golden lengths. I could die, now, a happy woman.

After we dry off, he pulls on Levi's, leaving his chest bare. I'll never make it out the door if he dresses like that.

He lobs me one of his T-shirts and a pair of sweats. "Not that I don't love that getup from last night, but I'm thinking this will be more comfortable for you today." He smirks, picking up my discarded garter belt and twirling it around his finger.

"There's my Mr. Thoughtful," I say.

Mick leaves to make coffee and I get dressed. Swimming in his clothes, I fold down the waistband on his sweats a few times, forming a bulky roll, and knot the shirt near my navel. It's not pretty but it'll have to do—and they smell like my ocean, which means I'm never taking them off. My change of clothes is at Remy's...and I'm not ready to think about him yet.

The pungent scent of freshly ground beans brewing wafts through the air as I enter the living room. Moving to those giant glass doors that beckon every time I'm here, I stare at the fog burning off over the bay, blue skies revealed little by little, as if the heavens are opening a curtain.

"It's ready," he says.

I make my way to the kitchen where he pours us each a cup. I add plenty of sugar and milk, and he laughs.

"A little coffee with your sugar?"

I smirk. "I'm sweet. That's what little girls are made of and whatnot."

He looks thoughtful and flashes a salacious grin. "You're delicious."

One look, two words, and my insides squirm.

We collect our coffees and sit outside on the deck. He lights us a couple of cigarettes, his Zippo snapping shut before he hands me one.

"Mick?"

He chuckles. "Fire away, woman. I can feel the questions rolling off you in waves."

"Last night was amazing."

"It was."

"But...what now?"

He rakes a hand through one side of his wet hair and takes a pull off his cigarette. "I don't know. Nothing's really changed."

I gulp. "You mean you still don't want to be together?"

"Jax. That's not it. I simply don't see how this can work. I'm living an hour away—and I'm stuck there in the worst circumstances imaginable. I can't drive across the bay at my whim."

"I don't care," I say, imploring him to return my gaze.

He stares at me hard. "I care. It's not fair to you."

"We could talk on the phone. I could come to your place. We have options." My legs cross and uncross, physical comfort impossible when everything inside me screams.

He tilts his head back, blowing out another stream of smoke, the curls dissipating into nothing. "I don't have any idea how long this situation will continue with the old man. My life is seriously fucked right now. Yours doesn't have to be."

I'm scared to ask, but it comes out of my mouth anyway. "Do you care about me?"

He nods, slowly and methodically. "Yes."

"Then let's *try*. I'm going into it with my eyes wide open."

He appears to consider. "And what about Remy?"

Ouch. "I...we...shit." My teeth worry my bottom lip before a heavy breath escapes. "It just happened. Look, you two are my best friends. I love you both so much, in totally different ways."

That earns me a wary glance.

"Remy and I were fucked up—me over you, and him over Karin. And..." I falter, a shiver coursing through me as the memory surfaces.

"And what?"

The air leaves my lungs in a harsh whoosh. "I got robbed at gunpoint at the station one night."

His eyes flare, brows knitting together. "Holy shit, Jax! What the fuck?"

As the relived events tumble from my lips, Mick's expression grows steely, then furious. I explain how Remy became a safe harbor, a protector, more...that is, until the party last night. My going off half-cocked. Gripping fear walking home alone. Relief at Mick finding me.

He listens quietly. I take a fortifying breath when I finish, sip my now-cold coffee, and wait for his response. It's a relief to purge it all, tell him the words stored up for him, even if I didn't realize it until now.

"I get it," he says. "I'm glad he was there for you. I sure as shit wasn't. Jesus..." His eyes fall closed. "What a fucking mess."

Reaching over, my fingers graze his arm.

He tugs on my hand. "Come here."

I crawl into his lap, and he holds me, one hand stroking my hair and down my back. We don't say anything, but words couldn't express any better what he already is to me. I know he doesn't realize it, but he's my safe harbor too. If he would just agree to dock his boat here, drop anchor, and let us be...whatever it is we're supposed to be.

"I'm sorry," he finally whispers.

I lift my face from his chest, and he kisses me with a yearning, softness, and intensity rolled into one. He may not be willing or able to say the words, but there's love between us—and he knows it.

He holds me until I reluctantly disentangle myself to call home. I'm thankful my mom answers. My parents think I slept over at Kendra's, and the lies pour from my mouth, continuing the charade and buying me a few hours.

After hanging up, I shoo Mick out of the kitchen and make us breakfast. Finding a box of Bisquick, I heat the waffle iron while whisking the batter then slice some fresh fruit, all the while ruminating over how to deal with the Remy conundrum. Honestly, I feel awful about it. At the same time, I'm fucking elated.

Like I said, *conundrum.*

After a quiet meal, Mick offers to call Remy. Right or wrong—or chickenshit—I let him.

"She's here," he murmurs. "Yeah, man." Pause. "We're headed over."

"Is he mad?" I prompt, guilt twisting in my gut. *What a stupid question.*

He nods, his gray eyes cool. "Worried as fuck too."

Of course he is. I disappeared without a word or giving him a chance to explain. If Remy screwed Karin last night, all this angst would melt away and wash away my sins (or would it?). Somehow, I doubt that happened, and I'm kidding myself if I think I'd be happy about it.

MY HEART RATE JACKS BEFORE MY ASS HITS THE Mustang's smooth seat. I'm jumpy, scattered, roiling inside. Ever perceptive, Mick squeezes my hand. This is why I'm fucking head over heels for him.

*Oh god.*

Fuck. Fuck. Fuck. Fuck. Fuck. Fuck. Fuck. Fuck. Fuck. Fuck. Fuck. Fuck. Fuck. Fuck. Fuck. Fuck. Fuck.

I chain smoke the entire way, pitching one out the window as Mick slides into a parking spot once we arrive. My Bug, facing us across the street, glares at me accusingly with its front end resembling a face.

Mick opens my car door and my body goes rigid, as if facing a firing squad. He takes my hand in his and we walk to Remy's apartment. He doesn't bother knocking, just pushes through the door and enters with a courage and bravado I don't share.

In a blink, I'm staring into the damning eyes of the other man I love.

# THIRTY-FOUR

Remy's glare fixates on our clasped hands. His intense blue eyes flash from Mick to me, then back.

"Dickwad."

"Asshole," Mick replies.

Remy shakes his head. "Fucker."

"Fucker."

It's like watching a tennis match. "We're all fuckers," I mutter. Literally and figuratively.

Mick huffs out a low laugh, but my copper-topped best friend-turned-lover impales me with a hard stare. "What the *fuck*, Jacqui? You up and leave the party without saying a goddamn word to anyone, and then don't show up here *all night*?"

"I—"

"Didn't it occur to you I'd be worried out of my *fucking skull*?" His eyes blaze. "Especially considering what recently happened to you?"

I avert my gaze, avoiding the pain and anger reflecting in his. "You're right," I say, defeated. "Totally a jerk move."

"Did your imagination run away with you a tad?" He hurls sarcasm my way like a fastball.

I glare back. "I don't know...did it? The last thing I saw was your ass as you ran after Karin without a backward glance."

"You know she's refused to speak to me since we split, and you know we had unfinished business. So yeah, when she showed up, I wanted my five fucking minutes."

"Whatever. It sure looked like you were about to fall on your sword and take her back, so excuse fucking me if I misinterpreted."

"That's one hell of an apology, Jacqui, especially considering it looks like *you* just screwed the guy you've been crying about for months...without giving *me* another thought."

Right again. "It wasn't planned," I say meekly. "I was angry and upset, and starting to freak out as I walked home. Mick intercepted me, helped me calm down. We cleared the air and then..." The words die on my tongue. I'm unable to force them out, hear them spoken aloud. But we all know perfectly well what ensued. Damn it though, if anyone understands how much I love and care about Mick, it's Remy.

It's hard to read Remy's response, and looking into his eyes is nothing short of excruciating. The three of us take turns eyeballing one another.

Mick breaks the silence. "That went well, don't you think?"

Remy doesn't crack a smile. "So, what's the deal, Mick? You moving home? You two lovebirds back together?"

My throat knots at the spite laced with hurt in his tone.

Mick glances briefly at me and answers. "No to everything. I'm here doing a favor for my mom and head back tomorrow. I'm in a shitstorm over there, brother. No idea when I'm getting out. The old man is bedridden, incapacitated, and spewing insults, only half of which I can understand. I'm mostly on my own with this situation. I already told Jax I'm not boyfriend material. I'm on the Titanic and won't drag her down."

The knots multiply and I swallow several times, my eyes welling.

Remy scrubs the back of his neck. "That's FUBAR."

Mick nods. "Exactly."

"I'm sorry, man. That really fucking blows." They share a long moment of what looks like understanding.

"Yep." Mick fetches his smokes and extends the pack in offering.

Remy ignores him and retrieves one from his own pack, the lighter bouncing when he tosses it on the coffee table. His gaze pins me once again. "What about you, Jacqui? Got anything left to say?"

I take a prolonged drag and exhale, willing my heart rate to slow. "I'm sorry, Rem. I don't know what..." Swallowing, I try again. "I love you...both. I don't want to lose either of you, or for us to hurt each other. Your friendship is the most important thing," my voice hitches, "to me. *Please*, can we all work this out?" A few tears escape.

The guys share another glance.

Remy's shoulders sag but he approaches, enveloping me in his embrace. "Damn you, girl. I can't stand to see you cry."

"I'm sorry," I blubber brokenly into his chest, his familiar warmth seeping into my battered heart. "I never meant to hurt you." A minute later, I reach my hand out. "Mick."

He complies, effectively sandwiching me between them.

"Don't even think of grabbing my ass," Mick mutters to Remy.

"In your dreams, Tinkerbell."

I exhale a ragged breath, a multitude of emotions swirling within.


MICK SLAPS HIS HANDS ON HIS JEANS AND STANDS. "I've got to split."

We've spent the last hour talking, avoiding emotional

topics. Despite the charged undercurrent, it felt almost like old times...except in this new universe, we now have carnal knowledge. I know exactly what's under their hoods and they sure as hell know what's underneath mine. How did this get so complicated?

I *think* we're going to be alright. Maybe I'm kidding myself.

"Me too," I add. I'm reluctant to leave with the future tainted with such uncertainty.

The boys give each other a rough, back-slapping hug while I drag my body upright.

"Take care of her," Mick mutters, so low I barely catch it.

"Have been," Remy answers.

Mick's words cement what he's already decided but I'd hoped he'd reconsider. He's leaving. Worse, I might never see him again.

Remy's arms wrap around me next, and mine grip him tightly. "I love you," I murmur.

"Love you too." He kisses me softly, reassuring me, giving selflessly despite his own injured heart.

Mick walks me to my car, and now I'm facing a different firing squad. Before I can gather my thoughts, he leans me against the driver's side door, presses his body to mine, and kisses me breathless. I'm floating, only tethered by where our bodies connect and his rough, calloused hands—one holding my cheek, the other guiding the back of my head exactly where he wants me.

We part, and my eyes find those bottomless gray pools, which melt me on the spot like his damn kisses.

"I love you, Mick Callahan."

It's a declaration I want him to hear—and believe.

He gives his head a rueful half-shake. "You are straight up heroin."

I didn't expect him to say it back or acknowledge it. He won't if this is it. "Don't let this be the end. I don't know what the future holds any more than you, but one thing's sure...we can still *try* and be there for each other. Don't disappear into thin air again. I'm here for you."

His earnest gaze finds mine. "Live your life, Jax. Tomorrow is promised to no one. That's never been clearer to me than now." His thumb strokes my jaw. "You are so beautiful. Caring. Giving. And your life is just beginning. You're meant to fly, baby, not be caged." He shakes his head like he wants to say more but doesn't.

"Mi—"

He cuts me off with his lips, kissing me until every cell in my body yearns for him.

*It's goodbye.*

Mick tucks me into my car, and I force myself to put it in first and drive away. As he's climbing into his Mustang, I drive past, already slipping into the abyss of fresh heartbreak. Wondering why I'm not enough for him. Why he won't fight for me, or for us. If I'm imagining how good we are together, like some dumb, lovesick girl. Why I desperately cling to his words, especially the last phrases he uttered, and the raw honesty with which he said them.

My head swims with all of it...the tsunami that is Mick. Everything he is and could be. The touch of his hands and mouth on my body and the fire they leave in his wake. His expression when he climaxes. His rare vulnerable moments. His chivalry. His penetrating gaze, as if he's staring into my soul.

My tears fall and I let them flow, blindly shifting through gears, my car steering itself home.

One thought resurfaces over and over.

He's called me heroin from the beginning, uttered it like a dirty secret, an admission, a weakness.

*But if it's true, how can he give me up so easily?*

# THIRTY-FIVE

Refusing to spiral downward, I funnel my energy into my future, researching universities I can transfer into and whittling my list to four. After considering the pros and cons of each, the winner is San Jose State. Known for its School of Journalism and Mass Communication, it also has a reputable English program with majors that could help me pursue writing careers.

Ninety minutes from Oakland places it far enough away to require living there, but still close enough to motor back and spend time with friends. I'll probably come home for holidays, but it's likely the only time I'll step foot back in Hall Penitentiary & Asylum for the Insane.

Hmm...is lovesick a mental illness? Because I can make a case for insanity.

SJSU is located only thirty miles from Menlo Park...where Mick stays locked in his own type of prison.

*Not that I'm thinking about it.*

There should be no issue getting in as a junior, I remind myself, when my fingers drop the envelope containing my application and (hopefully riveting) essay into the mail slot at the post office.

Remy and I weather our storm, patching our friendship together quickly. I'm still lugging around a mountain of guilt but can't do much more than show up as the Jacqui *before* she slept with her copper-haired, blue-eyed best friend. There's no denying the buzz between us, or how difficult it is to abstain from intimacy, but with everything that's happened—my reawakened feelings for Mick coupled with hurting Remy—I try to give our relationship the space to breathe without those convoluting strings.

To his credit, Remy's been nothing short of amazing, giving me more kindness and forgiveness than merited. I'm damn lucky.

He's the first person I tell about my college selection. We're on the sofa at his place—he with one arm strewn across the ridge, knees splayed in typical guy fashion.

"Happy for you," he says, leaning over and clanking his beer bottle against mine, something unspoken trapped in his sapphire eyes.

"But...?" I prompt.

He shrugs. "I'll miss you."

An imaginary noose cinches closer around my heart. Honestly, I'm shaky about leaving him behind. He's my rock, the only one I can rely on, trust, and believe has my back.

"I'm scared to be without you, and I'll miss you like crazy. It's the only bogus part of this entire deal."

He tilts his head. "You need anything, and I'll be there. Probably haunt your doorstep."

I nod, trying not to worry how this may cause us to drift.

He must sense my anxiety because he gestures me closer. Scooting into his side, I rest my head on his shoulder. His arm wraps around me and he presses a tender kiss to my forehead.

It's comforting and undemanding.

Reliable. Loving. Safe.

# THIRTY-SIX

The inevitable happens in December.

I'm at Remy's, as per usual, my favorite hangout. I'm relaxed, my body melting into the couch cushions, not remotely vested in the Monday Night Football game between the Jets and Lions broadcasting on the TV.

Remy strokes my arm, jolting me from narcosis. Goosebumps raise along my flesh, and a familiar warmth spreads through my center. My gaze swings, meeting his.

"I still crave you," he murmurs.

My breath catches. "Same." It's true, no matter how hard I've fought it.

"I want you to know something else."

My eyes blink slowly, tiny flurries beginning to swirl in my veins.

"I never cheated on you. Never once entertained it."

My mouth parts.

"And would never." He reaches over and strokes his knuckles across my jaw. "I haven't been with another woman since you."

His confession renders me speechless. Although we had no verbal commitment about our relationship parameters, he owed me no such promise. I never suspected he screwed around in the brief time we'd taken it to the next level, but it's not like I fully trusted him either. How could I, knowing his *modus operandi*?

Understanding dawns. *Remy's capable of fidelity.*

I'm momentarily floored—and flattered. Until struck with the damning realization *I'm* the asshole cheater in this scenario, regardless of how undefined our romantic involvement may have been. My head falls, unable to meet his gaze, as a fresh layer of shame knits itself into my skin.

"Remy," I rasp over the knot in my throat, finally lifting my head.

"I need you to know when you left me at the party and so easily went back into Mick's bed, you gutted me. It hurt me." Truth radiates from his beautiful eyes.

A few tears slide down my cheeks. "I'm so sor—"

Two of Remy's fingers cover my lips. "*Shhh.* I'm not trying to guilt trip you. Hell, I probably had it coming. Karma and shit?"

"Wai—"

He shushes me again. "I have real feelings for you, Jacqui. This isn't some mindless fling to pass the time. I don't want to be fuckbuddies. I want more with you."

More. He wants *more.*

He's laying himself bare and doing it despite how I treated him.

I allow myself the luxury of pondering what it could mean. His trust. His adoration. His touch.

A trickle of hope springs.

I'm not fully over Mick, but he *is* in the rearview, helped considerably by him not making any more appearances. Not that it truly matters. I refuse to spend any more time or heartache on Mr. Gray Eyes when he's made his stance clear and drawn his line in the sand. It doesn't matter that I disagree with Mick's choice. He left us no choice. So why am

I holding a torch for a man who refuses to walk toward the flame? Especially when Remy is sprinting to it?

Being with Remy feels right. He's attentive, affable, engaging—everything I want and need. He's not a rebound, a second choice, a runner-up. He's Remy in all his splendor, pulling me into his galaxy with his charm, wit, and ridiculous appeal.

Underneath the surface, my cells perk up from the attention, the admission I'm wanted, as they lean toward the man who professed it.

Deciding to take a chance, I throw caution to the universe. Climbing onto his lap, my arms drape around his neck and my eyes find his. "I love you, Rem. I want it too."

He lets his lips do the talking as he kisses me tenderly and we grip each other in a fierce embrace.

~

I HOLE UP TO STUDY FOR FINALS, JETTING OVER TO Remy's only for brief escapes—namely awesome sex or mindless television.

My last creative writing assignment is a short story featuring a protagonist and antagonist of my design. The main character must travel an emotional journey and come out better in the end. We're given free rein otherwise.

In some ways, it's my hardest final, but easily my favorite. I've learned so much about the constructs of writing—with a newfound understanding of characters and their arcs, plotting, pacing, conflict, and resolution. It's the first class in my entire school history to teach me something I *want* to learn, and which will aid me in pursuing my passion with bona fide, tangible tools.

I write about a woman whose heart was physically stolen by a deplorable man with magic powers. She spends her journey searching for a way to get it back and make herself whole again. Imbuing it with my own emotions makes it a powerful story, filling me with legitimate pride.


Tests complete, the semester ends. I whoop, full of gratification and a sense of accomplishment. This girl is going places despite the odds, crappy circumstances, and heartbreaks.

I'm stoked to have a few weeks off and time to spend with Remy and my friends, including a huge New Year's Eve bash at Terry's place.

I just have to get through Christmas, which isn't very merry in the Hall household. The weight of loss since my sister drowned drips from every twinkling strand of tinsel, dimming it so our guilt can continue to breathe and thrive. It's yet another reason I don't relish "the most wonderful time of the year."

My family suffers through, anesthetizing with booze and pills, but there will be a few niceties. A Christmas tree. Some presents. And often a decadent meal on the Spode china. Mom usually pulls herself together enough to cook a prime rib or crown roast of pork with the frilly paper hats on the ends, which strike me as weird (vs. fancy), like other house-wife conventions born in the 1950s. Still, it's one of few times of year she makes an effort.

Sometimes my grandparents join us. Those are better holidays, as my parents stay sober longer than usual. This is one of those years, thankfully, especially since Remy is joining us for Christmas dinner.

Truthfully, I'm not thrilled about it, but when he invited me to his family's annual Christmas Eve party, I capitulated. He wants to get to know my mom and dad, which is totally normal for a boyfriend. It's just...my family *sucks*. And economically, we register way below the wealth level of the Remingtons. Not that Remy's pretentious—quite the opposite—but now he'll get a microscopic view of my fucked-up home life, something I've absolutely shielded from him.

Shoving away my downer thoughts, I swing my VW into a parking lot in Montclair Village. It's close to home and quaint, with an assortment of restaurants, boutiques, and shops.

There's a snap in the air, enough to wear a sweater today, and my fingers button the front to hug it closer around me. Strolling along the sidewalk, the holiday decorations add a festive charm, boosting my enthusiasm over shopping for gifts. I'm not overly flush but saved sufficient funds to buy presents. Aside from my parents and grandparents, Remy's the only other person who matters.

Entering Le Bonbon, I'm instantly wrapped in the heavenly scent of fine chocolates. Salivating, I scan the vast display of oversized jars brimming with colorful candy and glass cases full of chocolates in every iteration.

I treat myself to small bags of dark chocolate caramels and gummy candy and select a fancy box of assorted confections for my mom, who loves them as much as I do. The tin of mints is perfect for my grandparents.

Continuing down the block, I pause at Curly's Liquors, venturing inside to study the rows of bottles. Might as well give my father what he likes best: booze.

I'm unsure what to get Remy. Something for the Camaro? He mentioned wanting a set of Hooker headers, but surely those are expensive, and my budget could only be called microscopic. Cologne? Junior high-level lame. I could take him out for a nice dinner in Jack London Square and wear some sexy lingerie...for dessert. Two ways to a man's heart.

I meander through a few more stores. At Bedazzled, a ring catches my eye, and I impulsively buy it for Kendra. Browsing through the eclectic products at Freeway Variety, I snag the January issue of *Cosmo* for myself. It contains the Bedside Astrologer, one of my favorite features of the year. I'm an astrology lover—and believer. It's astonishing how accurate it can be. I've become an avid reader of the magazine since dating two particular, hella fine mechanics, open to any advice, tips, or tricks in the bedroom to up my game. My final stop is McCaulou's, where I score a blouse on sale for my mother and a striped tie for my father.

Remy will probably never be the tie-wearing sort. What *will* he be? I don't know, and don't think he does, either. Maybe it doesn't matter right now. I'm a girl with zero expectations trying not to get her heart broken further.

I'm just unsure how to stay in that lane.

# THIRTY-SEVEN

On Christmas Eve, I arrive at the Remingtons' swanky home and jockey for a parking spot. The driveway and street are already jammed with vehicles. Walking toward the mansion, an incredible light display winds through the trees, illuminating my path. Tasteful, realistic reindeer pose on the lawn. Lit evergreens threaded with wide gold ribbon flank the front door. I ring the bell, shifting in my four-inch heels and smoothing my flattering black polyester dress. I'm excited to see the decked halls, while also swallowing my trepidation of how poorly my family will measure up in Remy's eyes.

A middle-aged woman answers the door in conservative, hired-help attire. Chatter and holiday music filter out as she gestures me in, offering to take my coat as I shrug it off in the spacious foyer.

She leads me into the vast living area, where I'm greeted by a glorious Balsam Fir brimming with lights and decorations towering at least twelve feet in the open space. Guests deep in separate conversations stretch from here to the kitchen, the nearest pausing to appraise me. This is no typical family get together—it's a small horde.

A handsome man bearing a striking resemblance to Remy approaches. I'm momentarily stunned by this copper-haired, twinkling-blue-eyed older version of my boyfriend.

His eyes crinkle at the corners as he grins broadly. "You must be Jacqui."

I grip his extended hand, shaking it. "That's me."

"I'm Randy's dad. Call me Rick," he says. Hearing Remy called "Randy" throws me—it doesn't fit him at all. "You're even prettier than he let on," he adds with a wink.

"Oh..." Awkward. "Thanks?"

He chuckles low, taking a sip of the rich caramel liquid in his tumbler. "Can I get you a drink? And if you're not old enough for the hard stuff, I have a 'don't ask, don't tell' policy." His lips form a Cheshire Cat smile as he slips me another wink.

It's obvious where Remy gets his charisma. His father's impossible not to like, and I suddenly empathize with all the women who've fallen for these Remington charmers. "I wouldn't turn down a gin and tonic."

He nods. "My kind of girl."

There's a hired bartender, but he shoos him away. Rick drains his own glass then makes mine at the well-stocked bar. Sliding it toward me, he cocks an eyebrow and waits for me to try it.

The crisp tonic bubbles down my throat along with the sharp, dry gin. A squeeze of lime provides a balancing hit of citrus. "Delicious. Thank you."

He beams. "Delicious indeed."

Before I can process his meaning, Remy sneaks up and envelops me in his arms, his lips grazing my cheek.

"Hi," I murmur, gazing up at him.

"Hey, beautiful. I see you met my dad."

I smile, holding up my cocktail as proof. "He's been most welcoming."

"Are you hitting on my date, old man? Because she's mine."

Rick's eyes fill with mirth, ignoring Remy's comment. "I'll leave you kids to it. Make yourself at home, Jacqui."

"I'm glad you're here," Remy says.

"Me too, but Rem…this is no small gathering. Who are all these people?"

He chuckles, shrugging. "It's family. We Remingtons like to procreate."

I pin him with a stare. "I know one who likes to *practice*."

His mouth finds my ear, his deep voice traveling straight to the apex of my thighs. "I've half a mind to drag you into my old room, lift this pretty dress, and *practice* all I want."

"Behave," I breathe, a hot flush burning my neck and face—and shooting again to my core. Damn him.

He laughs low and clasps my free hand in his. "C'mon, let me introduce you around."

First up is his mother, Virginia, a petite blond whose smile doesn't connect to those icy blue eyes. Her cream pantsuit, coifed hair, and professional makeup job scream "high maintenance." The silver spoon she grew up with somehow got lodged up her ass, but I shouldn't judge. Maybe she's stressed with dozens of relatives in the house.

I'm gracious, thanking her for including me before Remy whisks me off to meet his older brother (who's taller and fair-haired like their mother), cousins, aunts, uncles, grandparents, and family friends.

An hour later, the catered dinner buffet overflows with scrumptious choices—some which I can't identify, like the gelatinous mold which contains a combination of mystery meat and flecks of vegetables—and the alcohol flows like a river.

Remy remains attentive, and we join a table commandeered by his cousins. Our plates brim with holiday meats, trimmings, and warm rolls with tiny pats of butter molded into round balls.

Remy and his relatives regale me with colorful anecdotes from their childhood. I laugh hard and often at my now-grown scoundrel's younger antics and transgressions.

Excusing myself, I venture to the bathroom, remembering where it was from the infamous pool party. My thoughts immediately drift to Mick and our unexpected tryst in the gym downstairs. I make it through the portrait-lined hallway and into the powder room, sinking against the door once it's closed.

*Don't think about it. Push it from your mind.*

Those tapes replay anyway...me on the bench, Mick thrusting into me, his hands gripping my hips...*gah*. Why do I do this to myself? All it does is sting. I flush the toilet and wash up, staring at the girl in the gilded mirror. "Be happy," I whisper. "Be present."

Taking a fortifying breath, I open the door with renewed intention, nearly colliding with Mr. Remington.

"Fancy meeting you here," he quips, placing one hand against the wall, effectively blocking my path. The other grips the tumbler he never seems without.

Tucked in the hallway, his voice rises clearly above the din of clanking silverware, loud chatter, and holiday music. My laugh sounds fake even to my ears. It's a habit I've long loathed about myself, laughing when I'm nervous.

"You're exceptionally pretty," he slurs, making me wonder how much he's imbibed.

"Thank you." My eyes dart further down the hall.

He pushes off the wall. When he trails his forefinger down my bare arm, I flinch.

"If my son isn't man enough for the job, my door's always open." His gaze is heated, teasing. "I bet you're a hellcat in the sack." He fucking winks again.

Disgusted, my body recoils precisely as Mrs. Remington

comes into view. Her glare meets my startled gape. I move swiftly past Rick, wanting to get back to Remy as fast as humanly possible.

I don't know what his mother must think. Does she know her husband is a scumbag—or does she believe I'm flirting with him? Her withering stare flicks from me to Rick and back again while I do my best to calm my features and the rapid-fire beating of my heart, slamming against my ribcage like a SWAT team busting through the door. I offer her a faint smile as we pass, my gait speeding up as I round the corner.

Zeroing in on Remy—still at the table with his cousins, head arched back in a laugh—I ground myself in his image and force my feet to slow to a normal pace.

I zoom into my seat, inch closer to Remy, and reach for his hand. I'm rattled, trying not to panic about how all this looks or telling him about his slimy father. All I want to do, aside from leaving, is burrow into his arms.

His eyes find mine. "Everything okay?"

"Mm-hmm," I mumble noncommittally.

He cocks his head but lets it go, his question left unasked. The conversation picks back up and my renewed focus is on blending in—and blocking out the intrusive thoughts attacking me.

After enough time passes, my lips find Remy's ear. "I'm ready to leave. You don't have to...I'm sure you want to stay here and visit with your family."

"Not a chance. I want to spend time with you alone. Follow me home?"

I hesitate, but wanting the same, my head tips in agreement.

He kisses me lightly. "Let's make the rounds," he says.

We stand and he takes my hand. Steeling myself, I practice in my head what to say to his parents. After plenty of polite glad-handing along the way, we find his mother in the kitchen dispensing orders to the catering staff.

"Mom, we're splitting." He pulls her in for a hug. "See you tomorrow."

They part, my cue to say goodbye. "Mrs. Remington, everything was lovely. Thank you for having me."

Once again, she pastes on a phony smile. "It looked like you enjoyed yourself."

What is she implying? I fumble for a moment but pull it together. "I did. Thanks again...and Merry Christmas."

She tilts her head—exactly like Remy does—her sprayed helmet-hair not moving a wisp. "Merry Christmas."

On our way out, we find Mr. Remington by the bar refilling that bottomless glass.

"See you tomorrow, Dad. Jacqui and I are hitting the road."

"Ah," he says, slapping Remy on the shoulder. "Better keep a hold of this one, son. She's a looker." He waggles his brows, then fastens his glazed, skeevy blue eyes on me. "Pleasure to meet you, and I hope you'll come again soon. You're welcome *anytime*."

The SWAT team rushes back, my heart rate setting off alarms as I force myself to mutter a gracious thank you despite Mr. Remington giving me the creeps. *Total slimeball.*

Remy walks me to my car, tugging on my hand as I reach for the door handle. "What's wrong? Something's off with you."

I blow out a breath, willing my heartbeat to slow. My gaze lowers to the ground but Remy's fingers lift my chin and steer it back to his. There's nowhere to run or hide.

"It's your dad. He...said some inappropriate things."

"*Christ.* He's such a jackass," he says, shaking his head. "But harmless. He's a horny old dude. Ignore his ass."

His response irritates me. Why should I have to accept his father's bad behavior?

Remy appears to clue in, shifting to cup my face with

both hands. "I'm sorry if he upset you. You shouldn't be subjected to his bullshit."

He presses his lips to mine in a sincere kiss that calms me, steadies me, recenters me. My arms find their way around his neck, and we hold each other.

His deep voice finds my ear and issues a command. "Now follow me home, because I'm a horny *young* dude, and I fully intend to shower you with gifts."

I pull back with a smirk. "Aww, did you get me an orgasm for Christmas?" I say this like they're expected...because he delivers most of the time.

He chucks me under the chin, leans close, and runs the tip of his tongue over my full lips. "I got you several—and can't wait to give them to you."

My body clenches, heating from his promises, and a satisfied smile crosses my face. Little does he know I'm wearing a sexy black teddy underneath this dress as one of his gifts.

I follow Remy back to his place, rock cranking from KOME, obliterating all thoughts but the attentive lover whose limbs are about to tangle with mine.


I'M FRETTING THE NEXT DAY BY NOON. OUR FAMILY finished opening presents in the hour after breakfast, and the spiked eggnog's been flowing since. The TV blares *Miracle on 34th Street*, cranked to ear-splitting decibels since my grandfather is hard of hearing but refuses to wear a hearing aid.

The phone rings, and I jump up to get it.

"Merry Christmas, sweetheart," Remy says.

"Merry Christmas!" I answer, false cheer forcibly infused.

"I'm genuinely sorry to do this to you, but I've got to cancel coming for dinner. Please don't be upset."

My heart flips, then flops, relieved and mad at the same time. "How come?"

"My mom. She made a real fuss about me being here with our family. Went into full freak-out mode."

My stomach dips. Is this because of last night? Couldn't be. Could it? I wasn't the problem in that equation. But...

"Oh. I understand. It's Christmas and everything."

"Jacqui, I'm really sorry. Please apologize to your folks and tell them I'd love to reschedule another night soon."

Out of nowhere, my chest heaves and tears prick my eyes. *Pull it together*. "It's fine. I'll talk to you later, okay?"

"I don't have to go yet."

"I do," I whisper.

"I'll make it up to you, I promise."

"It doesn't matter. I'm fine." Except it does matter. And I'm not fine. "Gotta go."

"Jac—"

"Bye," I say softly, and hang up. Waiting a minute to ensure the call disconnects, I take the phone off the hook. If I know Remy, he'll keep calling until he feels better, and I don't give a shit about his conscience.

It's not even his fault, right?

I'm not trying to punish him. Or maybe I am.

Eying the booze sitting on the counter, I crane my neck and see everyone still glued to the movie, and quickly fill a glass halfway with vodka, the rest with cranberry juice. It's the best anesthetic at my disposal.

I'm so tired of disappointment. Of not being good enough for anyone. Of all the people who let me down. Each time inches me closer to a tipping point, and I don't know what's on the other side.

# THIRTY-EIGHT

In mid-February, after days of classes, schoolwork, and the mind-numbing joys of living at home, something epically fantastic finally occurs.

My VW engine whines as I race to the Chevron then sputters to a stop next to Remy's Camaro. I jog inside the shop, clutching the letter, and scan the garage, instantly flooded by the comforting scent of fuel, grease, and solvents.

Vinny yells out a greeting as I spy my boyfriend's long, coveralled legs shooting out from under a mint green Monte Carlo.

"Rem!"

He rolls out on the dolly, his arms gripping the underside of the car. "Hey, Trouble."

"I got in!" I say, waving my college acceptance letter.

A grin stretches across his face as he pushes all the way out and stands.

"Never had a doubt. Congratulations." His lips brush mine, but he's careful not to mar me—or my white jeans—with his greasy hands.

I'm beaming like the mothership and might never come

back to earth. This piece of paper is my ticket out of dodge. It represents *freedom*.

"Hear that, boys? Jacqui's going to San Jose State!" His pride coats me like a second skin.

Cheers erupt, and Vinny saunters over. "That's great, Jacqui! We always knew you were the smart one. Except for dating this guy," he says, jerking a thumb toward my redhead.

Remy punches him in the arm, hard.

Vinny pretends to wince. "Take it easy, Ali."

With a smug expression, Remy retrieves a blue rag from his pocket and cleans the grease from his fingers.

"Wait until you see the hoopties in San Jose," Vinny adds. "My buddy works at a hydraulics shop over there. Customizes low riders, trucks, the whole deal."

"Sweet." Another cool thing to add to the pile of fucking awesome.

*I. Am. Leaving. Home!*

My mental to-do list churns: finish out the semester, get through the summer months, secure housing, find roommates.

Remy slings an arm around my shoulders. "We should celebrate."


CELEBRATING TURNS OUT TO BE CRAMMING INTO Remy's apartment with nine friends he wrangled, a few cases of beer, and an eight-ball of coke. I don't mean to be a killjoy, but this routine's wearing thin, and I worry my life-of-the-party boyfriend is in trouble with drugs.

It happens more often, in bigger quantities, and with a cavalier attitude, as if tomorrow will never come. But tomorrow does come. And after these parties, mine arrive with a hefty price tag of hangovers, missed classes, and the taint of regret.

I'm on the cusp of breaking out of this oppressive life, of

pursuing a real degree in a field that exhilarates me. I don't know exactly what that looks like, how it manifests, or what I'll do with it, but I do know what nights like this get me (nothing), and where they take me (nowhere). Sitting around snorting lines, chugging beer, and playing drinking games— or attempting to solve the world's problems from our wasted, addled view—is not where I want to be in five years...or now. There's no trust fund waiting for me, but if there was, this isn't the roadmap to any life I want.

Amid this circle of friends that's more family than my own, I suddenly feel misplaced. Like what used to be a round hole turned square sometime in the night. As if the world shifted on its axis and my foundation crumbled.

It scares me to leave.

But for the first time, it also scares me to stay.

# THIRTY-NINE

My father shoves his third drumstick in his pie hole, tearing off a hunk of pink flesh. His lips shine with chicken fat like he's wearing lip gloss.

He blots the carnage with a napkin. "I have someone for you to meet. Possible roommates." He swallows another bite, chasing it with a few glugs of bottled beer.

"Really?" I dread whatever comes out of his mouth next. Or goes in.

"Two young women your age, already going to San Jose State. Our neighbors are friends with the father. Apparently, he bought real estate a year ago so they can live near campus, and they need a third roommate."

"Oh, um, great." It's already March and I'm still on square one. "Did you get a number?"

My father gives me a pointed, exasperated stare. "Of course. He's expecting your call."

"Did the girls go to Skyline?" If they're from Montclair, then probably, which doesn't exactly bode well.

"I believe so, and one of them is from India."

Nothing beyond a vague recollection skirts my memory.

"Sounds promising," my mother says. "It would be better for you not to live with strangers."

Except they are strangers. And if I do know them, odds are high they land in the asshole category. "Mm-hmm," I answer noncommittally.

After cleaning the dinner dishes, I dial the number.

"Hello?" A male answers with a thick accent and strong emphasis on the "o."

"May I speak with Mr. Singh?"

"Speaking." His voice has a deep melodic timbre.

"My name is Jacqui Hall. I'm searching for housing near San Jose State for the upcoming year and our neighbor thought your daughter might need a roommate?"

"That's correct," he says. "Jaswinder will have a room vacancy in a few months. We own a three-bedroom condominium fifteen minutes from campus by automobile. Rent is $250 a month plus utilities. Does this interest you?"

*Hell yeah.* "Tremendously. Can I arrange to see the place?"

"Yes, please contact Jaswinder to discuss. That would be best." He rattles off her number and politely bids me farewell.

I call her next.

"Hello?" Jaswinder's accent is scarcely detectable.

"Hi, I'm Jacqui, and I understand you're looking for a roommate." I explain the neighbor connections.

"Sweet," she says. "Our other roomie is moving back to Oregon after the semester ends, so we have a spot. It's just me and my best friend, Kit."

*These girls have the coolest names.* "Nice."

"Can you come by this weekend? If you like the condo, and we like you—because you're going to love us—we can set it in motion."

I laugh again, digging this chick already. "Sounds like a plan, Stan."

"No need to be coy, Roy."

Grinning on my end that she knows the Paul Simon song, we make final arrangements, hang up, and I report back to my parents.

Whipping out my homework, I smile again at the friendliness of my potential roommate. Hope pushes through the cracks of my heart like a seedling breaking ground. Maybe, just maybe, I'm getting the space to finally bloom.

Following the directions Jaswinder gave me, I drive to San Jose. I exit the interstate and skirt downtown, winding up on a busy boulevard. My grin spreads when hydraulics shops line several blocks. Vinny wasn't kidding.

I turn onto the expressway and soon segue toward the hills, passing nothing but suburban neighborhoods. Arriving at the gated development, I enter the code and the gate swings open, taking me into a maze of streets. Each one contains modern, double-decker condo units forming long rows strung together, their ivory stucco surfaces resembling moonscape, small rectangles of lawn serving as front yards.

A bright orange Monza Spyder sits in the driveway at the address scribbled on my directions. I scope out the giant arachnid graphic plastered on the hood on my way to the door. This unit features the same neatly groomed landscaping that many do, with iridescent white rocks and hardy plants lining the cement walk and front of the condo.

The door swings open before I can press the doorbell, and I'm greeted by a gorgeous, dark-haired girl half a foot shorter than me. Glass of wine in one hand, long lashes flutter over huge onyx eyes, matching her shoulder-length hair. She beckons me in with a big smile, a flash of white against her deep beige skin. She's dressed simply in red shorts and an ivory Esprit crop top.

"Jacqui, I presume?"

A genuine smile cracks wide as I nod. "Nice to meet you."

"I'm Jas," she says, shaking my outstretched hand. "Entrez-vous," she adds with a shallow bow.

I step inside and she closes the door behind us. I immediately notice the ultra-high, vaulted ceiling and modern design, every wall painted white.

"Let me introduce you to Kit and we'll give you the grand tour...which will take five minutes."

Chuckling, I follow her through a narrow entryway and past an opening to the kitchen before arriving quickly in the main common area.

A girl with long brunette hair and a curtain of bangs rises from the sofa wearing a casual, cornflower blue sundress. Her striking whiskey eyes welcome me warmly as she extends a hand. "I'm Kit."

I'm relieved they both seem to jive with my chilled-out style. "Good to meet you both."

"So...this is the living room," Jas deadpans while Kit does an overly dramatic, game-show-hostess hand gesture in accompaniment.

Kit opens a sliding door leading to a concrete patio surrounded by a fence. "This is where we drink and pretend to study."

A round iron table and matching chairs with cushions sit under an umbrella. A few potted plants wither nearby, and I'm not judging. I can kill houseplants faster than an uninvited spider in the shower.

They finish the tour with my would-be bedroom, and the girls eye me expectantly.

The stress drains from me so palpably, I almost hiss like a released pressure valve. I can easily make this work. Hell, I could make a closet work if it meant escaping my parent's house once and for all.

"It's nice, you guys."

They both beam, and we head back downstairs.

"Wine?" Jas asks. "And before you think you're getting Napa Valley shit, it's wine in a box...but at least it's Chablis."

"Sure, thanks."

We reconvene in the living room—the girls on the navy sofa that's worn but looks comfortable and me in an oversized chair that is damn comfortable.

Jas tucks one leg under the other, resting her wineglass against her knee. "Let's talk a bit, get to know each other. We need to find out if you're one of those catty bitches we hate, or if you're cool like us."

"God, I like you," I admit. "Most of the women I know are assholes, so I prefer hanging with guys."

Jas and Kit exchange a look.

"Are said guys good looking?"

"They're fine as hell. And built...solid muscle. And they're also ridiculously nice." I might be laying it on thick, but I'm not lying either.

Their eyes gleam as they share another glance.

"We like fine as hell," Jas says.

"And muscles," Kit adds with an airy sigh.

Jas fixes her huge onyx eyes on me. "Nice is a bonus. Is one your boyfriend...or are you shuffling through them like a deck of cards?"

I bark out a laugh. "I'm dating Remy. Before..." I falter, about to talk about Mick for some stupid reason. "Well, let's just say I don't kiss and tell. Are you two seeing anyone?"

Jas wags her finger. "I sense a story there."

I'm holding a can of worms and she's twirling a can opener. I arch an eyebrow and shrug.

Thankfully, Jas lets it go.

"I recently ended it with a guy who doesn't matter, and Kit—"

"Is happily single at the moment," she answers for herself.

*"I sense a story there,"* I singsong to Kit, who breaks into a grin.

"You don't know the half of it," Jas adds, rolling her eyes, "But that's a tale for another day."

Kit shakes her head like she wants to avoid the topic. "Jas thought you were a transfer student?"

"Mm-hmm," I murmur.

"What's your major?"

"English or journalism. I've got to nail it down fast. I want to be a writer."

The girls share another look, the way best friends do.

"*I'm* a journalism major!" Jas squeals. "I can totally talk you through some options, or simply use my persuasive powers to make you join me in educating the world on all manner of subjects."

I laugh, and Kit nods. "She's not joking. She's ridiculously persuasive. It's why I have hangovers."

My lips curve up again...these women are both so easy to like. "What's your major, Kit?"

"Marketing communications."

"So...*also* persuasive."

She snaps. "I never thought about it that way."

The two friends look at each other and high five.

"You girls are trouble, I can tell." So am I, according to Remy. "I want in."

They break into slow grins and go quiet as they share more friend telepathy.

"Deal," Jas says. "And if you want, you can move in this summer. The room will be available July first."

My heart cartwheels in my chest. *This is really happening.*

Now to sell it to my father.

# FORTY

Remy and I absorb the chaos as we wait for our turn at the keg. We arrived at Terry's for a massive celebratory party ten minutes ago, and hundreds of guests mill about. Terrence "Badass" Walton was drafted into the Major Leagues after four stellar seasons in centerfield for Cal, none better than his senior year, where he broke all-time records for stolen bases.

I'm celebrating my own wins—finishing up my last semester at CCC with a B-plus average and convincing my parental units to let me move to San Jose early.

Two more weeks, and I'm free. I don't know what the future holds, but I'm ready to take the plunge and hurl myself from the nest, even if I break my wings on the way out. My parents effectively clipped those suckers years ago and it only made me more desperate to fly.

Remy pumps the keg a few times and hands me a cup foaming with beer before turning back to fill one for himself. We maneuver to the other side of the backyard where it's less crowded and find Jeremy, who gives me a big squeeze. It seems like ages since I've seen him.

I nudge him with my shoulder. "How've you been, stranger?"

"Same old rise and grind, sweetheart. What's shaking with you?"

"All good things. In two weeks, I'm outta beer, outta here." I wiggle-dance in place.

He cocks his head. "Where to?"

"San Jose. I'm transferring to SJSU to finish my degree."

Jeremy touches his cup to mine. "Congrats, girl."

I smile broadly, experiencing the slightest twinge as Remy's grip on my hip tightens. It's hard to know how my move will affect us. I know he's worried I'll meet a bunch of guys all vying to get in my pants.

"Better lock that down," Jeremy tells Remy, as if reading my thoughts.

"Don't I know it. Every college puke out there's going to try and tap this."

I elbow my boyfriend in the ribs, and he feigns injury.

Vinny joins us, shaking his head like he's in shock. "Can you believe this mob?"

"Better get used to it—Terry's going to be famous," Remy answers.

"Hope he remembers the little people," Jeremy quips.

Remy scoffs. "Says the guy most likely to become a congressman."

Jeremy runs a hand through his hair, nearly as white as the teeth flashing in his grin. "Says the guy mostly likely to become a playboy with no job whatsoever."

"Well, well, well, if it isn't Mr. MLB himself," Vinny intones loudly as Terry approaches.

We swarm him with hugs, back slaps, and well-wishes, and I'm certain nothing could wipe the shit-eating grin off his face. We ply him for details, and although Remy already told me the insider info, we listen with rapt attention as he regales us with how it all went down, what it means, and how soon he leaves. He'll start in the minor league organization for the Pittsburgh Pirates and hopefully move through the ranks to be brought up to the bigs.

We all hoped he'd get drafted by Oakland, but maybe someday he'll be traded and wind up back in our hometown. We're awed he succeeded at such an incredible feat.

An hour later, I'm desperate to escape Leland, who's again pursuing me with dogged persistence after he found me filling a plate at the buffet. I spot Remy stretched out on a lounge chair near the pool talking to Vinny and make a beeline for him.

He pulls me onto his lap.

"Aw, jeez. Not him too?" Leland exclaims, his face pained. "You need to stop playin' with these boys and get yourself a man."

"Bye, Leland," I say, fluttering my fingers his way. Giggling, I meet Remy's gaze. "Hi, handsome."

"Hi, beautiful." He strokes my hair away from my face, expression somber.

"You okay?"

He nods, slow and shallow. "It's just...I'm missing you already."

A knot forms in my throat, and I gulp it down. "I know. Me too."

He shifts us so I'm pressed against him, my back to his front. His breath tickles my ear. "Promise me you won't find someone else. That we'll make this work."

"I promise," I whisper. "Now you."

"Sweetheart, I can't ever imagine wanting anyone else. You're perfect for me."

"I love you, Rem."

"I fucking adore you."

Later, in Remy's bed, we illustrate the depth of our shared

vows with our hearts and bodies, coming together with our familiar, fiery harmony—and letting any negative rogue thoughts recede into the shadows.

Our love will be enough.

Won't it?

# FORTY-ONE

The last week of June, I'm packing. And packing. Also packing. Figuring out what to take and what to store at home is tougher than I predicted.

With an abnormal display of energy, my mom arms me with cookware, dishes, and kitchen gadgets, which I've never needed before.

I open a checking account, and a kind bank associate shows me how to log activity and keep my balance in the register.

My father throws down lectures on various topics of responsibility with a litany of threats for noncompliance. Since my parents are paying for college, my housing, and providing a small monthly stipend for groceries and bills, it makes his warnings weighty—but wholly unnecessary. Once I exit this house, I'm never planning to live here again...and nothing is worth risking my permanent freedom.

Cramming another box with clothes, I wonder how many all-nighters he'll pull now that I'm leaving. If he'll continue cheating on my mother. Whether he'll drink himself to death, or choke after stuffing too much pie in his hole.

I'm more worried about my mom.

Trudging into her room a few days before my departure with every intention of confronting her, I find her propped up in bed in a state of narcosis, logging another "sick" day. My resolve bolsters absorbing the scene.

I gently nudge her arm.

She rouses from her stupor, eyes glazed as they finally swing my direction. "Hmm? Did you say something?"

*Nope.* "Mom, please listen to me."

"Hmm?"

"Mom!"

She startles, finally giving me her attention.

Staring into her amber eyes, mirroring my own in hue and shape, I force the words from the dark depths they typically lurk. "You're killing yourself. One pill at a time. One day at a time. You need help." It's a desperate plea I'm unsure she'll even hear, let alone take seriously.

She shuts her eyes tightly, as if she can block out my words, then slowly reopens them. "It's too late."

My hand finds hers, clutching it. "It's not. I don't get why you've stayed in this hole. I understand your grief, but it's been years, Mom. *Years.*"

She musters the merest of shrugs, as if it's an effort for her withered body, starved and drugged for decades.

"I know I've been a disappointment to you...failed you." She swallows. "I'm sorry. It's not what you deserved or needed." Her clammy hand squeezes mine.

My eyes well, chest constricting. "It's not about failing me. It's about living your life. Eat. Stop taking pills. Don't put up with Dad's bullshit. *You* deserve better."

"I don't have it in me," her voice quavers, "to start over."

"Why? Help me understand," I implore.

She lowers her head, saying nothing, her hand slipping from mine.

My body tenses, pulse ticking up. "So, you're going to make death easy?"

She huffs out a breath. "I'm going to do what I must to get through the day."

My head shakes—dismayed, exasperated, heartsick.

She lifts a frail hand and smooths the hair from my face, her fingers landing under my chin and lifting it to meet her gaze.

"You're our shining star, and I want you to shine so bright in your lifetime, honey. Don't make my mistakes. Stay away from drugs and boys who hurt you. Be self-reliant. Find your passion. Blow out the sky with your brilliance."

The backs of my eyes prick. "Your star could be bright too, Mom," I croak. "It's not too late."

Her grimace morphs into a wan smile. "My light dimmed when your sister died. Somewhere along the way, so did your father's. We don't seem to know how to find our way back."

"I don't want to lose you," I plead. Even though I already have.

She smooths the covers with bony hands aged forty years older than they are, her eyelids drooping. "I'm tired now, honey. Be a good girl and shut the door on your way out."

She shifts, curling her body into the fetal position, her eyes fluttering closed.

Free-flowing anger and disappointment roil inside. She gave up so easily. Abandoned me in the process. My father too. I don't grasp any of it. And she won't explain.

*Why and how could she do this?*

Gritting out a long sigh, I stare down at her lifeless form and unclench my hands, which balled into tight fists without me even realizing it.

Anger recedes as my heart fills with melancholy.

She's still my mother.

Bending down amidst the bottomless angst, I gently kiss her forehead. "I love you, Mom."

# Forty-Two

July first lands on Friday, and Remy borrows a truck and takes off work early so we can move my bed and a smattering of boxes to my new digs. The rest we'll get tomorrow with Vinny's help.

Jas and Kit greet me with excited hugs, and I introduce them to Remy.

After my boyfriend helps lug stuff up to my room and assemble the mattresses on a basic frame, we flop onto it, becoming lost in our own thoughts.

Everything about this feels foreign and strange and yet so right.

"How do you think your roommates will react to me making you scream while we christen this bed?"

I slap him playfully and roll to face him, propping on my elbow. "I think you'll meet their expectations."

"Only one way to find out."

He manhandles me, the joy-filled soundtrack of my laughter echoing off the walls.

WE RISE EARLY AND DRIVE TO OAKLAND. VINNY meets us at my house and between the truck, his car, and my VW, we manage to fit everything.

I hug my mother goodbye, trying not to focus on how feeble she's become, our last conversation, or my worries she'll fade deeper into oblivion once I'm gone. My father slips me a hundred dollars, instructing me to buy pizza and beer for my helpers. It's a nice gesture—and their help did get him off the hook to move anything. He expresses his thanks to the guys as he shakes their hands.

He pulls me in for a quick embrace, an unexpected act of tenderness. "I love you. Be safe," he says gruffly.

The desperate little girl buried inside me that aches for those words mumbles them back, overriding my shock. "I love you too, Dad."

Our convoy departs. Driving toward my next chapter, earlier memories of home sift through my thoughts, especially relating to my father.

He used to be attentive, paternal, personable, once upon a time. He took me miniature golfing in the early years, just the two of us. He taught me to ride a bike, shuffle a deck of cards, play Gin Rummy. We'd watched the A's countless times during the 1970s, sometimes side-by-side on the bleachers at the Oakland Coliseum, eating hot dogs and caramel popcorn as some of the greatest to ever play the game dazzled us. Catfish Hunter. Rollie Fingers. Vida Blue. Reggie Jackson. They'd won three consecutive World Series that decade.

I'd blossomed under his wing, a daddy's girl, a cherished daughter. Somewhere, it all went sideways.

Tears roll down my cheeks, hot and bittersweet, as I remember how my parents started fighting more, and with it, my father's drinking escalated. Maybe he thought I was old enough to care for myself—because he couldn't possibly miss how his wife had left the fucking building by then, aban-doning ship on me, on us, on life. My hand swipes the wetness from my cheeks, my heart hardening as it re-cloaks with protective armor.

When my father dispenses attention my way now, it's to order me around, keep me in line for some arbitrary plan he's concocted, or tether me with dictatorial rules—the irony lost how he also barely shows up as a parent. I guess his extended leash is still a restraint in his mind.

But his leash is sixty miles long as of today. He'll have no earthly way of keeping tabs on my daily doings any longer. With that cheery realization, I shove the nostalgia into the recesses, lock the box, and let out a loud, obnoxious whoop.

JAS AND KIT OPENLY GAWK AT VINNY BEHIND HIS back, and he's scoping them out every chance he gets. I can't blame them—his flexed, ample muscles are on full display from carrying my belongings inside.

Afterwards, the five of us sit around eating pizza, drinking beer—and some of us, flirting. I'm happy and relieved everyone appears at ease. I'm hoping my friends will come here to hang out or party sometimes.

Vinny's eyes noticeably flit between my roommates and me.

"What?" I ask.

He grins wide. "You girls are the new *Charlie's Angels.*"

Jas, Kit, and I regard each other—our hair color the requisite black, brunette, and blond—before busting into smiles.

"Only better," Remy agrees, pulling me securely onto his lap. "You're my angel," he whispers into my ear.

We sit around bantering until Vinny says he needs to motor. I hug him and offer my profuse thanks.

Remy and I retreat to my room, where we make love, trying not to think about the distance now separating us. When the sun lowers in the sky, my boyfriend readies to split, needing to return the truck. He kisses me long and hard, and then he's gone.

I'm contemplating the mountain of boxes waiting to be unpacked when Jas grabs me by the forearm and drags me into the living room.

"Tell me *everything* about Vinny. He is gorgeous. The whole Italian Stallion thing going on there is deee-licious. Is he single?"

Laughing, I say, "Riding solo. He's a real sweetheart and represents all the muscle groups."

She lets out an exaggerated sigh. "I could eat him for breakfast, lunch, and dinner."

"Don't forget snacks," Kit quips.

"The feeling's mutual. He already made it known he wants to come back."

"Dibs," Jas says.

"You know I steer clear of Italians," Kit adds.

My head tilts her direction. "Wait...why?"

"She's Sicilian and believes those handsome devils are serial heartbreakers," Jas explains.

Kit rolls her eyes. "I may or may not like them a little too much—and I should know better. But does he have any single, non-Italian friends?"

"Absolutely, but some are players. Where do you line up?"

"Giving commitments a wide berth, but I don't mac-attack with just anybody either."

I laugh, never hearing the term used that way. "Are you saying you like *two* all-beef patties with special sauce?"

She purses her lips and pretends to think about it. "It sounds like too many calories, but potentially a bang worth the buck."

We crack up, and the girls tell me to get ready because they're taking me to El Torito's for dinner and margaritas.

After my eyes open early the next morning, it takes one second to realize I'm in my new digs, not at my former address. I flip off the comforter and kick my feet into the air.

*I'm so fucking happy.*

With more energy and enthusiasm than I've ever displayed in the morning, I gather my hair into a ponytail, brush my teeth, and stupidly grin at my reflection in the mirror. *My* mirror. In *my* bathroom. In *my* condo.

Returning to the bedroom, I quietly organize the myriad belongings still in boxes. It shapes up nicely. My dresser, desk, bed, and nightstand all fit without dwarfing the space, partly since the closet holds so much. Fresh bedding and pillows, which my mother treated me to, add a welcome newness.

Opening the sliding glass door, I venture onto the small balcony and lean against the railing. There's not much of a view, but it's private with room for a couple of chairs and an accent table. I make a mental note to stay on the lookout. Tilting my face to the mellow sunshine, my eyes close as warmth coats my skin.

Movement downstairs interrupts my basking. Investigating, I find Kit hovering near the coffeemaker in a matching shorts and camisole pajama set. Her natural olive skin tone makes me antsy to deepen my tan, even though I've got a good base going.

"Good morning," I say.

She turns, her tousled hair adorable. "Morning. Coffee?"

"Sure, thanks."

"Getting settled?"

"Making headway." I accept the cup of dark brew and take a swallow, wincing at the bitterness.

Kit laughs. "Too strong?"

Nodding, I add in sugar and milk until it's palatable.

We head to the patio and sit in the cushioned chairs, After lighting up a cigarette and sipping my much-improved beverage, it strikes me this all seems very "adult." Self-satisfaction washes over me as I stifle the urge to pump my fist in the air.

Kit hoists her legs onto the adjacent chair and crosses her feet at the ankles. "You doing okay?"

"Are you kidding? Never been happier."

"I thought maybe separating from Remy would be hard."

My head bobs in agreement. "That part is tough."

"How long have you two been an item?"

"I've honestly lost track. We were on, off, then on again. We've been friends since last summer. I met him when I got a job next door to where he works. Vinny works there too." The memory of the first day I saw the guys pops into my head.

"What kind of place?"

My brain momentarily stalls while gray eyes pierce my thoughts for the first time in months. "A gas station and auto shop. They're mechanics."

"Grease monkeys...mmm. Are they all cute?"

My lips curve and I flick my ash. "Every damn one."

"Lucky you."

*Yes and no.* "You have no idea."

"We should beach it today."

I gasp. "Yes, please. Where do you go?"

"Two places, mostly. They're both awesome, but different vibes. Santa Cruz is all about crowds, the boardwalk, rides, and junk food. Half Moon Bay is less crowded but there are no concessions, so you need to bring stuff with you."

Easy choice. I've been to Santa Cruz plenty. And while I love riding the Giant Dipper and eating drippy chocolate dipped cones, I'm game for something different. "I've never been to Half Moon Bay, so I'd love to see it."

Jas pokes her head out the sliding door. "Hello, lovelies. Be right there."

"It's pretty, and full of surfers." Kit's eyebrows waggle.

Jas returns with a huge mug of coffee. "What did I miss?"

Kit catches her up. "We're talking about going to Surfer's Beach. Jax has never been."

My heart lurches as if stabbed and my head swivels, pinning my new roommate with an open-mouthed stare.

Kit cocks her head. "What?"

"It's...the nickname. Only one other person calls me that."

"Is it okay? I kind of like it."

"And doesn't it totally work we all can shorten our names to three letters?" Jas says. "Jas, Kit, Jax. And is it weird we're all J's and K's?"

"It's meant to be," Kit muses.

"Meant to be," I repeat, trying to thwart the hostile Mick takeover in my brain.

# FORTY-THREE

We drive up the peninsula in Kit's Honda Accord. When we pass the Menlo Park exit, which sits alarmingly close to San Jose, my eyes burn a hole through the sign, and I can't help scouting for a certain blue Mustang fastback the next few miles.

It takes about forty-five minutes to reach Half Moon Bay. We whiz by the surprisingly small town as we traverse the road taking us to Surfer's Beach, where surfers purportedly congregate. My roommates are here to ogle male bodies, and all the better if they're on surfboards. I love watching surfers, but for a different reason—I've always wanted to try it.

We park and grab our towels, bags, cooler, and snacks, then make our way to the large swath of beach. My nostrils inhale the familiar salty tang of the ocean. The wind whips my hair. My feet sink into the warm sand. Wetsuit-clad surfers dot the horizon. And the deep blue of the Pacific is on magnificent display, waves crashing on the shore, leaving white foam and vanishing footprints in their wake.

We survey where to set up, and I admire the breathtaking view of rocky cliffs and grassy bluffs jutting toward the ocean as far as the eye can see, colliding with a brilliant cerulean sky dotted with clouds. This, right here, is what I love about the Northern California coastline.

Staking our spot, we spread our towels and strip down to bikinis. I lean back on my elbows, legs stretched long, and track the surfers through my sunglasses. Over a dozen ride waves or sit waiting. How hard would it be to learn? Maybe now that I live closer to the ocean, I can take lessons.

My gaze travels to one in particular, his brown hair wet and hanging just north of shoulder length. He looks like Mick and moves like Mick. *Why the fuck am I thinking about him again?* It's like he's living inside my head in a rent-free bungalow.

Jas sighs next to me. "I love it here. Especially the view."

She's not talking about nature, despite its stunning vista. "Mm-hmm," I mutter in agreement, only I *am* referring to the environment.

I analyze the surfers. Why some enter a wave while others hold back. The grace they exhibit as they spring to standing, their bodies mimicking the wind. The way some carve the waves or milk the ride before cutting out. The dip they make, prone on their boards, as they paddle through undulating water to return to the starting position. My breath catches as one stashes and tumbles underwater, his tether snapping as his surfboard goes airborne then torpedoes into the murky depths.

Surfing embodies big sensations—from the scary to the exhilarating. I wonder if I'm brave enough to try.

As the waves turn flatter, surfers exit the ocean, unzipping their wetsuits, flipping hair out of their faces, talking to each other.

Not-Mick rides a wave all the way in. Once in the shallows, he grabs his board, carries it effortlessly to the beach and lays it across the sand. He unzips his black neoprene wetsuit halfway, revealing broad shoulders and a tapered back. When he runs a hand through his long, wet hair and we glimpse his profile, we all collectively inhale.

But my skin prickles. It looks a hell of a lot like my heart-breaker, although he's too far away to be sure.

Jas fans herself. "That is no man. He's a straight up Adonis."

"I could watch him all day," Kit murmurs.

The guy picks up his board and starts walking our way, and my mouth goes dry.

"Fuck," I mutter, my heart hammering in my chest. "Fuck, fuck, fuck, fuck, *fuck*..."

I'm reaching full panic mode. My roommates speak, but the noise in my ears deafens everything around me.

Our eyes collide at the same time, recognition dawning as gray smashes into amber.

"Jax?" His voice is incredulous.

The girls' stares burn into the side of my head.

"Mick," I gasp. My body goes rigid, as if suspended in Krazy Glue.

His mouth spreads into a heart-stopping grin, and I'm consumed by the vision he presents. Hair nearly black and dripping from the ocean, gray eyes popping from under those dark, wet lashes, muscles straining from carrying his surfboard.

"What are you doing here?" he asks, grin fully intact as my insides riot.

*Breathe, Jacqui.*

*In and out.*

*In and out.*

*In and out.*

I manage a return smile. "I'm...here with my new room-mates. Mick, meet Jas and Kit. Girls, this is Mick."

He rests his board on the beach and bends to shake hands with them, greeting them politely before his eyes zero in on me again. "Roommates? Where are you living?"

My heart threatens to leap from my chest, a faint roar still numbing my ears. "In San Jose. I transferred to SJSU. Start next month." It's like I can't conceive—let alone speak—an entire sentence. So much for being a writer.

"That's terrific." His hand rakes through his hair again, and I'm mesmerized, Micknotized, lost in his fucking spell, as always. "I'm happy for you, Jax."

His eyes trail from my face down my body. Recognition of my cherry-red bikini and the potent memories it evokes is obvious by his expression, and my cheeks burn, along with... other parts. His stare turns molten for a millisecond, then he glances away.

"How are things with you?" I vocalize with effort, my insides still flipping like a drunk gymnast.

He takes a breath, his gaze returning my direction. "About the same."

"I didn't know you surfed."

"My mom got us all lessons, my brothers and me, when we were young. It's been a while, but I try to make it happen once or twice a week, even if it's only for an hour. It's helped me...mentally...with this whole fucked-up thing."

I nod.

"You're seriously good," Jas says.

"Thanks," Mick answers, barely sparing her a glance.

"Want to join us?" I ask.

He seems to debate. "Can we take a walk?"

"Sure!" I practically leap to my feet, especially since regret at my ineptitude swirls in my thoughts. Why didn't I hug him right away? Now it would be awkward. It's like I don't know my right from my left, or up from down.

We move toward the ocean's edge where the sand is firmer. I'm quiet. He's quiet. I'm freaking out. Maybe he is too.

The wind whips my hair, and I tuck the right side behind

my ear, sneaking a peek at him. "It's good to see you. One hell of a surprise."

He laughs, low. "You can say that again."

"I almost had a heart attack."

"Me too," he confesses. "You look amazing, Jax. Happy. Healthy. And the whole college thing...it's fantastic. You're pursuing your dream."

My lips curve, my happiness irrepressible. "I am. It's only been a couple of days but getting away from my parents has been liberating. I was suffocating there, drowning."

He nods. I imagine he's the one drowning now. "I get it."

"I know you do. I'm sorry for your situation. It royally sucks."

He shrugs. "I'm still above ground. And hey, I got to surf today—and see you. It's shaping up to be a banner day."

A genuine smile emerges, the kind beginning in my center and radiating outward. "I think about you," I admit.

"I think about you too."

"Mick?"

"Yeah?"

"You okay...for real?"

He shrugs again, a clue he doesn't want to talk about it. "I'm making do. So, San Jose, huh? We're neighbors."

"It would seem so. You still in Menlo Park?"

He nods again.

"But you surf here often?"

"When I can. It's one of the better spots. I hope to get a place out here..." His sentence tapers off, unfinished, and I let it die.

"And what about your dream? To captain a boat? Florida?"

He gestures to the ocean. "Lots of opportunity to do it here or there. Once things change."

"With your father?"

He sighs. "Yeah. I've been talking to people, researching job options. I'm not giving up. It's only been delayed."

"I'm glad." I smile, leaning in and nudging him, a spark shooting between us at the contact. *Bad idea.*

"How's Remy?"

*Remy.*

"He's good."

"He must not be too happy about you moving so far away."

I tilt my head. "We're making it work. I know it's going to sound like bullshit, but he's committed."

He's quiet for a minute, a hand running through his nearly dry hair, those blonder ends framing his face. "I've been the shittiest friend ever."

"I think he understands, Mick. You're dealing with a lot."

"No excuse. He's my best friend." He fixes his gaze on the ocean. "I didn't want to drag him into this, especially after everything he's already done for me."

This admission guts me, an image of my two loves as little boys coming into view. One, bruised and battered. The other, his life raft. My eyes prick and I blink a few times to stem the tide. "He loves you. That will never change." *I love you too. And I don't think that will ever change either.*

"Would it be okay...?" he begins but doesn't finish.

"What?"

"Never mind. I have no right to ask you for anything."

"Mick. Just ask."

"I don't know, seeing you, knowing you live closer...can we, maybe, try being friends? Talk sometimes?"

It's like he dropped a bomb. An ooey, gooey, chocolate-covered explosive I could inhale, not caring one iota if it detonates. "Of course. I'd like that." I stop walking and he follows suit, swinging his gaze to meet mine. "You've never stopped being my friend, you know. We were friends first, and we still are."

*Best friends. And more.*

I don't know if I'm believing my own crap or if it's true, but I sense Mick needs me, *us*, and I *think* I can do it. After all this time, despite the way my heart reacted initially, I want his friendship. I want him in my life. There's a void there with his name on it. Maybe this can work.

He tugs at my hand, closes his around it and squeezes. "Thank you, Jacqui. It means a lot."

I ignore the jolt and welcome the warmth. It dislodges something stuck between us, freeing it up so it's more like old times...how it was before we became more.

We walk back, sharing more effortlessly, naturally—more *us*. By the time we return, a weight has lifted.

I scribble my number on a piece of paper for him and jot down his. My friends are wide-eyed with unspoken questions.

He wraps me in a sincere hug, his arms pulling me into his ocean. "Thank you, Jax," he whispers. "Seeing you is like coming home."

He leaves me standing there dazed by his words, his touch. He bids my roommates goodbye, retrieves his board, and walks away.

I flop back on my towel and let out a long, steadying breath.

"You've got a lot of explaining to do, girl," Jas says.

"A *lot*," Kit emphasizes.

# FORTY-FOUR

I regurgitate the entire story over the next hour to an enraptured Jas and Kit, who only occasionally interject with a question or exclamation. Giddiness free-floats through my bloodstream as I relive it for my roommates—but it's also a sobering reminder of all that's transpired.

The pop-top hisses when my fingers rip the tab on a cold 7UP. I inhale a few slugs, energy still pin-balling through my system.

"It's all so...romantic," Jas says with a sigh. "Both Mick and Remy are fine as hell."

"You could solve all your problems by turning that into a sandwich," Kit adds.

Soda sprays from my mouth and whatever makes it down my throat nearly chokes me. "Are you saying what I think you are?"

"Threesome it up."

"You're crazy, Kit! I could never."

I don't think. The guys would never either. There will be no sandwiches. No Big Macs with two all-beef patties smeared with special sauce. And yet...the vision persists, giving me a glimpse at being the filling between those slices—and burning a hole from my brain straight through my center. *Oh my god.* Stop this nonsense. Why am I contemplating it? Because undeniably, they're both incredible lovers.

My head shakes, almost violently. "Not happening." *Ever.*

"Why? It's 1983. We're in the age of feminism. Why not sleep with two hot men who love you?"

Jas leans over, staring pointedly at her best friend. "I don't see *you* leaping into a ménage à trois."

Kit shrugs. "Simply trying to problem-solve for our newest gang member."

I laugh. "For now, I'm going to attempt to be his friend again."

Jas fans herself. "Good luck with that. He might be the best damn looking man I've ever seen."

"I know. Better than anybody...I know." I take a long sip of soda and lean back on my elbows.

"You know, Kit has her own crazy love story," Jas says.

"Really? Out with it."

"Jas is making it sound like a bigger deal than it is," Kit insists. "And let's call a spade a spade: mine's an unrequited love story. I met Davis at fourteen. He was twenty-two, so he thought I was a twerp—"

"A gorgeous twerp," Jas interjects.

"Over the years, whenever our paths cross, he's always sweet, and pretends he's waiting for me—"

"He *is* waiting for her," Jas whispers to me. "Pining even."

Kit scoffs. "Whatever. He's probably married by now. I never expected it to become a thing."

Jas nudges her friend's shoulder. "Sure you didn't, *Kit Kat.*"

Kit's mouth purses before straightening into a hard line.

"That's what he calls her?" I ask.

"Yup," Jas answers.

Kit looks out at the ocean with another sigh, and I let the topic drop. It's obviously a sore subject. Isn't love always?

WHEN WE GET BACK TO THE CONDO, I CALL REMY from the privacy of my bedroom, fingering the scrap of paper with Mick's phone number scrawled across it.

"It's me."

"Hi, you. Where've you been? I tried you earlier."

"The girls and I went to a beach in Half Moon Bay. You won't believe who I saw."

"Who?"

"Mick."

Pause. "No shit." Pause. Pause. Pause. "At the beach?"

I move into rambling speed-talk. "He was surfing. Then he walked right by us after he got out of the water. I mean, I almost didn't recognize him, but as he got closer...and once we realized...well, we started talking and—"

"And what? Did you fuck him right there...or did you wait and do it in the parking lot?"

He's pissed.

"Remy, it wasn't like that. *We talked*. He's feeling like a shitty friend to you—"

"He's fucking *been* a shitty friend!"

"He's still dealing with his dad and everything. He said he missed you. It's clear he needs...someone."

Remy scoffs. "You mean you?" he spits out.

"No, I mean *us*. And I think we should try to understand. He's been in a crappy position, and yeah, he's been absent, but damn it, Remy, you know he loves you. Ju—"

"And you!" he yells. "Whenever it's fucking convenient."

I sigh, tamping down my frustration. "Can you just...forgive him? I am."

"That's rich."

"Rem—"

He hangs up on me and when the phone buzzes with the dial tone, I slam down the receiver. Not that Remy gets a pass for his behavior, but if one person understands his feelings, his fears, his bitterness—to a degree—it's me.

It's complicated between the three of us.

# FORTY-FIVE

Remy's on my doorstep two hours later with zero warning. "We need to talk," he grits out, his face a mask of steely anger.

He storms in, barreling past me and barely acknowledging my roommates as he marches to my bedroom. I follow, tempering my testiness and indignation while also summoning strength for this showdown. I hate getting blindsided, and this makes twice today.

Once my bedroom door closes, Remy spins, his voice low and full of rage. "I want to know what the fuck is going on. *Right. Now.*"

"Nothing is *going on*. I told you the truth on the phone."

"I'm not stupid. You and Mick are suddenly going to try being *just friends*?" He says "friends" like it's poison.

Luckily for me, my brain's firing on all cylinders. "Yeah...kind of like *you and I* did after *we* slept together!"

He stares straight into my soul, eyes blazing, cheeks and neck reddening by the second. "Really? And how'd that work out for us? We lasted a month. And news flash: I was in agony *the entire time*. You think I want to be *just pals* with you?"

His words cut deep. Averting my gaze, I wipe my sweaty palms against my cutoffs.

When I glimpse him again, his jaw ticks in time with his heaving chest, but he doesn't utter a word.

"I'm not denying I love him, any more than I deny loving you. You two..." I say, voice cracking, "are the closest thing I've ever had to family."

Remy looks out the window, crossing his arms.

"I didn't go looking for Mick." My voice is hoarse, and my eyes beg him to look at me. "None of it was planned. But, Rem, maybe it *wasn't* an accident."

His head swings my way now.

Swallowing back the flood of emotion, I pick up steam. "He needs us. He's hurting. You know he doesn't show his hand, but I saw it. I felt it. He's open to it, wants to let us in."

"You honestly think we can all go back to being friends?" The edge to his voice remains.

A part of me desperately wants to believe it. "Yes...yes, I do. And damn it, I think we need to at least try."

He unwinds his arms and runs a hand through his copper hair. "Fuck."

Stepping closer, I place my palm on his chest until he looks at me. "I love you, now and forever."

Pain crosses his face before his features smooth. He wraps me in a hug, gripping me tightly and melding us together.

"Okay," he breathes, and my body shudders with relief.

We fall into emotional make-up sex, letting our bodies do the talking—and healing.

Then he calls Mick, our limbs still tangled in the bed. Remy's hand strokes my calf, hooked across his chiseled abs. My smile and heart expand as I listen to him banter with his best friend like old times. There's name-calling, quiet moments as he listens, and eventually, a plan for us the following weekend.

Fears and trepidation vanish as the familiar warmth from

all three of us being back together spreads through me, comforting me like a warm blanket.


IT'S AN INTERMINABLY LONG WEEK OF WAITING, BUT Saturday finally arrives. Mick is driving to my place then we're going to some gargantuan club called The Saddle Rack recommended by my roommates. The Country Western saloon reportedly once had live bulls on the premises, until they escaped and wreaked havoc on city streets. They still have a mechanical bull for intrepid riders, plus multiple dance floors and bars.

I invite Jas and Kit to join us but they're heading to Oakland for Mr. Singh's birthday party. I'm secretly relieved, wanting the guys to myself.

"Sandwich," Kit quips on her way out the door.

"Stooooop," I chide, dragging out the word and hoping no sordid imagery manifests.

We need for this to work, and it's already primed for failure with our sticky threesome. *Not threesome!* Three Musketeers—the three inseparables, if my recollection of the translation is accurate. Yes, that's us. Except, not us. Because Athos, Portos, Aramis (and later, D'Artagnan), don't sleep together.

Remy arrives as I'm exiting the shower, lobbying (unsuccessfully) for a quickie. I shoo him away to finish getting ready.

Soon Mick and Remy's laughter and muffled voices filter upstairs. Winged things flutter through my system. This girl needs a drink—or ten.

After applying the last of my makeup, I whisper at my reflection, supplying a stern pep talk. "We're friends. Mick needs us. We've got this. Let's do it."

The guys stop mid-sentence when I emerge on the stairs. My heart stutters a beat when Mick's eyes meet mine, a smile inching up his lips, his gray eyes intent but warm. His hair and eyes pop against a black button down, rolled halfway up his forearms, paired with his usual Levi's. Remy's similarly dressed, his sapphire eyes offset handsomely with a navy shirt. They're two tall drinks of water, and I'm one lucky girl.

Mick stands and we share a hug. On my way to the kitchen, I press a reassuring kiss to the top of Remy's head. I'm fully aware we're in a live *Twilight Zone* episode of weirdness and pray I haven't bitten off more than my big mouth can chew. After pouring a glass of chardonnay from the wine-in-a-box that resides in our fridge, I rejoin the guys, hoping alcohol will relax said winged things, now viciously banging against my skeleton and making it impossible to concentrate, let alone breathe.

We share a grin and toast to being together again. I silently add *and not screwing it all up*. Downing my drink in record time, I launch to my feet, nearly falling in the process. I'm embarrassing myself. *Get a grip.*

"Y'all ready?" My country twang needs work, but it'll do.

"Giddy-up," Remy says.

Mick surveys us, shaking his head. "It's going to be a long fucking night."

We pile into Remy's Camaro and wind downtown, marveling when we realize the Saddle Rack takes up nearly a city block. Remy finds a parking spot in the packed lot, and we stroll to the entrance. I attempt nonchalance as a behemoth pro-wrestler-looking dude checks my fake ID, scrutinizing it before handing it over and letting me through.

The music pumps through the space, people swarm the dance floors, and my jaw drops as we walk through the various sections, taking in the sheer vastness of the club.

Spying a chair in the middle of a long wooden plank bar where patrons can get an "upside-down margarita," I practically skip to it. When it's my turn, I sit, tilt my head back, and open my mouth. A pretty bartender shakes salt in first, followed by a squirt of lime, then turns bottles of tequila and triple sec upside-down until liquid pools. The act of rising has the tasty concoction sliding down my throat, and I'm an instant fan who'll be back for more. The guys buy themselves a couple of beers, and me a bona fide margarita.

We find a table and absorb the scene. We have a partial view of the mechanical bull, with several people in the queue to take their turn.

Remy stands and leads me onto the dance floor. The music's unfamiliar but energetic, and we work up a sweat in no time. Mick takes me out next, guiding me backwards as we attempt to mimic the popular stutter step we see other couples doing. We botch it, laughing at ourselves, and keep trying. When line dancers take over, I'm captivated, wishing I knew the steps. The last time I remember line dancing was when The Hustle was all the rage in junior high.

After hours of tequila shots, drinks, and dancing, a sheen coats our bodies, hair clings to our faces, and music pulses in our ears. It's like déjà vu.

"I'm riding that bull," Remy announces after slinging down the last of his beer.

Mick raises an eyebrow. "This I've got to see."

The three of us traipse over and Remy signs a liability waiver. When his turn arrives, he straddles the brown leather bull with inebriated bravado and a gleam in his eyes.

He signals the operator and the machine starts slowly—rotating, bucking, giving its newest rider a taste. Then it picks up speed and intensity, sometimes rotating nearly three hundred sixty degrees before jerking back. Soon enough, Remy's flung onto the padded mats, laughing his ass off.

"I'm going next," I say.

Mick winks. "Show him how it's done, Jax."

Completely tanked, I pause a moment before signing the waiver. Could I seriously die doing this? *Pshh.* The operator prattles off instructions my brain scarcely comprehends, jarring me from contemplating death by drunken stupidity.

My feet sink against the padded floor walking toward the bull. I hesitate briefly upon reaching it as this thing is bigger than it looked. Holding onto the saddle knob for leverage, I swing my leg over and hike myself up. Damn it's hard to clamp my limbs around its smooth, broad sides. There's no way to gain purchase, despite my limber thighs.

Shrugging, I hitch my thumb that I'm ready. *Here goes nothing.*

Maybe the operator's taking it easy on me, but I manage to hang on through the first several swivels and dips, letting out some *yee-haws* the faster the mechanism rotates and bucks. Spectators hoot and holler, urging me on as my aching thighs clutch the fake bull.

A surge of cockiness erupts as I outdo my boyfriend's ride...until the dumb bull takes a big dip and I'm dumped unceremoniously onto the mat, landing with an unladylike thud. Remy's so busy laughing, Mick helps me to my feet. My legs protest, throbbing from exertion and unsteady from tequila.

"I'm gonna be sick," I mutter, and Mick half-carries, half-drags me to the ladies' room.

My head spins as my knees buckle toward the cement floor, and I hurl into a dirty toilet. *Gross.*

Once the retching stops, I clean myself up at the sink and exit the restroom, thankful the guys are waiting for me. They each grab a side, wedging me in the middle, and carry me to the car. I crawl in the back set and curl into a ball. Mick, the only sober one, drives us back to my place. The last thing I remember is the comforting roar of the Camaro.

I WAKE UP TO THE SUN STREAMING THROUGH THE open blinds of my sliding glass door and wince at every violation. The bright light. The pounding in my head. The horrific coating in my mouth. And the icing on the cake: dry heaves with tequila notes.

*I'm never drinking again.*

Remy snores softly next to me. How did I even find my way into bed, or undressed, or...what *is* the last thing I remember?

Propelling myself to sitting, my quads and hamstrings shriek. What the ever-loving fuck? *Ohhh.* The stupid bull. This is going to hurt. My legs wobble to standing and yup, it's brutal. Everything revolts as I take my first steps, but I make it successfully to the bathroom. I scrub my teeth, test out sips of water, and eye the commode warily. Bracing myself against the wall for support, I fall to the seat, zero control over my damn muscles.

I shuffle along the hall and down the stairs to drink something, anything, to abate this egregious mouth situation. That's when Mick's form comes into view. He's crashed on the couch, dressed in last night's clothes except for his shoes, neatly stowed on the carpet. One arm's thrown over his chest, the other under his head, peacefully depicting a fucking angel. My heart skitters.

*Mick is sleeping in my living room.*

On its heels comes a self-satisfied peace. *We did it.* We all went out, had fun, stayed friends. We really can do this. Psyched, I give myself a mental high five.

My aching legs make it to the kitchen, where I pour a glass of apple juice and take a minuscule sip. And another. Nabbing a sleeve of Saltine crackers, my behind thuds into a chair at the table.

Ten minutes later, Mick shifts, rolling onto his side and gifting me a sleepy, lopsided grin. *Be still my heart.*

"How're you feeling, party animal?"

I scrunch my nose. "Indescribably bad."

He chuckles, stretching his tanned arms overhead and

flashing those biceps...that I acutely remember having wrapped around me.

"How are you not destroyed?" Annoyance laces my tone.

"I paced myself."

"I hate you." *Lie.*

He grins, eyes tracking me, probably noticing I'm a hideous mess. Except those gray depths don't recoil—they soften. "Thank you," he says.

"For...?"

"Everything."

A smile lifts my lips as understanding grows.

He pushes upright, scrubbing his hands over his face. "I've got to bail. Can I grab a gl—"

"Help yourself to anything."

He coasts gracefully into the kitchen—smart people don't ride mechanical bulls—and pours a tumbler of orange juice, downing it in seconds. He rinses his glass and places it in the sink with a soft clink. Returning to the sofa, he pulls on his sneakers and stands.

"Tell fuckhead I said goodbye." He saunters my way and when he reaches me, kisses the top of my head. "See you, Jax."

The affection in that kiss travels all the way down to my toes.

# Forty-Six

Jas, Kit, and I settle into a booth at Original Joe's, a San Jose landmark serving obscene portions of Italian food my Sicilian roommate vouches for with her life. These are huge selling points for a "starving student."

I'm not technically starving, but not flush either. My parents may foot the bills, but my spending allowance remains tight, so I'm on the lookout for a part-time job that's manageable once school starts. Only two more weeks of summer remain until classes begin, and for the first time in my life, I'm eager to start the semester.

The restaurant bustles between the wait staff hustling food and the patrons packing the joint, while Dean Martin croons about *amore* in the background. The aromas wafting from the visible kitchen make my mouth water. I ogle the armloads of chow whizzing past: large plates heaped with spaghetti and meatballs, thick wedges of lasagna, or slabs of juicy prime rib.

"Told you," Kit says, a satisfied smile on her lips.

My stomach growls, and I suck down some of my cola. There's a maraschino cherry resting on the bottom, which speaks to the old school hospitality.

"So..." Jas stares at me pointedly. "What's the latest with the two men in love with you?"

I shake my head. "Mick and I are just friends." That's understating things a tad, but it's true the three of us are making this work. It's already been a month, and I'm calling it a success. Although I can't deny a powerful gravitational pull to Mick—the force is strong with that one.

Jas guffaws. "Oh, so you won't mind if I date him?"

The burn is instantaneous and raw, blazing through my chest, breaths coarse as I capsize and start to drown. My eyes lift to meet hers as I'm swallowed by rabid jealousy.

She smirks. "That's what I thought."

*Holy shit.* I deep breathe myself off the ledge, my heart rate still skyrocketing. "It's complicated, okay?" My voice sounds strangled.

Jas hikes her eyebrows, tilting her head.

Except how do I explain? "Listen, we're finally regaining our footing. The three of us were—*are*—best friends. We screwed things up by letting it get physical, but we're trying to find our way back, and so far, so good."

"You love him though, don't you?" Kit asks softly.

"Remy? Of course."

She shakes her head. "Mick."

I worry my bottom lip between my teeth. "For better or for worse, I love them both. Fiercely."

"But you're *in* love with Mick, right?" she presses. "Not Remy."

Double fuck. Is it that obvious? Heat creeps up my neck and cheeks and sweat trickles down my armpits.

"I fell hard for him," I admit, my hands rubbing the icy surface of my glass. "Then he jumped ship and had to leave Oakland. But he had a good reason, which had nothing to do with us." Or did it? I sigh. "He's...maddening. And broken...and beautiful."

"Aren't we all?" Jas muses.

"I'm grateful we're getting along, making it work, seeing each other again. That Mick realized he can let us help him carry the load." All true.

"You're not worried this geyser's about to blow?" Jas says, snickering at her choice of words.

Great. Now I'm picturing Mick's cock—and all the ways he knows how to wield it.

"You're thinking about his dick right now, aren't you?"

"Fuck off, Jas." I stare at her, my mouth curling into a tight-lipped smile. "And I say that with all sincerity."

She barks out a laugh. "Touchy."

"Touchy indeed," Kit mimics. The two girls share a look.

Our food arrives, interrupting the inquisition, and we dive into our respective plates. Our collective groans erupt as we inhale a few bites before eagerly sampling each other's dishes.

I don't vocalize it, but I struck gold with these roommates. They're shaping up to be exactly the kind of girlfriends I've always wanted but never thought I would find.

The three of us split an order of heavenly tiramisu bursting with coffee, chocolate, and cream, laughing over our shared worst date stories.

On our way out the door, I spy a help wanted sign for a hostess and snag an application. The evening hours will work with my school schedule, and a paycheck will augment the rigid stipend from my parents and provide some breathing room.

A few days later, two hours after driving to the restaurant for my in-person interview, the job's mine.

# FORTY-SEVEN

"I have some news," Mick says, his tone light—buoyant even—through the phone.

My insides twinge, and my attention shifts away from the stack of textbooks I'm reviewing for my upcoming semester. "Tell me."

"I got a job at a boatyard in Half Moon Bay."

"Mick, that's fantastic!"

"With my mechanic background, they're giving me maintenance duties. But," he says triumphantly, "they'll also teach me how to operate their fleet. They've got fishing and recreation boats, plus some yachts and cabin cruisers."

"I'm *so* happy for you. You deserve this. And you can manage it with your dad's situation?"

"Only part-time, but I'm making this work, Jax. I need it for my own sanity."

I lean back on my bed pillows, crossing my legs at the ankles. "I know," I say softly. "It blows my mind how well you've coped. Especially with how long it's already gone on." His Florida dream crashed and burned, but this gets him back on track. It's something. More than something.

"You've helped me a lot."

My insides melt—as they do anytime he throws a tidbit of affection my way. I don't want to admit how pathetic that is, or how it might be a giant, crimson-colored warning flag. "I'm glad."

"Want to celebrate?"

"Hell yeah."

"Can you come my way? I need to stay close to home tonight."

"Sure thing." As I'm jotting down the directions, a voice murmurs to call Remy even though he can't meet us. He's at his parents' house and I want to dial that number about as much as I want to stick porcupine quills in my eye. The odds of getting the bitchy Mrs. Remington or the horny Mr. Remington clinches my decision.

Besides, the three of us have successfully navigated this rebooted friendship over the past six weeks, restoring trust and love. Mick and I haven't been alone yet, but I'm a big girl. Responsible. Large and in charge.

After pulling on and off an absurd amount of clothes, I settle on an outfit. The fallout looks like Esprit, Casual Corner, and The Limited blew up in my bedroom. I tease my honey locks with a comb, add some light hairspray, and apply eyeliner, mascara, blush, and a coat of lip gloss. *Not trying too hard at all.*

My Bug zooms toward Menlo Park, and I sing along to cranked tunes, attempting to tamp down the jitters jetting through my system. When I arrive at Mick's father's house, the jitterbugs are swarming. I'm being let into the inner sanctum, a BFD—big fucking deal. I pause a minute to get my bearings.

Mick materializes at my car door, smiling with his enchanting dimple and making me forget...everything. "You coming in—or are you going to sit here and look pretty?"

*Gulp.* "Both?"

He chuckles in his disarming way and extends a hand. "We won't eat you."

Images of him feasting *down there* flash unbidden in my mind. Heat zings irritatingly right to command central.

His gray eyes widen, a knowing laugh leaving his lips. "Hmm, obviously that's not happening."

I shouldn't feel disappointed by that.

Taking his proffered hand, he helps me from the car, and promptly drops it.

I shouldn't feel disappointed by that either.

We pause outside the front door.

"My dad's not often lucid. He sleeps a lot. Sometimes he's a dick. I doubt he'll wake up while you're here." Gauging my wide-eyed expression, Mick adds, "Relax."

He opens the door, and I follow him inside. I'm about to see the man who both created and harmed one of the people I care about most. My stomach knots further. If he's awake, what am I going to say... *'Nice to meet you'*?

We enter a small foyer where a narrow, glass-topped table displays an empty ceramic vase. An antiseptic smell permeates the home, combined with a mild funk I associate with old people. We pass the living and dining rooms where the bland décor continues—everything's white or beige. Stopping in the kitchen, he offers me a beverage and I snag a soda.

"Be right back," he murmurs. "I'm going to check if he's awake."

My head bobs. Curling my finger under the aluminum ring tab, I pull it off, leaving it on my index finger like jewelry. Fizzy bubbles tickle my nose when the can reaches my mouth. Leaning against the Formica counter, my eyes graze the avocado appliances and dark wood cabinets, but truly, I'm listening for signs of life. It's eerily quiet aside from the hum of the refrigerator, the tick of a wall clock, and some incessant, unidentifiable beeping.

Mick returns, motioning me over, and leads me down the hall to an open doorway.

"That's him," he whispers.

His father sleeps in a hospital-style bed, attached to a monitor that chirps at regular intervals, showing vital signs in colored numbers and graphics. My eyes sweep over his father, finding a withered shell of a man—bony, pallid, weak—not the virile, strong version he likely once was.

The tableau fills me with sadness. A man who mistreated his sons and wives now lays here, his life over for all intents and purposes, still dragging down the life of Mick, never to take responsibility or atone for his sins. I pity his father—but I grieve for Mick, his brothers, his mother, and everyone subjected to this unrepentant dirtbag's abuse.

I bite my lip, trying to hold back tears. Mick doesn't need them, and this man isn't worthy of them.

We back out of the room, my exhale harsh on my way down the hall. Once in the kitchen, I fling my arms around him, not saying anything. The steady thud of his heartbeat pulses against mine. He's rigid at first, but then grips me in return, his face burying into my hair.

There are no words to make this better, and Mick wouldn't want to hear meaningless platitudes anyway, so I let my embrace say it all. His ocean scent overwhelms me, and I cling to it as hard as his sturdy frame. Add in his rare display of vulnerability and it makes for a potent combination, his forcefield drawing me closer as we stay glued together for several minutes.

A knock on the front door jolts us apart. He leaves to answer it, returning with someone he introduces as Jerry, a thirty-something male nurse sporting a beard and stud earring. They discuss Mr. Callahan's current condition and Mick confirms we'll return in a few hours.

We step outside into the night, tangibly relieved to escape. My fingers glide over the louvers on Mick's fastback, one of my favorite features, as I follow him to the passenger side of the Mustang.

He holds my door open. "Ready to get the hell out of here and have some fun?"

"Absofuckinglutely," I beam.

His gray eyes flicker back to life, and he cranks up the car, the idle pulsing through my veins with familiarity. He lights us a couple of smokes, messes with the radio until landing on a song he likes, and heads back out to the main boulevard. I don't know where we are or ask where we're going. None of it matters.

Mick pulls into the parking lot of a joint called The Big Griller. The second I'm out of the car, the heavenly scent of chargrilled meat assaults my senses. We order from the scant menu offerings at the counter and slide into a booth in the cramped dining area. Our food arrives in minutes: a double cheeseburger for him, a single for me, and a grease-stained bag overflowing with fries we share.

My fingers grapple with the oversized burger. Ketchup and beef drippings snake down my hand, and when I lick them with my tongue, Mick tracks every movement. Our eyes catch, and his burn into mine, stealing all the air from my lungs.

He schools his features, downcasting his eyes beneath those magnificent lashes, and I try to remember we're skating on ice thin enough to crash through.

We polish off the meal and I duck into the ladies' room to clean up. Once we're back on the road, it's only a few miles before we're swinging into the parking lot to Tiki-Tavi's, a tiki bar with kitsch written all over it.

He grins after opening the passenger door. "Wait until you see this place."

The interior brims with an explosion of bamboo, thatched straw, totem poles, and colorful lights to a backdrop of tropical music. A hostess seats us next to a running water feature near the middle, rainbow hues illuminating the fountain.

Without even perusing the cocktail menu, Mick orders us something called a Sidewinder's Fang.

"Trust me," he says.

Ten minutes later, the waitress places a gargantuan brandy snifter-style glass in the center of the table. Two long straws protrude from the boozy mixture, along with an impressively vertical fruit display speared with a fuchsia cocktail umbrella.

A laugh spills. "What on God's green earth is in this?"

Mick shrugs. "A lot of alcohol and a little fruit."

"It's nutritious? Bonus."

We lean in to sip at the same time, me curious, him amused.

Strong rum hits my throat, and I sputter out a cough. "This might put hair on my chest."

He smirks. "That would ruin a good thing."

Glancing away, his words echo inside me. Choosing not to read more into the statement, I meet his gaze. "Congratulations...since we're officially celebrating now."

"Thanks. And thanks...for coming."

My head nods, disarmed by his sincerity. "Mick..."

"Let's not talk about me, okay? Tell me about you. Are you stoked about school?"

We're back to this. I don't blame him with his life so screwed up right now. My questions aren't important, not when he probably has no answers, existing in purgatory.

"Totally. I'm hoping to learn how to earn a living from writing. You know, so I don't wind up a pathetic, starving artist working in a tiki bar or something her whole life, waiting for the magic to happen."

He cocks his head, a half-smile playing at his lips. "Believe you can and you're halfway there."

"Philosopher Mick is back!"

He rolls his eyes. "Can't take the credit. Teddy Roosevelt

said it. He was big on action, *trying* instead of fearing failure. You're already there, so you're way ahead."

I mull over his words. "Jas is a journalism major, and after talking with her, I switched my minor to that because it's bankable—and opens the door to other types of writing gigs. I'm stoked about starting. Maybe I'll need to interview a boat captain one day." I raise my eyebrows. "Better expect my call, because I'm coming to you, buddy."

Mick chuckles, shaking his head. "If that day comes, I'll be happy to accommodate you."

Beaming, I slurp up more of our drink, and we talk and laugh about easygoing, safe topics through another Sidewinder's Fang. By the time we head back, the alcohol has loosened my defenses—and tongue.

My cheek rests against the leather seat, taking in Mick's handsome profile. His chestnut hair flowing from the open window, his dark features, the stubble on his jaw, his potent masculinity.

"Want to hear my poem about you?"

His surprised eyes catch mine briefly. "I don't know...do I?"

I giggle. "It's not, like, a hate poem."

He pauses, seeming to consider. "Knock yourself out, Jax."

Shutting my eyes, I clear my throat theatrically and recite it from memory.

"'My Ocean,' by Jacqueline Hall.

"Cloudy gray clashes with the night,

"He comes in mighty waves, stealing all the light.

"Lapping and receding, I tumble in his wake,

"I give him all of me, uncaring what's at stake.

"But he's a tsunami in disguise,

"The danger a warning in his eyes.

"I can't avoid the storm, even if I should go,

"Forever trapped in his compelling undertow.

"Like the sand beneath my feet as tides begin to shift,
"He disintegrates, pulls away, until I am adrift.
"Yet I feel his strength...his pulse...his love,
"No matter how intently he tries to shove.
"I wait at the ocean's edge, hoping he'll return,
"Never knowing if my heart is destined just to yearn."

Opening my eyes, I venture a furtive glance. His face, cloaked by night, makes it difficult to gauge the effect of my poem. I'm far too tipsy to know whether I should be embarrassed, but the artist in me craves a reaction. Validation. *Something.*

He swings into his driveway and the car shudders to a stop. "Goddamn," he mutters.

"Hmm?"

He turns in his seat. "Your poem is beautiful, Jacqueline Hall." He scrubs his jaw, his eyes darting away from me. "And reminds me I never deserved you."

That one sentence crushes my heart—and whatever flimsy cage was protecting it. Instinctively, I reach for his hand. "Yes, you did," I whisper. "You deserve all good things."

He laughs ruefully, head shaking. "You're nothing but good."

"I thought I was heroin."

"Straight-up. It's been hard to kick the habit."

This garners a smile—and more. It's a jumpstart to my broken vessel, a sign maybe it hasn't been as easy for him as I thought.

"C'mon, let's sober you up or else you need to crash here."

"Okie dokey."

When I'm deemed unfit to drive, Mick tucks me into his bed, clothes and all. I pass out, his salty scent the last thing I remember.

# FORTY-EIGHT

Yelling jolts me into consciousness.

"Where the fuck is your lazy, good-for-nothing ass?"

Seconds later: "Goddamn imbecile. Don't you know how to do anything? Worthless as the day I brought you into this world!"

My eyes widen, heart thumping erratically as I listen to Mick's father berate his son.

"Not *that* one, you idiot! Jesus H. Christ, I could do it faster myself!" Mr. Callahan bellows.

Mick responds, but I can't make out what he's saying.

Wide awake now, I log a few details:

I'm in Mick's bed.

*Oh, shit.*

Dressed.

*Thank God.*

With a headache.

*Sidewinder's Fangs certainly sank its fangs into me.*

I can only imagine how many times Remy has called, and what kind of shit sandwich I'm in there.

Except I didn't do anything.

*And Mick gets all the credit for that, not me.*

Fuck...did I recite my poem last night? My head hurts even more.

"Get my breakfast. Before the goddamned sun goes down!"

What to do. Stay? Go? Help? Pull the covers over my head?

Scanning for my sandals, my insides jackhammering, I wonder how to get out of here, or what Mick wants, needs...and knowing Remy's probably furious and requires attending as well. What a mess.

I stand, wincing, as Mick comes through the bedroom door, his face unreadable.

"Welcome to club paradise," he deadpans.

"Mick..."

"I assume you're ready to split...unless you want to stick around and join the old man for breakfast? He's in rare form today."

"Except he's not, is he? This is what it's like for you all the time."

"Does it fucking matter?"

I step forward. "It matters to me."

"Just go, Jax."

"Fine." I hate being snippy, but goddamn him.

He levels his gaze, eyes flaring. "Are you really copping an attitude?"

"I only want to help!"

"You can't! No one can!" He flings out his arms and traps me in his frustrated stare.

My eyes brim.

"Don't you dare feel sorry for me," he grits out. "This is exactly why I left and didn't put you through this bullshit. Isn't it bad enough one of us has to deal?"

A few tears spill, and I swipe them away.

He's in front of me in an instant, cradling my face with

both hands, eyes imploring. "You are a kind, beautiful, special person. I'm talking about how you are on the *inside*. I know you want to help, to be there for me, to shoulder the burden, but I've never wanted any of this ugliness to touch any part of you. If you love me, you'll understand."

He presses his lips to mine, searing them and showing me exactly how he feels. I press back, arching into him and answering him completely.

Our kiss is profound...leaving me stupefied, breathless, and standing at the ocean's edge.

Honoring his request, understanding him better than I did five minutes ago, I walk out the front door and back to a life that no longer rings true.

# FORTY-NINE

There's no fallout with Remy, who's oddly distracted and vague when we talk on the phone. He grumbles about his mother meddling in his affairs but won't elaborate, telling me after he left his parents, he got shitfaced with Terry at some Berkeley dive and slept in his Camaro.

Equally distracted, I explain my evening—hearing Mick's good news, meeting up to celebrate, and witnessing his stark reality—stressing our friend needs our support and saying little else.

Words are woefully inadequate, my equilibrium incinerated. The blunt reality and honesty revealed in the last twenty-four hours makes everything else seem like a charade, and I don't know how to act as if nothing's happened.

I love these guys more than anything or anyone, making the pain in my heart greater than its actual size. When one of them hurts, my heart capsizes. Mick's slowly drowning in murky, deep water, and I ache for him, with him, over him.

Yet I'm powerless to do anything helpful or meaningful. And any angst, resentment, or self-pity I've held onto over his decision to spare me from the misery he's forced to dwell in evaporates. It leaves a crater of a different kind behind.

The name of the game becomes distraction—pedaling faster than my rioting emotions can catch and staying well ahead of thinking too long or hard.

My hand itches to pick up the phone and call Mick, but I don't, respecting the space he's asked me to give him, waiting for him to reach out when he's ready. He's never far from my thoughts. How could he be?

Classes begin and I throw myself headfirst into them and my new job. On my off nights, I hang out with my roommates getting lost in episodes of *Cheers* and *Taxi*—frequently with a glass of wine in hand to take the edge off. A murmur in the recesses of my mind whispers *that's how you get from the shallow end to jumping off the diving board,* but I'm too tired, too fragile, and too broken to listen.

Living is all-consuming, the screaming so loud in my head, it hurts. And I don't have any answers.

They say time heals all wounds, but that sounds like a load of sanctimonious crap nowadays.

I'm wounded.

Mick's wounded.

My heart's fragile, broken, bleeding out, and I don't think time will do a fucking thing to mend it.

Maybe some of us don't survive these travesties of the heart.

# FIFTY

For my twenty-first birthday, Remy, Vinny, and my roommates take me to a club in downtown San Jose. Before we leave the condo, I hack my fake ID into pieces with a pair of scissors and ceremoniously dump them in the trash. I'm not a baby anymore but a legal, of-drinking-age adult.

I'm giddy handing my driver's license to the doorman at LA Rocks, and when he spies the date, he lobs me a smile but warns, "Don't get too crazy or you'll puke your guts out."

It's possible the evening will end that way, but you only turn twenty-one once, right?

The drinks flow, dance music pumps through the dark club, and we're a collective, sweaty, drunken group hours later —except Kit, our volunteer designated driver. Vinny and Jas are all over each other, grinding on the dance floor, and doing risqué tequila shots where they suck the lime out of each other's mouths. Plenty of guys ask Kit to dance and no wonder—she's a dark-haired beauty with a killer smile.

Remy's attentive, putting me at ease, but the undercurrent that turned me upside-down since seeing Mick remains. I long to flick it off like a mosquito you find crawling on your arm, but its fangs are lodged deep, far under the surface.

Once again, my method of coping is drinking and denying. Especially remembering the sound of Mick's voice when he called to wish me a happy birthday. And my parents, who called right after him. Sentiment coats me like thick honey as I recall my mother's kind words, my dad's too. And...Mick's.

Flicking the air with my fingers on both hands, my drunken compatriots wonder aloud what I'm doing.

"Mosquitos," I slur.

I'm greeted with blank looks and guffaws.

When last call is announced, we slug down our final shots and stumble out of the club. Kit, who only had one drink to toast the auspicious occasion, drives us home.

As soon as we're inside, Jas and Vinny disappear into her bedroom, as predicted.

I make it to the bathroom in time to hurl, as the doorman predicted.

Within twenty minutes, I pass out next to Remy, both of us too inebriated to undress other than kicking off our shoes.

And there's not a damn mosquito in sight.

# FIFTY-ONE

When a weekend frees up, I drive to Remy's for a party. There's distance between us, both physically and intimately. Our responsibilities, combined with living in different ZIP codes, make it impossible to spend much time together. I can't deny the fissure forming after my last Mick sighting, try as I do to bury it deep.

I'm hoping time with Remy will at least patch up whatever's falling apart for a while. Somewhere inside, I'm aware a patch can only work so long. If you don't address the actual reason for the breach, you're asking for a blowout.

My heart speeds up when I coast my Beetle into a parking spot in front of Remy's. Jogging to his front door, I push through it, jumping into his arms at first sight, my legs wrapping around his waist. He laughs and crushes me to him before our lips meet, greedy and hungry. The awareness and ache slams into me like a bus: I've missed him. He's my best friend, my lover, my guy.

"Damn, you feel good," he groans, his breath tickling my ear.

"I've missed you so much," I say between peppering his face with kisses.

"Guess we better do something about that…"

"Hurry," I whine.

With me still clinging to his frame, he walks us into the bedroom and deposits me on the bed, his blue eyes blazing. The longing is present for us both.

We don't even bother fully disrobing before Remy's inside me. We cry out at the rightness—and long absence—of our two bodies joined at the hips.

"Fuuuuuuuuuuck," he utters, thrusting slowly.

"Oh god, Remmmmm," I cry.

He picks up the pace, our eyes connected. Our breathing ramps up with every plunge he drives into my depths. I'm near tears at the intensity, everything in me missing everything in him, needing his touch with the ferocity he's delivering it. Remy dips down, his lips claiming mine, tongue probing, mine answering, until the need for oxygen prevails. Our bodies move in sweet symphony, creating an exquisite composition. With such exalting perfection and bliss, angels must surely be singing.

"Damn it," he murmurs right before he explodes, face contorted in pleasure as we grind out the final contact.

Our foreheads touch, warmth spreading through us, intimacy restored. Our breathing calms, our hearts finding their familiar rhythm.

Remy rises enough to kiss me tenderly. "I'm not done with you yet, but that couldn't fucking wait."

"I know. It…" I lose all words.

Remy merely nods.

"I love you."

"I love you, sweetheart," he repeats.

WE PREP FOR THE PARTY BY STRAIGHTENING UP HIS place then running out to score cases of beer and a half ounce of blow. In and around these activities, we steal kisses and more. He ducks his head between my legs and brings me to orgasm with his tongue and fingers. While I'm bent over vacuuming, he tugs my jeans down and takes me from behind. In the shower, I give him head, worshiping his cock like it's the second coming (or third or fourth, but who's counting?). By the time friends arrive, I'm already high on sex, my worries about us subsiding.

Seeing familiar faces is the best homecoming, a prescription I didn't know I needed. Nothing—and everything's changed. Vinny has a new girl by his side. I'm unsure whether this would bother Jas, as she and Vinny have kept it casual. Kendra appears with her new beau, and I'm elated to see her happy after a tough break-up with Terry. Jeremy arrives sporting his next female victim. There are also a few unrecognizable people, guys Remy has befriended who give me the creeps. They stare too long and look borderline dangerous.

Aside from Terry, who's playing minor league ball and reportedly holding his own for the AA team, the only person missing is Mick, holed up across the bay with his cantankerous father. Thoughts of him invade my mind throughout the night but I've become an expert at shoving them into my murkiest depths.

WHEN MY EYES OPEN THE FOLLOWING DAY, IT'S afternoon. I'm hungover and sore in my nether regions, my body abused from all angles. Remy's not in bed, but conversation drifts from other room. I peek out the bedroom door and take in the scene. Vinny and his girlfriend are *still* snorting lines with Remy while a football game flashes on the television. Shaking my head, I limp into the shower.

Cheers erupt thirty minutes later when I enter the living

room. My comrades look strung out: bloodshot eyes, matted hair, and the kind of dopey belligerence that comes from an all-nighter.

"Want a line, baby?"

"How do you still have coke?" I ask.

"Scored another eight-ball!" Vinny says proudly.

*Holy Mother.* They'll be up another twenty-four hours, for sure. "I'm good. I need to bail. You know...homework and responsible shit?"

Remy's expression contorts into exaggeratedly sad.

Hovering over his face, I move an errant lock. "Go to bed soon. Save that for another day."

"Don't think so, *Mom*," he answers, and the trio snickers.

I roll my eyes. "I ain't yo mama."

"Damn right you aren't," he leers.

"Call me later." I plant a kiss on his waiting lips and squeeze his shoulder.

Walking out into bright sunshine, I squint and hurry to the car, where my sunglasses await. Putting them on only brings mild comfort.

Driving home to San Jose, I'm plagued by questions. Is this how I want to conduct my life? Is this the best I've got? Is Remy the guy I want to do it with? Have I even thought—with a shred of intention—what the hell I'm doing?

Mick's words come back to me from months ago. *"Live your life, Jax. Tomorrow is promised to no one."*

As do Remy's: *"You only live once."*

Two similar statements each are adopting in totally opposite ways. Mick, trying to make his dreams happen despite the nightmare of his reality. And Remy, living for the moment, pissing his life away without a fucking care, perhaps because of that trust fund parachute strapped to his back.

The burning question is...what do *I* want?

# FIFTY-TWO

A week later, I fly out to Surfer's Beach early on Saturday morning. Mick usually surfs weekend mornings, and I don't give him a heads up, taking a chance he'll be there.

I make my way to the beach, the fog showing signs of lifting as brief moments of light filter through the dense gray. My tension lifts when the Pacific comes into view, more when I spy my ocean catch a wave, tracking him as he rides it gracefully. He makes it look effortless.

Breathing in the fresh air, the still-chilled sand cools the soles of my feet as I near the shore. I lower myself to sitting, allowing the stress of the past weeks to release.

Mick methodically surfs unruly waves in various sizes, carving the water, kicking out, eating it once. I'm glued to his every move as he paddles out, noses under oncoming sets, and crests the surface time and time again.

I'm calmer as he rides one in, my heart no longer compressed as if trapped in a vise. Surprise registers on his face the minute he realizes it's me, then a grin lifts those perfect lips into a big smile, popping that dimple.

He's fucking gorgeous. And sopping wet? Devastating.

He lays his surfboard on the beach, unzips his wetsuit, and peels it to his waist. "What are you doing here? Everything okay?"

"Not happy to see me?"

He grins and sinks next to me. "I'm always stoked to see you, Jax."

My lips curl briefly before fading like a wave against the shore. "I'm worried about Remy."

"What's the idiot doing now?"

My fingers sift through the sand, silky and gritty at the same time. "He's partying way too much. Regular all-nighters. Tons of blow, drinking. Plenty of friends who want to do it all with him."

"Who...Vin? Jeremy?"

I shift my gaze to the ocean, hoping the rhythmic crashing of waves will bring the usual peace. "Yeah, but also some new guys who totally skeeve me out. I'm worried he's in too deep."

"And you want me to talk to him?"

I find his gray eyes and get lost for a moment. "I don't know, Mick. I guess I want you to help me figure out what to do...if there *is* anything to do. I can't sit by and watch him do this shit."

He raises an eyebrow. "You know he's a hardhead, right? And reckless? And acts like a rich playboy?"

My teeth rake over my bottom lip. "I know."

"I can try...but he'll probably tell me to go fuck myself."

He's right, of course, but I don't care. I'm scared Remy's crossed some invisible point of no return or is damn close. "Thanks—for trying."

He nods, staring out at the sea.

"How was the surf?"

Mick sighs. "Superb."

"Don't you mean ripper?" I tease.

He shakes his head and breaks into...Valley Girl speak. "Ohmigod, it was *so* totally gnarly, you know? Like, if ripper and rad had a baby, it would be *so* completely *tubular. So choice.* Like, no duh."

My mouth drops then breaks into a goofy grin. I'm literally speechless. This is a whole new side to Mr. Wonderful, and *I like it.*

He winks at me, smirks, and stares down the beach so I can no longer track his expression.

I nudge his shoulder with mine. "Just when you think you know a guy…"

"You know me," he says quietly, seriously.

My insides liquify, his words melting me with their tender honesty. I'm ninety-nine percent certain there's a short list of people who've earned this privilege.

I inhale a salt-air breath. "How are things at home?"

"Funny you should ask."

That perks me up, and my eyes swing to his.

"We're about to move the old man to a facility. He had another stroke."

"That's…a load off, isn't it?"

He gives his head a vigorous shake, flipping his damp hair out of his face. "A huge load off. He needs round-the-clock care now, so he's parked at the hospital. The doctor said he doesn't see him living out the year."

"I guess that's a blessing." My fingers find more sand to sift, merely for something to do.

"Goddamn right it is."

"I'm sorry," I say, hugging my knees to my chest, my eyes fixed on the horizon. "I shouldn't be out here burdening you with my problems. You already have enough on your plate."

"Jax."

I glance over. His stare bores into mine.

"I'm glad you're here. You're never a burden, so stop thinking it. I want to know if Remy's fucking up and help if I can."

My head bobs, my throat swallowing the lump there.

He cocks his head. "Want to get some breakfast? There's a great diner near here."

A slow smile reverses my frown. "I'd love to."

OVER HEARTY, HEAPING PLATES OF FOOD, MICK'S eyes light as he fills me in on how it's going at the boatyard. He's already learned to operate some of the boats, and one of the guys is showing him how to sail. If there was any question he's in his element, it's gone.

He prods me for updates about school and my job, and I invite him to eat at Original Joe's because he won't be sorry.

"Written any more poems lately?"

My neck heats, and I'm momentarily flustered. "No, but I'm writing a short story. Not for class...for myself."

"Do I get to read it?"

"You want to?"

"Hell yeah. I want to read everything you write."

I'm tongue-tied. No one's ever expressed anything I compose might have value. It knocks my damn socks off.

"Thanks," I say softly.

His eyes lock with mine. "I'm proud of you. Not like my opinion counts for shit. You, on the other hand, should be proud of yourself...because that does count, that does mean something."

It's a new way of looking at it. I've always wanted everyone else to be proud of me, validate me—but they haven't. Perhaps I need to give those *attagirls* to myself and stop hoping others will verify my self-worth. It's enlightening.

Reaching across the table, I cover his hand. "You always have something profound and wise to say."

Mick barks out a laugh. "I don't know about that."

# FIFTY-THREE

Over the next month, Remy and I split further apart. I'm immersed in school and work. He, on the other hand, is majoring in Getting High and Frequently Unreachable—and he was furious with Mick for confronting him about it, and me for instigating it.

When Remy and I do connect and I deign to question his whereabouts, he's vague and defensive, omitting details about where he goes and with whom.

My worries he'll wind up in trouble or dead amplify. We fight and argue. He makes me feel like a nag then I blame him for turning me into one.

We see each other less and less, and it becomes harder to find common ground. The divide widens between us, one I'm clueless how to bridge.

Conversely, Mick and I draw closer together.

I call him with funny stories, to complain about a professor, or to laugh over the Pinto some guy lowered with purple undercarriage lights.

He leans on me over getting his father resettled and regales me with animated tidbits about working at the boatyard.

I show up at said boatyard, and he gives me a tour. He takes me out on a small sailboat—handling it like he's done it a million times, his joyful expression contagious.

Another night, Mick shows up at Original Joe's with my roommates, and I sit with them for twenty minutes during my break. They stuff themselves and linger, drinking and chatting until I'm off work. Mick's eyes track me around the room, which I know because mine constantly swing back to his.

We walk a slippery slope, our feelings like the arms of two octopuses, reaching and retracting, our tentacles desperate to suction to one another.

We don't act on any of it, remaining platonic best friends, but it's akin to a ticking time bomb.

# FIFTY-FOUR

It's a glorious Saturday, temps already in the high seventies and climbing, a beach day sculpted by the universe—a gift as fall begins.

Jas navigates the winding highway to Santa Cruz with me as her copilot. Kit's working or she'd be cruising in the Monza with us. I'm fighting with Remy—again—and trying desperately not to think about it.

When Jas pops in a Boston tape and cranks it, "More Than a Feeling" blasts from the speakers. My resentments take a back seat as I slide my bare foot out the window and tap my hand against the rooftop in time with the music. We sing along, hair flying on the breeze as we speed toward the beach.

We hit bumper-to-bumper traffic, shamelessly flirting with guys in an old pickup truck who are not-so-ironically trying to pick us up. We ditch them before exiting the highway, drive through downtown Santa Cruz, and park in a metered spot.

We walk through an opening in the boardwalk, instantly bombarding my senses with all the sights, sounds, and smells, infused with a hit of nostalgia. Squeals erupt from various rides, and the familiar crank of the chain lugging a new batch of riders up the Giant Dipper roller coaster is music to my ears. Once they hit the drop, more screams serenade us and I smile, knowing how you fly out of your seat enough to hit the lap rail holding you inside the cars. Buttery popcorn, caramelized spun sugar, and other heavenly aromas waft through the air.

We descend the stairs to the beach, and I kick off my flip-flops, eager to feel the sand beneath my bare feet. My soles burn in seconds, and both of us scurry to an open spot to quickly make camp.

An intermittent wind whips hair in my face and challenges us to get our towels unfurled, but minutes later, we've stripped down to our swimsuits, slathered on tanning oil, and are soaking up the rays.

A comfortable sigh leaves my lips. "I love the beach."

"Kill me now and I'll die a happy woman," Jas murmurs.

"If only there was a ripped lifeguard to serve us beverages and wait on us hand and foot."

"Definitely. And another to massage me."

"Nothing else?"

She giggles. "Oh, I can think of a few more *duties*."

I laugh, but the combination of the sun's heat and where this conversation takes my imagination shoots straight to my bikini bottom.

"How's everything with your boy toys?" she asks.

My lips quirk. "They are not my toys. But they *are* my boys." I pause. "Things with Remy have been weird for a while."

"Because you don't see each other much?"

"That's part of it. He parties too hard too often. I'm worried he's in trouble with drugs, mostly the coke. And he's been evasive lately...but I guess those go hand in hand."

Jas hums.

"I knew it would be tougher once I moved to San Jose.

We both work, and I have school, and it's hard to coordinate our schedules. It just...really sucks."

"Do you want it to work out?"

My brow furrows. "Why wouldn't I?"

Jas clears her throat. "Mick. You know you love him."

"I love them both. I'm pretty sure they both love me. Things have gotten...messy." I pause, considering that statement. "Maybe they've always been messy."

She snorts. "That's what I like to call a problem of prosperity."

A chuckle escapes even though our situation is far from funny. "I'm worried someone's going to get hurt. Namely me."

"Sounds like you need to talk to Remy, sort things out."

"Yep. Except every time I try, we wind up arguing. We're fighting now."

"Ugh. That's the worst."

"It's totally unsettling." And what if he's intentionally, or unintentionally, pushing me away? What if he's...I bolt upright. "Oh, shit."

"What?"

"It just dawned on me that with Remy being evasive, and such a jerk, maybe he's cheating on me." I fish out my cigarettes and lighter, puffing hard once I've got one lit.

"That seems like a big assumption, Jax."

Reconfiguring myself to sit cross-legged, I glance her way. "Remy used to be a real player, shamelessly unfaithful—without any obvious guilt. So much that I never saw myself getting involved with him."

"And yet, here you are."

I take another long drag, talking through the exhale. "He pledged the loyalty card, and I believed him. But damn if something doesn't smell rotten in Denmark."

"Or Oakland."

"Shit!" I mutter, flicking the ash and staring out at the waves.

"Don't jump to conclusions. You need to talk to him."

Nodding, I stub my cigarette into the sand, extinguishing the cherry. "I'm going up to the boardwalk to get a dipped cone. And before you ask, yes, I'm drowning my sorrows with chocolate. Want anything?"

"I'll come with you."

SKIN CRISPY FROM A DAY IN THE SUN AND SALTY from wading in the Pacific, we head home. I've already decided to call Remy tonight and get us back on better footing...but I also can't shake this latest revelation. Is he fucking around on me?

Nothing else fully explains his behavior. And why wouldn't he? He never stayed faithful to Karin—or anyone prior, if memory serves. Now our relationship takes effort. I'm not around nor am I in proximity to bust him, which probably makes it more tempting. Put it all together and Remy's defaulting to...Remy.

Jas slams on the brakes and my upper body jerks hard against the lap belt, snapping my neck at a painful angle. Brake lights flare before us and we screech to a halt, barely missing the car's bumper. A paralyzed breath releases.

*That was fucking close.*

A car rams into our rear end, smashing us into the car in front of us. Metal squeals, crunching and mashing all around us, combining with Jas's screams. My head knocks hard against the window frame, stars flickering in my vision.

The world spins then slows. Dazed, my eyes swivel to Jas. She stares back, equally shook.

"You're bleeding," she says, her voice strained.

My fingers drift along my scalp until landing on a sticky patch where the hairline meets my forehead. Swiping through it, I bring my fingers into view, observing the crimson evidence. Dizziness washes over me.

Blinking slowly, my breath labors. "Jas," I rasp, "are you okay?"

Her eyes flit wildly, terror reflecting when they land on me. "I...don't...know." Her voice breaks and tears trickle down her cheeks.

My hand finds her forearm and gives a reassuring squeeze, pain radiating from my neck. "I'm right here. We're going to get out of this. We're going to be alright."

Forcing calm, measured breaths from my lungs helps me stem the panic coming at me from all sides.

The giant spider decal on the Monza stares at us, deformed atop the mangled hood, now pushed toward the windshield at a disorienting angle. Steam rises from underneath, making it look like a deranged horror show.

I shift to survey our predicament, my neck throbbing from the movement. Traffic's at a dead stop, cars skewed at various angles, a scary mess involving what appears to be many vehicles. A painful glimpse behind us confirms we're wedged between two cars, and a fresh wave of wooziness forces me to look straight ahead.

Sweat breaks out across my skin, and a high-pitched whine rings in my ears. We're trapped. Sitting ducks. Like I was at the gas station.

I fumble for the door handle and give it a push. Shock waves echo through my body, my efforts yielding zilch. Using more bodyweight, I bang into it harder, but the door stays firmly shut, keeping us imprisoned. Hysteria knocks louder and the pain smarts like a sonofabitch. Defeated, my back slumps against the seat, quiet tears sliding down my cheeks. *Calm. Stay calm. We're going to be okay. Please let us be okay.*

Sirens wail in the distance, a smidgeon of relief coursing through me. "Help is on the way, Jas. Hang tight."

The two of us clutch hands and wait.

# FIFTY-FIVE

Firefighters, paramedics, and law enforcement zoom onto the scene, sirens and lights blazing. A flurry of activity plays out around us. Jas grips my hand—her tension palpable even as the shock wanes.

In the time it takes anyone to address us, the sky's warm hues fade to black, the swirling lights turning more vivid.

Finally, a firefighter assesses our vehicle situation and crouches low enough to talk through the driver's side window.

"I'm John, and I'm here to help you," he says evenly, sea green eyes flickering between Jas and me underneath his helmet. "Are either of you injured?"

"My neck hurts," Jas answers, wincing when she tries to turn her head his way. "I think that's it. I'm not sure." Fresh tears coat her wet cheeks.

"What's your name?"

"Jas."

"Jas, I'm going to reach in and place my hands on your head. Don't fight it, just go with my flow."

John performs a cursory exam and seems satisfied with whatever he finds. "Try not to move your head. We're going to get you out of here as soon as possible and into an ambulance so you can be properly assessed at the hospital." John's gaze lands on me. "And what's your name?"

"Jacqui."

"Looks like you knocked your head pretty good, Jacqui. Are you hurt anywhere else?" His voice remains calm and warm.

"My neck is stiff, and I have a massive headache. But nothing's broken or anything."

"Have either of you attempted to get out of the car?"

"I did," I volunteer, "but my door's stuck. I didn't body slam it or anything though."

John's lips quirk. "Maybe leave the body slamming to the pros. We'll do a vehicle extrication, essentially cut what we need to safely remove you from the car, then get you on your way to the hospital."

"Can we ride together?" Jas pleads. "Please? I want her by my side."

"I'll see what I can do. This is a multi-car accident, and we're getting everyone taken care of as fast as we can. Sit tight a while longer. I'll be back." He raps his knuckles once on top of the car. "You're doing great, ladies."

John leaves and relief spreads palpably through me. We're getting out of this mutilated heap of metal soon. We've been trapped here over an hour. I fantasize about a shower, food, sleep...Remy. My worries recede considering death knocked on my door. I just want to feel his arms around me.

"He was cute," Jas says, her breathing shallow.

A snort leaves my lips. "I knew you were going to say that."

"And seems super sweet. Do you think he's single?"

I start to shake my head and think better of it when I'm met with a rigid resistance. Note to self: Stop moving.

"One way to find out," I grit out, pain throbbing from the shoulders up.

"Look at my Monza," Jas whimpers.

"I know, sweetie. It's a sad sight." And clearly totaled.

"I fucking love this car."

My fingers grope blindly for her hand again. "Me too. If it's any consolation, you can replace the car. Can't replace you, Jas. This could have been so much worse."

She sniffles. "I know."

WE CALL KIT TO PICK US UP FROM THE HOSPITAL after getting released. She goes into a fretful tailspin upon hearing about the accident, calming when she's reassured our injuries aren't life-threatening.

Jas sports a flesh-colored padded neck brace for severe whiplash and thankfully, nothing worse. A bandage covers the six stitches on my head, and I'm still spacey from a mild concussion.

When Kit arrives, we limp outside...beleaguered, drained, and decidedly not enthusiastic to ride in another vehicle. She hugs us gingerly before we get into her Honda. We fill her in on the gory details and cute firefighter as she drives us home without incident.

We enter our condo, relief consuming me again. *I'm alive and intact.*

All I want to do is shower the sand and fear and blood from my body, put on comfy loungewear, and hear Remy's voice. I imagine he'll haul his ass out here to care for me and wrap his arms around me all night, waking me up every few hours because of the concussion. There's no better nurse than Remy. Renewed chills roll through my body thinking about that horrible stick-up for the second time tonight, but also a surging warmth when I think about how my boyfriend rescued me—and cared for me.

Sniffling back tears, I shuffle upstairs, disrobe, and let the shower's warm spray coat my skin. After standing for several blissful minutes, I carefully clean my body, keeping the bandage covering my stitches dry as ordered. Washing my hair around the dressing is a bitch, but manageable.

I'm stiff and sore and would kill for a few aspirin chased by a tall glass of wine, but that's off the table for another two days until I'm cleared of this head injury.

I'm not complaining.

My soft T-shirt and sweats cradle my body in a pillowy heaven, my mood considerably improved after getting clean and comfortable. I sink into my bed, propping my head on the pillows, and dial Remy's number.

It rings several times, the sound lonely and hollow.

*Fuck.* My chest hurts, also lonely and hollow. I need him. Where is he?

Knuckles rap softly on my door. "Jax?"

"Come in."

Kit enters, her gaze focused on my face. "How ya doin', train wreck?"

"Tired. Sore. And now bummed. Remy's not answering his phone."

She gives me a sympathetic smile. "Looks like I'll be your personal nursemaid for the night. Try and rest. I'll be back in here every few hours to wake you up and make sure you're still alive."

"No sponge bath?" I joke, my eyes already closing.

"Maybe for you, princess," she murmurs, the door snicking quietly closed seconds later.


As promised, Kit wakes me every three hours, turning on the light to check I'm conscious, test my eye movement, ask if my head hurts, refill my water. She's a good roomie—a hell of a lot better than my absent boyfriend, who doesn't answer the phone *all night*.

Am I pissed? Fuck yes.

*Where is he?*

Am I suspicious? Heartbreakingly so.

*Who is he with?*

Am I out of my mind with worry? That too.

*Is he dead in a ditch?*

I'm also stuck here, unable to drive or operate machinery (do blenders count?) for another day. My head and body ache like I spent the night tumbling in a dryer. My neck is painfully stiff from a minor case of whiplash—nothing as bad as what Jas must be enduring. And my stitched head gash is tender, but at least my scar will be hidden by my hairline.

Placing the receiver back on the hook after another unanswered call to Remy, I'm about to go check on Jas when the phone trills. *Finally.* My emotions battle, expecting it to be Mr. Missing In Action. It will take a herculean effort not to scream in his ear.

I answer, going for steely but failing. My voice only sounds rough since they're my first spoken words of the day.

"Jax?" It's Mick.

"It's me." The air whooshes from my lungs, sensations rioting at the sound of his voice. It's almost pathetic the way I sink into believing—hoping—he cares. Anyone. Fucking someone. My nose burns, throat working to dislodge the thick knot already there.

"Did I wake you?"

"No," I croak.

"What's wrong?"

Get a grip. Get a grip. Get a grip. "I'm a little messed up right now. Jas and I got into a car accident last night. It was scar—"

"Are you hurt?"

"Just a little banged up. Needed stitches on my head. The doctor diagnosed me with a mild concussion. And I'm sore, but I'm okay, really. Jas too. She's got a bad case of whiplash, and her poor car is totaled."

"Shit. When did this happen?"

"Last night coming back from Santa Cruz. You know the twisty part of Highway 17? We were in a multi-car crash where everyone rear-ended each other, a real mess."

"You know you can't sleep with a concussion, right? Did you...is Remy with you?" He sounds tense.

Well, that answers one question. Remy's clearly not with Mick. "I've tried getting a hold of him all night. No answer. But Kit woke me up every few hours and I seem to be in the clear on the concussion thing. I've got a headache, and my cut is tender but no blurry vision or weird stuff."

"Thank fuck you're alright," he mutters, his tone turning softer. "I'm sorry this happened, baby."

My heart swells with such intensity, I'm not sure my chest can contain it. *Stop it, stupid heart. Your heart belongs to another now. Another who is probably out fucking some other broad.*

"Shit," he huffs. "Old habits die hard."

It's not even an old habit. We had so little time together. Agonizingly short and yet...sublime.

"I don't mind." Mind? I'm over here bathing in it. Time to change the subject. "I know what I'm stuck doing today, but what about you?"

"Going for a sail. Thought if you and Remy were game, you might like to come."

"Let's pour lemon juice and salt in that wound. Oh yes, that's much better."

He laughs. "Hey, my intentions were to show you a good time."

A smile tugs my lips wide. "Just can't help sticking your foot into it today."

"My intentions were purely honorable," he clarifies. I can hear the smile in his voice.

"Of course they were. You're a gentleman."

He coughs. "I try, although if I'm honest, my thoughts are not always gentlemanly when it comes to you."

I laugh, hiding the palpitations that surge.

"Do you want me to come out instead?" He offers, getting our conversation back on safe ground. "Do you need help?"

*Yes. And yes.* And Nurse Mick? *A million percent yes.* I'd never survive, plus I'm not about to ruin his Sunday. "You're sweet to offer, but I'm fine. Kit's waiting on me hand and foot. I'm taking full advantage."

"You sure?"

*No.* "I'm thrilled you have your life back somewhat. Go sailing, El Capitan. I'll think about you with the wind at your back, hand on the wheel, living large in your happy place. Have a cold beer for me."

"There's my writer. That sounds damn poetic, Jax."

My volatile heart goes all mushy again, leaning into his every word. "That's me."

"I'll call and check on you when I get back. Try and rest."

"I will. Thanks for calling, Mick."

We hang up, his words filling me with warmth, and keeping me forever tormented in the muddled abyss that exists between us.

# Fifty-Six

Jas, Kit, and I lounge in the living room Sunday doing little except eating, watching TV, and occasionally dozing. Jas admits being miserable in her cervical collar, unable to move her head much or find a comfortable position. The ER doctor said she may have to wear it for three to six weeks and if that's true, she may claw at the walls, not just her foam brace. She's doubly depressed about her Spyder.

Kit caters to us invalids all day, even venturing out to score our favorite junk food: McDonald's cheeseburgers and pints of Häagen-Dazs Chocolate Chocolate Chip ice cream. They're the perfect accompaniment to my pity party and by the look of Jas, hers too.

I've long given up on Remy, no longer bothering to try tracking him down. He can fuck the fuck off. I did call my parents. They'd eventually see the insurance bill and I figured they'd want to know. Shockingly, for the second time in a couple of weeks, they expressed appropriate sentiments smacking of genuine concern. Maybe I've judged them too harshly. Or perhaps now that I'm no longer living at home, they appreciate me more. I'm not stupid enough to hope, although a tiny part of me does anyway.

KIT ROUSES ME FROM SLEEP, AND I SHAKE OFF THE cobwebs, realizing I'm on the living room couch.

"Remy's on the phone," she whispers, peering over me.

My reaction is instantaneous, the adrenaline already surging. I haul myself upstairs and into my room for privacy.

"I've got it, Kit," I say once the phone rests against my ear.

She hangs up and Remy's resulting "Hey!" sounds loud and obnoxiously cheerful.

"Where the fuck have you been?" My tone remains flat, devoid of cheer, the opposite of his.

"Yosemite!" he says belligerently. Jesus, is he coked up? *Again?*

"What the hell are you doing in Yosemite? And with who? When?"

"Vinny and I got a wild hair yesterday and thought why not drive down, see a few sights?" He laughs—but nothing, absolutely nothing, is funny about this.

"Are you high right now?"

"We're rolling, baby! Been rolling since Friday night."

That's almost forty-eight hours of snorting blow and probably drinking and definitely not sleeping.

"You're such an asshole. I needed you last night. I was in a fucking car accident!"

"What?"

"Yeah, Rem. I could have died." It's a bit dramatic, but still true-ish.

"Are you hurt?"

"Of course I'm hurt. I have stitches, a concussion, whiplash. I *needed* you! Not to mention being worried out of my damn mind when you were MIA. And all the time, you were high on cocaine down in fucking Yosemite National Park? *Awesome.*"

"Jacqui..."

"What?" I snap.

"I didn't know something was going to happen to you. It sounds like you're alright."

"Whatever. I've got to go."

"Don't be a bitch."

The incredulous huff leaving my mouth says it all. "Fuck you, Remy."

I slam the phone against the cradle, then pop it off the hook once the call disconnects. Absolute motherfucker. He can go straight to hell without passing go or collecting his two hundred fucking dollars.

Punching my fist into the bed pillow, pain rocks me from spine to skull, accompanied by a burn roaring straight through my blood at the injustice of it all. The accident. Remy. My life.

Carefully laying back against the pillows, I calm my breathing. Remy's selfishness and lack of empathy surprises me. How can he treat me this way? He's totally in the wrong here. Completely fucked up...again. And acting like a prick.

Yosemite? On a drunken, drugged-up whim?

He's unhinged. Beyond irresponsible. He's left the proverbial building.

And party boy's not here for me. Nor is he running straight home to comfort me.

*He doesn't care.*

*How can he not care?*

# FIFTY-SEVEN

Another two weeks pass, and I'm fully healed physically. Emotionally, I'm on less stable ground. Remy drove out the week after my accident and spent the night. We talked, cried, and made love, putting another flimsy bandage on our relationship.

It's clear something's out of kilter between us, the divide widening as one day bleeds into the next. I don't know how to fix it—or how badly I want to, but the tension keeps my guts churning and mind whirling.

When we're together, the love thrums between us, and we're connected. It reminds me of pulled taffy—stringy and near breaking when apart, but strong and sweet when it binds and solidifies.

There's no denying how deep my caring runs. He's my best friend—every bit as much as Mick—even when he's fucking up or wasting his life.

But since a fissure formed, I'm questioning his honesty, integrity, and certainly commitment—all topics I've skated over like they're under a solid plane of lake ice. One that's cracked and about to swallow me if it breaks.

These are the thoughts washing over me while I'm

standing in the shower on Saturday afternoon—and stay with me as I dress and blow-dry my hair. It's time to face it head on. We need to talk, really clear the air, and be honest.

*No more pussyfooting around.*

Grabbing my keys, I make a rash decision: I'm going to Oakland unannounced.

REMY TOLD ME HE HAD A PARENTAL OBLIGATION, but I swing by his apartment first anyway, hoping to catch him and avoid the Remingtons. Wishful thinking—he's not home.

I drive to his parent's house next, painfully aware I'm clueless about what he's doing today, which speaks volumes and fortifies my resolve.

When I arrive, his unmistakable Camaro sits parked out front. I drum my fingers against the steering wheel, silently debating. I'm showing up uninvited and I'm already uneasy about Remy and me as it is—but as my boyfriend once advised: *carpe diem.*

I walk to the door, ring the bell, and wait.

Mrs. Remington answers, surprise etched across her face, which she quickly composes into something akin to a bitchy queen lording over her serfs.

"Good evening, Mrs. Remington. Is Remy here?"

She stares at me intently, openly appraising my faded jeans, peasant top, and flip-flops. "*Randy,*" she emphasizes, "is unavailable right now."

My brows furrow. "I don't understand. I've driven over an hour to speak with him, and it's important. Apologies if I'm interrupting your family time but I'm sure you can spare him for a few minutes."

Her coiffed hair doesn't budge as she inclines her head. "It's unfortunate you've wasted your time, but that does not mean I have to waste mine. I'll let him know you dropped by," she says, shutting the door in my face.

My body immobilizes as if turned to stone, and I stand there, stunned. The slow burn from my neck heating gives way to the hot flame of anger. "Fucking bitch," I mutter. My teeth grind together as I turn and stomp toward my car. Halfway there, I pause.

Then I stalk back and ring the bell three times.

Mrs. Remington answers again, and this time, there's zero pretense. "I already said you're not welcome here. To be absolutely clear and direct, I mean ever."

My arms cross, chest heaving, even while a part of me shrinks. "Why?"

"You're not good enough for my son, and never will be. You're nothing but a trashy gold-digger."

I gasp, my mouth falling open as my eyes widen. I'd love to wipe the smug expression off her face with some clever retort, but my manners war with the idea.

My limbs are so tightly crossed, my fingernails dig into my skin. "You don't know me."

The self-satisfied smile inching across her face belies her true nature. "I know everything I need to about you. You're nothing but a little tramp," she hisses.

Indignation spreads through me like molten lava. "That's..." I sputter. "You're way out of line, and you couldn't be more wrong." My voice cracks on the last word.

Her expression turns almost pitying. "Doubtful, but no matter. Randy's dating other women. We're working on a suitable companion."

The air leaves my lungs at this unknown tidbit and Mrs. Remington's stature inflates, visibly pleased with herself.

*Fuck her. Fuck Remy. Fuck this.*

I'm about to shove off before I say something I'll regret when Remy appears. His sapphire eyes bug out when he sees me on the doorstep, a multitude of emotions crossing his face.

My glare could burn holes through his eye sockets.

"What...what are you doing here, Jacqui?"

I jut out my left hip and place my palm against it. "Apparently, ruining your *date*."

Mrs. Remington stands proudly, not ruffled in the slightest, but I barely spare her a glance.

"Mom, I need a minute alone," he says.

"Don't be long, and do *not* keep your date waiting."

"Mom!" he implores. Turning back to me, he steps outside, shutting the door behind him.

I've half a mind to leave him in the rear view. Instead, I recross my arms and glare, waiting for his explanation. For the first time, I catalog how he's dressed: navy button-down shirt, khaki slacks, and Sperry Topsiders, as if he's at a fucking country club. My pulse-point twitches against my neck.

"Your mother," I seethe, "called me a tramp. A fucking *tramp*, Remy. And a gold-digger. *And* she said you're *dating*! What the fuck is going on?"

"Christ," he mutters, his hand scrubbing his jaw. "I'm so fucking sorry, Jacqui. My mom had no right to say that."

"Which part?" I grit out.

"Any of it."

"Are you dating?" I ask from between clenched teeth.

His head hangs. "It's not what you think."

I snort, wholly impatient for him to explain this shit, and already preparing for lies.

He takes a step toward me, one hand outstretched, and I retreat. Pain flickers in his eyes, but he stops and shoves his hands in his pockets.

"My parents—mostly my *mom*—are worried about their precious money and where it's going to end up. They've made marriage another stipulation to get my trust fund, another hoop to jump through, and they're growing irritated with me on, well, every front. So, they've been forcing me to come over here on weekends to meet families—"

"And let me guess...their daughters?"

He stares at the ground, kicking a pebble with his stupid leather boat shoe. "Something along those lines. But I'm just going through the motions. I'm not doing anything."

I flash him a withering glare. "Not. Doing. Anything? You lying, two-faced motherfucker. Fuck you! And fuck your bitchy mother. And fuck your totally inappropriate father, who was ready to screw me in the bathroom last December."

I turn on my heel to leave.

He lunges, latching his hand to my wrist. "Jacqui, wait! Please!"

"I'm such an idiot. I've been wondering what the hell is going on with you. Why you've been distant. I've tried not to think the worst. To believe you're not lying and cheating and fucking other wom—"

"I haven't—"

"I've been worried about you because I *care about you*. Despite how you've gotten pissed at me for it, called me a nag, made *me* out to be the bad guy." I shake my head. "And all the while..." My throat knots, and the dam threatens to break.

"Jacqui, don't leave. Please..."

I'm not waiting—or wasting—one more second. Stalking away, I lift my right hand and flip him the bird. He's not worth any more words.

# FIFTY-EIGHT

Hurt and outrage rain down, deluging me as my VW careens around turns, my foot pressing the accelerator and speeding recklessly through the straights. The ugly words and allegations—and Remy's deceit—replay with every mile. I should pull over, but don't, gassing it onto the freeway and heading to the only place my heart pulls.

Mick's.

Maybe because as of this moment, there's no one in this world who cares more about me than Mick. An hour ago, I would have said Remy too, but we all know that yacht just sailed with his trust-funded ass sipping champagne off the bow.

Puffing hard on cigarette after cigarette, my mind whirls, memories from the last several months rolling around in my head. The pieces assemble, reconfiguring into a fresh, unveiled truth, and everything in me longs to torch the fucking puzzle.

What I thought was true was a lie.

The adrenaline ricochets furiously through my bloodstream. After fumbling to light another smoke with shaky hands, my free hand switches on the radio, scanning for a tolerable song. Like a sick joke, it lands on "Lyin' Eyes" by the Eagles, and I scream into the night, violently twisting the selection knob.

Upon arriving at Mick's, I'm drained, sagging with relief when I spot his Mustang sitting in the drive. I'm guessing it's in the vicinity of eight p.m. and once again, I'm showing up somewhere unannounced—which went pretty fucking badly an hour ago.

*Please, please, please don't let him have a date in there.* It'll destroy me if this night goes any further south.

Limbs leaden, I heft myself from the car, trudge up the walkway, and knock on the door.

The outside light flickers on seconds before Mick opens it.

"Hey," he starts with a grin, which slowly fades as he assesses me. "What's wrong?"

I step inside and sink against him, unable to speak for fear tears will fall... and *fuck crying.*

His arms wrap around me, bringing me close, as he kicks the door closed.

My chest heaves a few times, but I stave off the waterfall, submerging into the comfort and safety of Mick Callahan's arms.

"Talk to me, Jax," he murmurs, breath ruffling strands of my hair.

"I just need a minute," I whisper.

"Take your time. I'm not going anywhere."

Mick's embrace is a reprieve, allowing me precious minutes to ignore the ugliness, the stinging words that ring true, the way Remy allowed it. The weight of my expectations and disappointment may as well be an anvil tied to my foot. Vacillating between *I've been wronged* and *I'm worthless* makes it tough to cling to my righteous indignation, even though traces remain.

We break apart and he fetches me a glass of water and waits patiently for me to speak.

I drop onto the sofa, clearing my throat and taking a restorative breath. Then I start at the beginning and regurgitate it all, including the roiling inner turmoil I'm desperately wishing would fade.

Mick listens attentively. He doesn't interrupt or ask questions. When I'm finished, he looks thoughtful, nodding his head.

Then he gives me a pronounced shrug. "Virginia always was kind of a cunt."

Something cracks inside me, and I burst into laughter—the uncontrollable, unstoppable variety—until happy tears dampen my cheeks.

Mick starts laughing at me, then with me, and soon I'm aware the anvil's gone, its tether cut loose by an invisible blade. Mood lifted, I'm filled with the giddy satisfaction that comes with having a friend on your side. Versus one who doesn't even defend you to their mother.

"Don't shoot the messenger, but you should hear Remy out. This smacks of his mother's BS, and maybe he told you the truth, or tried to."

I scowl.

Mick pretends to scowl back.

We share another laugh.

"I'm glad you were home," I say with all sincerity.

"Makes one of us," he jokes.

"Screw you."

He smirks. "Is that a proposition?"

My lips clamp together. I don't have the strength to fight...this. Him. Us. Or flirting that veers from harmless toward hazardous.

"What *are* you doing here on a Saturday night? Since you're a free man?" I leave out single and devastatingly good-looking.

"Packing." He flashes a big grin, and his dimple winks at me—a proposition all its own, without Mick even knowing it.

I clap my hands. "You got the place?"

He nods. "Wait until you see it. It's fucking great. I'd take you out there now, but it's too dark to see anything. Want to stay over and go in the morning?"

"Hell yes."

I don't have to think twice. I don't want to be alone tonight, even if I'm throwing caution to the wind with Mr. Dimple...who hasn't been an asshole in a long, long time.


MICK FIXES ME A SANDWICH AFTER MY STOMACH growls. He returns to packing, and I help. It takes my mind off my life and the questions I'm not prepared to answer.

We finish around midnight and we're both ready to hit the rack.

"You want to sleep in my bed?" he asks. "I can take the couch or—"

"I want to stay with you." We share a loaded look, but he blinks it away.

We crawl under the covers, and he turns the radio on low. A Peter Frampton song ends and the telltale opening guitar riffs from U2's "Two Hearts Beat as One" filter in. It's my new favorite song, and I haven't told Mick it reminds me of him, of us.

Bono's potent vocals give life to those lyrics describing everything Mick and me, and hearing it in such proximity to my ocean overwhelms me and my fragile, splintered heart.

He settles next to me, energy crackling between us, thunderous despite the fact we're not talking and barely touching. I'm acutely aware of our minimal clothing, especially when our bare legs collide, sending the volts flying.

"Come here," he whispers.

I roll onto my side, resting my head in the crook of his arm, every nerve ending supercharged—and wide fucking awake. His arms circle me, holding me snug. He kisses my forehead, and my breath catches. I wait, wondering if he heard, or if it can be shoved back into the cave from whence it came.

Suddenly, I don't care.

I let go, give in. *I'm so tired of fighting.*

Raising my head, I offer up a silent invitation he accepts.

In the dark, with only a dim glow coming from his clock radio, his hand cups my face, drawing me to his mouth. When our lips meet, heat blazes through me, igniting nerve endings, my entire being twinging with want. But it's the jolt to my heart, the recognition, stealing my breath.

*Sweet surrender.*

His lips press softly at first, deepening by the second, and when I whimper into his mouth, he consumes me, taking what's his. His tongue dances along my lower lip, and I throw open the doors, wanting him with every cell in my body.

*I'm yours. Forever yours.*

"I've never stopped wanting you," he says, the timbre of his voice low, his words caressing me in wholly different ways.

My words flow easily, releasing what I've kept so desperately trapped. "I've never stopped loving you."

The scant light gives me a glimmer of those compelling gray eyes. "And I've never loved anyone the way I do you. You are everything to me."

How I've longed to hear these words. My hand cups his cheek, coasting along the razor stubble, and I swallow down the emotion lodged in my throat.

Mick pins my body to the bed, hovering above me, and our lips meet, sealing our sentiments, searing into me as my heart soars from his confession.

"I want to feel you, all of you," he murmurs.

I nod, still bereft of words, and we quickly shed our clothing.

Both yearning for one thing, he merges us together, and a few tears slide down my face unbidden. I tremble beneath him and am astonished to realize he's trembling too. The intensity lays thick between us as we savor the sensation of how he fills me utterly and completely.

*Two hearts beating as one.*

His eyes stay locked on mine as his thrusts begin, slow and decadent. It's a love letter, one requiring no words.

He turns hungrier, driving into me with need. Longing. Desire. He possesses me, leaving no question in either of our minds we belong together.

He reaches the crescendo, meshing our bodies still closer. We free-fall over the cliff, clutching each other and absorbing the profundity of what we just consummated.

# FIFTY-NINE

In the morning, after a quick breakfast, we load up the Mustang with boxes and Mick drives us to his new digs in Half Moon Bay. We're in a sunny mood, and the temperature matches, giving us a mid-seventies, blue-sky day—even in late October.

My window's down, bare foot propped on the dash. "This is why I can never imagine leaving California."

He cocks his head. "Never say never."

Mick pulls up at a small, two-story cottage near a larger house, explaining his landlords live there. It's far enough away to give both privacy and space, yet still clearly connected.

We head inside. Light filters into the floor-to-ceiling windows overlooking the cliffs and vast ocean. The main level is one big room with a kitchen taking up one corner and plenty of space for a dining table and living room furniture. There's also a bathroom and closet. A loft bedroom and full bathroom claims the upstairs. I love everything about it, and my heart swells. Mick needs this. For a man who lives and breathes for the outdoors, especially the water, he couldn't have found a more apropos dwelling.

It's easy to picture him here, at peace.

I'd be lying if I didn't admit picturing myself here with him.

Reaching for him in front of the windows, my fingers curl through his belt loops on either side. "It's perfect, Mick."

He grins and nods.

"You deserve it."

He shrugs, ever the humble one, but lets out a long sigh as we both return to gazing at the incredible vista.

"Come on. Let's go down to the beach," he says, tugging my hand.

A smile spans my face. "You don't have to ask me twice."

He kisses me quickly, leading me by the hand to the edge of the bluff, where a crude trail is worn into the cliff. My breath catches at the view below. Stretching out the size of a few football fields is a private beach, shielded by towering cliffs and greeting the Pacific like a welcome mat.

Going first, Mick guides me down the rocky path. It's slippery and treacherous in places, but all worth it once my toes hit the sand and I get a close-up of every magnificent detail.

"Private, you say? What could you do here, I wonder?" My eyebrow arches.

He grabs me around the waist and throws me over his shoulder. "I could plunge your pretty ass into the water."

"Don't you dare!" I shriek.

He howls and continues toward the ocean.

"Mick!"

He stops and slides my body against his until my feet sink back into the sand, his dimpled smile meeting my glare. "Or," he says, inches from my lips, "I could worship you for hours anywhere on this beach whenever I want."

My insides melt and swirl. He cradles my face in his hands, kissing me passionately, and all is forgotten except this, and now.

We walk the windy shoreline, me dipping down to scoop

up colorful seashells on occasion as Mick tells me how he found the place through a guy he works with and other boat-yard happenings.

We've avoided talking about what occurred yesterday with Remy, and I'm trying not to think about it even though it's not going to miraculously resolve itself.

I'm not surprised when he brings it up.

"How are you doing today, Jax?"

I'm honest. "I'm not actively thinking about it."

"Fair. Any regrets...about last night?"

My gaze flies to his. "None. Why...do you?"

He shakes his head. "Nope. Just checking in with you since this is something we've got to deal with at some point."

"I know." My hair whips around me, the long strands obscuring my vision.

"Are you going to talk to Remy?" Mick's tone is soft, but direct with an undertone of something...pressure? *He cares. He wants this...us?* He squints at me through his own wind-tossed waves.

"I guess that's the right thing to do."

He moves closer, wrangling my tresses behind an ear. "It is. Tell me what you need, and I'll do it."

I swallow the knot forming and nod.

"I'm going to unpack the car, but after, do you want to go boating?" His eyes gleam with the offer, and again, I'm struck by how handsome Mr. In-His-Element is when he's happy.

"I'd love to."


We arrive at the boatyard around noon after stopping for beer and snacks. Mick disappears inside the office to see about borrowing a boat and returns ten minutes later.

We collect our refreshments, and I follow him to a beau-tiful vessel docked in their marina, rocking gently with the current. It's gorgeous—a gleaming white fishing charter with navy accents, a covered cockpit, a smooth hull, and plenty of seating. But it's also enormous, with room for a dozen or more people.

"You realize I'll probably be of no assistance, right?" I say.

He shakes his head like I'm ridiculous and extends his hand to help me aboard *Seas the Day.*

I roll my eyes at the name. The way that phrase follows me is downright karmic.

"I don't need you to do anything—"

"Except give you a blow job while you're at the wheel?" I say sweetly.

He chokes on a laugh. "I mean, if you're offering..." He tilts his head my way with a smirk. "What I was going to say is you don't need to do anything unless you *want* to, in which case, I'll show you."

"What if I *want* to give you head?" I offer him my best sexy-but-innocent look.

"Christ," he mutters, bringing me flush against him and kissing me. "Can't say no to heroin."

I smile against his chest, marveling at the sensations of his arms wrapped around me...and all that's transpired in the last several hours.

He kisses my forehead. "Now stop baiting me or we'll never get out of the marina, and we require privacy if you're going to make good on that promise."

We part and he busies himself with unlocking the cabin area and unsnapping the thick plastic windows from the cockpit before leaving to prep the boat.

I scope out the craft top to bottom. The cockpit area is generous, with long, padded benches on which anyone could easily stretch out full length, along with the captain's wheel, console, and a complicated instrument panel. The stern is mostly open, catering to fishing clientele with several pole holders in strategic spots. Rails along the sides help with maneuvering on deck and my fingers glide along the smooth metal as I make my way past the expansive hull to the bow. Standing there, I imagine the waves undulating underneath like a ride. Making a full revolution, I proceed below deck. It's surprisingly spacious—including the headroom—with more bench seats and cabinets. Tiny appliances fill up the galley. A bathroom scarcely big enough to use is behind one closed door. Another reveals a bedroom molded to the shape of the bow and there are other beds tucked into the starboard side.

This impressive ship includes room to eat, lounge and...other things. A telltale tingle murmurs from within, and I ponder whether he'll drop anchor so we can do *other things*.

A nagging cry from the heart persists—the Remy situation, of course—but I swat it away like a pesky fly. Not yet. *Just...not yet.*

I make my way back to the stern, prop my knees on a low seat, and lean against the smooth fiberglass. My hair dances as my lungs inhale the salt air, my gaze scanning the boats peppering the horizon, excitement rising we'll be out there soon.

I turn to say something to Mick, fixating on his flexed biceps working with a rope, when a flash of copper steals my attention—and Remy jumps on deck like a fireball of fury.

# SIXTY

Remy's steely gaze darts between Mick and me, but I refuse to wither. All the anger from yesterday's fuck-show bubbles up with renewed force, even as my heart jackhammers, deafening everything around me. My lips flatten into a thin line, arms crossing like armor, and I laser beam a death-glare right back.

Mick bolts upright, addressing him directly. "Hey, man."

"What the fuck?" Remy snaps, assessing us warily.

"Exactly," I repeat. "What the fuck, Remy?"

His blue eyes soften. "You didn't give me a chance to explain. Instead, you tore out of there like an emotional psychopath—"

"Are you *serious* right now?" If incredulous could be a fashion statement, I'm rocking it.

One hand rifles through his hair. "Shit," he mutters, staring at the ground. "Look, I know you think I cheated on you and—"

"Do you blame me?" My hands fling into the air. "With your track record? Then I learn you're being groomed to find a suitable future fucking wife because I'm—and I quote—'a tramp'?"

A stab of truth pierces me: I've slept with them both. I love them both. Does that make me a slut? *Yes, yes it does.*

Out of my periphery, Mick's calm gaze volleys between us, poised to intervene if needed. The intensity of my thoughts and feelings attacks like machine gun fire. I'm not sure how any of us will be left standing.

"My mom's an asshole. I should have told you, but the whole charade was stupid and meant *nothing* to me. I couldn't risk how you'd react. I figured you'd think the worst, and I'm right. You do."

"You didn't even defend me in front of your mother." My voice quivers. "And that hurts the most."

"Jacqui," he pleads. "I'm sorry. I fucked up."

My eyes cast back to the ocean, tears welling.

Remy steps close, forcing my gaze to his, the pain reflecting in them gutting me. "But tell me this...when it all went down, did you run right out here to Prince Charming?"

My throat constricts, emotion lodged so thick I might choke.

Remy's tenor changes, quiet and tortured. "How long have you two been sleeping together?"

"Last night was the first time," Mick says, dishing it up straight.

My knees buckle and drop to the deck, unable to shoulder the weight of this emotional burden. A part of me wishes the ocean would swallow me whole.

I love these two men from the depths of my very being—despite the heartbreaks, history, problems.

I never planned to fall for them both.

I never meant to hurt them.

I never thought we'd wind up here.

*All I ever wanted was to love them and be loved in return.*

Now I can't see a way where any of us will come out unscathed.

# SIXTY-ONE

This is the moment I've dreaded. The day I lose my two best friends. They're all I have, all I want. *I need them.*

But there's no way we're making it through the pain of this. Our collective deception. Our back-and-forth. Our crossed hearts.

I can't have the proverbial cake and eat it too. We can't be best friends *and* lovers, even if I love them both. The idea of choosing is abhorrent. And I can't come between their own lifetime of friendship. I'm the odd woman out here.

Anguish storms through my body, raining hail as the seconds tick toward my impending execution. My breath comes in fits as I struggle through my sobs.

"Take care of her," Mick barks, his footsteps growing distant.

Remy lifts me into his arms and cradles me, collapsing on a bench seat under the canopy as the engine cranks to life.

Through blurred vision, I glimpse Mick taking the wheel and guiding us out of the marina. "Calm her down."

"I'm trying." Remy's hand strokes my hair as he pleads with me to stop crying.

Their voices fade under the avalanche of emotions burying me. I have no shovel, no way to dig out, everything eclipsed by this dark weight.

"Take the helm," Mick says. "Go straight."

I'm jostled as the two switch places.

"Jax, baby, listen to me," Mick murmurs. "I need you to breathe. In through your nose, out through your mouth. We're going to do it together."

I try and fail, unable to stem the hyperventilating.

"Breathe, baby, please."

Inhaling through my nose takes effort, and I cough when jagged breaths leave my lungs. Tears drench my face.

"That's it. Try again," he says, his tone soothing, calm, just like his hand rubbing my back in long, sure strokes.

More barbed inhalations lead to easier, steadier exhalations.

His hands steady their grip around me. "Good girl."

Through wet, thick lashes, my eyes find his. I see nothing but love and reassurance in those gray pools.

A spark of hope flickers inside me. My gaze swings to Remy, who stands tall, forearms gripping the wheel, the wind riffling through his longer locks on top. Sensing my stare, he meets it, his full of concern and...more. His deep affection is obvious, but also his plea.

Maybe it's not over.

Maybe I—we—haven't ruined it.

Stray hiccups erupt as my breathing evens. My head drops to Mick's chest, and he presses a tender kiss to my forehead.

"We're going to work all this out," he murmurs.

Are we?

I sink into the safety net that is Mick. The groan of the engine pushes the boat through the ocean, the force of the wind thrashing against the ship's flags, coercing them to furl and unfurl, snapping to attention at random. The occasional cry of a gull screeches overhead. My thoughts and worries abate as I breathe in his familiar scent, now mixing with the Pacific, his steady heartbeat pumping under my ear.

But peace is far from my grasp.

What's going to happen?

What do I want?

Can we all come out of this on the other side?

Can we stay friends? More?

I can't lose them.

*I can't.*

My life is unclear without them in it. Worse than unclear...I'm not sure I can go back to how it was before or that I'm strong enough for something so monumentally depressing.

"You good?" Mick asks.

*No.* I lift my head and nod yes anyway.

"I need to do some captaining now." He gives me a one-sided smile, lifts me gingerly off his lap, and slides out. I miss his warm presence immediately.

He takes the wheel, steering the ship while explaining he's about to drop anchor and assessing the instrument panel for inputs. Once he's positioned *Seas the Day* where he wants, he turns off the engine and heads toward the bow.

My eyes collide with Remy's, which shine with concern, or perhaps regret, or sadness, probably all of it. "Jacqui."

I swallow, my heart still lodged in my throat.

"I'm sorry."

Nodding, I manage a few shaky words. "I know. I'm sorry too." The chain releases and my gaze jerks at the sound.

Fifteen minutes later, the charter boat bobs in place. A surge of pride sneaks through my doom at seeing Mick so comfortable in his element. My ocean is meant to be on the ocean, and *he's doing it*.

Mick returns, stopping to pull a six-pack of beer out of a bench cooler in the stern. He doles them out and takes a seat next to me. Remy sits across from us, and my pulse ticks up, readying for confrontation. We inhale the beers and light up cigarettes, releasing an ounce of steam from the pressure cooker threatening to blow.

"Let's hash this shit out, away from prying eyes and ears," Mick says. "I suggest we all take a turn and say our peace." His gaze lands on Remy, then me. "One way or another, we're not leaving this fucking boat until we're cool."

Remy nods. "You going first, Mr. Feelings?"

"Sure will, douchebag." He leans back, slinging an arm across the seat, his wavy chestnut hair dancing in the breeze. "I love her."

My heart shocks back to life with defibrillator force.

Mick takes my hand. "I love you, Jax, and I'm not willing to go back to the way it was. I'm aware I've done some shitty things since we met. I was only trying to protect you, but I hurt you in the process, and never want to be responsible for doing that again."

He huffs out a breath and turns to Remy.

"I love you like a brother, and I don't mean to hurt you either, or be a dick, but this is how I fucking feel, so you're going to have to deal with it."

My fingers squeeze Mick's hand. I'm reeling with sensations and absorbing every syllable.

Remy shakes his head, eyes darting side to side. "Well, that's great. Where does that leave me? I love her too." He scrubs his eyes. "I knew this was going to happen the minute we tried to make this 'we can all be friends' bullshit work."

I reach over and grasp Remy's hand—now I'm holding both of their hands, connecting us all together, even if tenuously.

"Jacqui, I don't give two shits what my parents want," Remy says. "I want *you*. I love you."

"What about your trust fund? You're not going to just throw it all away," I answer, not stating the obvious that *I'm not worth it.* I also squash voicing my other concerns, because the core issue isn't his trust fund, or drug problem, or making time for each other. It's that there are three of us in this baffling equation.

He waves a hand in the air. "That'll shake out over time. This won't. What we have is better than anything I've ever experienced. You can't deny our chemistry—or how we click on every level."

That only cements my thoughts, bringing us to the root of our unsolvable riddle.

My heart bleeds both directions.

It's not fair to either of them. Or to me.

There's a pulsing silence, aside from the snapping flags and lapping waves, and the faint roar in my own ears from my heart splintering.

"What do *you* want, Jacqui?" Mick finally asks.

*You.*

I glance at Remy, eyes pleading. *And you.*

"I love both of you," I whisper.

Their hands fall from mine.

"With my whole heart." My gaze shifts from my copperhead to my brunette. "You changed my life, forever altered it, and my heart beats more for the two of you than it does for myself. I've never felt so loved or cherished by anyone than I have by you. But don't ask me to choose." I falter only a second before picking up steam.

"*Because I choose us.* I know that's selfish and unreasonable and probably hideous from your point of view, but it's the truth. We started out as friends. Became lovers. But it's the love we have for each other that makes choosing one untenable—and unforgivable."

Mick's head cocks. Remy expression remains guarded, unreadable.

"I'd give my life for yours any day. I can never repay what you've given me, which is belonging. Acceptance. Adoration. Love." My eyes prick with more tears. "You guys are my family," I say beseechingly, "and I don't want to lose you."

No one speaks for a few minutes as we come to grips with a no-win situation. The boat rocks gently in the sunshine, completely opposite of the raging emotions deluging us.

"Wait, are you saying..." Remy begins.

"You want us to share you?" Mick finishes.

I blink, confused. No, that's not what I was thinking. I'm spitballing, shooting from the hip, speaking from the heart.

"Um...that's not what I meant." *Or is it?*

"Sounds like a potential solution to me." Remy says, flicking his butt overboard.

My mouth forms an O.

"Can you share, Callahan?" he asks.

Mick is thoughtful, churning this around. "We've already been sharing, asshole. Now it would just be completely out in the open."

*He's right.*

We've shared each other all along, a potent thought that takes seed and grows. My heart lifts. Perhaps it's not breaking today after all.

"Jacqui?" Remy's sapphire eyes find mine. "You on board?"

I turn to Mick, searching those mesmerizing gray eyes. There's conflict warring there, but before long, he dips his head in assent.

"Yes," I breathe.

# SIXTY-TWO

I'm stunned into silence after hearing myself green light...well, I'm not exactly sure what the hell this means. Do we need ground rules or something? Figure out some sort of...schedule? Is this the worst idea ever? *Are* we all good with this, really?

Mick passes us another round of beers and I chug mine down, attempting to buffer my raw, exposed nerve endings crackling with the unknown.

The second I set my can down, Mick's lips claim mine—infusing my head and heart with reassurance—and heat. My pulse accelerates with every sweep of his tongue, pulling an involuntary moan straight from my throat...while my body tingles with awareness.

I barely have the wherewithal to worry what Remy's thinking before he turns my chin toward him and presses our mouths urgently together. Sensing his longing, I return it, my insides pinging with sexual tension.

*Holy fucking crazy helloooooooo.*

We break apart and I'm panting, flushed, and way off balance.

Remy stands and whips off his shirt. Mick's eyes snap to

his, blue and gray facing off and boring into each other. I vacillate staring between the pair, catching Mick's lips quirking on one side, head lowering as he rakes his teeth across his lower lip. When his gaze meets Remy's again, his head nods ever so slightly.

I'm confused, still whirling from their kisses, until Mick stands and slowly peels off his shirt too.

And then their hungry eyes fixate on me.

*Wait!* my head screams.

Their exposed athletic chests taper to nothing but promise under those bulging blue jeans. My gaze flicks between them, stuttering my thoughts.

I'm overwhelmed by the sight of them and my love for them—and their declarations of love for me. *Me.*

"You good with this, baby?" Mick murmurs, taking my hand and pulling me upright.

"Speak now or forever hold your peace," Remy adds, hope swirling in his eyes.

I nod, my throat tight as desire flares, a rogue wave-type of freak-out rocketing through me.

This is either going to ruin us or ruin me.

But I can't—won't—stop it. I couldn't if I tried.

We're on a freight train, headed downhill with no brakes. We can hang on and enjoy the ride or crash and burn when it goes off the rails.

Mick lifts my shirt over my head and removes my bra, kissing the pulse point on my neck. Remy peels off the rest, leaving me naked and on display.

"Gorgeous," Mick says.

"A stunner," Remy agrees.

Their praise cloaks my vulnerability. The covered cockpit helps block would-be gawkers, but no other boats are nearby. And I trust my guys implicitly. With my body, my heart, my life.

Growing dizzy from their hard, heated stares, my cells crackle with the sexual energy surging between us.

"Don't even try and stop me from eating that pussy," Mick declares, guiding me to the padded bench. He kneels before the V separating my thighs and spreads my legs wide.

"Jesus," Remy groans, claiming his own view. "Look at how wet she is. How much she wants this. She's glistening. Let me feel her."

Mick grants him enough access to push in two fingers. I gasp as they slide in easily, sending a fresh jolt of yearning through me. They come out soaked, and through a lust-filled, surreal haze, I make out Remy lifting them to his mouth and sucking my essence.

Mick's tongue plunges into my depths. I cry out, panting as his fingers and tongue work their dual wizardry. He groans at my responsiveness.

I let go of everything—the judgmental labels, craziness of this idea, foreboding whispers.

My fingers sink into Mick's hair as I surrender, bucking toward his beautiful mouth. Remy positions himself next to me, leaning over to suck one of my nipples, stiffened with desire and peaked in offering. His lips and tongue work pure magic, rolling and gently biting to the point of pleasurable pain. He alternates between kissing me and worshipping my breasts, a dizzying parade of flicks, nips and sucks. The combination of both men indulging me is almost an out-of-body experience except *I feel everything*...more toe-curling ecstasy than ever in my life.

An untethered wail rips from my throat—the only warning—before I combust against Mick's mouth. He fuels my orgasm with more tongue while Remy keeps up his delicious assault on my twin peaks, providing rocket fuel as I drown in wave after delirious wave of pleasure.

"That's my girl," Mick murmurs appreciatively.

"Watching that was one of the sexiest fucking things I've ever seen, sweetheart," Remy whispers in my ear.

I glow under their praise as my breathing slows.

Although out of my depth, I'm thirsty to pleasure them next...and have one specific thing in mind.

Shifting to sitting, still dazed, my lips spread into a slow smile. "My turn."

They stand and shuck off the rest of their clothes, leaving me marveling at my two beautiful men and their robust erections. I beckon them closer, wanting to worship, relish, and please...both.

This is new territory—and I dive in, taking Remy's sturdy length in my mouth first while stroking Mick's thick, velvety shaft in tandem, then switch. Our collective moans ring out, and my insides twitch with anticipation and rekindled fire.

"Fuckkkkkkkkk," Remy groans.

"So fucking good," Mick agrees, breath ragged.

Minutes pass, the three of us lost in this unique, first-time experience. It's inferno-level *hot*.

Mick shifts me to standing and takes my seat on the bench. "Keep sucking me off, baby. Remy's going to take you from behind."

My center floods, and every cell in my body is awake and alert, a part of me still in disbelief we're doing this. I brace myself on either side of his legs and work to take him fully down my throat, eliciting guttural sounds from my gray-eyed lover. He fists his hands in my hair, guiding my strokes, while Remy lines himself up at my entrance, fingering me first as if he's unsure I'm ready.

*I've never been more ready.*

"Goddamn," he murmurs, teasing me with his crown. "She's soaked."

He thrusts inside to the hilt, my cry muffled by Mick buried deep in my throat as my walls stretch to accommodate Remy.

"Good girl." Mick touches my cheek with one hand, his eyes hooded, dilated pupils obliterating the gray. "And the way you look right now...damn."

"I've never seen anything so fucking hot," Remy grits out. "You should see the view from here."

Holding my hips, Remy drives into me, my core embracing his penetrating length while Mick thrusts into me from below, guiding me through murmured encouragement and praise.

We find a steady, dizzying rhythm where I'm suspended in a heady, sensual cloud. Grunts and pants punctuate our carnal threesome, adding a soundtrack to the symphony. It's an assault of the senses. They are everywhere, have all of me.

They both quicken in intensity, still moving in synchronicity, and I'm hanging on for the ride of my life. Mick loses it first, shooting his essence down my throat with a final groan. Remy follows, pumping his release deep inside me as he grinds to the finish line. It's dirty. Erotic. Electrifying.

We disentangle and flop onto the opposing benches in various poses, a sheen of sweat coating our bodies as we catch our breaths.

"You okay, baby?" Mick asks, his fingers caressing mine.

*How I love this man.* I nod, flashing a slow, satisfied smile.

"Good. Because we're not done with you yet," he promises. The simmering pot of desire within me responds, increasing to a low boil, despite being thoroughly, deliriously manhandled.

"Not by a long shot," Remy agrees.

Mick passes out cigarettes and Remy a round of beers, and we grin at each other like cats who've eaten a cage full of canaries.

We shift from the cockpit to sit in the rear of the boat. Basking in the fall sun, we prime for round two with cold brews, affectionate touches, and perma-smiles. This shouldn't feel so natural...but it does. I'm shocked my brain isn't slamming me with judgments and labels, but it's not. And if I hadn't witnessed firsthand my two men seemingly all in with this arrangement, I wouldn't believe it.

Mick gets up to use the head and when he returns, calls us over to the expansive, flat hull.

Sun reflects off the sparkling white surface, but there's nothing angelic about this scene. We're blatantly exposed, but with zero boats in the vicinity, I don't care about anything except what's happening *right now*. Maybe it's the risk of getting caught, or the risqué, smutty porno we're starring in, but I've given myself over to it, and the two men who have my heart and soul.

Mick sits on the smooth fiberglass. "Come here, baby."

I stretch out horizontally, laying my head in his lap. Heat from the sun's rays coat my body. Anticipation stokes the fire inside to scorching.

Mick's gray eyes caress mine. Reaching my hand up, I palm his cheek and coax his strong jaw to my lips, our tongues twining and dancing. His hands cup my breasts, fingers roving, stopping to fondle my rigid nipples. His erection hardens against the back of my skull with promise, and I ache to slide him back into my mouth and feel him come apart again.

My gaze travels to Remy studying us intently, the bright blue of his eyes eclipsed by his pupils. His fingers trace the apex of my thighs, which I've spread wide, granting him full access. My pussy weeps for him, *them*. When he presses a finger inside and drags it up to rub concentric circles on command central, I'm so turned on I can hardly breathe.

I'd think their dual focus on me might be unfair except they're clearly enjoying every minute. I'm in another stratosphere—heart soaring, chest heaving—as waves of pleasure crash through me.

Remy brings me right to the edge and stops. My body

sputters—delirious with need and anticipation...and greedy for more, more, more.

The guys switch places.

Mick's eyes meet mine as he lines up with my entrance. He thrusts his beautiful cock inside me, and I moan loudly, euphoria rocketing me skyward. He begins a familiar rhythm my body craves like a drug.

Remy kneels by my face and palms my breasts. "I love the way these bounce when you're getting fucked. I've got plans for them next."

I moan and his tongue probes my mouth like he's fucking that too.

What they're doing is deliciously mind-blowing.

"Goddamn," Mick utters, probably referring to the flood between my thighs, the squelch obscenely audible each time he slams into me.

Remy releases his hold on my mouth, enraptured by my face. I scream as Mick climaxes with a vengeance, spilling into me with long drives and grinding hips.

He pulls out, leaving me panting, and Remy straddles my chest.

"Push those magnificent tits together, sweetheart," he says.

His eyes hood when I've wrangled them and he pistons his hard length into the valley I've created. Through my gasps, I spy his face, unmasked with feverish gratification and focus.

Mick's fingers fondle me below, jolting me into a new fervent realm when I'm already soaring. I'm fully at his mercy —and happily, deliriously so—as Remy keeps me pinned, his straining erection thrusting through my breasts.

"I'm not going to last," Remy warns, his gaze shifting from my face to my breasts.

"I'm..." I pant, teetering on the edge.

"Come for me, baby," Mick's gruff voice commands.

I cry out seconds later, waves of release ripping through

me as I erupt. Remy falls fast, his hot release spurting across my throat.

"Jesus," Mick says, awe in his tone.

Remy dismounts, breathing hard. Mick grabs a roll of paper towels, pressing a handful to my chest before disbursing more from the roll as we mop up.

Reclining with our backs against the hull, me sandwiched in the middle, we savor the aftermath. I reach for their hands, and we lie side by side, connected, until we're ready to move again.

I'm the first to break the silence.

"Thank you," I murmur. It's all I can manage after being so thoroughly loved and worshipped. I'm awash in gratitude we're still...intact. This may be a new iteration, but I'm not losing them.

Remy cackles. "Uh...thank *you*."

I rip my fingers from his and elbow him in the ribs.

Mick chuckles and squeezes my hand, full of reassurance, and brings it to his lips for a prolonged kiss.

Remy retakes my hand, serious now. "You're incredible, sweetheart. Mick and I are the luckiest SOBs on earth."

My ocean hums in agreement.

Eventually we get dressed. On our way back to the marina, we're all grins and kisses and touches. No jealousy. No judgments. No pain.

Just...love. Friendship. A newfound closeness, if that's fathomable, one I've never known before.

A lingering question remains, though.

*What now?*

# Sixty-Three

The answers to all my questions are found in the easy way the three of us coexist from that point forward. Whether I'm with Mick, Remy, or both, we share our friendship like we always have, only now with added pleasure and open affection—and without guilt, lies, or jealousy.

I love them. They love me.

We simply...work.

Maybe because at the heart of it, we recognized each other as kindred spirits from the beginning. We're the family we never had—but chose instead. Our bond feels solid and unbreakable, a life raft on a stormy sea. We're stronger as one.

And with their love, I'm on sturdier ground than ever. Instead of tiptoeing around earthquakes and fault lines, I'm strong, confident, alive. The very picture of a lion with wild honey tresses framing my face...roaring, leaping, and reveling in my power.

I guess that makes the three of us a pride. Loyal, devoted, protective, caring...and hungry.

I'm not blind to the landmines lying in wait. Mrs. Remington will eventually make demands. Mick may move to Florida once his father dies. Remy's escalating party habits are concerning.

But I'm foolish enough, for now, to believe love conquers all.

The alternative is unfathomable.

And so, I don't fear the undertow. Or the sand collapsing under my feet. Standing front and center on the bow of this ship, rocking on the surging waves of this magnificent ocean, I take solace in the eye of the storm.

# EPILOGUE
## 1989

"Did you get in okay?"

His deep voice is a salve after a long day of travel. I cradle the hotel phone, curled on my side in the middle of a massive king-size bed. "I did, baby."

"I've got a surprise for you when you get home."

My heart performs a little flip. "Really? What is it?"

He chuckles. "Yeah, like that's going to happen."

*I know.* He's like a fucking vault when it comes to secrets. Something I love about him. "A girl can try."

"Don't bother to guess."

My mind whirs, then slows. I'm exhausted—and if I'm honest, anxious. There's no energy to mentally sift through a list of presents I could want. "I miss you."

"I miss you more."

"I'm too tired to argue." I stretch my legs, joints cracking in my ankles.

"Just how I like my women...pliant."

I bark out a laugh. "Pliant my ass."

"I like a pliant ass too."

"Well, that's true. You *are* an ass man." A loud yawn escapes my throat.

"Get some sleep, Sundance. I'm sure tomorrow will be tough. What time is the funeral?"

"Midmorning."

He pauses. "I should be with you."

*God no.* Potent images of Mick and Remy flash unbidden in my mind. "That would be like coming to my high school reunion, a total drag. No one cares about the plus-one. You're just the guy everyone is morbidly curious about because they're nosy and want to know if I wound up with a hot guy or some balding loser." *And I need to do this alone.*

"Which one am I?"

"If you have to ask..." My lips curve into a smile.

"Ouch."

"I'll call you later tonight, hot guy."

"And then you better get your pliant ass back home."

"Soon, baby. Soon."

# Up Next

**Up next**
*When There Was You*
Book two in the California Dreaming series
The story continues. Get your copy now.


**Want a little more to tide you over?**
It's Christmastime for our happy trio—and Mick, Jacqui, and Remy are spending it together in Half Moon Bay. Read the satisfying, steamy bonus epilogue showing how the best presents come in all shapes and sizes!
*(Download or see Bonus on my website)*


**Other planned books in the series**
Book three is from Mick's point of view. Book four finishes this epic love story. Book five is a standalone spinoff featuring Kit and Jas—and Kit's super cool age-gap love story.


**Never miss an announcement or release**
Subscribe to my newsletter. *(See website)*

# Playlist

## In order of appearance

- "Shoot to Thrill" by AC/DC, live version
- "Going to California" by Led Zeppelin
- "Beautiful Girls" by Van Halen
- "You Can't Always Get What You Want" by The Rolling Stones
- "Since I Met You Baby" by B.B. King
- "Love Stinks" by the J. Geils Band
- "Precious" by The Pretenders
- "Tube Snake Boogie" by ZZ Top
- "Don't Stop Believin'" by Journey
- "Looks That Kill" by Mötley Crüe
- "The One Thing" by INXS
- "Mad World" by Tears for Fears
- "You Dropped A Bomb On Me" by The Gap Band
- "Flash Light" by Parliament
- "50 Ways to Leave Your Lover" by Paul Simon
- "That's Amore" by Dean Martin
- "More Than a Feeling" by Boston
- "Lyin' Eyes" by the Eagles
- "Two Hearts Beat as One" by U2

# Acknowledgments

A humungous, really-can't-say-it-enough thank you to my husband Greg, who loses countless hours with me when I'm "in the bubble." That's what he calls my office, where I spend a whole lotta hours writing, immersed with my characters and doing other acrobatic feats necessary to keep this vibe vibing and lifelong dream happening. I also appreciate his consults on muscle cars, even if he had to endure the absence of Mopars in book one and adding insult to injury, the main car stars are a Chevy and Ford. I've got you covered in book two, baby—I promise!

Thank you to Josie Juniper for her insightful editing prowess of my first draft. Some of her comments had me howling out loud and caused me to reconsider making Mick more likable. And man, is he likable. Too f*cking likable. The book is much better because of your early comments.

Thank you to beta readers Natalie Eckvall, Renée Kerns, Kim Maeda, and Amber Tischio. Your feedback was invaluable, helped me improve this book, and I appreciate you. Especially your enthusiastic feeling of all the feels.

Thank you to Chris Remer for the consult about emergency protocol for California firefighters and medical personnel on the scene of an accident. But more so for a decades-long friendship filled with laughter, shenanigans, and respect that's endured.

Thank you to romance authors everywhere. I have voraciously consumed romance novels of all types for the past few years as I readied myself to start telling these stories myself. After writing for decades in other genres, I realized how satisfying it was to read a book knowing full well the ending would be happy—and why that's a very good thing in today's world.

Readers, you are my friends for life. We are kindred spirits. It doesn't matter if we read the same books, or like the same book boyfriends, or have TBRs in the tens or thousands, YOU ARE MY PEOPLE. Thank you for reading my book, being willing to swoon, and sharing your love of books and reading with the world.

# About the Author

K.C. Lake writes angsty, realistic love stories packed with heart and heat. *When There Was Us* is her first romance. An avid romance reader, her shelves are lined with trophies, and her TBR is out of control (then again, size matters). She lives with her grumpy, touch-her-and-die, non-billionaire husband and dog in the beautiful woods of Virginia. Find more info, subscribe, and connect at www.kclakebooks.com.

Your review on any book site or social media platform is greatly appreciated.

tiktok.com/@kclake_romance

instagram.com/kclake_romance

amazon.com/author/kclakebooks

bookbub.com/authors/k-c-lake